THE WATER DRAGON

ANDREW WOODWARD

By the same author:

In the DI Chambers 'Elements' series –
The Fire Walker
The Silverbird's Sign

For mum,

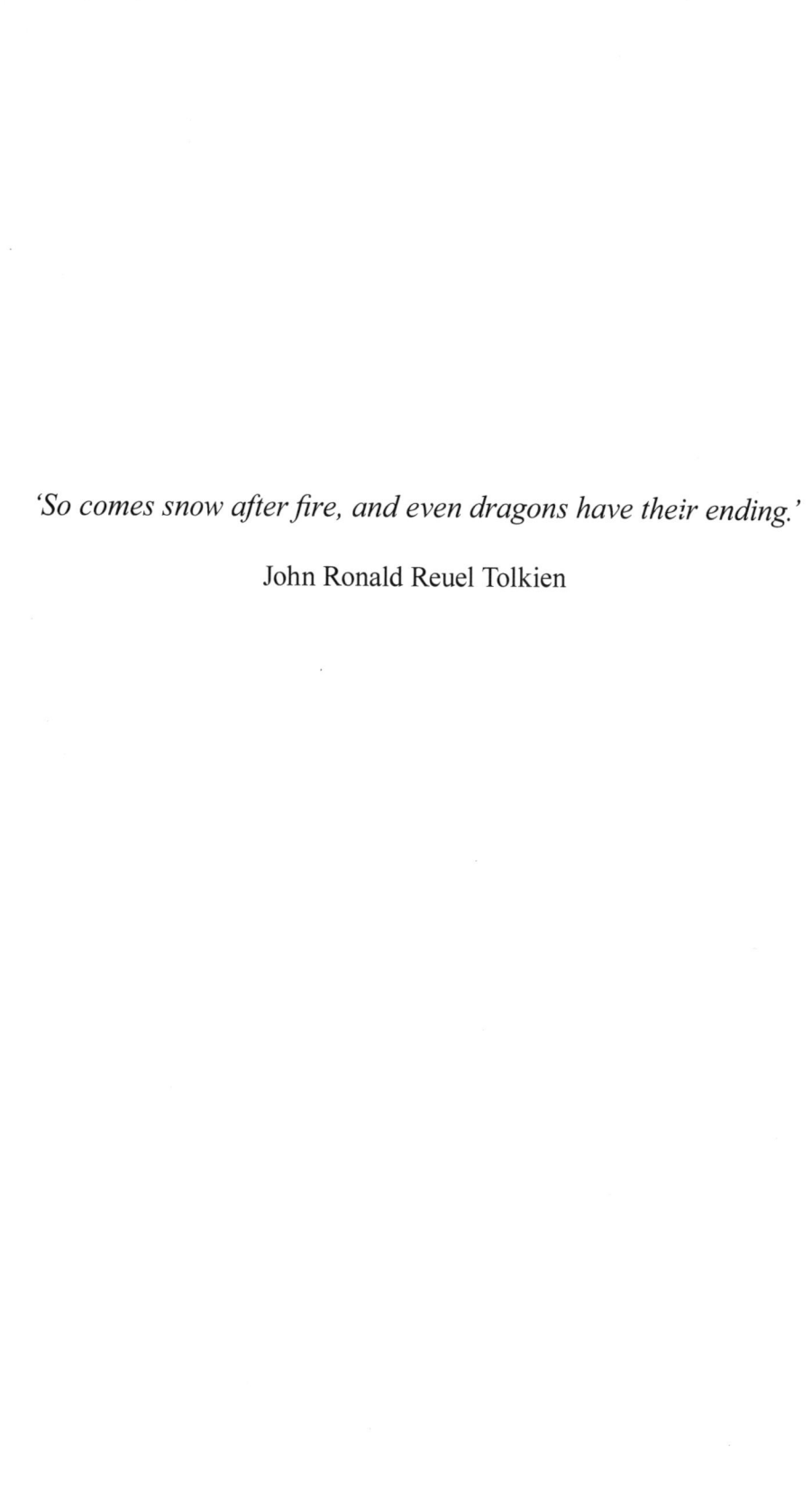

'*So comes snow after fire, and even dragons have their ending.*'

John Ronald Reuel Tolkien

Prologue

Friday 5th August 2011

A man with a crooked smile stood in the shadows of an alley watching the proceedings. His face intermittently tinted blue from the strobing lights of the emergency services' vehicles that further congested the already busy street.

It was a hot summer's evening in central London. Most of the people on the streets were dressed in T-shirts, short-sleeved shirts, many of the Friday night partygoers were wearing shorts or miniskirts. The thermometer had barely to register 20°C for the majority of Londoners to bare their flesh, wrapped up as it was for most of the year. But the people the man was watching were not smiling or having fun. Most were holding pint glasses or bottles of beer down at their sides as they gawped, open-mouthed at the scene laid out in front of them.

The bodies of two men lay butchered in the road, large pools of blood surrounded the victims, the head of one almost completely severed from his body, the other bleeding profusely from several large gaping holes in his chest. There was a host of police and ambulance personnel buzzing around the scene, the former trying to get the crowd to back away as they attempted to put up tape to cordon off the area, the latter trying desperately to resuscitate the lifeless figure.

The man had seen enough. Careful not to make eye contact with anyone, he slipped out from his hiding place and joined the ever-growing crowd. Here in London's Chinatown, he was just another Asian man among the thousands that thronged the surrounding streets. He was satisfied for now – another job had been successfully completed. His face once more contorting into a crooked smile as he walked casually away, invisible among the evening crowd, towards the nearby Piccadilly Circus tube station.

◆◆◆

Chapter 1

Monday 15th August 2011

Detective Inspector John Chambers reached for the air conditioner's controller and jabbed furiously at the luminous button with the 'up' arrow. He wasn't sure if you should press up or down. His drowsy logic told him you should press down because you wanted the room cooler, but then maybe pressing up would instigate more cooling power. He bashed the button a few more times before dragging himself to the bathroom and running his head under the lukewarm water pouring out of the 'cold' tap. How many more months of this could he take? Surely the humidity had to ease off at some point.

He grabbed one of the large, soft white towels that were folded neatly on the metal rack, drying his hair as he sat on the edge of the bed. He could feel the sheet damp against his legs from his own sweat. He glanced at the alarm clock, the bright green numbers contrasting sharply against the dark background: 6.37am. The gloominess of the room was slowly dissipating as the first rays of sunrise seeped in through a gap at the top of the curtains. He sat for a moment in his boxer shorts, idly scratching at his leg. Too late he became aware of what he was doing. As he looked down he saw he had woken two mosquito bites an inch apart on his calf.

'Bastards,' he said out loud to the empty room.

He stood up and walked over to the window, dragging the heavy curtain as wide as the runners would allow. He instinctively put his hand up to cover his eyes as they adjusted to the bright sunshine that flooded the room, still aware of the intense itch radiating out from his calf.

The scene that unfolded below was truly breathtaking. He drank in the view of the famed Victoria Harbour, already bustling with early morning activity. He let his eyes drift across the panoramic view and could make out islands off in the distance to his left, while across the harbour was the concrete jungle of the Kowloon Peninsula. He took in the towering building on the opposing shore and the ludicrous number of tall buildings that went back as far as he could see. He could just make out the ring of hills way off in the distance that gave the area its name, Kowloon – the nine dragons. His gaze drifted down to the water, revealing all manner of craft from enormous cruise liners to tiny sampans bobbing around in the wake of the plethora of passenger ferries criss-crossing the narrow stretch of water that separates Hong Kong Island from the mainland.

Chambers had been in Hong Kong for a week. Not long enough, evidently, to get used to the humidity. He recalled his introduction to the climate the previous weekend. He thought he had walked into a hot air dryer as he stepped through the automatic doors of the airport to find a cab to take him to his pre-booked serviced apartment in Causeway Bay. These few minutes that he spent in the morning enjoying the view were definitely his favourite time of the day since he'd been in Hong Kong, before the city's combination of heat and pollution imposed its life-sapping drain.

He had to continually towel the sweat from his body as he looked out of the window. He thought about how the view from his flat at home didn't compare to this. His flat, he couldn't get used to saying his 'apartment', like he'd noticed a few of his more upwardly-mobile neighbours calling theirs, was located just off the Goldhawk Road in Shepherd's Bush in West London. It wasn't a bad view and was one that was fairly common for most Londoners. His second floor living room overlooked a tree-lined street that was a mixture of terraced houses and small blocks of flats; his view was of his block's small 'private' car park. His place was on the right side of a U-shaped block so he could, if he so desired, look back across to his left into his neighbours' windows. Or, if he looked to the right, watch the traffic coming up the narrow car-lined street and listen to the grind of an exhaust pipe as it scraped on the oversized speed bump that seemed to catch out every motorist who had the misfortune of taking this route.

Although his place was close to the action around nearby Shepherd's Bush Green, his street was fairly quiet. Most sensible drivers knew to avoid using it as a short cut as the amount of traffic control devices made any kind of time saving irrelevant, let alone the cost of repairs the speed bumps caused to the vehicle's underside. Most of the traffic was made up of motorbike delivery drivers and couriers. But, more annoyingly, it did seem to feature as some kind of drunkard's cut-through to and from the local area's pubs and bars, so served as a noisy, late-night thoroughfare for the homeward journey of the many resident revellers. Plus the Tennessee Fried Chicken shop on the corner meant the hedge that surrounded his car park was often filled with all manner of greasy paper boxes dripping their congealed carcinogenic contents on to the pavement.

Chambers checked the clock and decided it was time to shower and shave. He turned and within two steps was in the small shower/ toilet/bathroom. Everything at a cost he thought, the greatest view in the world, but you have to accept living in a shoebox to enjoy it. He turned on the shower and only waited for a couple of seconds for the water temperature to adjust before he stepped in. As he enjoyed the cool water he wondered if today would be the day he'd catch a break, something at least, to go on.

≈≈≈

Pausing in the lobby, Chambers wanted to maximise his time in the deliciously cold air pumping out of the a/c unit directly above the glass front doors. After almost 30 seconds he saw someone coming towards him from outside. He waited until the last moment before pulling the door open. The man and a blast of warm air came in simultaneously, both rushing past without acknowledgement. Chambers slowly left the chilled confines of the lobby behind him and set off towards his workplace. He thought momentarily about hailing a cab, but decided to walk for several reasons. Firstly, it was less than a ten-minute walk away; secondly, the traffic on Gloucester Road was already quite heavy; and thirdly, he thought he might get a cab driver who spoke no English. This had happened a couple of times already during his short stay and it was quite frustrating for all involved, especially when the driver finally understood he only wanted to go a couple of blocks up the road – they usually, and completely understandably, weren't too impressed. He added basic Cantonese to the growing list of things he needed to get a handle on, as communicating with cab drivers was going to be imperative in this town. 'Here, straight, stop, right and left', these would be a good start.

First things first, he knew he needed to slow down. His rapid walking pace was just something all Londoners did, they were always in a hurry. In Hong Kong, all it caused him to do was sweat profusely and constantly walk into the back of people who were moving at a speed slower than his; although he wasn't sure the latter was all his own fault. The locals didn't seem to notice him that much either, which he thought was strange as he was six foot three and a fully paid-up member of the 100kg club. This morning he decided to take it at a more casual pace, but he'd only travelled 50 metres when he felt the first pin pricks of sweat moisten his brow. He knew before long he'd have his trademark crescent-shaped sweat mark above his stomach, the mandatory soaking wet armpits, despite slapping on the anti-perspirant, and a completely wet back. He crossed a few narrow dank and shabby side streets. As it was still relatively early most of the shops were still closed.

The general ramshackle mess and the unpleasant smells baffled and slightly irritated him. Gloucester Road was pretty much a motorway, there was little to be done about that, but the piles of refuse under the flyover and pedestrian bridges made it look like the dustmen were on strike and the rancid reek from the festering rubbish was almost overwhelming. As he waited to cross the road he looked up at the building directly across the way, it looked ancient, like most of the others he'd seen, but that was probably because it hadn't been cleaned since it was flung up several decades previously. It was his overriding impression of the city so far – like the whole place could do with a good scrub and a lick of paint. The view from his room high up above was incredible, but down here at street level the city looked cheap, old and grubby. He picked up his pace as he reached the cool embrace of his destination, the Wanchai Police Station. On his way to the lift he waited for the influence of the lower temperature to impact on his sweating. By the time he was in the lift he was totally drenched; much wetter than he'd been when outside in the humid grip of midsummer.

However, he was learning fast. He headed to his desk and grabbed the spare shirt from the hanger on his cubicle wall and headed to the bathroom. After confronting his colleagues with matted hair, a red face and unsightly sweat patches for the first few days, he'd tried taking cabs with mixed success. It was then Chambers had come to the conclusion that the best solution was to arrive at the station half an hour earlier and simply change at work. At the sink, he took off his wet shirt and grabbed some paper towels from the dispenser. He knew he'd have to wait for a few minutes until his body began regulating its temperature back to something that it considered to be a little closer to normal. He took the time to check his physique. Not bad, a few lumps in the wrong places perhaps, a hint of love handles, but for a man in his early- to mid-40s Chambers thought he looked OK. He had all his own teeth and hair, now that was definitely a good start. But he was noticeably greying at the temples, a couple of years ago he hadn't seen a grey hair. How things had changed. Only last week he'd been faced with his first grey chest hair, a particularly sobering thought. He flexed his muscles and pulled a couple of comedy poses like he imagined he was in a Mr Universe competition. As he was reaching his finale with fists clenched, arms pumped and showing his best grimace to the mirror, the door to the bathroom swung open framing the not inconsiderable figure of Chief Inspector James Pang, who immediately took on a pained expression.

'Ah Detective Inspector Chambers, I see you are learning our quaint Hong Kong customs already,' he said in a gently mocking tone. 'But we Hong Kongers like to do our T'ai Chi in the park … while wearing something more suited to the occasion.' He turned on his heel, chuckling to himself as he went, leaving Chambers even redder in the face than he'd been a few minutes previously.

≋

It was bad enough that he was the only non-Cantonese speaker in the department, but this was just another in what was becoming a long list of embarrassing situations he'd found himself in with his colleagues and he'd only been here a week. Most of them were caused by his lack of awareness of the local etiquette. His transfer from the Metropolitan Police had come at very short notice. So short in fact, that he'd not even had time to pick up a Cantonese language book, not that it would have made much of a difference, he was terrible at linguistics. He could order a beer and count to 10 in several languages but that was about it. In reality, that wasn't much use unless you're buying beer for a group of 10 people or less in a handful of specific locations around the world.

He had picked up the Hong Kong and Macau: City Guide, since his

8

arrival, where he'd learned that the language had six tones, that was more than enough to stop his feeble attempts at study in their tracks. Even worse, when he'd been chatting with one of his new colleagues about it, he was reliably informed that there weren't six tones but nine. This led to an all-encompassing office discussion on how many tones there actually were. Although the conversation took place mainly in Cantonese, he decided if the locals weren't sure, and seeing as they spoke it, there was little chance for this particular monotone Englishman to master it. He convinced himself that he was only here for the duration of the case, and being naturally optimistic, he would soon be back in London and in no need of the six or nine tones of Cantonese. If he needed any further convincing, his new colleagues told him he'd be better off learning Putonghua, as it only had four tones – something they all agreed on – it would be much easier for him to learn. Chambers wanted to point out that you wouldn't go to France to learn Spanish, but wasn't sure how his logic would be appreciated. Plus the English he spoke had only one tone, and he was happy enough as long as people could understand his particular West London drawl.

≈≈≈

He put his shirt under the automatic hot air dryer and held it there with one hand while using his other to wipe down his body with the paper towels. When he was as dry as possible he put on his clean shirt and returned to his desk. He hung the damp shirt up on the hanger, content in the knowledge that it would be hopefully be perfectly adequate for use the following day. He pressed the button to turn on his IBM computer. It was evident the machine he'd been allocated was at least ten years old. In computer years it was a relic. They'd given it a modern touch by adding a Benq flat screen monitor, a little bit like putting alloys on a Morris Minor. He didn't mind as long as it served his purposes: email; web and the other usual suspects found in MS Office.

If he needed access to the organisation's mainframe there were several communal terminals in the office that he could use instead for faster service. As the machine booted up he went in search of his first caffeine boost of the day. The sheer number of options had amazed him on the first day when he'd been shown the pantry. There was the normal water machine with hot and cold taps and inverted five-gallon plastic water bottle. An ancient Zanussi coffee machine that allegedly vended 16 different types of hot beverage, so far so good. But it was the array of kettles and other instruments for keeping water warm or boiling hot that made his mind boggle. There was a huge gallon urn, three kettles, two automatic water heaters and four jugs just for hot water plus pots of concentrated Chinese and English tea.

Chambers grabbed a coffee from the Zanussi and returned to his desk. He opened one of the manila files on his desk and removed the packet of photographs. He flicked through them again. He'd looked at these pictures at least once a day since the multiple murder case he was working on had got its first and only break two weeks previously. The photographs were a series of eight sequential shots of the man suspected of being behind the gruesome killings. The pictures showed the suspect exiting a black London taxi and heading into a building. The images weren't of the best quality, mostly blurred beyond recognition, but the fourth one was clearest. It was taken as the man crossed the street, half of his face was in sharp focus, his features clearly defined; unfortunately a signpost obscured the other half of his face. This was the best they had. The man responsible for the pictures was a fairly reliable informant, but regrettably not a professional photographer. The information filtering back soon after the photos arrived at the department was that the man they were looking for had just boarded a flight to Hong Kong. The natural course of events meant the lead investigator on the case, DI Chambers, was sent to find him with the help of the Hong Kong Police. So here was Chambers, looking for a man with half a face and only the nickname, Hak Loong, to go on.

~~~

Chapter 2 – Rice-spoon Head

Thursday 3rd February 2011

Dear diary,

It was easier than I thought it would be, the murder, I mean. The rest of it, making sure that I hadn't left any evidence and the distribution of a 'clue' or two was a bit more time consuming, but on the whole my first murder went well. I'd planned it as much as possible; as much as you can plan the murder of someone you've never met. You see I have this thing I need, no, not need exactly, more like this thing I want to do. It's been inside me for a long time, slowly distilling, all the time gathering momentum. It was like an epiphany if you will, how I finally figured out what I would do, I felt filled with a dynamic energy something I had never experienced before. Everything in my life became clear. Everything that had happened to me, I now understood. These things were necessary, they had happened for a reason, and that was to get me to this point in my life. To where I am right now. I knew what I needed to do and just how I needed to do it. For the last few weeks I've been actively preparing for this day. And as I said, it was much easier than I thought it would be.

ΞΞΞ

I had taken the *Xui Ze*, the 3.30pm boat from Central Pier 5 to Mui Wo on Lantau Island. The ride over on the First Ferry Company's orange and white open-deck passenger boat took about 35 minutes, the only concern I had at that stage was that the vitally important contents of my bag remained in situ. The boat had the usual mixture of loud locals, bloated expats plus a host of Filipina and Indonesian helpers all going busily about their futile existence, ordinary people doing ordinary things. I was glad I was no longer part of this pointless way of living, people moving blindly through an uneventful bland life to their inevitable demise. Not for me, not now, because my life has a purpose. I always knew I was different, but I had finally realised what my raison d'être was and what my full potential could really be. I'm destined for fame, of that much I'm certain.

I had dressed casually, but warmly, as it was a relatively cool winter's day. I wanted to blend into the crowd as we disembarked from the ferry pier. Although no-one's going to look twice at a man coming off the boat wearing standard hiking gear with a medium-sized black rucksack. Why would they? Mui Wo is a popular entry and exit point for hikers looking to explore the high hills of Lantau Island, but you'd never guess it from the ugly and depressing concrete mass that confronts you on arrival. I headed across the sprawling grey bus depot leaving most of the recently disgorged ferry passengers waiting for their connections to more remote parts of the island. I crossed the road past a few rundown restaurants and walked along the footpath that curves around the bay that embraces a wide stretch of sand. The only people visible were a man with a young boy and their dog walking along the water's edge. There was another passage that ran perpendicular to the beach alongside a small water channel. I followed this through a dilapidated village and on to the disused silver mine. The distance between the traditional three-storey village houses was already beginning to increase. While the number of locals, who all seemed to ride around on pushbikes, was becoming equally sparse. I was already fairly 'off the beaten track' as I rounded a corner past several buildings that must have dated back hundreds of years, awaiting the return of their rightful owners who, like their offspring, are long dead overseas.

From here it was unlikely I'd see more than a handful of hikers on a busy day and even less chance this late on a Thursday afternoon. I took the Olympic Way, the steep concrete path that bisects Lantau Island and goes all the way across to Tung Chung. It was on this path I passed the last person I would see before my victim, a young man heading back in the direction of Mui Wo. The hood of my jacket was up and I diverted my eyes, appearing to be suddenly very interested in the grove of banana trees on my left. I continued steadily uphill, occasionally having the odd moment of concern about the precious and dangerous cargo that I was carrying on my back – if it got out, it would be perilously close to my neck.

On my left, Sunset Peak loomed up out of the low cloud that seemed to permanently shroud its summit. A small break in the low trees on the top of the ridge indicated another, less travelled, route. I turned right onto it and headed through the woods. From here the hiking path heads up along another ridge out of the tree line and eventually on to Sunny Bay and Hong Kong Disneyland. I always find it amazing that in such a populous place as Hong Kong, there are so many places where you can be completely alone with your thoughts – whatever those might be.

I'd walked here a lot when I was younger and I liked to return from time to time, it was a great place to escape my shitty life at home, and it was a place where I always felt free. I'd come up here with my dogs, they loved the open space, running in the long grass without a care in the world. I envied their simple lives. Here I would sit down on the top of piles of scattered rocks and watch as eagles soared overhead, the occasional wild dog standing boldly on a distant outcrop, and depending on the season and weather, there was a selection of brightly coloured insects. I loved the solitude and would often stay up here for hours before heading back to the lousy existence I knew would be waiting at home, as it always was. You realise there is something wrong in your life if you think a dog has a better existence than you. I suppose if I had to point to a moment then I'd say that's where it all really began for me.

I stopped to make one last check of the contents of my bag: the bulky Timberland shoebox containing the naja atra was still sealed and the air holes were clear. I took a long drink of water and put the bottle back at the bottom of the bag. I removed my jacket and also placed it in the bag. I donned my black Thinsulate gloves, as the temperature was beginning to drop, and although it never gets that cold, when you've lived in the tropics for so long, you become a bit more susceptible to the weather. I noted the time was nearing 5pm as I put my watch in one of the side pockets of the rucksack. I took out my Swiss army knife and also removed an item that I had bought at Toys 'R' Us in Causeway Bay the week before. I wanted everything to be at hand when the time was right.

I continued along the path until it skirted the golf course that ran along the lower plateau. Here the trees became scarcer, while the path headed sharply upwards. I kept an eye out for what I needed and it wasn't long before I found what I was looking for at the edge of the path. I carried on for several hundred metres until I found my ideal viewing point. This was where I waited for my victim. I had come up the weekend before, to refresh my childhood memories and to see where the best place would be. I had my Canon Sx200 camera with me, so I could capture the location; I also took a panoramic record on the movie setting so I could review it at my leisure at home to confirm this was the best location with the best view of the surrounding area. On weekends there are always a few hikers out and about, and it's not uncommon for people to be up there taking pictures, as on a clear day the view from up there is amazing.

I scrambled up a nearby boulder that was about 20ft in diameter, so I could see back down the way I had come, but I was still a long way out of sight and hearing range of any golfers finishing off a late round. The course had looked fairly quiet when I passed by earlier. From here I could see along the plateau to the north in the direction the path continued and where my victim would have a fifty percent chance of approaching from. To the East, it

14

was clear enough to make out planes taking off from and landing at Chek Lap Kok Airport with a comforting regularity. The site is a fascinating testament to man's triumph over nature as the whole structure is built on reclaimed land; it's an amazing feat of engineering. I sat on a nearby rock and watched the planes for a while, occasionally scanning the surrounding barren slopes for any sign of life. As there were no trees up here on the ridgeline, just the long, dry, brown grass swaying on the plateau, it would make any human traffic easy to see. The sun was gradually moving to the horizon offering the first intimations of the orange hues that would later become a deep and vibrant red. After an hour or so I made out a figure approaching from the way I had come. I was a little surprised, I don't know why, but I had just assumed they would come from the other direction. It's funny how you see things in your imagination; you just expect that's how it's going to be.

He was still too far away to notice me as I hopped over a couple of smaller boulders, putting me on the plateau side of the ridge. I arranged the items I'd removed from my bag earlier, rolled up my trouser leg and lay down flat on my back to wait. My new position afforded me a clear view along the path ahead, so I could see if anyone was approaching from the other direction, in case I needed to abort. After several minutes of waiting and listening to the gentle rustling of the grass, and going over what I'd say and what I planned to do again and again in my head, I finally heard the sound of heavy footfall on the sun-baked earthen path. I began to make fairly low moaning noises while keeping my body movements to a minimum. I took a quick look towards the direction of the sounds and saw the top of a head come over the crest. I quickly looked away to shield my face from his view and continued to moan softly.

The man called out, he was obviously quite shocked to see me. He quickened his pace and soon his face was looming over me. I could smell beer on his breath, while his thinning, mousy brown hair was matted against his brow with his own sweat. His cheeks were ruddy from his exertions or the cold. His eyebrows were knitted in anxiety, and his pale, slight lips pursed in an exclamation of concern. Little did he know it was his own safety that he needed to be concerned with.

'Are you ok? What happened?' His voice sounded odd, a mixture of apprehension and confusion.

'Snake' I whispered, 'bitten', I slurred and let my head loll in the direction of where the man would have headed had he not met me. This allowed me to keep an eye on the path to make sure no one was coming from that way.

'Help me,' I rasped and nodded carelessly at some stones about 10 metres away. 'Threw stones, think it's dead.'

'Christ,' he called out as he looked off towards the rocks 'is that a … is that a snake?'

He took several slow and measured steps towards the metre or so of thick, black, rope-like object close to where several fist-sized stones were strewn.

'Careful,' I croaked, 'it's poisonous'. My real fear was that he was an amateur herpetologist or that he had keen eyesight.

'Jesus!' The man called out. He had a telescopic metal walking stick that he had extended to its greatest length and cautiously began reaching out to poke the body of what he must have assumed was a dead or badly injured snake. As I sat up watching the man, I had a sudden realisation that the setting sun could upset my carefully laid plans. I hadn't factored on this as when I had come here a few days previously, it had been much earlier in the day. He still had his back to me as I got up, picking up the large rock I had collected on the way up, and in two quick steps covered the distance between us. He appeared to notice something and took a step back, whether it was the huge shadow my body cast that he saw stretching out over the grass in front of him, or the simple fact that he realised the snake was actually made of rubber, I guess I'll never know. I like to think it was a combination of both.

My memory of the entire day is crystal clear, so it's easy for me to write about, but for some reason I can only recall the next part in single frames, like one of those early attempts at movie making.

16

I can see him standing up. He begins to turn. His mouth opens. I hit him on the temple with the stone. He slams to the ground. I hit him again. He lies still. Then it's like the slide show finishes and the film whirs back into real-time action. I checked the paths in both directions, and felt relief that there was no sign of life, only the wind blowing patterns into the tall grass on the plateau. My heart was pounding as I pulled out a plastic bag from my pocket and slipped it over his head, tying it as tight as I could around his head. I could see from the condensation that formed in the bag that he was still breathing, but at least it helped to contain the blood that was seeping from his head wounds. I needed to act quickly. I carefully removed the shoe box from my bag and placed it down next to the inert body. I rolled up the leg of his jeans. Now came the tricky part.

I took the elastic bands and the tape off the box and slid the lid off. The real snake was coiled in the box. As I slowly moved my hand towards the snake, it flicked its tail. Not a lot but enough to make me step back. This part was essential to my plans and couldn't be overlooked. After several minutes of trying I eventually managed to grab the snake by the back of the head. I used my free hand to untie the string that bound its nearly two metre body and it whipped its tail at the freedom its body had been awarded. The tip from the pet shop owner in Mong Kok had been a huge blessing. His binding of the snake had rendered this deadly Chinese Cobra relatively harmless. Well harmless to me anyway.

I squeezed the back of the snake's head to force it to open its jaws, revealing its curved, grooved fangs that were razor sharp. As I pushed the head towards the victim's leg, I could feel the muscles of the snake's hood trying to expand in my grip. I made the snake bite the exposed flesh, holding the head as the fangs pierced the skin. After several seconds, enough time for the poison to enter the bloodstream, I lifted the snake clear and walked back a few metres and off the path to my left. I then bent over and carefully released the snake into the undergrowth, keeping a careful eye on it to make sure it slithered away from me, pleased that it had decided against coming back to trouble its malevolent captor.

I returned to the body. He was still breathing, just. I looked at the snakebite; there were two smallish red piercings on his left calf. I pulled down the leg of his jeans and, with the corkscrew blade of my Swiss army knife, punctured the fabric of his trousers, making two small holes, to correspond to the bite marks on his leg. I just needed to do one last thing. I took out a box of matches, struck one which the breeze quickly blew out. I then placed the dead match in the hem of his trouser leg and folded it twice. I then turned up the other trouser leg to align them both.

I dragged the body back to the ridge crest. The path swung away to the left, roughly in the direction the snake had taken. It was an effort to hold the body as straight as I could; he was quite heavy, 85 to 90kg I guess. I ripped the plastic bag off his head and gave him a slight push, allowing gravity to take its natural course. I watched as the body dropped down the rock face, colliding with a few boulders before coming to an abrupt stop several metres below, in an awkward and painful-looking position. His blood-smeared face was looking away from me. The blood was almost a perfect colour match for his red polyester jacket.

If he wasn't dead now, it surely wouldn't be long. The bite from a Rice-spoon Head snake, or Chinese Cobra as it is more commonly known, was likely to be fatal. When combined with a bad fall landing head first into a pile of rocks, there was surely little chance of survival if he was exposed to the cold for the night. It was unlikely anyone else would be passing this way before it got light the next morning.

I retraced my steps. As I did so, I took the blood-stained bag and wrapped it inside another plastic bag. Before tying the end I picked up the fake snake from the pile of rocks and held it by the neck. It wasn't a bad replica of a cobra, and it had certainly played its part well enough. I coiled it around my hand before putting it in the bag and tying up the end. I took my jacket and the water bottle out of the rucksack, put my gloves back in the bag, washed my face and hands off the side of the path and then put on my jacket. I surveyed the scene, picking up my equipment and packing it in my bag. The path was too hard to leave footprints or to leave any sign that a body had been dragged around. There was nothing to say I had ever been there, except the dead or dying man slumped somewhere down the ravine.

The sun was close to setting as I hurried along the plateau. I wanted to take a turnoff that was located further ahead and it was easy to miss in the failing light. I didn't want to follow the main path down from Tiger Head as it was very steep, slippery and potentially dangerous in the dark. I found the turnoff in the long grass and made my way along a tight and twisting narrow path until it eventually led me out to a disused reservoir.

By now it was dark and the road was lit by streetlamps that led up to the golf course on the right or down into the Stepford Wives-like town of Discovery Bay to the left. I turned left and headed down the long and winding road back to civilisation, if you wanted to stretch reality and describe Discovery Bay using that moniker. More like another Hong Kong in a parallel universe. One in which the expat still proudly rules the city. I strode down the road accompanied only by the sounds of the chirruping cicadas and the nearby stream. About halfway down I walked past a couple walking their dogs and soon after a solitary runner pounded his way up the steep hill. The occasional golf cart went by, although none of these peculiar non-golfing drivers gave me a second look. As I approached the final stretch, the paved footpath ended abruptly and continued on the other side of the road.

I stepped out without looking as the night was whisper-quiet. Suddenly I realised a cyclist was bearing down on me at high speed, he made a quick swerve missing me by inches. Imagine, my carefully laid plans thwarted before they had really got going. Killed by a lycra-clad cyclist flying down the road with no lights. I felt a rage well up inside me and nearly screamed some abuse at the arsehole, but managed to contain my rage as the most important thing, I told myself, was not to draw unnecessary attention. When I got to the junction at the bottom of the hill, I took the quieter route to the ferry by avoiding the central plaza on the right. This was a more circuitous route that went past the fire station and came in to the pier from the other side. I took this way to avoid recognition from anyone at the bus station or exiting from the ferry.

It was now coming up for 7pm so the ferry coming in would be packed with commuters. I swiped my Octopus card on the reader, slipped through the barriers and found a quiet corner in which to wait for the incoming ferry to empty its load of passengers. I took my seat near the front of the boat and within 30 minutes I was getting off at Central Pier 3. As I strolled along the harbourfront, I opened my rucksack, took out the green plastic shopping bag and casually dropped it in a nearby rubbish bin. I zipped up my bag, headed towards the Star Ferry at Pier 7 and continued the rest of my uneventful journey home.

EEE

Chapter 3

Monday 22nd August 2011

A week on and little had changed for Chambers. His new life in Hong Kong had settled into a routine of working, eating and sleeping. He hadn't had much spare time to have a look around the city at this early stage; in fact, the only time he been off Hong Kong Island was when he arrived at Chek Lap Kok Airport on Lantau Island when he arrived. He was getting a better understanding of how the department worked; the Organised Crime and Triad Bureau that he'd been seconded to would, he hoped, hold the identification of the man he was looking for somewhere in their copious records of all of Hong Kong's gang members.

The week before, on his first day, Chambers had been sitting at his new desk when a young, uniformed constable approached.

'Excuse me, Detective Inspector Chambers?' The officer asked with a hint of what Chambers took to be embarrassment.

'That's me, how can I help?' Chambers offered the junior a friendly greeting, despite the cracking headache he was suffering. He'd had it since he had woken that morning, he'd put it down to dehydration, making a mental note to drink more water.

'Sir, I have been told to ask you to report to Chief Inspector Pang in Meeting Room 1 immediately.'

'Sure thing, can you just tell me where that might be?'

'End of the corridor. It's the last door on the left.' The young man pointed, then turned and walked back to his desk.

'Thanks, and by the way there's no need to call me sir,' Chambers called out to the constable's back. Aware his raised voice was drawing inquisitive looks from his new colleagues, he spun round in his chair, picked up his notebook and made his way towards the Chief Inspector's office. He stopped outside the solid wooden door and knocked, he had already seen through the floor to ceiling window that there were five people in the room and he could hear the sing-song sound of their Cantonese conversation. As he knocked the chatter died away.

'Come in.'

As Chambers entered the brightly lit room all the members of the group stood up. The room had all the standard office equipment, a large plain white table with seating enough for eight, plus a whiteboard with three non-permanent markers in the primary colours. There was also the all-pervasive smell of old coffee plus another odour, not altogether unpleasant, that he couldn't quite put his finger on.

'Hello DI Chambers, I hope you have settled in OK, I'm Chief Inspector James Pang, we've been liaising by email this past week so it's good to put a face to a name. Let me begin by welcoming you to the OCTB, and just to confuse you further, we refer to ourselves as the O Gai – don't worry, it's just the Department's Cantonese nickname. But I'm sure you will hear it used a great deal.'

Chambers recognised this as the voice that had invited him into the room a moment before. His English, he thought, was very good, although he seemed to put the wrong emphasis on certain syllables, but as Chambers spoke no other languages, he was in no position to criticise anyone else's linguistic capabilities.

Before Chambers could respond, the Chief Inspector continued, 'OK, let's get the introductions out of the way; this is DI Brian Tang, Sergeant Stephen Tsoi and Station Sergeant Peter Yuen.' He indicated the three men around the table. 'And this is Detective Lucy Li,' he gestured to the only female in the room.

Whether it was his innate sense of manners, or some other force at work, Chambers found himself with his hand outstretched. He noticed too late he was blushing, something he was aware he hadn't done for a very long time.

'Jo saan', he heard himself mumbling, this was his first attempt at saying good morning in Cantonese to another human being rather than his comical attempts in the mirror. She gave him a warm smile as she offered her hand in return, and said, 'jo saan. Good morning DI Chambers, welcome to Hong Kong. And you speak Cantonese, how lovely.' Chambers shook her hand, had he detected a slight Australian accent? More than anything he hoped his palms were drier than the rest of him.

Pang saved him from the awkward silence that ensued. 'DI Chambers, I've assigned Detective Li to assist you. She's your first point of contact for whatever you may need.'

Chambers took this to mean CI Pang was not to be disturbed by his every whim and that Li was to effectively be his go-between and buffer, not just for the street but also for dealing with pretty much everyone and everything. Either Pang didn't like Chambers' chances on his own or, more than likely, he doubted his London skills would easily transfer to Hong Kong. Either way, Chambers felt Li's help could only be a blessing. She was tall, attractive, with a slim figure, about 30-years-old and had long, silky, jet-black hair. It could be worse, he found himself thinking.

Pang continued, 'there's obviously a lot of other members in the department, but those gathered in here are the only ones who know about your case, and the ones whose expertise I think will come in very handy to you. Brian here is our resident Triad symbol expert, our Triad cryptographer if you will, anything from the significance of the colours worn by the gang members to the type and symbolism of their tattoos, he's your man. If you need ground support from our Emergency Units – the uniforms or plainclothes officers – then talk to Stephen. Finally, Peter is on hand to liaise with any of our other bureaus. Whether it's armed response, harbour police or the Police Tactical Unit, just ask him. Of course, if you need to get Peter involved you had better clear it with me first. At the moment most of our resources are tied up in a major ketamine investigation. The streets of Hong Kong are awash with the stuff and it's taking up a lot of our resources. So as much as possible these people are here to help you, but please understand there are limitations of what we can offer.'

Chambers thanked the team and shook hands with the others. When it was clear the meeting was over, for him anyway, he excused himself and left the room. He was a little bemused by this show of support. Having everything available to him at his behest was definitely not something he was used to at the Met. As he headed back to his desk he tried to keep any cynical thoughts at bay. He was the new guy here, was this common practice or just a way of fobbing him off? Only time would tell whether the offer of support was genuine or not.

His first week had been spent familiarising himself with the OCTB systems and procedures. One thing was clear, Chambers concluded, police forces all over the world, had a shared love of paper work. Li, whose desk was opposite his, had been quick to point out to him that the name Hak Loong meant Black Dragon in Cantonese. Chambers knew this from the dedicated Triad team back at the station where he was based in the West End of London, but deferred mentioning it. He didn't want to sound like a know-all in front of her. His intuition told him she was going to be essential in his navigation of this case and the city in general. He wanted her onside from the outset.

'OK, that's a good start, so do you have a folder of images, either hard or soft copy, that I can begin to work through?' he asked her. 'I mean, if he's got form in the UK, there's a good chance he's already on your books, right?'

'The only problem with that is the name 'Black Dragon', more than likely, is a reference to the Triad group he's involved in. It's more likely he's in a subdivision of a gang like the K19, or it could simply be a reference to a tattoo or even a childhood nickname. But I seriously doubt it's a nickname, and it's certainly not a reference to his rank. Ranks are usually numeric.'

She obviously saw his look of disappointment. 'Don't worry; if he's in Hong Kong we'll find him, you needn't worry about that'. She gave him a reassuring nod. 'I'll send you a link to the photographs we have of all known Triads in Hong Kong. I'll email you a link to the 'O' drive where they're kept.' She paused. 'Assuming he's from Hong Kong, that is,' she tailed off.

'What do you mean?' This was definitely not good news. He was under a lot of pressure from his superiors to 'get a result and get it fast'.

'Well,' Li continued, 'there's no guarantee he's a Hong Kong Triad, he could be from the mainland, across the border in Shenzhen, or even from one of the many Triad groups in North America, Europe or anywhere in the world.'

'All the information we received at the Westminster Chinese Unit from various sources say he's come to Hong Kong.' Chambers didn't feel the need at this stage to explain to his new colleague that he worked for the Metropolitan Police out of the West End Central Station that was also the home of the Westminster Chinese Unit, the team responsible, among many other activities, with keeping tabs on local Triad activities.

'Look I'm not saying he's not here, and if he is, we'll find him. I just think you need to face facts. The longer this investigation drags on the greater the chance that he's moved on. Especially if this isn't his home city, he might just have made a detour on the way to his final destination, wherever that is.'

Chambers thought about this. The only information was from the usual snitches. How reliable was their information? As reliable as ever, he guessed. That meant anywhere from hard fact to pure fiction. He knew when he was sent out to Hong Kong that this case had the potential to be a major blot on what was until now anyway, an impressive record. It could also be a career killer. He was the lead investigator on a double murder in Chinatown. The London papers were referring to them as the 'Rupert Street Slayings' predicting this was going to be the start of a Triad turf war in central London. Two local Chinese traders had been shot and hacked to death, supposedly by the man in the photo. So now Chambers was in Hong Kong looking for the proverbial needle in a haystack. He just didn't know if the needle was in this particular haystack.

≈≈≈

Chapter 4 – Mr Jolly Rides Again

Friday 4th February – Saturday 5th March 2011

Dear diary,

I've decided to use this journal solely for the purpose of recording all the necessary information about my new 'hobby'. I need to keep meticulous notes of the events as they will be essential to what I plan to do with them later. I'm putting down the facts as best as I recall them, but maybe from time to time I might tell something that didn't really happen, slight embellishments from time to time. After all, your brain can play tricks can't it? My brain in particular has a funny way of processing information. But my memory seems to be very clear; my recall of events is crystal, maybe it's the amount of adrenalin pumping through my system when I'm at it. I don't really know. Or maybe it's the omnipotent power that I feel; the total and absolute control. As I have a lot to do, I want to write this down as soon as it happens, that way I can avoid any confusion later. I've got a feeling I'm going to be making a lot of entries.

The discovery of the body was reported in the *South China Morning Post* on Saturday, because the body was only found on Friday morning. Turns out he was called Michael Watson. He lived in Discovery Bay with his wife, Mrs Ellen Watson, 38, and child, Russell Watson, 8, according to the paper. I like how they go into so much irrelevant detail. Like the age of his son is in someway important. Apparently he told his wife he was hiking over to go drinking in Mui Wo with friends and she had gone to sleep expecting him to return later that night. When she woke at around 6am and realised he wasn't back, she had called a couple of his friends and when they could not confirm his whereabouts, she had phoned the police. The body was found at 8am by Mr Jan van den Hauwe, also a resident of Discovery Bay. He had been on a training run with his dogs as he prepared for the upcoming Standard Chartered Hong Kong Marathon in a couple of weeks' time. The victim's red jacket had caught his eye as he descended the path from the plateau. It wasn't too far off the path, among some rocks. He had called the police and by 9am the place was alive with local police including a helicopter brought in to remove the body. It was taken to nearby Tung Chung police station for identification. The police issued a statement: 'The body of a 45-year-old man has been found on Lantau Island. The matter would be thoroughly investigated and the findings announced after a post mortem had been carried out.'

I kept an eye on the *South China Morning Post* over the next few days, as a dead gweilo, or expat, was big news in Hong Kong. There were interviews with the victim's wife, leading police figures, and of course, in true Hong Kong style, a battery of politicians angling to maximise their department's cause by somehow muscling in on the story or for self-righteous newspaper editors looking for someone to blame so they could sell more papers. The list ranged from the usual whipping boys at the Tourism Board roundly getting criticised for not making the island's hiking trails safer for visitors, to the Parks committee's need for more funding to make all of the natural areas of Hong Kong better for all, the police departments calling for more police and hardware, and green groups looking to further the cause of looking after the region's native fauna. The amount of people with an axe to grind was seemingly endless.

On the following Saturday, the *South China Morning Post* announced that a toxicology report confirmed Mr Watson had died from a snakebite complicated by exposure and head trauma. 'The venom', the report showed, 'had come from a Chinese Cobra that normally preferred to evade rather than confront humans, although it could rear up, spit venom or bite if surprised'. Whether the toxicity alone was strong enough was complicated by head injuries the victim had received in the fall. The article continued on by hypothesising that, 'the victim was incredibly unfortunate to have alarmed the snake, possibly by standing on it. This type of snake could be found all over Hong Kong, although it was quite a rare species. Its reaction was to strike out and bite Mr Watson on the lower extremity. In a state of shock, it appears he had taken several steps back before tumbling down the rock face behind him. The coroner had concluded the victim had died by misadventure.'

I read the article several times, then put the paper down and noticed my hands were shaking. Although I'd been confident, the plan had worked better than I really believed it would. After I had got home that night, I'd been left with a nagging doubt that he might have regained consciousness and been able to get down the mountain. I'd forgotten to frisk him, something that became clear to me at 3am the following morning, when I woke in a cold sweat, suddenly recalling I never checked the body for a mobile phone. I was left with a gnawing sensation in the pit of my stomach until the weak light of dawn signaled it was time for me to rise. In fact the first time I was rid of that uncomfortable feeling was when I read the article about the body's discovery on Saturday morning, as I enjoyed my breakfast at the Starbucks around the corner from my apartment.

I thought afterwards that I had been lucky on the day. First, there were even fewer people around than I had thought, the victim had been alone, I'd not had any problems with dealing with him, or with the snake. But I also knew I had been lucky that he hadn't regained consciousness and my failure to check for a phone could have been costly. Also I hadn't run into anyone else just before or after the incident – the only close call had been with the cyclist when I was crossing the road. I could afford to laugh about it now, but at the time that could have put an embarrassing end to my plans, and that way no one would ever get to know about what I was up to, and that's the part I'm really looking forward to.

But I knew that they all wouldn't be so straightforward, especially as my next assignment was on Hong Kong Island.

ΞΞΞ

I was wearing practically the same clothes as I had been the last time. Not for any superstitious reason, the weather was a fair bit warmer, so I'd left the jacket at home. I left the Star Ferry and took the steps up to the pedestrian bridge that leads to the side entrance of ifc, that enormous consumer Mecca. I bypassed the place and continued on the network of raised walkways that span most of the lower end of the Central district, before I dropped down to street level, crossed the road at Ice House Street and headed to the tram stop outside the Burberry store on Des Voeux Road. A couple of trams came along before the one I wanted. The familiar yellow and green destination sign was visible from a good distance away. The tram was crowded as they always were on weekends. I pushed my way to the top deck and stood at the front.

I needed to sit by the front window, it's important to me, and after staring long enough at the old woman who occupied the position, she eventually got up and went downstairs, cursing me under her breath. Personally I think she should think herself lucky – on another day when I wasn't as busy, I might have been paying her an unexpected and unpleasant visit. Once in the seat I pulled the window down and enjoyed the scenery of downtown Hong Kong. The tram has long been a favourite mode of transport for me on Hong Kong Island. I didn't mind the speed, or the fact that every other road user took advantage of its lack of acceleration to box it in or slow its progress. It's like everything else in life, give someone an inch and they'll take a mile. Well, I was in no rush; I had all day to take care of my particular business. When we were rattling along I quickly checked my rucksack's contents: matches; rope; gloves; gaffer tape; plastic bag; camera; T-shirt; and a hammer wrapped in cloth. I was careful; I didn't take anything out of the bag, because you never know who is watching. There are a lot of nosey bastards about.

When we came to a halt at the terminus, I took my time leaving, making sure not to bang my head on the low ceiling of the old tram. I swiped my card and exited at the front of the tram. I took a quick look around, The Jockey pub nearby was suprisingly full but not nearly as busy as it would be on a Wednesday night. I crossed the road and headed towards the main stand. Saturdays were normally pretty quiet around here, as most of the residents would be in nearby Causeway Bay, satiating their shopping addictions. I slipped into the main stand through an open turnstile, there was fortunately no security guard in sight. There was a lot of activity on the inside section of the racetrack as there are several football and rugby pitches that were always busy on weekends. A running track circumnavigated the inside. But this was of little interest to me as I headed towards the stables underneath the main stand. I had no specific target in mind, knowing this was going to be about taking advantage of whatever opportunity would present itself to me.

Don't ask me how or why, but since I started on my new path, life has just got a little bit easier. Like when I was on Lantau Island last month, things just lined up, as if they were just meant to be. The same thing happened today. First the lack of security on the turnstile, then as I was passing one of the small blockhouses that act as stables for the horses on race day, there was this old guy sitting on a small stool in the doorway reading the paper. There were no horses or jockeys around as the racing on weekends took place up in Sha Tin in the New Territories, so the likelihood was there wouldn't be too many people in the vicinity. I took a quick look around and when I saw there was no one about I slipped the bag off my shoulder, put on my gloves and unwrapped the hammer, dropping the cloth on the floor.

The old man was still reading the paper oblivious to my presence as I approached cautiously, took one last look around to make sure no one was coming. I hit him several times on the back of his head. I'm not sure why, but I thought the hammer might have got stuck in his skull. The first blow knocked him forward, and I felt

31

the jolt through my arm, like a badly played golf shot. The noise, as I recall, and the sensation reminded me a little bit of cracking a boiled egg, just on a bigger scale. The second blow knocked him onto all fours in the straw on the stable floor. By the fifth hit he was lying motionless. I wheeled around, there hadn't been much noise, well he'd been quiet anyway, just the dull thump of the hammer on his skull. I stood still for a moment to listen. I could make out the shouts from the football pitches several metres or so away.

I took a few steps forward and collected the cloth. Wiping first my face, then the hammer. It had a bit of blood on it, not as much as I thought it would have. I then wrapped the hammer in the cloth and put it in the plastic bag and back in my rucksack. I took off my jumper and put on the spare T-shirt. I turned back and leaned in close to take one last look at the man, who lay perfectly still. I noticed he had fallen face first onto what I could now see was the racing section of the South China Morning Post. Among the blood splatter, hair, bits of skull and brain that was spread over the newsprint, the headline was referring to a story about the return to form of a locally bred horse. It read, 'Mr Jolly Rides Again'.

Before I took my leave, I took out the box of matches, struck one and blew it out. There were a lot of flammable objects in there and I didn't want to go starting any unnecessary fires, now that would be irresponsible. As he was lying on his front, I pushed the dead match into the dead man's back pocket. I picked up a horseshoe from a pile in the corner of the shed and placed it on the man's lower back. I made a quick survey of the scene to make sure I hadn't left any signs. When I was confident there was nothing, I took my leave, removing my gloves and stuffing them in my pack. Keeping my head down I went back out the same way I had come in, but instead of going back to the tram stop by the pub, I followed the Wong Nai Chung Road along the back of the main stand to the next stop which was conveniently empty.

I waited about five minutes for the tram I needed. When it slowed down, I got on and took a seat on the lower deck this time. As I sat down on the bench, there were a couple of Filipina maids opposite me. They were staring at me, I looked away and after a while I just looked down at my hands, that's when I noticed the blood on my trousers. Not a lot, and my trousers were dark blue so it showed up more as a damp patch, but enough for me to notice. I looked back at the women opposite, they were talking loudly even though they were sitting inches apart. Had they noticed? Two stops later at the wet markets they got up to alight. One of them had looked at my trousers as she was getting up, then she looked me straight in the eye before she exited the tram. During the next 30 minutes that it took for the tram to trundle its way back to Central, I was careful not to touch the blood. I placed my rucksack on my knees until I got off near where I'd got on earlier in the day. My breathing and heart rate had returned to normal by then. I took a quick walk along the raised walkway that links back to the Central Piers, making one diversion to the same rubbish bin on the waterfront to deposit my plastic bag before I returned to board the Star Ferry.

ΞΞΞ

Chapter 5

Tuesday 30th August 2011

Chambers took the free newspaper from the vendor's outstretched
hand as he made his way patiently to the police station. It was
Tuesday morning and his head was pounding. This was his third week
in Hong Kong. His frustration was obvious to himself and his new
colleagues. He was no longer being over-friendly to the other officers
in the bureau, and apart from the morning jo saan and nei ho his
interaction was limited. He spoke only to Lucy and even then it was
sparingly. He had searched through the entire 'O' drive. Checking
and rechecking thousands upon thousands of mug shots from minor
level Triads to the so-called big hitters. He'd been through folders
of photographs that dated back over a decade. Nothing. He hated to
admit it, but at the beginning of the search, he had a fear he might end
up with a lot of possibilities. He knew if he mentioned this to anyone
he'd be strung up for racism, the white policeman's worst nightmare.
But he was genuinely concerned that by looking at the multitude of
images of predominantly young Han Chinese men, that there may be
an element of repetition. He was surprised that he'd barely seen five
pictures that could even be slightly confused with the man he sought.

Chambers slumped into his chair and opened the newspaper. He'd taken to reading it every morning over the past week; it gave him a way of starting the day with things unrelated to his case and he hoped would give him a better feel for the new city. He sipped his coffee as he browsed the pages without expecting to find any insightful articles. His experience of *The Standard* was that it was a good overview of what was going on in the world for those people who didn't have Internet access. It reminded him of the free papers that for a few years seemed to be multiplying back in London. After rush hour on the tube the inside of most carriages was wallpapered with the flotsam of commuters' cast off newsprint, thankfully the authorities had clamped down on it before the whole tube system ground to a halt under the weight of discarded paper. One of the major differences was, he concluded, that at least the London papers had a little bit of interesting content, the back pages might be filled with the clichéd sound bites of premiership football managers, but the listings for gigs and events were almost always reliable.

The Standard, on the other hand - well he was yet to find its redeeming qualities. It was an odd mix of biased editorial, weird news from the mainland, European football reports that were at least two days out of date and some very odd columnists. The overall result gave Chambers a sense that if they were reflective of the readership, then the average Hong Konger couldn't be quite the full quid. It was also one of those newspapers that have given up the pretence that it is a bastion of the truth, determinedly searching out stories that can topple governments, providing its readership with informed, thought provoking and exciting opinion pieces, and if that meant selling a few more adverts then so be it. Whereas *The Standard* had no qualms about selling out wholeheartedly to the advertiser without any attempt at advertorial subtlety. Every day that he'd picked up the paper, the front page was dedicated to a real estate company or a high street jeweller. Tuesday's paper was no different. A huge wraparound advert for some new and expensive tower block in a part of Hong Kong he'd never heard of.

Chambers was expecting to break his own record for reading the paper cover to cover in less than 15 minutes. He was hopeful, as early in the week the paper had fewer pages. No wonder it's free, he thought, you can't charge people for 32 pages that include about 16 full-page ads. But as he turned the page, all thoughts of a quick read vanished. The headline read 'Murder in the Park'. The article was light on facts. Peter, Ho Man Kwok, had been found with serious head injuries in the aviary at Kowloon Park the previous evening by a park employee. Kwok, 21, was believed to have died from blunt force trauma. There was no mention of the weapon used or whether it had been found.

He put down the paper and leaned back in his chair for a moment. 'Lucy,' he called across the desk, 'did you hear about this murder in the park?' leaning forward he showed her the relevant article.

'The one in Kowloon last night? Sure. Why? What about it?' She barely took her eyes off the flat screen in front of her.

'Why would this be front-page news? Does the paper think it's a Triad-related crime? I don't see the significance of it. Or is this guy Kwok famous or something? Does he have some form? Is he in our files?'

'I doubt it, to be honest; we've not had any requests as yet from anyone on the investigating team from Kowloon. It just sounds like a robbery to me.'

'So, if it's a robbery gone wrong, how come it's front-page news? I mean it's tragic, but apart from that, I don't see why it's so prominent, is there no news in Hong Kong?'

'Well Detective Inspector,' she adopted a heavy Chinese accent, 'that is because you come from the big smoke, dangerous city like London town, manee murders, manee crimes.' She was laughing now as she reverted back to her normal voice. 'Hong Kong might be famous for its Triads, but to be honest, the crime rate for most things here is very, very low. For example, in 2007 the number of murders in Hong Kong was only 18. That's for the whole year. You probably get that in London every month, or maybe a week! So yes, a murder here will likely get front-page coverage.'

Chambers pondered for a moment on the figure. Eighteen murders in a year? That was incredibly low. He racked his memory for the murder stats back home. He tended to try and forget the real numbers as they didn't make for pleasant reading. But if he remembered correctly, it was just somewhere near 200 a year, and that was just for London. That would explain why they were not on the front page, with that number there'd be little room for any other stories.

'Maybe it's due to your small population,' he replied, not wanting to let her in on what he knew.

'Well, Hong Kong has about seven million people, so it's not that much smaller than London. But I'll bet you whatever you want that our murder rate is a lot lower than you've got in the UK. What's the population of London? Eight, ten million?' She was giving him a knowing look. Chambers felt defeated already. He decided to change tack.

'Do you think this might have anything to do with our case?' He appreciated that deflecting her challenge sounded weak.

'I don't see why it would.' She gave him a puzzled look. 'We can check his details; see if he's been a naughty boy. In fact, I have a better idea.' She picked up the handset from her desk phone and pressed three numbers.

'Hi Brian, can you do me a huge favour? Can you run a check on last night's murder victim? Just see if there's anything that might be of interest in relation to his, er, connections. Thanks so much. I'll call you back later for an update.'

Chambers watched Li. There was something intensely attractive about her. Even now, as she spoke to a colleague about a work-related issue, she had an aura that he found completely captivating. He'd noticed that nearly every day she wore her long hair in a different style, today it was hanging down in loose yet perfect curls. In his eyes she was beautiful enough to be a model. She was certainly more attractive than the models he'd seen in the ads plastered all over Hong Kong's advertising hoardings.

She snapped him out of his musings. 'OK partner, grab your coat, I'm taking you on an adventure. You're about to get your first taste of Kowloon-side Hong Kong.'

~~~

Li hailed a cab on the slip road in front of the Wanchai Police Station. The driver swung in and the old red box-shaped cab stopped abruptly in front of them, the back left passenger door automatically popping open. Chambers held the door for Li; he followed her in and saw the door close behind him. Hong Kong taxis were quite different to anything he had seen before. Most of the ones he'd seen were made by Toyota, but the design looked very dated maybe as far back as the 1980s. The old-style seemed acutely at odds with the rest of the ultra-modern cars that cruised the roads of Hong Kong. On closer investigation, Chambers could see the steel bar contraption that allowed the cabbie to open the back door for customers.

Li told the cab driver their destination in Cantonese. Chambers decided against starting a conversation with her, as the combination of the music blaring from the speakers and the crackling voice of the taxi controller repeating the same phrase over the radio every ten seconds rendered it nigh on impossible anyway. He looked out of the window and enjoyed the view as the taxi merged with the heavy traffic on Gloucester Road heading in the direction of Central. The road passed close by to some historical colonial-style buildings that contrasted sharply with several futuristic buildings set a block further back that looked like they came from a different world.

Li followed his gaze, and pointed out to him the sharply angular

Bank of China building and the red and white neon-framed HSBC head office building. The cab entered a tunnel and a couple of minutes later pulled up alongside Pier 7 at Central. Before Chambers could get to his wallet, Li had paid the driver the HK$30 fare.

'Up or down?' Li asked him as they took their leave of the cab, the door closing of its own accord.

'What do you mean?'

'Have you been on the Star Ferry before?'

'No.'

'Really? Have you seen any of Hong Kong's famous landmarks?' She gave him a look of astonishment, shaking her head slowly. 'Upper or lower deck? Which one would you prefer? Traditionally the gweilos, sorry, the colonials, would travel on the upper deck and the poor Chinese workers would travel on the lower deck.' She stared at him before flashing a smile that had the effect of rendering him almost speechless and not in a position to point out her unnecessary anti-colonial sentiments.

There was little Chambers could do personally, he felt, to mitigate what had happened as a result of Britain taking Hong Kong from the Chinese in the Opium Wars, the best part of two centuries ago.

'OK, let's go downstairs, I'm not fussy.' Chambers felt himself getting frustrated. He liked her, but she always seemed to be making fun of him. He had noticed over the past few days that he'd catch himself idly looking at her. Every now and again, she would turn her gaze to meet his, and of course, he would immediately look away, embarrassed. God only knew what she thought of him. For all he knew, she probably just thought he was some kind of lecherous older man.

She led the way, swiping her card and walking towards the gate at the far end of the short pier. Chambers was left fumbling for the HK$2.20 fare to get through the turnstile. When he caught up with her, she was holding out a multi-coloured plastic credit card towards him.

'You really ought to get yourself one of these. It's an Octopus card, it allows you to swipe your way onto all forms of transport and pay for stuff in convenience stores and supermarkets. I'm pretty sure almost everyone in Hong Kong has one. Saves a lot of hassle,' she said with a slightly patronising tone, again offset by one of her winning smiles.

'Thanks for the tip. I think I've got a lot to learn about living in this city.' He was interrupted by the loud and abrupt buzzing of the gate as it swung open.

Other passengers started down the wooden ramp to the open-sided ferry that was bobbing next to the pier. They tagged along and entered the lower deck. Chambers followed her to a row of wooden seats. She yanked the back of the seat across, changing the direction the seat faced so they could look at the view of the harbour that opened before them. Chambers looked around the boat; it was like going back in time. The deckhands were dressed in old-fashioned navy outfits that would look more at home on a child in a picture from the eighteenth century. The ferry emanated an innate sense of history and tradition. There were huge pipes with large steel rivets and brass plates lining the sides of the dark green and white-coloured vessel. The deckhands were furiously coiling large snakes of rope and getting ready to cast off. The walkway was raised by a series of thinner ropes and pulleys, and within a minute of boarding, the ferry was sliding away from the pier.

Chambers craned his neck to get a better view. From the little bits of information he had gleaned from his cursory reading of his Lonely Planet guide, this was an essential excursion for any tourist visiting the city. He had planned on taking the following weekend to do some of the touristy stuff. But this was a pleasant interruption into what was turning out to be a frustrating case. He could see why this excursion was so popular. As he enjoyed the stunning views of the surrounding harbour, Li leaned towards him.

'Do you know this old ferry service has a very romantic history?'

Chambers continued to stare out at the harbour. He didn't know what to say.

'The Star Ferry Company was started by an Indian merchant back in 1888; he named the company after his love of Tennyson's poem, Crossing the Bar.' She paused for a short while before reciting:

'Sunset and evening star,

And one clear call for me!

And may there be no moaning of the bar,

When I put out to sea,

But such a tide as moving seems asleep,

Too full for sound and foam,

When that which drew from out the boundless deep

Turns again home.'

She spoke the final two lines almost in a whisper.

Chambers who had been looking out to the water, turned to face her but she was looking out past him as if lost in thought. He was struggling to find any words that would suit the occasion, he said: 'How lovely,' aware of how pathetic it sounded after Li's moving rendition of the poem.

His words seemed to snap her out of the spell, she looked straight at him.

'It has a romantic history. I really love coming down here and taking the ferry. Sometimes I just turn around and come straight back, there's such a magical quality about gliding across the harbour. It is like all the problems in your life, no matter how troublesome, for a few minutes anyway, they all seem to disappear.'

They sat in silence for the rest of the short journey. She somewhere else deep in thought, while he was aware how banal anything he said would sound after her beautiful soliloquy. He had a hunch there was something troubling Li, but was it right to pry? He didn't feel he knew her well enough yet to be asking any personal questions. The whole crossing lasted less than ten minutes. By the time they walked up the ramp she was back to her usual self.

'Welcome to Kowloon,' she said and within seconds the first of what would be many salesmen from the subcontinent approached him offering the latest in 'good copy' watches and the 'finest' tailored suits. He followed her, fending off vendors with a range of ripostes from downright ignoring them to firm refusals and the occasional fearsome scowl – well as fearsome as he could muster. She was ahead of him, not necessarily moving quickly, but gracefully weaving in and out of the crowds, while he blundered along behind her. He eventually caught up with her at a set of traffic lights.

As they crossed she gestured to the building ahead of her to the right, 'The Grande Old Dame'.

He looked up and saw the name 'The Peninsula'. The name meant nothing to him, but he didn't want to admit to his ignorance, so he just nodded while making a mental note to read more of his guidebook when he got home.

She took a left at the end of the hotel on to a broad street that was buzzing with action. For the first time since he'd been in Hong Kong, Chambers became aware of a change in the demographic. Where he was now living and working was predominantly Chinese, at work he was the only foreigner, and walking around the streets of Causeway Bay the ratio of Chinese to others appeared to be about 100:1, and those were mostly Caucasian. Here was completely different. Apart from the multitude of Indian 'traders' there was a large number of African men and women. He walked on, mesmerised by the sheer volume of pedestrians, and the vibe of the place – it was akin to Oxford Street during the January sales. He passed a shop selling, well he wasn't sure, there were some dried fish, dried lizards pegged out on sticks, but there were also plenty of other dehydrated things. He could not envisage what they would have been when they were alive, some might have been vegetables and there was definitely some dry mushrooms and what might be dried plums, but the shop fascinated him. Not the sort of thing you see every day he thought, until he saw there was another open-fronted store a few doors down trading in exactly the same kind of things.

He looked across the street. The shops there seemed to be selling mainly cameras and other digital equipment. His eyes scanned the neon signs. This would be an interesting place to come back and visit after nightfall. He continued his exploration while keeping an eye on Li up ahead. After several hundred metres, she took a left near the train station. Along this street she took a right and Chambers found himself walking up a steep slope into a city park. It took a minute for him to catch up both physically and mentally.

'Kowloon Park right?' He said as he drew level with her.

'Got it in one,' she replied without turning to look at him.

She took the path to the left and stopped at a fence that encircled a pond. He stopped and leaned on the metal railings as he regained his composure. He wasn't in bad shape but walking in this heat in the middle of the day had taken its toll. His armpits were damp along with his brow and back. He looked over quickly at her. Not a drop of sweat on her or a hair out of place. How do the locals do it? He wondered, returning his gaze to the pond. At the far end was a mass of pink.

'Hey are those ...'

'Yes,' she interrupted. 'Flamingoes. Cool eh? Right in the middle of this dense urban sprawl is a park with a pond full of pink flamingoes.'

He was taken aback, and began walking towards them. This time it was her turn to follow. He took up a new position closer to the large crimson birds. Most of them were standing idly on one stick-thin leg.

43

It looked incredibly uncomfortable, and the more he thought about it, particularly hard to do with such a high centre of gravity. But they stood as motionless as statues, evidently at one with the world around them.

'How the hell do they do that?' he asked of the approaching Li. 'And what are they doing in a pond in Kowloon; they're from Africa aren't they?'

'Ha ha, good question. I'm sorry to tell you I don't know how they do that, or in fact why. It looks so awkward, doesn't it?'

They stood in silence for several minutes admiring the birds.

'Come on. Follow me,' she said, making for a flight of stone stairs off to their right. They passed an enormous Banyan tree that had grown into the 10-metre-high wall next to the stairs. The roots of the tree had become a part of the wall; the result gave the structure a look like something found in Angkor Wat.

They walked up the stairs together; Chambers realising they were now standing in a raised aviary encircled by the high stone wall with the canopy of the Banyan trees cutting off most of the natural light. The place had reopened to the public and judging from the assortment of tourists gawping at the colourful selection of non-native birds, he guessed that none of the other visitors knew this was the scene of a grisly murder less than 24 hours previously.

'Why did you bring me here?' he asked her at last. 'There's nothing to see.'

'Look, to be honest, I just wanted to get you out of the office for a while. I've sat opposite you and seen your face grow longer and longer every day that you've been poring over those files. I thought it would do you good to get out of there. To see a bit of Hong Kong and get you more familiar with what this city is all about.'

'Right, OK. So what now then?'

'Come on John, you need to relax a little bit. The case isn't going to be solved in a day. Take the murder here last night, I'm sure it has absolutely nothing to do with your case so let's just enjoy a few hours out of the office. If you want, we can take a cab and have a drive around some of the more recognised Triad hangouts. Knutsford Terrace, Mong Kok and back to TST where we got off the ferry. I think at this stage it's about you being able to visualise the places you're reading about. Most of the Triad-related action takes place over on this side of the harbour, so you need to get familiar with here.' With that, she circled the walkway of the aviary and exited down the stairs on the other side.

Chambers followed, scanning the area as he went. If he didn't know there'd been a murder the previous day, there was nothing discarded by the investigating police team to show anything had happened. He took one last look around at the noisy, colourful birds in their bizarrely located miniature rainforest enclosure in one of the most populous places on the planet. He bounded down the stairs after Li, marvelling at this quirky city and wondering what other strange sights he might see before the day was over.

≈≈≈

Chapter 6 – A Battering Ram

Sunday 6th March – Monday 4th April 2011

Dear diary,

Things are really progressing! The murder was on the front page of the *South China Morning Post* the day after it happened. The Sunday paper's cover story was about the brutal slaying of a retired stable hand at the Happy Valley racecourse. The report stated that the body had been found at around 4pm. A colleague had called round to the stables to invite the victim for a drink when he found the body. Police were appealing for witnesses to what they described as 'a heinous crime'. The main article stated 'the deceased's name was Mr Cheung Man Keung, known as Felix; he lived alone in a small apartment near the racecourse. He had worked at the Hong Kong Jockey Club for over 25 years and was a popular character around the racetrack', "he always had time for people," Mr Tsang, an ex-colleague was quoted in the paper as saying.

Salt of the earth, no doubt. Isn't it amazing how no one bad ever gets killed? The newspaper said the police were investigating whether Mr Cheung had any enemies, a history of gambling or any other debts that might have had something to do with his sudden demise. Mr Cheung had died almost instantly from blunt force trauma. The weapon, police suspected, was a standard, household-use hammer, but further tests were to be carried out.

The article read like they had no real leads to go on. No eyewitness accounts. I knew I hadn't been seen actually doing it, but I couldn't forget the women on the tram, had they seen the blood on my trousers? The write-up in the paper stated that on initial investigation the police believed the murder took place at around 3pm. I was on the tram back to Central at 3.15pm. There was certainly a risk one of the women could go to the police, but what could she tell them? That she saw a man on the tram that might, or might not, have had blood on his trousers. Anyway, I was taking no chances. I took the blue trousers I was wearing that day and the rucksack and carefully cut them both into strips. I mixed up the pieces and distributed them into four plastic bags; I tied the ends of the bags tightly. I would place them in rubbish bins around the area over the next few days.

I had known my second murder was going to be more problematic than the first, just by its very nature. There are not many quiet places on the north side of Hong Kong Island. But to have been lucky enough to find almost the perfect setting then realise my own stupid carelessness could have put the whole plan in jeopardy … I need to be much, much more attentive to detail in future as the next one's going to happen in a very busy place.

☰☰☰

On the day of my third murder, I got up late. Unlike the first two, this time I knew the victim, where he'd be and at what time he'd be there. The problem lay in getting the job done and getting away unseen.

His name was Daniel Lam, or in Cantonese, Lam Yin Yik. His routine was like clockwork. He had his third and final cigarette of his morning commute on the steps of the office building at 9.05am. Arriving at his desk at 9.15am, he was not the first in but by no means the last. A couple more cigarettes over the next few hours to accompany his morning pint of black coffee from the nearby Uncle Russ Coffee shop. Then the ritual of lunch with his fiancée who worked around the corner. Same boring restaurant, same boring dish, same boring chat. So far he was the only victim I actually knew, and there was something about him that made me feel I was actually doing him a favour. I had spoken to him a few times while I worked there. Like with most places, I hadn't lasted long. I didn't miss the tedious chores they made me do every day. These square heads telling me what to do when some of these cretins could barely tie their own shoelaces.

Daniel wasn't a bad guy, he wasn't management yet and so, in theory at least, he still had plenty of time to turn into an arsehole. During one of our infrequent conversations I had inadvertently picked up some critical information. We were talking casually, him blowing that hideous nicotine breath of his all over me, while at the same time revealing his giant false front tooth that was so out of place – not only was it enormous compared to the rest, it was also a different colour. Maybe these days dentists were using tar-resistant false teeth, now they just needed to come up with a solution for his other unsightly yellow fangs. Just to keep the conversation going and to appear friendly I asked him where he lived, and he gave me a long lecture on his neighbourhood, where he'd grown up and where he would live out the rest of his predictable and tedious existence. At the time neither he nor I could have realised exactly short a time that would be, or that we'd both be there to see his demise, right there in his own street as well, as luck would have it. For some reason it stuck in my mind and when the time came for number three, he just ticked all the boxes. Knowing who the victim was, had made my planning a little more long-winded. I needed to check for certain how he travelled to and from work, what his pattern was, how reliable this was. Fortunately for me, he was a dull creature of habit.

ΞΞΞ

I was sitting at the Tung Tat restaurant on Pitt Street by 7pm. It's right outside Exit A2 of the MTR Yau Ma Tei Station. He would be coming out of here any time soon. I had already walked the route. Up to the end of Pitt Street, a left on to Waterloo Road, past Kwong Wah Hospital, the junctions with Dundas Street and

Yim Po Fong Street and the next left was where the action would take place. I checked my new bag. I had bought a large sports holdall earlier that afternoon at the nearby Fa Yuen Street area that specialises in all sorts of sporting goods. I paid cash, I always pay cash. I've read too many stories about stupid people getting caught because they'd bought a weapon or something they used in a murder at a local store using their credit card. I mean how dumb are these people? Learn from other people's mistakes. That's what clever people do.

I wanted to get my weapon from the same street. My first thought was that a baseball bat would do the job nicely, but, as I was in Hong Kong, there might be something more accessible, and when I went into another sports shop I saw something that would work just as well. When I saw the brand name on it, I knew the fates were smiling on me. This was the clincher and a sure sign things were going to work out just fine. By the time I was at Tung Tat, I had transferred my other equipment to the holdall. Only the handle of my weapon was sticking innocuously out of the bag.

I was dressed casually, this time in tennis shorts, white socks and tennis shoes. I had a thin windbreaker-like jacket on over a polo shirt. I zipped the jacket right up to the collar; it just looked like I was getting ready to go for a game of tennis unless you looked too closely at my back-up racquet. I had chosen a seat a few rows back that offered me a clear view of people coming out of the exit. I checked the contents, the usual things were in the side pocket: camera, gaffer tape, box of matches and gloves. I took the gloves and put them in one pocket and the matches in the other. In the main part of the bag was a tennis racket, some tubes of tennis balls, baseball cap, my weapon, two red and white checked dishcloths and a pair of jogging bottoms. I folded up one of the tea cloths and placed it in the waistband of my shorts.

I'd been there maybe fifteen minutes, taking my time over a cup of strong milk tea, when my target exited the station; I recognised his profile under the flickering neon lights of the restaurant's sign. I called for the bill and left a HK$20 note on the table. I knew his route, so I was in no rush. I headed on to the pavement after I

49

made sure he had a 30 metre-or-so head start. The street was quite busy with both cars and pedestrians, so it was easy to follow at a safe distance. He hadn't seen me and why would he be looking? He lived an innocent life and I doubt whether he thought someone he worked with six months ago had been spending the last two weeks tailing him to and from his workplace and was planning to kill him tonight.

As I made my way along the predetermined route, I slipped on the gloves and put on my newly purchased navy blue New York Yankees baseball cap. I put my right hand through the holdall handles and then put my hands in my pockets. Dusk had turned to night and the road was lit up by street lamps and car headlights. I closed the gap between us to less than 20 metres as we approached Yim Po Fong Street. True to form, he swung into the McDonald's on the corner, which gave me my opportunity to go on ahead and wait for him. I darted across the road and under the train bridge, nearly stepping on a tramp who was sprawled on the floor. He hadn't been there when I passed earlier in the day. It wasn't common to see beggars in the city and his presence, or maybe his seeping leg ulcer, unnerved me momentarily.

I took the left into Peace Avenue – the irony of the name wasn't lost on me – and headed for the alley that was several metres up on the other side of the road. The alley went back a little way to a flight of ten or so steps and another path leading to the emergency exit of an apartment block. The alley was in near darkness, and I knew from earlier investigation that there was a recess in the wall just before the stairs. I put the holdall down and took out my weapon. I looked around then took up my position at the entrance to the alley and waited. He would cross near here; he lived a few doors further along the road. A few people walked past but I was in the shadows. From watching this alley on a few occasions previously, it only seemed to be used to dump rubbish in the big bins off a side entrance, so it was unlikely anyone would be turning into it. After a few minutes he crossed diagonally, puffing away on his cigarette, his free hand holding the top of a brown paper bag. I checked as best I could up the street. Almost directly opposite was a minibus stop, thankfully no one was there, and the street appeared quiet, apart from a couple walking towards the far end of the road.

I moved back to the nook and as he walked past the gap I called his name. He stopped. I called again, softer this time. I could see him smile, he obviously thought I was a friend or neighbour having a joke, I'm quite sure he wouldn't be expecting an ex-colleague was about to bludgeon the life out of him. As he turned into the alley. I took my chance. I stepped out and swung the weapon. He caught the full force straight in the face. I rained blows down thick and fast. Maybe 15 or 20, I don't know exactly. I dropped the club and pulled out the tea cloth. I wiped my face, then my shoes and turned back to open my bag. I removed the tracksuit bottoms from the holdall and was careful to unfurl them out of the way of the quickly spreading pool of blood that was threatening to cover the whole width of the alley. A car horn blared somewhere up the road to the right. The vehicle was accelerating down the road towards the junction with Waterloo Road. I was momentarily startled and fumbled as I put one foot into the waistband I was holding. I nearly fell over as one of my feet caught in the material.

I took the matches from my jacket pocket and was about to strike one when I heard the sound of a voice from behind the door up the short flight of stairs. At least I thought it was a voice, it was hard to say, the blood was pounding in my ears and the car horn had made me jumpy. I threw the matchbox at the body, the container was half open, and so the matches flew out in all directions. I turned, skirted the body and ran out of the alley, took a right and continued to move quickly along the road. The car I'd seen had passed by and there was no one in front of me. As I went, I took off my jacket and then my gloves, forcing them into the bag, keeping my face looking across the road to my left, as it was just a railway embankment on the other side, while on my right were a mixture of shops and entrances to apartments, some with security guards sitting in booths with nothing better to do than stare blankly at the street.

A right turn took me onto Liberty Avenue where I slowed down to a walk as it was lined with shops. The next left and I continued my escape on to Victory Avenue, a much busier road with several cars, minibuses and quite a few pedestrians. I tried to regulate my breathing and blend in with the other people walking or staring into the multitude of pet shops that lined both sides of the street. My first thought is I should have kept my cap on, but I didn't know if it was showing anything incriminating, blood or brains perhaps. Fortunately for me, most of the people were more intent on watching the pets cruelly imprisoned in their tiny cages, than to bother to look at the man striding past. I kept my head down and walked to the junction with Argyle Street, a left here and within a couple of minutes I was back in Mong Kok, enjoying the anonymity that the huge crowds offered. I made my way to the MTR Station and headed down the stairs to complete my getaway.

ΞΞΞ

Chapter 7

Thursday 22nd September 2011

Chambers woke up with a particularly sore throat. Every time he swallowed it felt like he was trying to eat shards of glass. The day before he had moved to the window to enjoy his morning view, but he'd been confronted by a wall of grey. This was no overcast day; the cloud was thick, like some unseen giant had laid an enormous grey blanket over the city. He couldn't see over to Kowloon, and from his lofty height, he could barely see the main road directly below his building. He made his usual way to work, but by the time he was at his desk, his eyes were stinging and his throat sore.

'Lucy, what the hell do you call that outside?' He asked motioning towards the office windows.

Li looked up from her screen. She rotated in her chair and looked out of the large windows that faced towards the harbour. She took her time, as if this was the first time she had seen it and she was trying to work out what this new phenomenon was. She turned slowly back towards him.

'Ah,' she said at last, 'welcome to Hong Kong's infamous pollution. The air quality has actually been really good since you arrived so I didn't want to draw your attention to it. I mean you could have solved the case and been back home in wet and windy London before we had a bad day.'

They were interrupted as one of the constables passed by. He was wearing a light green mask more commonly seen in operating theatres.

'And what is that all about?' he whispered, gesturing towards the back of the passing constable.

She followed his gaze, and then said in a soft voice, 'some Hong Kong residents are a bit paranoid about germs. Having said that, it could be the pollution, or it could be that he's got a cold and doesn't want to pass on the germs. Have you not seen the signs in the lifts?'

Chambers pictured the laminated sign in the lift that read: 'These buttons are disinfected every 15 minutes for your convenience and safety.' Chambers hadn't paid too much attention to it, as often when he was in the lift he got to witness a unique Hong Kong phenomenon. Whenever anyone entered the lift they naturally pressed the button of the floor they wanted to go to, followed quickly by jabbing the 'close door' button. No matter if it was rush hour and there were people running for the lift. If the person getting in the lift didn't press the button, then sure as anything, other lift passengers would be quick to intervene to get the door closed as quickly as possible. This behaviour intrigued Chambers, as surely no one could be in that much of a rush to get to their desks that they couldn't wait a few seconds for the doors to close automatically. But he'd witnessed the same behaviour in every lift he'd been in, so he could rule out members of the constabulary as being the only impatient ones.

'Yes, but are you telling me he might be wearing a mask to stop catching germs, to stop spreading then, or to cut out pollution? That seems a touch on the paranoid side. If he's really sick, surely he should just stay home.'

'Ah, this is another quaint local custom. Unless you're on death's door, and even then, you are expected to come to work. Simple as that.' She smiled at his look of displeasure at the thought of coming to work obviously sick.

He was secretly pleased to see her happy. He found himself inadvertently making comments to her to try and get her to smile or laugh, although he had an inkling that more often than not she was laughing at him, not with him.

Since his initial visit to Kowloon several weeks previously, Chambers had taken to going over there every couple of days. She was right, he needed to get better acquainted with the area, and while the chances of actually running into the suspect were slim, they couldn't be ruled out completely. He had taken to visiting in the evening as well, as there would be more obvious gang activity at night around the bars of Mong Kok and TST. He'd given up trying to say Tsim Sha Tsui. When he listened to how the locals pronounced it, the name sounded more like Chim Sha Joy or Jim Sha Choy. Either way, he found TST worked just as well. The other thing that he liked about going over in the evening was it was a bit cooler, so he didn't get a sweat on immediately, and the colourful lights and street signs came alive. He particularly liked Nathan Road, the street was a vibrant and industrious place where much of the action was not all above board, Chambers was sure of that. But at the southern end of the road it seemed like a multitude of small-time furtive operations, the nefarious ways of the vendors further enhanced by the garish neon lights.

Chambers had spoken with Li about getting access to the bureau's informers, and he knew from experience this was the best way forward. The problem was, he couldn't talk directly to them on the street, it was bad enough being seen with a white guy who looked like a policeman, it would be even worse with a translator in tow. No, he needed to hand this over to someone with more experience dealing with them. Li or even better Brian Tang, he was the go to man for Triad information.

He felt things were a little awkward between him and Li. The previous Friday he had invited her to join him for a drink after work. He'd meant it in a casual Friday drink scenario. It was very common at home for people to let off a bit of steam after work at the end of a tough week, and depending on their responsibilities, it could, and often did, turn into an all-nighter. Most of the team he worked with in London would normally be available for at least one drink. Since Chambers had become a single man again a few months previously he'd been one of the stayers. But he wasn't a big drinker, apart from the standing joke that he was six foot three, so actually he was quite a big drinker. He was by nature an early riser and a belly full of lager and early mornings do not make amiable bedfellows, or so Chambers felt. He had asked Li to join him for a drink. He'd not had the inclination to go for a drink since he'd been in Hong Kong, and the only bars he knew were the ones he'd seen when he was doing his research over on Kowloon-side.

He thought it could be a good opportunity to get to know each other better, and Chambers knew he was developing a crush on Li. So it might be a chance to find out if there was a Mr Li knocking about. He had surreptitiously checked her wedding finger and found it was tantaslisingly free of jewellery. He didn't want to enquire with another colleague as that would surely lead to further embarrassment. No, he thought a couple of glasses of wine and a subtle line of questioning regarding her marital status would be easy to pull off for a man with his interrogation experience. Well it would have been if she hadn't turned him down flat. She told him she had a prior arrangement, and if he wanted some fun on a Friday night he just needed to walk round the corner from their office to enjoy some of the best bars Hong Kong had to offer for a man of his stature. When she smiled at this point he should have realised she was making fun of him.

Chambers had thanked her profusely for the tip and left immediately, keen not to show his embarrassment on being rejected to the rest of the team in the office. He exited the building walking along

Gloucester Road for a couple of blocks before the heavy traffic and blaring horns made him turn left into Luard Road. On the other side of the road he saw a sign for a bar called Mes Amis and headed in for a pint.

Chambers didn't get home late, but he was pissed. Not from the drink, but at Li. She'd 'advised' him to go for a drink in Wan Chai, which from what he could work out from the few hours he'd been there, was full of 'fallen ladies' and dodgy lap-dancing bars whose main clientele and that of the plethora of 'normal' pubs, were fat, forty and foreign to Hong Kong. As he was walking down Lockhart Road, the neon signs were advertising such delights as Cockeye among many less creative names. He was certainly no prude and would normally have seen the funny side of it, if she hadn't thought this was what he was all about. He'd been trying to impress her. He realised that now. The reason he'd been so thoughtful, chosen his words carefully and had tried hard not to say or do anything that might cause offence to the locals or anyone else for that matter, was because of her. In short he'd been on his best behaviour and she had simply pigeon-holed him along with the other older, overweight expats who came down to Wan Chai on a Friday to get smashed and get their titillation or more from the scores of whores.

Monday morning was awkward.

'Did you enjoy your night on Friday?' She enquired with one eyebrow slightly raised.

'Yes it was great.' Chambers answered in a deliberate monotone.

'Oh really? You liked it?' She seemed genuinely interested. This alerted Chambers. Had she not grasped his obvious sarcasm? Well two can play games.

'Yes, I loved it, I had a fabulous night.' He gave her a cheesy wink and returned to looking at the folder that was open on his desk.

'Oh good, I'm pleased for you.' She got up and went to the pantry.

Chambers wasn't sure if he should deceive her. Maybe she did like him. He really had no idea. He couldn't read her at all. It was like she had a barrier up when it came to showing her emotions. The rest of the day passed with little communication between them. The following day Chambers took himself off to explore the backstreets of Mong Kok. He found it hard to believe he could find another place busier than where he was living in Causeway Bay, but Mong Kok was on a totally new level. It was physically impossible for him to walk more than two steps without bumping into someone. He had to walk on the side of the road, as he could make no headway on the pavement. He could see this endeavour wasn't too safe either with the amount of traffic, especially the minibuses hurtling along at breakneck speed. He gave up and headed back to the office. Li wasn't there, so Chambers could get on with his work without further distraction.

On the Wednesday, the day of the bad pollution, things were a little better in the office. When he engaged her in conversation she chatted quite freely, but he noticed she wasn't instigating as many conversations as she had previously. On Thursday, he'd come into work with his sore throat; he had bought some lozenges at the chemist but had declined the shop assistant's offer of a mask. He didn't have a temperature or a running nose so, he hoped, his colleagues might not notice he was sick, especially if he kept wolfing down the throat sweets. She wasn't at her desk when he came in. He called Brian Tang and invited himself over to the DI's office.

Detective Inspector Brian Tang had an infectious smile. He was 45, five feet five inches tall, had neatly parted hair and a pair of wire-framed glasses that sat low on his nose.

'Come in and please take a seat DI Chambers. How can I be of assistance?'

'Thanks Brian. I need your help. I think the only way I'm going to get close to the man I'm after is through an informer. You're the man with all the contacts so I'm hoping you can help me.'

'Of course, we've got over 200 "assistants" on our books.' He paused, clicking on his mouse several times. 'Just bear with me a moment. We've got plenty of people on the street, in all of the major Triad districts.'

He was obviously looking for something on his computer. 'Here,' he said after a few minutes' search in which Chambers idly looked around Tang's office. He was pleased to see that his desk was not spotless, there were files all over the place. Chambers didn't trusted anyone with a tidy desk. There were also a couple of pictures of his wife and kids. On the wall behind him were several framed qualifications and a small crucifix.

'This file contains the most recent information we've received. I've been keeping your case in mind. But there's been nothing that seems of any relevance so far.' Tang turned his monitor round so that it faced Chambers.

'As you can see, all the reports are in traditional Chinese.'

Chambers looked at the file that was on the screen. It was neatly laid out, times and dates he guessed at the top, the informant's name followed, no more than a number if they were following protocol. The elegant script looked very pleasant on the screen, a shame he couldn't decipher any of it. Would this be another dead end?

'Look,' Tang continued, 'the easiest thing is for me to have a word with a few of our guys, see if they've heard anything. Or if something comes up I'll let you know straight away.' He smiled at Chambers. There was little else he could offer at this stage.

'Thanks Brian, I really appreciate it, anything you get, please, if you could pass it on.' He nodded as he got up from the chair. Chambers was thinking of his next step as he returned to his desk. He was quickly running out of options. There was no record of his man on the system, no one had heard about him coming back to Hong Kong, or if they did they weren't letting on. What next? He noticed a steaming cup of coffee on Li's desk, she had evidently returned in his absence. He sat down idly twiddling his pen and staring into the distance.

'A penny for them.' Chambers turned to see Li standing there. 'Everything OK DI Chambers?' She looked really beautiful he thought. Today her hair was pulled back into a ponytail.

'Everything's fine, if you consider I'm no further on than I was when I arrived. I'm going to have to let the big bosses back at home know this little excursion was nothing more than a waste of taxpayers' money.'

'Come on, cheer up, it could be worse. You're stuck in Hong Kong and you have a wonderful partner.'

'Who's that?' he joked.

She ignored his comment. 'I was just visiting a colleague, Jenny Greening. She's with the Forensics team. She's invited me over for dinner with her family on Friday night. You can be my plus one if you like.' She paused; Chambers knew what was coming next. 'Unless of course you have other plans in Wan Chai perhaps.' He grimaced and quickly changed the subject.

'Greening? You mean there's another …' he paused realising his next words would dig the hole that he'd just dug for himself, even deeper.

Li hesitated; it appeared she enjoyed prolonging Chambers' agony. 'Another what? DI Chambers, another foreigner? Another white person?' She stared at him, showing absolutely no indication whether she was annoyed at him or not. 'No unfortunately for you, Jenny is just another Chinese person. She just had the misfortune to marry a gweilo.'

Before Chambers had the chance to say anything Li continued, but this time her expression had softened. 'Hey, don't let Ian, that's her husband, hear that I said that! He's a nice guy really, just a bit of a windbag when he's had a couple of bottles of wine, but apart from that he's completely harmless.'

Chambers cracked a smile to show, outwardly at least, he didn't mind the joke being on him. 'What does he do?' he enquired more out of politeness, than genuine interest.

'He's a barrister with one of the big firms in Central. If you join me for dinner, you'll get to hear all about it first-hand ad nauseum. I'm kidding, it won't be all bad as Jenny's a great chef. Well I say that, what I should say is her Filipina helper, Chu Chi, is a creative genius in the kitchen. They're a nice couple and they've got a couple of kids at Uni age.'

What was with Australians shortening everything? He definitely knew she must have lived or studied abroad.

'Hey, while we're on the topic of universities,' he couldn't bring himself to say 'Uni'. 'Where did you study? Australia?'

'Correct, UNSW, to be precise. Four great years, sharing a flat just off Coogee Beach. I loved it there.' She stopped and looked at him. 'Are you making fun of my Aussie accent?'

'Oh no, not in the slightest. I'd be delighted to join you. Friday you say? You mean tomorrow night. Hang on, let me check my diary.' He flicked through an imaginary notebook. 'Friday's good with me, what time and where?'

'They live out in Discovery Bay, have you been out there yet?' She then said 'what?' reacting to Chambers shake of the head. 'How long have you been here now? And you've not been out there? Discovery Bay is where most of the expats live. I thought you westerners had some kind of magnetic ability to stick together. It certainly seems the case in Wan Chai or Lan Kwai Fong. Don't tell me you've not been there either.' She looked incredulous at his apparent lack of knowledge. 'Well, you are getting on a bit; it's more of a young person's place.'

Another unsubtle dig, she didn't seem to care too much about his feelings. Was she doing this deliberately? He refused to rise to the bait.

'OK, so where is this Discovery Bay, is it Hong Kong side or Kowloon side?' he said, wanting to show he was at least familiar with some of the local lingo.

'Neither, it's out on Lantau Island. We need to take a ferry. Not far from where we caught the Star Ferry from. I suggest we take an early mark, and head out there about 5.30pm. We can pick up some wine when we get there. Dinner is planned for 7.30pm. If you want to go and change, you can leave earlier, it's up to you. It's an informal thing so I wouldn't worry too much.'

'Great, well I'm going to spend the day tomorrow over in TST, so lets say I meet you here at 5pm.' He had taken to going over to the other side of the harbour during the day, casing out places he had read about in the files. This allowed him to act more naturally on his return when things were busier during the evening trade. Mostly he took a seat at one of the bars, nursing a beer and taking in the faces, hoping he might see someone in particular.

Chambers' phone rang. It was Brian Tang.

'Hello Brian. Good news I hope.' Chambers said, popping a blackcurrant-flavoured throat lozenge into his mouth.

'Hi DI Chambers, I just had word from a colleague that one of our informants, who has been very quiet recently, has just popped up on the radar. It might be nothing but the word is he was in London and just got back to Hong Kong a couple of days ago. My source says he was there at the time of your murders. It might be nothing but I'm going to try and meet with him tomorrow if you want to tag along.'

'Brian that's great news, count me in.'

'Good. Keep your mobile on and I'll call you the minute I have a time and location.' Tang rang off.

Chambers turned to Li, despite his sore throat, things were looking up. 'Looks like tomorrow is going to be a good day in more ways than one.' He leaned back in his chair and gave her a big toothy grin. As he did so the lozenge slipped out and the sticky purple sweet adhered to his shirt front.

Li burst out laughing and turned away leaving Chambers to remove the offending sticky sweet from his shirt and curse his luck.

≈≈≈

Chapter 8 – Rhesus Pieces

Tuesday 5th April – Tuesday 3rd May 2011

Dear diary,

It took me a long time to find my balance after the last one. Heading through the hordes of people in Mong Kok was a blur. I kept waiting to feel a vice-like grip on my shoulder, or hear someone shouting for the police. The mistakes screamed out at me from the dark recesses of my brain. Even though my previous success in Happy Valley the month before had long vanished from the front pages, I was initially pleased to see that there was no immediate link in the newspaper coverage the next day. Of course this story got me back on the front page. There's not that many murders in Hong Kong, it's not like it's New York in the eighties or Mexico nowadays. I think every murder guarantees you at least some real estate on the front page of the South China Morning Post. The big difference between this one and my last cover story was that this time they had the murder weapon. There was a picture of a suitably sombre-looking policeman holding a golf club, a putter to be more precise, and to be even more specific, a RAM SDX–2. A good club with a nice heel-toe balance, a shame I'd never got to use it for its intended purpose. I certainly hadn't meant to leave it at the scene. The less unintentional clues the better, it clouds the waters and leaves the real clues that much harder to notice.

I read the article a few times; there was no mention of any suspects, nothing from the crime scene. The copy was too busy ladling on the horror of the scene. I didn't recall it being that bad, a lot of blood perhaps. The journalist used phrases like 'frenzied attack', 'shocking bloodbath' and 'work of a psychopath'- it's just this kind of sensationalist journalism that's the problem with the media these days. , Oddly, there was also no mention of the matchbox or its contents. I can still see in my mind's eye, the box arcing in slow motion towards the body, disgorging red-tipped matches all over the place. I can see literally thousands of them blanketing the whole scene. It's funny, the tricks the mind plays.

The police had roughly established that the body was found by Mr Ma Chi Hung, a neighbour, who had come out of the apartment block approximately 10 minutes after the crime had been committed. Ma had been on the way to his work as a night shift manager at the 7-Eleven store close to Mong Kok MTR Station. Later he told police that 'he hadn't heard any noise and when he opened the front door he wasn't paying attention as he was putting on his tie and hadn't been looking where he was going. He made his way down the stairs in the dark as he had done a thousand times before; it was here he had come into contact with the body. He had actually slipped and fallen in the pool of blood surrounding the corpse.'

A passerby, Mr Li, approaching from Waterloo Street, heard the screams and had run into the alley. At first he thought he was witnessing a murder, as Ma was now covered in the victim's blood and kneeling over the body. Li told police officers 'the man [Ma] was screaming like a banshee'. Li had taken to his heels and called the police from a safe distance. When the police arrived 10 minutes later, Ma was quite understandably a quivering wreck. Some kind of normality had finally ensued when Ma's proof of address was established by the police coaxing him to show his Hong Kong ID Card.

I knew they could get no fingerprints off the putter, but what I couldn't be sure of was the matchbox. I hadn't intended to leave it at the scene. I had no reason to believe that anything would show up, as the box wasn't very big and I had been wearing gloves at the time, but the nagging doubt remained with me.

I almost forgot to mention the victim. He was dead by the time Mr Ma had quite literally stumbled on the body. The police were actively pursuing some leads, was all the article reported. I just hoped those leads weren't fingerprints. My guess is they would have maybe got a description from one of the dull-eyed security guards from a nearby building lobby. I mean, if you're the kind of person who is working as 'security' in a residential building in a side street on the edge of Mong Kok, my guess is it suggests that they probably failed the police entrant's exam.

However, it never pays to underestimate a person, that's something I've learned the hard way over the years. Definitely never trust anyone and never underestimate anyone either, or you'll only come off worse. The next few days the papers were filled with the usual invective: 'abhorrent crime', 'poor family', 'hard-working son', 'frenzied attack' blah blah. The police were under increasing pressure to find the culprit. No one was seriously linking the crime to the previous one in Happy Valley the month before, only in the sense of mentioning an increase in serious crime. A week later and the story had been replaced by the usual rhetoric that follows the politicians around. I started to get the impression that for all the huffing and puffing, there was little substance to what was being said. It gave me an odd sensation. I felt strangely deflated that no one was making any connections. I could feel my frustration building. Well, soon they'd have another body. Only time would tell if they would start putting the pieces together.

三三三

I set off early this morning and caught the bus from outside MTR Prince Edward Station. The weather was quite hazy which was a shame, as it meant I wouldn't get to enjoy the views when I arrived at my destination. The bus dropped me off on Tai Po Road. I walked almost the full length of Section 6 of the McLehose Trail, until it turns off into the forest for the last stretch along a narrow wooded path. I had completed the whole thing once; the full 100km of the McLehose Trail all in one go, back when I was a bit fitter. It took me nearly 24 hours; I was sore for days afterwards. But that was back when I was more concerned with keeping fit and looking my best. That never got me anywhere. I still come up here from time to time, as the rugged scenery, forests, series of reservoirs and the great views are quite breathtaking. Well today for someone it literally will take their breath away – permanently.

I headed back from the turn off and worked my way along the road until I came to the rest area on the side of Golden Hill. I wanted to make sure there were no workmen around. From time to time there were repair parties on stretches dealing with rock falls or erosion to the steep-sided cuttings, and I wanted to make sure it was as quiet as possible up here. There were no workmen that I could see and as it was an early morning in the middle of the week, I knew foot traffic would be light. However, several cars and minivans had already gone past. This wasn't the best news, but as the road wound its way up the hill, most drivers wouldn't get a good look at me, and anyway they'd probably be distracted by the scores of monkeys that have completely taken over this small part of Hong Kong.

I had come out here the week before, similarly dressed with my freshly laundered baseball cap and shades on, so that the bus driver or any other busybody that might possess a photographic memory would have little to go on. I was also getting a better idea about blood splatter from victims that I had hit with heavy or solid objects. So I knew what I had to take off, wipe down or change into or out of to give myself the best chance of not showing any obvious signs of blood; wearing dark coloured clothing helped as well.

The last time I'd been up here I had stopped at the same rest area, so I knew the resident monkey troupe wouldn't be far away. I guess they hung out here as visitors to the country park were always discarding stuff, plastic bottles, food wrappers, you know the kind of crap humans can't help leaving behind. These inquisitive macaques weren't slow on taking advantage. Whoever coined the phrase 'there's no such thing as a free lunch' had never seen a group of wild monkeys in full flow. They were so game they'd steal the eyeballs out of your head. Saying that, I wonder if they did that to the victim?

I took a seat at one of the benches and turned to enjoy the view or not as the case may be. The haze was so bad I could barely make out anything, which was a real shame as it would have been nice to relax while I waited for the action to start. I opened my pack and took out one of those contraptions similar to the ones the SPCA uses to catch feral cats: a handle with a noose on the end that you can pull tight. I got some bananas and my knife out as well. I checked the road for hikers. The benches were positioned a bit back from the road so drivers wouldn't get much opportunity to see what was going on in the rest area. I'd be lucky to see 20 people, even if I had to stay up here all day. I peeled my banana and broke it into several pieces, scattering them on the ground around me, making sure a couple of pieces were not much more than an arm's length away, throwing the banana skin down the steep slope behind me. I waited, it wouldn't be long, that was for sure. Maybe a minute went past before I heard a familiar sound. I couldn't see them, but I knew that they would know perfectly well where I was. Another few seconds and one appeared about 10 metres away, its face twitching as it evaluated the danger level. A couple more arrived, checking the bins and generally enjoying the run of the place. They squawked and chirruped, stopping occasionally to bare fangs at each other and me. Their quirky mannerisms and how they acted generally reminded me of a group of ADD-suffering, delinquent teenagers.

I counted eight of them in front of me in a range of sizes, mothers with babies clinging to their stomachs, some with bright red faces like old gweilos who are too fond of their red wine. There were probably a couple more behind, but they were no threat. Although they were wild and could be quite confrontational, they weren't as aggressive as the ones I'd seen attacking people at Monkey Forest Road in Bali. Now those critters were mean bastards, that was for certain, they seemed to have absolutely no fear of humans. No, these were almost tame in comparison; I just wasn't one hundred percent sure how they would react to what I was going to do. They picked off the outlying pieces of banana, but were getting quite wary about the last two pieces.

Eventually one of them gave in to its greed and darted forward. Quick as a flash I had the noose around its neck and pulled the trigger to tighten the plastic loop. It let out a shriek as I lifted it clean off its feet. The other monkeys initially took flight for safer ground, shrieking and caterwauling as they went. I picked up the Swiss Army knife that had the scissor attachment open, and carefully I tried to turn the monkey around. It was kicking out and flailing its arms and legs – it put up a terrific fight – so in the end I had no option. I flipped it over, forced it face first into the ground and put my foot on its back. I bent down and made several cuts, then I held the rod out as far as I could and let go of the trigger. The noose loosened and the monkey screamed off at full pelt towards the nearest tree, which was a great relief to me. I bent down and scraped up all the fur and put it in a little plastic bag I had in my pocket. Without further ado I carried on along the path, in case the monkey or its troupe decided to get revenge on their uninvited guest and impromptu hairdresser.

I carried on along the path for about 400 metres until I came to another rest area. This is where I waited for my victim. A little off to the southwest of the rest area was the Shek Lei Pui Reservoir. The reservoir was at the foot of the slope of Golden Hill, home to more of my friends from earlier. They would unwittingly serve as bait. I took out a few things from my rucksack and placed them on the table: My Canon EOS 50D Camera with its 100mm-300mm lens, water bottle, gloves and the cat-nabbing tool. While I waited for the first passersby, I fiddled with the settings on the noose. It was possible, I discovered at home the week before, to adjust the amount of plastic loop to play with. I made sure I had let enough out by placing it over my own head. Just after I removed it, a couple of hikers came along the path towards me. I turned slightly so I was facing away from them and took a great interest in my camera. They shouted a hello as they passed and I gave them a wave back, hoping they would think I was too caught up in my photography to be sociable. It annoyed me, I had been hoping the first person I saw would be alone, and that way there'd be no witnesses. But you can't have it all your own way, right?

Another hour passed and it was around noon when a smallish man made his way up the path. I looked beyond him down the trail and then quickly checked the other way.

'Hello' I shouted. 'Are you interested in seeing a white macaque? I just saw one down at the reservoir.'

'Really?' He paused a moment, as if he was about to say something, before changing direction and heading off the path towards to me.

'Yes I saw it just now, down there at the water's edge, completely white except for a yellow tuft of hair on its head. I just came back up to change the lens on my camera to get a better shot', I nodded towards my Canon on the nearby table. 'I've been coming here for years taking pictures and I've never seen a white one before.'

'Albino,' the man corrected me as he set off down the hill in front of me fumbling with the straps on his bag, evidently focused on removing something. I took my gloves out of my pocket and slipped them on.

'What was that?' I called out as I followed him down the grassy slope leading away from the road and out of sight between some trees, down towards the reservoir.

'Albino, the white one is called an alb ...'

I had the noose around his head and pulled it tight before he could get his words out. I had my knife in my pocket, just in case. The attack had caught him totally off guard and with my height and weight advantage I forced him onto his knees. His hands were grabbing wildly at his neck much like the macaque had earlier. Except this time I wasn't going to let my victim go. Oddly enough, he wasn't putting up as much of a fight; maybe it was because he could only use two of his limbs. I transferred my grip from the noose's handle to get a better purchase on his throat. I increased the pressure and after a couple of minutes his body relaxed. My arms were aching from the exertion. I rolled him over and checked his breathing. It had stopped. I took a few steps back up to survey the path, feeling relieved it was still quiet. I went back to the body. He appeared dead but disconcertingly, his eyes were still open. I dragged the body out of sight behind some trees that were on the edge forest that stretched back a few kilometres.

I went back to the table where my bag was and took out the sachet of hair and another banana, putting my knife and camera back in. I returned to the body. He lay slumped on his side. I unfurled his fingers and placed some of the hair from the macaque in his left palm and then re-clenched his hand. I unpeeled the banana and smeared it across his face, placing a few more bits around the body. I pushed his body further down the forested slope, it would be out of sight to all but the most inquisitive. To be honest, I didn't really know what might happen, but hopefully the monkey fur in his grip would cause some confusion later on. Before I left the corpse, I pulled a cheap, steel lighter out of my trouser pocket and pushed it into his other hand. Although there wasn't much I could do about the red welt around the man's throat, the other 'clues' would surely cause a fair bit of speculation and head scratching. Well I could leave that to the experts to figure out. See what they would make of it all.

I went back up, grabbed my bag, took off my gloves and checked the scene. There were no obvious signs of a struggle and it wasn't possible to see the body from the path. I checked one last time before quickly heading down the trail to the Kowloon reservoir some two hundred metres ahead, avoiding any more contact with the hordes of monkeys. I took the left fork of the trail along the Lion Rock Country Park path that would eventually arrived in Sha Tin. As I descended the path I started to see more and more people and by the time I arrived at the MTR Station I was back in the usual hustle and bustle of Hong Kong street life. I swiped my way through the barriers, on to the concourse and took the escalator down to the platform for the short train journey home; contemplating as I went just how few of the people around me knew exactly who I was or what I was capable of doing to them.

ΞΞΞ

Chapter 9

Friday 23rd September 2011

The meeting with DI Tang and his informant, E121 was not as productive as Chambers had been hoping for. He'd got the call late the night before telling him to meet at the Pacific Coffee Shop in the ifc mall in Central at noon. Chambers got to the mall half an hour before the meeting time and took his time wandering around. He was amazed how busy it appeared, it wasn't even lunchtime and the shopping crowd was already in evidence – plenty of dolled up, 'older' local ladies marching around with handfuls of luxury brand bags. He found it hard to tell the ages of Hong Kong women. The ones he had seen seemed to be either under 40 or over 60. One thing was clear, there was certainly a great deal of cash sloshing around.

Eventually, after he had completed a full circuit of the mall, he located the coffee shop. As he entered he was lucky enough to see the last of the large red sofa and table sets that were available in what appeared to him to be some kind of offsite meeting room. Every other table either had someone busily typing away on a laptop or a group of people in suits deep in discussion. Chambers was about to go up and order when he realised that if he did so, he'd lose the table.

He decided to stay put, attracting annoyed looks from the stream of people entering looking for a place to sit. He only had to undergo a few minutes of not catching anyone's eye before Tang entered with a young man, who walked in like he owned the place.

'Ah, there you are.' Tang gestured to the young man to sit down at Chambers' table. 'Look we'll skip the pleasantries, you don't know his name, which is how he wants it, and you're better off if he doesn't know yours. OK, before we get down to business anyone want a coffee?'

The man answered in Cantonese, Chambers was sure the man said 'gaa fay' that sounded familiar to him. Maybe this Cantonese language is easier than it looks, he thought. He made a mental note to question Li on some basics of the language. He realised Tang was waiting on his order.

'Oh, just a coffee with milk and sugar, cheers.' Tang shook his head as he made his way to the counter. Chambers took the opportunity to have a good look at the informant. He was in his mid-twenties, cockily slouching back in his chair, and he had, Chambers decided, what could be classed as a good old-fashioned mullet. Short on top, and long and thick at the back. He had a diamond in one ear like some kind of premiership footballer or American gangster. His face was contorted in a permanent sneer and he was staring hard at Chambers. A face you wouldn't get bored of punching, Chambers found himself thinking as he held the man's gaze until the informant looked away. The rest of the man's appearance was the usual street wear: gold chains, white vest under a red and white striped shirt, black jeans with deliberate holes in them and a pair of Nike Air trainers. But it was the way he held himself that fascinated Chambers. He knew from what DI Tang had told him, that this guy was real low level. A bit of dealing, a bit of leg work perhaps. Looking at his thin frame he certainly wouldn't be used as muscle. He'd been an informant for a couple of years after he'd been busted with a bag of ecstasy tablets. Not a huge amount but enough for a short stretch. So, he had rolled over and was now feeding bits and pieces of information to the bureau. Chambers reflected on his attitude, surely a man in his delicate position would be a little less abrasive to the rest of humanity, if he really knew what was good for him.

Tang returned to the table with the receipt. He sat down and asked Chambers for the list of questions he had asked him to prepare for this meeting. Chambers handed him the typed sheet. Tang began asking the informant the questions in Cantonese. Chambers could see him translating them as he went, occasionally pausing to find the right words. He never ceased to be amazed by people who could converse easily in more than one language. His questions were fairly standard. He was here in case an answer elicited any kind of leads, that way he could push him further. After a couple of minutes of questioning, Tang handed Chambers the coffee receipt to go and collect the drinks. The three paper cups were sitting on the counter. He grabbed a couple of red plastic stirrers and a mixture of white and brown sugar sachets before making his way back, placing the drinks down and tossing the sugar in the middle of the round, wooden table.

Tang took his reappearance as a sign to pause the questioning. 'Look Chambers, so far he says he was in London, he heard about the killings but he doesn't know who did it.'

Chambers pulled the envelope out of his jacket pocket and removed the photo. He placed it face down on the table in front of the informant, his hand still on the picture. 'Tell him to turn it over when I take my hand away.'

Tang passed on his instructions. As Chambers took his hand away he kept his eyes on the man's face. The informant casually flipped the photograph over. Then he picked it up, gave it a cursory glance and turned and said something to Tang, dropping the picture as he did so. 'He says he's never seen him before.' Chambers knew he was lying.

He leaned forward and flipped the photo over leaving it face up on the table. 'Ask him if he knows anything about the two guys that were murdered.' All the time Chambers kept his eyes on the informant.

'He says no. He says he wants to help but he doesn't know anything about the murders that he didn't read in the paper. But if we want any information about a big ketamine deal, now that's something different. That is something he can help us on.'

'Look Brian, if he's got useful stuff for you on another case then by all means carry on. I'm finished with him.'

'No, I can talk to him later about that.' He turned back to the informer and said something in Cantonese. The man got up, nodded nonchalantly at Tang, picked up his coffee and walked out without acknowledging Chambers.

'So, what do you think?' DI Tang asked him.

'He knows him definitely. Did you see how he checked the photo again as he stood up? And another thing, he said he knew nothing outside what he read in the paper. So he can read English?'

'Sure, he speaks it as well. He just wanted a bit of power over you. His way of showing you he's superior I guess.'

'Right, I want you to put the squeeze on this guy; he knows a lot more than he's letting on. It's not much but now know Hak Loong has connections here.'

Chambers spent the remainder of the afternoon back at his serviced apartment. He took a long bath and spent a relatively long time getting ready for his unofficial date. He played it casual, white linen shirt, jeans and loafers. He toyed for a few minutes about how many buttons to open on his shirt, deciding two was the way forward. He put a bit of wax in his hair.. He sprayed on a little Dior Homme aftershave, and loaded on the deodorant. He was good to go. Taking no chances, he grabbed a cab to the station at 4.30pm and was at his desk by 4.45pm. Li was nowhere to be seen. She came in just before 5pm. Chambers looked up. It was hard to say what she had done, but she looked impressive. Her long hair was tied back, maybe that was it, and he could see more of her face. She was dressed casually – to his eye – she made it look effortless and had on skinny faded jeans and heels, plus a loose fitting, low-necked long T-shirt. As usual she had a way of putting him on the back foot.

'Wow, it smells like the perfume counter at Lane Crawford in here.' She theatrically sniffed the air, before turning her gaze on Chambers. 'Is that you John?' She paused to give him the once over. You don't scrub up too bad now do you? Are you ready?'

He nodded and got up from his chair. 'Let's go.'

They took a taxi to pier three and this time Chambers was ready with his recently acquired Octopus card. They were in good time for the 5.30pm ferry; the taxi ride just early enough to miss the onset of the main rush hour.

They got on the sleek white catamaran ferry. It was enormous and ultra-modern compared to the ancient Star Ferry, and this one had no fresh breeze or the smell of the engine, the oil, the sea or the authenticity he'd experienced on the older boat. This was hermetically sealed, white, clean, sterile. Almost as if the passengers were not to be reminded they were actually on a boat on the water. Chambers spent most of the crossing staring out the window. He could never take this view for granted. He was amazed that most of the other passengers were reading magazines, or playing with their mobile phones or iPads. Hardly anyone was enjoying the view. It was a beautifully clear day and the sun was gradually turning orange and sinking low in the sky. The high hills of Lantau Island beckoned towards the boat. As they came into the bay, they passed a bizarre looking castle on their right.

'That's Disneyland.' Chambers realised this was the first time Li had spoken during the journey. She had been busy reading the free magazine from the seat pocket in front of her. They got off the boat and he followed her into the main plaza.

'Welcome to Disco Bay,' she said.

'Are you going to introduce every place we go?' he teased.

'OK, OK, no more tourist guide,' she laughed, 'let's just relax tonight and have some fun.'

'Disco Bay, I like that,' he said more to himself than to her.

'Most people call it DB, the ferry company which is owned by the resort management company calls it DBay, my favourite though is 'Dogs and Babies'. You'll see why in a minute.'

As they entered the circular plaza he understood immediately. There were children everywhere, running in every direction, riding bikes, skateboards, kicking footballs or just screaming their heads off, the noise was terrific. There were a multitude of benches set out with parasols ringing the area. Every table appeared to be taken, with a mixture of locals and expats who mostly, judging by their collections of cans or bottles, seemed to be well on their way to getting smashed. There were also a great many dogs in all shapes and sizes that either sat staring intently at all the activity and the temptation presented by the mass of balls that were being kicked around, or lay asleep on the floor oblivious to the pandemonium that engulfed them. The plaza had no vehicular access therefore it allowed the younger generation to run riot, while their parents seemed happy enough to let them, as they seemed to be focused on letting their collective hair down. They were well supplied with opportunities. There were three 7-Elevens selling alcohol, a wine store, two bars and a pub, not including the restaurants that all probably held liquor licences.

'Come on,' she led him away to the right. They passed several restaurants and several kamikaze children on scooters, before turning the corner and entering a bar with a large seating area that looked out onto the beachfront. The bar was relatively quiet in relation to the pandemonium that was occurring round the corner in the nearby plaza. Chambers appreciated the change of tempo. As they sat down on the stylish black wicker furniture, he gazed up at the verdant green hills he'd seen from the boat coming in; they led almost right down to a perfectly manicured beach. He wasn't sure what surprised him the most, the beach, the lush jungle slopes or the contrast of Discovery Bay to every other part of Hong Kong he'd seen so far.

'I told you that you'd like it,' she said as she picked up the wine menu, 'you need to learn to trust me more.'

'OK, I promise.'

They ordered some drinks: a glass of merlot for her; a bottle of Asahi for him. They sipped in silence as they watched the sky change colour from burnt orange to a deep, dark blue.

Every twenty minutes a passenger ferry eased into the pier and deposited a new batch of commuters, some of whom passed by the bar on their way home. Chambers wanted to find out more about his elusive partner, but he was struggling to find the right questions. Put him in an interview room with a murder suspect and he knew what questions to ask, using just the right amounts of coercion and incentive to gain even the smallest of clues that would often crack a case. Here though, he couldn't find the words. Opening up wasn't easy for Chambers. He'd been single now for several months since the messy split with his fiancée just weeks before their wedding day. She'd left him for one of his oldest and best mates. Of course friends and family knew, and as much as he'd tried to keep it quiet, it was common knowledge at work. It had been impossible to keep something like that from circulating the office, especially as he'd been off work for a couple of weeks while he got his head straight. When he returned he'd been aware of the looks he received from colleagues, the awkward silences when he went to the canteen but no one had ever mentioned it and that was the way he preferred it.

It was coming on for six months, he contemplated, that was the longest time he'd been single since he'd left school over two decades before. He felt that a part of him had simply shut down. It was only since he'd met Li that he realised a component of what made him who he was had been effectively dormant. He though back to his ex-girlfriend, he'd known her for years before they got together. Her family had moved to the UK from Zanzibar when she was a little girl and they'd been to the island together several times when they were dating, staying with her uncle in Stone Town. That's where they had planned to get married and have their honeymoon. To help him 'move on', his friends had unsubtly tried to introduce him to female friends in that clumsily obvious way that immediately put him on his guard. He hadn't been annoyed at their meddling, he just felt distanced from the whole dating thing. Now he sat with a beautiful woman, enjoying a drink and the right words, any words in fact, had become elusive. He had positioned himself where he could look out over the beach, not in her direct eye line. There was something about her that made him nervous. He'd never had a problem around women, so what was it about Li that always made him feel like a naughty schoolboy?

Eventually it was Li who broke the silence and snapped Chambers back to reality. 'I like coming out here; it's a chance to escape from the intensity of Hong Kong Island. Jenny has membership of the club over there.' She gestured to a building nearby that was set back from the beach. 'I come over in the summer, laze by the pool – it's like a holiday from Hong Kong without leaving. My friends and I call them staycations'.

Chambers nodded but didn't respond. He was thinking she said friends, not boyfriend.

'Do you like fireworks?' She asked.

Chambers thought it an odd question. 'Er, yes I suppose. I can't say I actively go in search of them. Why do you ask?'

'It's just that's Disneyland over there,' she pointed to the brightly lit building across the bay, 'the place puts on a firework display every night, it's for their visitors but you get a superb view from here as well.'

He had no interest in Disneyland, or fireworks for that matter, but he

79

decided to humour her. She was making an effort so it was the least he could do.

'Have you been?'

'Yes, a couple of times, it's actually not as good as the other ones.'

He looked non-plussed. Euro Disney? One in Florida? Was there also one in California? He couldn't be sure. 'Have you been to the States?'

'No, I've not been yet. I went to the one in Japan; it's much bigger and better. This one here is too small; they are planning to expand it, so I'll go again when they complete it.'

'But you said you've been to this one more than once. Are you a secret Mickey Mouse fan?'

'No, friends come and visit from overseas. My uni mates from Sydney, that kind of thing. You know how it is.'

He didn't. If he had mates coming to visit, never in a million years would he think about whisking them off for a weekend at Euro Disney. He nodded anyway.

He changed the subject. 'Another drink?'

'Sure, one more then we should head over.'

Chambers got up and went to the bar. He needed to take the initiative. He really wanted to get to know her and he wouldn't get a better opportunity than this. He was still thinking about some interesting topics to speak to her about that had nothing to do with the case. As he put her drink down, she excused herself to go to the bathroom. By the time she had returned, a group of Australians had taken over a nearby table.

'Do you miss Australia?' he asked, nodding his head in the direction of the new arrivals.

'Sure, I loved it there. I met some wonderful people. The Aussies really know how to enjoy themselves; it's such an outdoor place.

People say that Hong Kongers are never at home. You know, extended families living together in tiny apartments, so they are always looking for something to do away from home. That's why the city always seems so busy I guess. But Sydneysiders are always out, at the beach, on the water, hiking, biking and watching sports. It's a great way of life. I really do miss it.'

'What's stopping you going back?'

'A few things. It was a real eye-opener for me. I saw a different side to life. One that isn't completely dominated by work. But my family is here and my friends from school and I love Hong Kong, I really do. But I do think I'll go back to Australia one day. I'd like to retire there.'

'Retire? That's a long way off for you.'

'Who knows? I might meet a wealthy Australian, and then I can be a rich tai tai,' she smirked.

'Tai tai?'

'In Cantonese it means wife. Normally a rich wife,' the smirk turned into a broad smile.

Chambers nodded, surely if she was saying that she must be single. That meant there was still hope.

She suggested they finish their drinks and go to the bottle shop, off licence, he had corrected her, to collect a couple of bottles to take with them. He let her choose while he insisted on paying. She led him along the paved path beachfront to a house with a garden that led out almost to the sand.

'Hello,' Li called in through the open patio doors.

'Hi, Lucy, come in, come in, this must be DI Chambers. Hi I'm Jenny, I recognise you from back at the station.' She held her hand out. Chambers shook it and passed her the wine carrier containing the two bottles.

'Thank you. Very kind of you. Please come in.' She ushered them into the spacious apartment. 'Ian will be home any minute. Take a seat and make yourself at home.'

The living room that opened up on to the garden was about four times as big as Chambers' serviced apartment, dispelling the myth that everyone lived in a shoebox. It was much bigger than Chambers' flat in London. The place was like a showroom, beautifully decorated and spotlessly clean. There wasn't as much as a coaster out of place. He recognised Greening from the office though they had never been formally introduced.

'What can I get you to drink?' Jenny called from the open plan kitchen.

'Let me give you a hand.' Li was already on her way to the kitchen.

'Anything is fine for me,' he called back. Jenny brought over a beer for him, setting it on a coaster on the small side table, before she returned to the kitchen and her Cantonese conversation with Li. Chambers got up and wandered over to the paintings adorning the far wall. Some sort of modern art, he had no idea, but he could tell they were originals, probably, judging by the rest of the ornaments and furniture, very expensive. There were also a lot of family photographs in frames, some on the wall and some on top of the sizeable mahogany-coloured hutch. Many of them were carefully posed family photos obviously taken in a studio with various artistic touches or moody shots in black and white. Nearly all of them featured all or a combination of Jenny and a man, that must be Ian, along with two Eurasian children across their childhood and teenage years. The only picture that was different was one of Ian and another teenager, who looked slightly off camera with a sullen expression.

'Ah DI Chambers, you're an art lover, jolly good.' Chambers started at the well-spoken voice. He turned to see an older version of the man who appeared in the photographs, entering through the patio doors. He was heavy set with a ruddy complexion and thick grey hair, dressed in an immaculate fawn suit, crisp white shirt and a red, patterned tie.

'I'm Ian Greening, Jenny's better half. I'll just close these; don't want any of those nasty mosquitoes coming to spoil our little gathering. So DI Chambers, or can I call you John? How are you enjoying Hong Kong?'

Chambers made the best of the evening. Li was right, Ian was a pompous old windbag. He guessed Ian was in his late 50s. He was amazed at how many opportunities the man took to mention his, by Chambers' standards, grossly inflated salary. He wasn't sure that anyone should be making a salary like that; it seemed to be about five times as much as what he earned and that wasn't taking into account Hong Kong's attractive 15% maximum tax rate that his host was also happy to mention on several occasions. Greening was happy to talk at length about his spectacular career as a property lawyer. During the dinner they were joined briefly by the couple's two children. Eliza, the elder, was a recent graduate who was working as an intern at one of the big banks. Richard was finishing his last year at a local university. Chambers was impressed by his size and not surprised to hear he was part of the university's rugby first team. They both seemed pleasant and, luckily for them, appeared to have got their mother's looks and charm.

As the evening wore on, Chambers found himself more and more isolated in the conversation. They talked about work, but mainly about Hong Kong life, politics, the media and the arts. These topics held little interest for Chambers even when he was back in the UK. He preferred to get out and explore, hiking or in the old days playing a wide variety of different sports. A good weekend for him a few years ago was a trip down to Newquay for a bit of kite surfing or sea kayaking, and SCUBA diving if he went abroad. All the physical team sports he'd played when he was younger were catching up with him, so now he was content to go on hikes around the home counties with a few friends, some of whom, if truth be told, seemed to be more interested in the post hike drinks. At least he didn't have to worry about his lack of knowledge on these matters, as a visitor to the city he could hardly be expected to know his Donald Tsang from his Shanghai Tang. At around 11, Li began to wind the night down. She had picked up on Chambers' discomfort, although he was trying his hardest not to show his boredom.

Eventually, after much arm-twisting and inebriated hugs from Ian to Lucy, they slipped out and on her word ran for the 11.30pm boat. They just made it and slid into an empty row of seats. The ferry was pretty quiet. Li was more intoxicated than he was.

'You didn't enjoy tonight?' she asked, looking him straight in the eye, but with a faint smile curling the edge of her lips.

'Look, Jenny is really sweet and a genuinely lovely person. Their children seem to be really nice as well. But to be honest, Ian is not really my cup of tea. I like money, we all do, but that guy is seriously obsessed with it. I mean how many times did he mention his salary?'

'Well, you know what they say about old guys and flash cars,' she interrupted, laughing at her own joke. 'Maybe it's the same with talking about their money. Saying that, he would probably have talked about his car. But cars aren't allowed in DB. I never showed you that, as we only saw the beach and the plaza. But it's only buses and golf carts on the road.'

'Golf carts? That's crazy; you make it sound like some crackpot island out of a James Bond film!' He was laughing now too. He was glad he wasn't as drunk as she was, as he had an overwhelming desire to lean over and kiss her. She seemed unaware of the moment, or maybe she had picked up on his intention as she subtly changed the subject.

'Ian loves to give off this image: big earner, perfect wife and kids, collector of great art, fine wine enthusiast.'

Chambers interrupted 'Yes, I mean, I've met my fair share of wankers in the city, but most of the time I don't let them get under my skin. I move in a different world to them. But there was something about Ian tonight. It makes you question yourself. Jenny's really nice though.'

'Oh oh,' it was Lucy's turn to interrupt, 'is there something you want to tell me? That's twice in as many minutes you said that.' She gave him a saucy wink.

'Not at all, she's a good-looking woman, intelligent, patient, but she's a bit old for me. What is she, 45?'

'I can't tell you that!' she exclaimed. 'But it's older than that,' she laughed. 'But don't tell her I said that!'

Chambers continued, 'well there he is, making a fortune out of other's misfortune, I'm sure. He's got the picture-perfect family; I mean those two look like they're out of a catalogue.'

'Yes, but he didn't mention his other son. Sometimes when he gets drunk he launches into some maudlin talk. I think we got away at a good time.'

'Yes, thanks for saving me, I was getting a bit bored towards the end.'

'Yes, I could see your eyes glazing over during the entrees.'

'No! It was great, honestly. I appreciate you inviting me. I thought Jenny said they only had two children? That would explain the picture I saw on the sideboard of Ian and another young man.'

'Eliza and Richard are their two children. But Ian has another child from before he met Jenny. He'd be 23 or 24 or so now. His name is Brad. He and his father have had a, let's say, difficult relationship to say the least. I've met him a few times. He just seems a little lost to me. I think his dad has always pushed him hard and he's never quite got to where he should be, or where his father wants him to be. Ian's life is far from perfect; there's definitely a few skeletons in his cupboard. He has never mentioned Brad's mum and he's banned Jenny from speaking about it.'

'That's sad. So I take it Brad doesn't live at home?'

'No, he moved out to go to uni overseas, I think he was studying medicine or to be a doctor, something pretty heavy duty. When he dropped out he came back to Hong Kong but never returned to the family home. He's the proverbial black sheep. Well so he thinks anyway. Apparently he hates his father's blatant materialism, yet he can't survive without his daddy's handouts. His confidence seemed shot the last time I saw him. He was a good looking kid and it seemed he had everything on a plate. I think he might have had some kind of breakdown that either caused him to drop out or happened because he did. He's a mess, poor kid.' She said this even though Chambers figured there couldn't be more than a few years between Li and Brad, maybe there was something she wasn't telling him.

'I feel sorry for him, which is saying something if I haven't even met him.' Chambers wanted to lighten the mood of the conversation and take advantage of Li's state of intoxication. 'So what about you, DI Lucy Li? Any sordid skeletons in your cupboard?'

'Now that would be telling, you must think I'm drunker than I am.' With that she rested her head against the seat and closed her eyes.

~~~

Chapter 10 – A little Chicken for the little chicken?

Wednesday 4th May – Thursday 2nd June 2011

Dear diary,

Can you believe that this time the body wasn't discovered for a week? On the following Tuesday afternoon a man walking on the trail had been intrigued enough by the foul smell to go and investigate. I'm sure he wished he hadn't. When he realised it was a decomposing human body he called the police who soon arrived and closed off the area to prying eyes, although I'm not sure that macaques understand the relevance of Police – Do Not Cross tape. The *South China Morning Post* on Wednesday carried the story low down on the front page. It wasn't the cover story, but the headline 'Hiker's body found near popular trail' suggested the police were yet to confirm it was murder. I felt a little skeptical about that as I imagined the choke marks, whether from the plastic noose or my hands would have shown up quite clearly. I'm no expert in body decomposition, so maybe that was the case. I mean he died on Tuesday at lunchtime and was found a little over a week later. Who knows what kind of changes the body goes through exposed to the elements and the hungry monkeys. The temperature had been pushing 30 for most of the week, plus it had been raining over the weekend. I guess whatever they found can't have been too pleasant and it made no bones to me whether they thought it was murder or not at this stage. Sooner or later, well later at the rate they were proceeding, they might just piece something together.

They released the victim's name. Mr Chan Chung Hing, Trevor. He worked as a guide at the Hong Kong Wetland Park. It just said he was survived by his partner. I almost felt pity for him; he was probably not a bad person. Then I remembered he had unnecessarily attempted to correct my English, so in actual fact he was just another arsehole in a world that was crammed full of them.

When I'd embarked on my little plan last year, I had mapped out a timeline. Dates were of the utmost importance as was the theme. The setting wasn't particularly relevant, well some more than others. But the one I had thought of straight away, the one I was most looking forward to was this one. This one and the one I'd do in late September. Always have a plan, I understand that now. I wish I'd thought about that more when I was younger. No one told me that. That's what your parents are for right? They're supposed to help you. Not try and make life difficult for you. It wasn't my fault they'd had a tough upbringing. I wouldn't have wished it on them. Why would they wish it on me? Why have children if you want them to fail? I can't follow the logic.

呂呂呂

Today I'm ecstatic! Everything worked like a charm. I had been imagining this one for a long time; maybe that's why it worked so well. I'm going to go down to see an old friend of mine tonight. I say 'old'; she's actually quite young and very, very attractive. I'll be having a good time with pretty Kitty tonight. It'll cost me of course, it always does. No such thing as a free lunch, well not to a prostitute anyway. But that's the way I like it, no strings attached, 'love 'em and leave 'em', that's my motto.

I had spent the afternoon waiting for my victim. Again I didn't have a specific mark; I would know them when I saw them. I'd been to the wet market on Electric Road in Tin Hau, and bought a few dozen specific bits of frozen chicken. The man wrapped them in paper and I asked him to put them in a plastic bag. I folded the bag and put it in my rucksack, alongside my usual equipment for my 'special' day trips. Incidentally, I had previously worked close to this wet market with the unfortunate Daniel Lam. I used to get my meat from one of the stalls along the road but I didn't want to take the chance of being recognised, so I used the wet market instead. I didn't like the place normally. They had whole pig carcasses hanging up and sometimes you saw a pig's head with the skull removed, it looked like some kind of freaky Halloween mask waiting to be worn. The place unnerved me, something to do with all those poor innocent animals waiting to be slaughtered for nothing else than some undeserving human's greedy enjoyment.

I crossed the road and went to nearby Victoria Park. I wandered about, enjoying the flowers that were in bloom, eventually settling on a bench at the slightly raised part of the gardens. I could see down to the miniature boat enthusiasts. What kept them racing their little speedboats around the small pond? I say racing, they never actually seemed to compete with one another. A few high-tempo laps then take the boat out of the water and have a little tinker, then back in and round and round again. Very strange behaviour. Maybe one of them perhaps? I pondered the question while I watched. Certainly not to be ruled out and almost guaranteed to be single, that would make it much easier. The more I thought about it I could see the obvious flaw; these people were bound to live at home with some interfering parent. I turned to survey the park from my elevated position, to see if there were any other options; it was getting too hot for me so I moved to another bench in the shade.

From my new viewpoint I saw the man destined to be my next victim. He was walking briskly through the park speaking loudly on his hands-free phone. From a distance he looked like a fool shouting at no one in particular. He was wearing a well-tailored suit and his hair was teased into what was considered the latest fashion. Well, he had already ticked a couple of boxes on my 'arsehole' checklist. The world had to be a better place without him in it. I let him get a head start on me of 50 metres or so then

I casually set off after him. He was walking from Causeway Bay back towards Tin Hau, not ideal as it increased my chances of running into a familiar face, but most of the people I knew around here would be dying slowly in some anonymous cubicle in a faceless office.

I followed him as he exited the park near the tennis courts. He darted out into the traffic on Hing Fat Street and entered the small car park of a green-fronted building opposite. I stayed on my side of the road by the bus stop; he didn't pass through the courtyard but ducked into one of the cars. I heard an engine fire up and saw a bright yellow Audi TT pull out on the far side and roar off with a wheel spin onto Electric Road. Another box ticked on my mental checklist. That meant he had to drive back around in front of me on the one-way system. I had no need to mark down his number plate, there couldn't be too many arseholes driving around in canary yellow TTs, could there? There was a slim chance he didn't live in the building where he was parked, as the sign on the wall of the Viking Mansions building informed me that the block rented out parking spaces. But I had an intuition this was where he lived.

After the car had passed by, taking the left up the slip road that led back to Causeway Bay, I crossed over and walked through the small parking lot. It was open to pedestrians on one side and had the vehicle access on the other. I forgot that there was also a ramp leading to an underground car park, strange, as I'd walked past the block plenty of times on my way to work. There was no security guard visible so I darted in and down to the lower level of the car park. There were a few empty car spaces and a lift. I went over and, pulling on my glove, pressed the lift button. The door pinged open. I got inside and hit a random button. The doors closed and I was transported up towards the seventh floor. This was a good sign as a lot of buildings had a security card system these days, but I guess Tin Hau wasn't the most salubrious of areas. When the doors opened I leaned out. There were three apartment doors and another one that looked like it was the fire escape. That was all I needed to know.

I returned to the basement level and walked up the ramp onto

Electric Road. I went to the nearby hardware shop and bought a coil of nylon washing line and a pack of bin liners. Everything else I needed was already in my rucksack. I walked back towards the park, crossed the road and sat on the low wall near the bus stop where I had watched him from earlier. This would serve its purpose: I could see the parking space, so I'd know when he returned. I tried to think of another less visible place where I could see his car approach, but couldn't think of one. Although here would get very busy at rush hour, there was still an hour before that would begin and if he hadn't returned by then I'd have to find somewhere else to wait. In the meantime, it afforded me a perfect view while I just looked like I was waiting for a bus and anyone seeing me there would soon be getting on a bus themselves, so I shouldn't arouse any suspicion.

Fortunately, I didn't have to wait long. I heard the car before I saw it, some hideous Canto-pop blaring out of the speakers as he revved his way into the car park. I took a quick look before I ran across the main road, up a side street and round the corner before descending into the basement and calling the lift. It opened vacant so I jammed the door ajar with my foot for a minute. While I did this I put on my gloves, pulled my cap low and slipped the eight-inch knife up my sleeve, pinching it near the tip, holding it out of sight. I stepped into the lift, the doors closed and the lift jolted up one level, the doors opened and in stepped my victim. He gave me a look that reeked of disdain as much as his aftershave stank of effeminacy. It was as if I'd wasted a vital few seconds of his valuable life, well I guess I had, seeing as he didn't have that long left to live. As the doors closed he leaned over and pressed the number nine button with one of his perfectly manicured fingers. He seemed to pause, maybe he noticed that the stranger in the lift hadn't pressed a button. He turned and faced me.

'Shhhh.' I said, 'you don't need to say anything'.

W-Why, what?' he stammered.

'I said, don't say anything. Now if you play along, you won't get hurt.' I let the knife slide down and grasped it by the handle, revealing the end of it out of my sleeve.

'What do …'

I cut him off. 'This is your last warning, you utter one word and it'll be your last. Just do as I say and I'll be out of here in five minutes …'

I was interrupted by the ding of the lift and as it juddered to a halt, the door slid open.

'Out you go.' I put my arm on his shoulder and forced him to turnaround – marching him out of the door. I could tell from his reaction there was no one there. 'Not a word, remember. Now get your keys out and open the door. And while you're at it, give me your phone.'

He fumbled in his pocket and handed me his mobile, before fishing out his keys and proceeding to 903.

'Hang on.' I whispered. 'Put your hand up if you live alone, we don't want any nasty surprises'. His left hand moved upwards. Not so cocky now are you? I thought.

'Open the door'

He leant towards the lock and fumbled with the key, eventually using both hands to stop his shaking, he unlocked the door. I moved in quickly, pushing him into the centre of his living room, stepping in as the spring-loaded door snapped shut. I quickly took in the room. It looked like a bachelor pad, albeit a very fancy one. There was the large LCD TV, PS3, black leather sofa, designer lamps and an assortment of fancy trimmings to show this man had money even if he didn't have particularly good taste. The curtains were open, offering a view onto the park. On a high floor like this one, there was no way anyone could see in. He had turned to face me, his eyes wide with fright and his hands trembling. He opened his mouth as if to speak. I put my finger to my lips.

'OK sit on that chair,' I indicated the high-backed wooden chair at the dining table. 'I have to tie you up. Stop you from doing anything stupid that could end up hurting one of us and we don't want that, I can assure you.'

He was compliant now. I guess he thought I wanted to rob him, steal his car maybe. Just play along and this lunatic might leave

92

me alone, he was probably thinking. He stepped towards the chair. As he did so I chucked his mobile on the sofa in the other corner of the room. Took my bag off my shoulder and took out the duct tape and nylon cord.

'This will be over soon. Just take it easy.' I reassured him; I quickly bound him with the cord to the chair. I taped his hands together at the wrists over his shirt cuffs. Then stuck some tape over his mouth and round the back of his head. I don't think his eyes could get any wider. Snot was coming out of his nose as his breathing got harder and faster.

'Calm down.' I demanded, but I knew it would be of little use. When I was sure he was secure, I quickly looked about the flat. I needed something heavy. I looked in his kitchen drawers and found a rolling pin. That would do nicely. He was craning his neck round to see what I was doing. Hoping, maybe, that I was rifling his belongings for money. I approached him from the back and gave him a crack on the back of the skull with the rolling pin. His slumped forward, obviously unconscious. I took the packet of chicken out of my bag; it had thawed out sufficiently. I returned the rolling pin to the drawer and found a frying pan that I put on the stove and began cooking up the bits of chicken. They were nicely browned in a few minutes; I put the bits on a plate and brought them to the dining table. There were already some condiments and candles on the table.

I stood behind him, and then grabbed him round the throat. I pulled the tape from his mouth and with my free hand picked up some chicken's feet, I forced them into his mouth. I managed to fit five in before his body started gagging. I forced his mouth shut and held it there, pinching his nose at the same time. His body seemed to be in spasm. I held him tight so he couldn't move or breathe. When he stopped jerking and twitching a few minutes later, I figured he was dead. So I let go off his nose and opened his mouth, I took out four of the chickens' feet and put them back on the plate. I opened his mouth again and forced the remaining foot deep into his throat then carefully leant the chair all the way back, so he was lying with his back on the floor. I removed the tape from the cuffs of his shirt and the cord from around his body, putting the pieces back in my bag. I couldn't see any marks left by tape on his clothes. I took his door keys from where he had dropped them on the floor and put them in his hand. My final touch was to take the Zippo lighter from next to his pack of Pall Mall cigarettes and light one of the candles on the dining table, leaving his lighter next to his body. I went over and drew the curtains nearly all the way across, then turned on a sidelight. It was time for me to depart.

I made my way over to the door and looked out the spy hole. No one was on the landing. I slipped out of the door and called the lift. I turned my back to it in case there was anyone inside. The doors opened; fortunately for me it was empty. I took the lift back to the basement. Exited on to Electric Road. I turned and took one last look at his yellow TT and set off right to make the short walk to the MTR Tin Hau Station. It was all too easy. I couldn't believe how this big-balled, strutting peacock had given in so easily without a fight. I was sure I'd have to use the blade. Well it was much cleaner this way. It was hard not grinning all the way home. That was my fifth and you know what that means? I'm now 'officially' a serial killer and I'm destined to be famous no matter what happens next.

ΞΞΞ

Chapter 11

Tuesday 27th September 2011

Chambers' mobile vibrated on the side table next to his bed. He'd only just come into his serviced apartment after work and was looking forward to getting into the cool stream of the shower after another hot and sweaty day on the streets. Although the humidity had begun to show signs of decreasing, he was still forced to take a minimum of three showers a day. He contemplated leaving the phone to go to message bank. But finally he decided to shut off the water and step the couple of paces to the table to pick up the phone. He saw DI Tang's name on the caller ID.

'Hi Brian. What gives?'

'Some major news. You know the man we had a coffee with last Friday?'

'Sure, what's he done, got himself arrested for his bad attitude?' Chambers realised the joke sounded poor as soon as he said it.

'We've just received word that he's been murdered.'

'Shit, really?' That sounded even dumber, as if DI Tang would phone him up and tell him the only informant that possibly knew where Chambers' man might be, was now dead, just as a joke. 'Where, when?'

'News is a bit sketchy, at the moment. I just got a call from a colleague in the OCTB in Mong Kok, said his team had been called by the local police. They'd been investigating a complaint of a flooded apartment in East Mong Kok. When they went upstairs and no one answered, they broke the door down. That's when they found him face down in the bath. They checked his ID and called it in. My colleague called me to run some background checks on him. I couldn't believe it when I saw the match.'

'Can we get access to the crime scene?'

'I can ask as it's relevant to your case. I don't think it should be a problem. Let me call you back. Give me ten minutes.'

Chambers decided to take his shower. He was out in a couple of minutes. When he went back to his phone he saw a missed call from Brian. He called him back.

'Sorry I missed your call. How did it go?'

'Fine, we're good to go. I'll grab a cab. Meet me downstairs on Gloucester Road in five minutes, OK?'

'No problem.' Chambers threw on the same trousers but changed his socks, pants and shirt. The last one was still damp. He slapped on some deodorant, grabbed his camera and headed out. The cab was already waiting downstairs.

They arrived outside the block after 8pm. The ride had taken the best part of an hour, even though Chambers figured it was a journey of less than five miles. The driver had no choice than to go through the Central Harbour Tunnel which, slow moving at the best of times, was a virtual gridlock during rush hour.

The lobby of the apartment block was teeming with police and crime scene officers. Tang waved his badge at one of the uniformed officers who motioned them towards the lifts. He and Chambers manoeuvered their way past some moth-eaten, fake leather sofas and entered the lift. Tang pressed button 15. There were more police inside the apartment, that much was visible through the open door. Chambers could also hear the click of the flash and the whine of the batteries recharging, presumably from one of the forensic team's cameras. Again Tang flashed his card and said something in Cantonese to the young uniformed officer on the door. The policeman leaned back and held the door wide open for them to enter.

Chambers had been to more murder scenes than he cared to remember. This one didn't look noticeably different. He did notice a slight smell of something rotting, mingling in with the smell of mould, or mildew to be more precise. He went straight into the bathroom. The body had already been taken away and the water drained from the bath. He knew there would be little evidence to be gained from the bath water. He would need to get to the morgue and take a look at the body. The lurid green mat in the bathroom and the colourful rugs in the hall and living room were sopping wet. There was no sign of a struggle in the bathroom. That would mean the victim was already dead or at least unconscious before being put in the bath, Chambers figured as he returned to the living room.

'Hey Brian,' he called over to Tang who was deep in discussion with another officer.

'I'll be with you in a moment.' Tang went back to his conversation.

Chambers noticed several black objects scattered around the floor. He took out a pen and bent down to get a closer look. It looked like a rat. He rolled it over with the point of his pen. Yes, it was definitely a dead rat, and one that didn't smell too pleasant either. He turned as he heard the sound of a metal object hitting the floor. He saw an old-fashioned stove top kettle rolling on the linoleum, its lid was missing and what he presumed to be another dead rat was hanging out of the opening. There was a uniformed policeman standing next to it, with a look of shock and displeasure on his face, staring down at the kettle. Chambers guessed the policeman had lifted the kettle and opened the lid, getting a nasty surprise for his trouble. Chambers had seen enough. He signalled to DI Tang, who'd finished his conversation, that he was ready to leave.

~~~

The following morning Chambers was already at his desk when Li arrived.

He acknowledged her arrival with a 'jo saan.'

'I see your Cantonese hasn't improved much,' she said disdainfully, not making eye contact as she booted up her PC.

Chambers was surprised at the criticism. She was obviously in a bad mood about something. With him or someone else, he wasn't sure. What he knew for certain was that he needed her onside and focused.

'Everything OK?'

'As you're asking, no.'

'Trouble at home? Do you want to talk about it?' He was trying his best to sound sensitive and caring.

'That's got absolutely nothing to do with you, DI Chambers,' she snapped again.

After a few minutes' hiatus, she added, 'if you must know, it's you.' With that said she got up from her desk and walked off to the pantry.

Chambers got up and followed her.

'What did I do that's pissed you off so much?' He asked

'I thought we were partners. I've been at your beck and call for the time you've been here. Anything you want, any help you need I'm there. I've put my other cases on hold to help you on what even you think is a wild goose chase.'

'Hey, I know that, and you know I'm grateful for everything you've done. So what's the problem?'

'Last night.' She said, turning and looking him straight in the eye for the first time. 'What you did last night is the problem.'

He realised what he had done.

'I'm here helping you with everything,' she continued, 'and the moment DI Tang gives you something, you're off with him. Didn't you even think to call? Don't you think this case is important to me too?'

'I'm sorry, I wasn't thinking. It was very short notice. We just went out to have a look.' He paused; he needed to choose his words carefully. 'Look, Brian was pulling a few strings to let me in there. I didn't want to make a scene and turn up with too many people. I just wanted to tread lightly.' He knew that wasn't the best way he could have put it.

Li seized on it. 'Tread lightly? That's rich coming from you.' She spat the words at him. 'You're blundering around here; you have no idea how to tread lightly. You think bringing me along would have been a problem, but you being there wouldn't? You can't even speak the language!'

'I'm sorry that just didn't come out right. I just didn't think last night ...' Before he had the chance to finish, Li had stormed out.

He waited in the pantry for a few minutes. He decided to make a coffee for them both. It wasn't much, but he hoped she would appreciate the effort. He brought the steaming hot cups back to their desks, placing her drink on the corner of her desk.

'Here's a peace offering. Skim milk, no sugar. The way you prefer.' He moved back round the desk to his seat.

A few minutes of silence ensued between them, where the only sound coming from Li's side of the desk was the sound of her fingernails tapping on her keyboard.

'Look, I'm really sorry, I need you on this case, your help is essential to me,' he offered.

This was met with more silence from Li's side.

In the end Chambers decided to ignore her petulance. 'I thought it was a bit of a long shot. It's the first potential clue for us in this whole case. I just wanted to see if there was anything out there. The chances of getting a lead are more than likely going to come from forensic evidence anyway. I wanted to get a feel of whether our man was the murderer. I don't know what, exactly, I was expecting to find. From what I saw I don't think our man did it. I can't say for sure he wasn't involved, but I don't think he was actually there.'

'Why do you say that?'

Chambers hesitated. Why was he sure his man wasn't there? He couldn't just say it was his intuition. 'The murders in London – a professional did them. This one, well, it was messy. It wasn't like a contract killing. Also there were some odd elements at the scene. Hopefully, the forensics team will come up with some DNA or something more concrete to go on.'

'What do you mean, "odd elements"?' She was fully focused now, her body language had changed, she had turned to face him.

'When I was coming back with Brian last night, he assured me that certain facts won't be released to the press.'

'John, don't piss me off even more,' a hint of anger still in her voice, 'I'm not the press. What are you talking about?'

'From what I saw there was evidence of a struggle at the door. Another more violent one a few steps into the flat. There was blood splatter on the wall and carpets. The body had been removed by the time I was there. But there was no evidence of a struggle in the bathroom where the body was found. Face down in the bath. So that means the victim was either dead or unconscious when he was put in the bath.'

'But there's nothing in what you just said that would need to be kept out of the papers. What else was there?'

'Hang on. I'm getting to that. The murderer deliberately left the bath running.'

'He could have been disturbed,' she interjected, 'or maybe he just wanted to make sure the body was discovered.'

'That's right. But if the man is already dead, then why go to the trouble of drowning him? And if he's not dead, why not just strangle him or carry on beating him to death, he's unconscious anyway? Brian told me the police at the scene said the victim had severe head injuries. It just doesn't make sense.'

'What else? Surely the press would know about the flooding from the neighbours below.'

'Yes. What they are keeping out of the papers is that a number of dead rats were found at the scene.'

'Well that's obvious, you said yourself the victim is … was an informant.'

'Exactly, that was my first thought too. A message for other informants and even for us perhaps, just to let us know that the victim was being watched. They knew precisely where he'd been and whom he'd been talking to. But, there was also something that just didn't sit right.'

'Like what? It seems quite obvious to me that someone finally got tired of this guy's antics and wanted his mouth closed, permanently. Whether it's your guy covering his tracks, well that's a different matter. It could be good news in a twisted way. It could mean he's here, and if he is, then someone out there must know where he is.'

'Yes. But the odd thing about the dead rats is that one would have been enough to convey the message. But there were eight. Mostly they appeared to be casually thrown about the place. But one of the plainclothes guys got quite a shock when he found a dead rat in the kettle. There was another one in the fridge, one in a saucepan on the stove top and another in the bath with the corpse.'

'Gross.' She pulled a face. 'I wouldn't like to have found that. Whoever did must have got the fright of their lives. It reminds me of those two murderers from the eighties. What were their names? Dennis someone?' She paused a moment, 'the other was Dahmer. Yes Jeffrey Dahmer. They murdered homeless people and hid body parts in their houses. Didn't they find a head in a fridge and body parts in a kettle?'

'That's right, Dahmer was the American. Nilsen, Dennis Nilsen, was the other. He murdered at least 15 people, not all homeless though, and boiled body parts in his saucepan.' Chambers paused, 'Did you know he was one of ours?'

'Meaning?'

'Well he's British for starters, but also, and more embarrassingly, he used to work for the Met Police. Not something we like to admit to. Having a serial killer in the ranks isn't something you want to advertise. In our defence, he had left the force a few years before he started committing the murders.'

'So what's that all got to do with this murder?'

'That's exactly my point. We need to establish whether this is about killing a snitch or a tit-for-tat gang killing. What we do know is the victim was a police informant. We also know he was was a Triad gang member. Those two are facts. What we're not sure of is if he knew our man the Black Dragon. Maybe yes, maybe no. But let's say it's one of these three things that got him killed. I can understand why the murderer left a rat at the scene. Again that's clear. But why eight? And more importantly, why one in the fridge and one in the kettle? That's says to me it's either one hell of a coincidence or that this murder has more to it than meets the eye.'

'So,' she was looking off towards the huge windows that looked out towards the harbour, tapping her pen against her chin. 'Why would a contract killer murder a known police informant, then leave some evidence at the crime scene that appears to be some kind of twisted homage to a couple of serial killers from three decades ago. It seems too bizarre for words. Could it just be a coincidence? A warped sense of humour on the killer's part, perhaps?'

'Could be. But you and I both immediately thought of the Nilsen-Dahmer thing. So there could be something in it. But just as likely the killer was having a bit of fun. Brian is putting the word out among the other informants that this wasn't targeted at them, no matter how it's reported in the papers. He's selling it to them that this guy annoyed too many of the wrong type of people, and got what was coming to him. Anyone that knows him will know that's not too far from the truth. The important thing for us is to get feedback from the street as quickly as possible as to who is behind this.'

'What can we do in the meantime?'

'I recall you telling me Hong Kong has a relatively low murder rate. Have there been any other bizarre murder scenes recently? Can we check the database? If your figures are correct, then there shouldn't be too many others. Also we need to get a look at pictures of the body.'

They spent the rest of the day sifting through soft copies on the police database. They went back to the beginning of August at Li's insistence. By 5pm they'd found, and done their research on, four other murders that had occurred in Hong Kong in the previous three months. There had been one report of a husband murdering his wife. One instance where the wife had murdered the husband and two apparent robberies where the victim had died from head injuries as a result of the attack. One of these was the attack in Kowloon Park that they'd visited the day after the murder took place. The other was the death of an 84-year-old grandmother who died after being hit on the head and having her purse stolen. Tragic, but hardly the work of a Triad hitman. The images taken during the autopsy had also been sent to them. Apart from the injuries to the head and neck that Chambers attributed tot the struggle they revealed little else.

Chambers and Li went over the case in Kowloon Park once again.

The victim was 21-year-old Peter Kwok, a very junior member of the K19 according to his records on the OCTB database. He'd died from blunt force trauma to the head. There were no witnesses. He'd been found in the aviary in Kowloon Park on Monday evening, 29th August. At the scene the investigating officers had found a large bottle of water, a children's book and a pair of sunglasses around the body. On further investigation, they found he had his wallet on him, with HK$450 in cash plus all his credit cards and his HKID card. He had some gold jewellery and a pair of sunglasses folded into the V-neck of his T-shirt.

Chambers sat back in his chair and addressed Li. 'You mentioned before, it's a relatively common mugging style here. Hitting people on the back of the head before stealing the handbag or purse. Knocking them out cold so you can go through their pockets, that way if they do wake up they can't ID the attacker.'

'That's right. So why does this victim have his wallet, cash and cards still on him?'

'Again, maybe the killer was disturbed. Or maybe it was just meant to look like a robbery. What does he have in common with our rat man?'

'John, we know the victim from last night's name is Eric Cheng. I'd prefer it if we can call him by his real name. I just feel it's a bit disrespectful to refer to him as the rat man.'

'Fine, sorry. What do these guys Kwok and Cheng have in common?' he continued.

'They're both K19. They were both killed in a way that could at first look be seen as something straightforward. A mugging that went wrong, or someone silencing a rat.' She realised what she had said.

Chambers acknowledged her slip up. 'Right, but again at this scene there's some anomalies. The murderer left the wallet. Also why the second pair of sunglasses? They have to belong to the killer. At the time of the initial report they didn't know for certain what the murder weapon was.

'But it's been confirmed since that it was the bottle of water. It would have been frozen at the time and would certainly have packed a punch. Therefore we know this was premeditated. No one in their right mind is going to carry around a frozen bottle of water on the off chance they might murder someone. '

'Do you think he was being followed then?' Li asked.

'It certainly looks that way. What about CCTV? Do they have cameras at the entrances to the park? Can we get one of the uniforms to get on that?'

'Sure.' Li picked up the phone and punched in some numbers. Chambers heard the ringing from the other end, then a voice. Li began speaking in Cantonese. He thought back to the night before. Brian had confirmed that the old building didn't have a security guard or any cameras. It was most unfortunate. There were some cameras further up the street covering the junction. DI Tang was getting the local force to coordinate assessing the tapes. The problem was, even though they had an approximate time for the murder, the cameras only covered one end of the street. They'd be knackered if the murderer came from the other direction.

Li snapped him out of his thoughts as she put the phone down. 'They're on it. Apparently there are cameras on most gates in the park. It just depends on how long they keep the records for. It's been nearly a month since it happened.'

'Fingers crossed then that we might get something out of this. Who knows?' He knew from Li's translation of the file notes that the detectives working on this one had no leads so far. He just hoped that they wouldn't tread on anyone's toes and that there just might be some link to his man, as so far he had very little to write home about. And speaking of writing home, he knew his boss, Inspector Asbury, was getting very anxious about the lack of headway. He had been in touch with Chambers both by email and by phone, constantly reminding him of the pressure 'from above' to bring this home. And 'what a feather in the cap of the department' the arrest would be. Chambers knew it wasn't all Asbury's fault. Of course he was under pressure, they all were. But emailing every other day wasn't going to help him solve the case. Chambers needed time, something that evidently he didn't have much of. Eventually the killer would show himself. Maybe this was now the time.

'What about the other items? The sunglasses on the ground have to belong to the killer, right?' he asked her.

Li had the file up on screen. 'Yes but they came back negative for fingerprints.' She let out an exasperated sigh.

'What about the book?' He asked. 'I've never heard of it, but it's a kid's book, that's what you said earlier, right?'

'Yes, McDull, he's a bit of a Hong Kong celebrity. He's a cartoon character that, for want of a better explanation, is a bit silly. You know there is even a statue to his honour at the Avenue of Stars in TST, next to one of Bruce Lee. Hang on. Let me call him up on the web.'

As she began typing, Chambers went round the desk and stood looking over her shoulder, thinking as he went there must be a shortage of local celebrities to honour if a cartoon character had it's own statue.

As the images appeared on screen he leaned in for a closer look. The first one was of a cartoon pig with a baseball cap on. The pink pig had an orange circle around one eye.

Chambers couldn't see anything cute or funny about the drawing. He put it down to another incomprehensible cultural difference.

He took a moment. 'So who is the target demographic for McDull?' He realised he sounded like his boss, talking official jargon straight out of the training manual.

'All ages like him. Sometimes the cartoons have a bit of an edge;

you know political jokes, satire, for the adults to appreciate. But on the whole, I guess it's aimed mainly at kids.'

'So why do you think he has a copy?'

'Perhaps he has a younger brother or sister? Maybe he just likes the character, it's hard to tell.'

'He's a wannabee gangster. There's no way he's going to be walking around with a kids' book unless it's a gift. Can you check his file? See if it says about his siblings.'

Li pulled up the file. 'Yes, one sister. Hang on. Date of birth says 23 June 1985. That makes her an older sister. An unlikely present for a woman in her mid-20s. I wouldn't rule it out completely though. Even some thirty-somethings buy McDull merchandise.'

'OK, let's leave it as a possibility. But even if he had bought it as a present, there's no bag or receipt for it. Also we know the attacker didn't steal his wallet and appears to have come with a prepared murder weapon. I don't know how this is linked to the other murder or even if it is. But there are too many loose ends with both of them. Let's see what we can get from the CCTV.'

'What about the times of the murders? Anything in that?' Li said, she was already scanning the notes. 'The one in the park took place at dusk on a Monday. Yesterday was a Tuesday. The murder took place around lunchtime. There's no obvious similarity.' She looked over at Chambers. He had a look on his face that reflected how she felt – that unless the CCTV footage came up with something then they would be quickly approaching another dead end.

≈≈≈

Chapter 12 – Dog Day Afternoon

Wednesday 3rd June – Sunday 31st July 2011

Dear diary,

Now for a little admission. You can see what I'm doing here right? If I ever get picked up for any of these crimes, I've got my book all ready to go. It can be printed and on the shelves before the trial has even started. Imagine what I could charge a publisher for that? It would make me a fortune. I'd do a couple of years in prison for sure, but I'd get it reduced on some kind of plea bargain or insanity defence, I know a fair bit about the law. I'm still young; I'd be out living the good life before I'm 40. But don't think I haven't thought it all through, I'm not stupid you know. And this will show my parents that I can make money. I mean, that's all they've ever been interested in. How much you're worth. Not what you're like as a person or any of that caring nonsense. It's all about the money with them.

Disappointingly for me, although the article appeared on the front page, it was not the lead story. There's not that much happening in Hong Kong that this shouldn't be the major event of the day. In fact I'd been beaten to the paper's pole position by a mug shot of some trashy D-list model/celebrity/singer who'd been busted for carrying a couple of milligrams of a prescription drug, or some other bullshit. It's ridiculous. The amount, her, and the fact her make-up-less ugly face should be spread across the front page. But then it's a fair reflection on the state of the world these days when some 'famous for 15 minutes' wannabe gets more coverage than a murder. Just goes to show where society is heading when it's lost all perspective on what's important. I mean you'd expect that from the tabloids, but from the *Post*? I'm thinking of writing them a letter to comment on how their editorial integrity is slipping. All I got was one measly column on the bottom half of the page.

Body Found in Apartment

A local man was found dead in his apartment in Tin Hau, Hong Kong Island.

The body was discovered after police were called to the Viking Mansions building on Electric Road in Tin Hau.

Neighbours had reported a foul odour emanating from the man's apartment. Police said there were no signs of a break-in and no arrests have been made.

The body was found in the living room of the apartment. It is thought that Mr Fung, 25, could have been dead for up to five days.

A police spokesman said he believed the man lived alone and that a preliminary forensic examination has been carried out.

ㅌㅌㅌ

Reading my article again, I realised there was no mention of it being a murder. This struck me as odd. It's feasible a man could choke to death on a chicken's foot, but could he get such a serious head injury from falling backwards? I wouldn't have thought so. If the body was stinking enough for the neighbours to complain, maybe the body was a bit of a mess. Funnily enough, nearly a week had passed before the police had been called. That surprised me. The man had a Bluetooth hands-free earpiece. He was surely a very busy individual or at least he was keen to be perceived that way.

Over the next few days there were snippets in the paper giving a few more details. One of the pieces explained the deceased, Mr Fung Chun Kit, was joint owner of a small but thriving software company. His business partner was in Thailand and was not due back for another couple of days. Police had checked and confirmed his alibi was solid. According to colleagues the victim, known as Tony, didn't appear at the office regularly, so his prolonged absence wasn't unusual. Eventually one of them would have got round to calling the police. Reading the quotes attributed to his colleagues, it seemed they were actually enjoying the time away from Tony; maybe more than one person out there shared my sentiments. It's strange isn't it? You can have a successful business, expensive wardrobe, flash car and all the latest gadgets, but when you're dead, who really cares?

I'm just not sure why the police aren't suggesting there was any 'foul play' involved. From an investigative angle the reports were sparse on information. That was my fifth murder, officially a serial killer, although I'm not sure how that works. Killing four people is bad but at least you're not a serial killer. Very strange. Anyway, the papers reported my first as an accident, second and third as murder, fourth and fifth, well it hard to say. I was really going to have to make things a bit more obvious for them. So I decided to take a bit of a risk with the next one. I was going to go back near the scene of my last crime.

ΞΞΞ

It didn't go very well. In fact I had to abort. Things just didn't work out the way I planned. I had seen this guy around near Victoria Park; he always had this dog with him. It was in a terrible condition, a lot of hair missing, its ribs visible through its skin, the poor thing looked like it was on death's door. The man who is walking it has one of those lean, angular faces, the ones you simply can't associate with ever doing anything good for anyone. You know the sort. Well, I took to following him as he did a circuit of the park. Outside you understand, not inside. If you want to hear something ridiculous, animals aren't allowed inside; people are too concerned they might what? Piss on the grass? Whatever next? Anyway, I'm following this dog abuser along the waterfront where all the sampans are located. He keeps going, all the time I think he's about to turn round and head back. But the pair of them just kept plodding along. They pass the noonday gun on the waterfront near Causeway Bay. Along here a multitude of multi-million dollar yachts have replaced the sampans. Some absolute beauties are moored here. I wonder what kind of arseholes own them?

He carries on his journey opting to go through the marina rather than up and over the pedestrian walkways. Quite a long hike for that old dog, the only thing I could think of is there's a tiny stretch of grass further along, maybe they were heading there. My plan had been to follow him back to his apartment and 'help' him meet with an accident. He crossed over at the traffic lights away from the park. I lost him briefly as I was too far behind to make the crossing in time. As the green light came on and the heavy traffic drove past I caught a glimpse of him taking a right turn. It was a minute or so before there was a break in the traffic allowing me to across the road. I peered round the corner just in time to see the pair enter a building further up the street. Then it dawned on me and I realised I couldn't execute my attack on him, not now, not ever.

I carried on up the street and took the same door he'd taken. I'd been in here quite a few times. I took the lift up to the third floor and went straight to the reception desk. The man I had seen was further down the corridor opening a cage. I asked the lady sitting at the desk about the dog that had just come in. She asked if I was interested in adopting the dog, as she wanted to warn me it was quite old and sick. The dog had been dumped with them a year previously she explained. It turned out the man I was following was a volunteer who came in several times a week just to walk this particular animal. He couldn't take the dog on full time as his apartment was too small. I made my excuses and quickly left the building. It's strange how every now and again something can come along and change your preconceptions. How was I to know

111

the man with that hard-looking, angry face would turn out to be a volunteer for the SPCA in Wan Chai? I guess you can't always judge a book by its cover.

ΞΞΞ

As luck would have it though, I'll get a second chance. It's just fate I suppose, without it I would have been forced to amend my plans the other day. Twice in a month only happens once in a blue moon, and this was the month so I better make the most of it. And doing it this way will give me a nice round number at the end.

I was already pretty confident about my back-up plan. So I wouldn't make the same mistake twice. This one had other risks, but then don't they all?

ΞΞΞ

My second opportunity came today on what has so far been the hottest day of the year. By Hong Kong standards next month will be hotter and a damn sight more humid. I don't really mind the heat but at times it can get a bit oppressive. A lot of people head off at this time of year and with the success of today I might well take a break myself. I've been working hard and I think, reflecting back on the past six months, I deserve a little treat. I took care of business today. No mistakes and fairly tidy. I was happy with how it all worked out. I had seen this woman selling newspapers from her little stall in Tai Hang. I had passed her a few times when I was going for lunch. She had a dog tied up to her stall and always seemed to be scolding the poor thing for no apparent reason. The plan was simple. Follow her home and kill her. If there's one thing I really can't stand its cruelty to animals. I mean what sort of sad arsehole has to hurt a defenceless creature? Well, there's one fewer of them in the world now.

After I called off the last attempt, I got round to thinking about who would be my next victim, and although there's a lot of people on my list, the target has to fit certain criteria. That's how I decided on her. I began checking up on her; what time she started and finished, where she lived, when and where she had lunch, where she stored her publications, that kind of thing. So by the allotted day the plan couldn't have been easier. I knew she'd make the 10-minute walk home. She lived in an apartment block in the back of Tai Hang. So it was a simple matter of wearing a cap and sunglasses, plain dark-coloured T-shirt and shorts and my running shoes. I wouldn't need much else.

She was one of these women you see of a certain age. Who knows what they would have looked like when they were younger, but now they have shortish hair, a face like a bulldog chewing a wasp and wear clothes that look like pajamas, sometimes with a waistcoat thrown on for good measure. They're starting to get that bandy legged gait and have a body shape that can only be described as a cube. She always had a cigarette clamped between her thin lips; you could smell the stale odour of nicotine coming off her as you walked by.

She'd be dragging the little dog home and every time it tried to stop and sniff something or have a pee, she'd yank it by the collar and nearly throttle the poor thing. I'd like to throttle her, I thought, but there would be an easier way with this one. She let herself in through the metal barred security door. As the door was about to swing shut I got my foot in to stop it locking shut. She was climbing the dark stairway to her apartment, located on a floor somewhere up above. I raced up the stairs, pushing past her as I went; she howled some invective at me. But I was already up on the first landing and heading up to the next. I waited at the top of the second flight of stairs, crouching down behind the low wall of the second floor landing. As she approached my position, I jumped up in front of her.

She put her hands up; I'd obviously given her quite a fright. One hand was holding the dog's lead. I quickly grabbed the lead from her hand dragging it towards me with my right hand, while at the same time putting my foot behind her knee and pushing her firmly and squarely in the chest with my free hand. There was a short pause as she flailed her arms, trying to grab at me before she tumbled back over my outstretched leg and went arse over tip down the 20 or so stairs.

I managed to get the dog out of the way as that falling lump of lard would surely have crushed it. I pulled the collar over the dog's head and left the animal on the second floor landing, cowering down behind the low wall. I reached out and stroked its head and offered it some comforting words then I headed down to check on the woman. She was out cold. I pushed her along with the sole of my foot, no easy job as she wasn't exactly light, until she was at the top of the first flight.

I forced her round so her head was facing down the stairs. I pulled her head up by the hair so it was out over the first step, then slammed it down. I heard a crack. Something had broken anyway. I made sure there was no one either coming in or coming down the stairs then quickly pulled an old silver-coloured lighter out of my pocket and put it in hers. I'd bought it the day before from one of the so-called antique stalls at Cat Street Market off Hollywood Road in Central. When I knew there was no one around I braced myself against the wall and levered her off the top with my foot, her skull lolling spasmodically as it banged against every step as she slid down head first into a crumpled heap at the bottom.

I went down after her and quickly wrapped the dog's lead loosely around her ankles. I moved quickly to the exit and put my hand inside my T-shirt to turn the handle so I could open the main door. I exited and took a sharp left, and another left at the corner of the block. There were people around and the nearby garages were busy with people so the best thing was to get out of the area quickly. I pulled my phone out of my pocket and put it to my ear, put my head down and strode purposefully to the tram stop that was located a few hundred metres away on Causeway Road.

I climbed on the first one heading towards Central. I knew I had rushed the job slightly, but I was extremely concerned someone was going to come into the building. The security door was only a series of parallel vertical bars with a lock, and although it was fairly dark inside the hallway where the victim lay, you could see in if you looked hard enough. I just needed to be somewhere else when the body was found, assuming she was dead. I never even stopped to confirm that. It's been the same in all the murders –

114

easy to plan in the calm surroundings of your home, but when your blood's pumping all manner of little mistakes creep in. Imagine, not even checking she was dead! I kept my head down on the tram, trying to regulate my breathing, at least this time I didn't have any blood stains on my clothes. By the time I was on the Star Ferry heading home I was relaxed enough to turn my thoughts to my forthcoming holiday. When I got off at the other end, I stopped in at a couple of the small travel agent's booths that line the ferry pier to make some enquiries about my holiday.

ΞΞΞ

Chapter 13

Wed. 27th September to Friday 14th October 2011

In the two weeks since Chambers had been to the scene of Eric Cheng's murder in the flooded flat, his case had hit a new level of frustration. He knew that the chances of the murders being linked directly or otherwise to this target were slight. There was a chance the informant was known to him, and he had possibly been seen with a policeman just before his death but apart from these tenuous leads, Chambers had little else to go on.

He had been trying to find links between Cheng's murder and the murder of Peter Kwok in Kowloon Park. No other detective was making the connection, probably, Chambers reflected, because there wasn't one. There was no tangible evidence. He just had a hunch, a gut feeling, call it what you will, but he'd been wrong before. It was more likely that Chambers was a good detective with a knack for solving murders and if he was drawing a blank on his own case then he had no qualms about spreading his net a little wider. After all, it seemed a waste to be here in Hong Kong and not help out where he could. That's how he saw it anyway and he'd continue to involve himself until someone told him otherwise.

That hadn't been long coming – but not from one of the team members in Hong Kong. Chambers had received a call from Inspector Asbury back at the Met, telling him that if by the beginning of November no headway was being made, he'd better pack his bags and return to London. Chambers had pleaded his case, putting more emphasis than was strictly true on the link between the murder of the drowned man and his suspect. He even embellished his story to suggest there had been a sighting of their target. Chambers knew he was on thin ice. He didn't have unlimited credit with Asbury, they both knew it, so he'd have to tread carefully. Chambers pleaded for longer. Asbury finished the call explaining to him in no uncertain terms that he was expected back at his desk by the first week of November unless he could come up with some hard evidence. When he rang off Chambers was deflated. He knew that Asbury was only doing his job and that he had a valid point. He'd been here for ten weeks already, and the case hadn't moved forward in any way.

Even the other murders he'd become involved in were no further along. The CCTV for both cases had drawn a blank. The footage from Mong Kok only covered one end of the street and offered them nothing to go on. As for the cameras covering the park entrance, the only good news was the park kept the tapes for a month before reusing them. They managed to get hold of the tapes the day before they were due to be erased. One of the uniformed constables had tracked down the victim entering the park. However, when they ran the tape on there was no likely suspect following. They ran the tape back to a minute before he entered the park, again nothing. Some people on the blurry black and white tape were seen with bags, or carrying water, but they were mainly tourists or couples.

Chambers came up with two possibilities. The first was this was a random attack. The second and more likely, was that Kwok had arranged to meet someone in the park for a potential bit of business. What that was he couldn't be sure. Again Chambers enlisted Li's help to get the phone records of both the victims. These took several days to come back, but again drew a blank. Neither Kwok nor Cheng had called a common number; in fact, Cheng hadn't made any calls on the day of his death. Kwok's list of numbers appeared to be limited to his girlfriend and a restaurant that he'd called around lunchtime. There was little else for Chambers to do except wait for a break.

The department was busier than usual. Chambers noticed there was more excitement in the office. There was more chatter and more meetings were taking place. When he questioned Li, she had told him the department was gearing up for China National Day. Since the handover in 1997, Hong Kong was now a Special Administrative Region of China, and as such marked the National Day on the first of October with a flag-raising ceremony in Wan Chai. The exact location was at the Reunification Monument at Golden Bauhinia Square. It was on the waterfront by the iconic wave-roofed Hong Kong Convention and Exhibition Centre, just over the road from the Police Station where Chambers was sitting. The solemn sounding ceremony was to be accompanied by the police marching band and shows put on by the protective services including a fly past and a sea parade by the Harbour Police.

This year the official flag-raising duties fell to the Hong Kong Police and Li's department was to be one of the supporting cast of 15 groups, each consisting of 15 members. Li, Pang, Yuen and Tang were all part of the team. Chambers was impressed. He wondered what his team back in London would make of it. There were always a few who enjoyed getting the uniform on, but for most of his colleagues, they had been all too happy to be able to ditch the uniform for plain clothes as quickly as they could. He was a little surprised that the ceremony team was comprised solely of volunteers from the department. This year the event fell on a Saturday and knowing how many hours they all put in, he thought it might have been an enforced request. Li explained to him that it was a great honour. She personally enjoyed dusting off her police uniform and she was looking forward to the day, which was also popular with friends and family as well as Hong

Kongers in general. She invited him to come and watch the event that would be taking place in a few days time. The team was planning a Cantonese banquet afterwards with family and friends. He was delighted to be asked and accepted immediately.

On the morning of the ceremony Chambers guessed it was going to be a particularly formal lunch. So he'd dressed smartly but, as he was going to be outside for what he presumed would be quite some time, he chose a light blue shirt, chinos and a pair of brown boat shoes. He didn't want to look too out of place at a table full of uniformed officers. He used the series of raised walkways that crossed the busy confluence where the road coming from the cross-harbour tunnel joined Gloucester Road below. He could see from his vantage point that his destination was already packed. The walk should have taken him little more than 10 minutes, but today, with a maze of metal barriers and what appeared to be the entire population of Hong Kong all making for the same place as he was, it took him nearly 40 minutes to get down to the waterfront. The place was heaving with people.

He had learned enough during his couple of months in the city to know what to do. He had one hand raised in front of his face to prevent the loss of an eye from a carelessly waved umbrella. He marveled at just how many locals would carry an umbrella, no matter rain or shine. Only on the city's infamous smoggy days was he safe from these dangerous weapons. If his height caused him potential injury from the sea of umbrellas, it had other advantages. He was 10 people back from the barrier; but his height allowed him a reasonable view among the raised hands clicking cameras, the mass of umbrellas and the occasional child hoisted on a parent's shoulders.

The flag-raising ceremony was done with much pomp and ceremony. The 60-person silver band was creating a din only matched by the volume of the tannoy announcements that seemed intent on making sure the crowd was tested to its limits of aural endurance every couple of minutes. The temporary grandstand on the other side of the parade ground was solid with spectators. Eventually the group of his colleagues hove into view, immaculately presented, as they marched past the crowds and took their place alongside representatives from the other services. The event culminated in the flag-raising with a simultaneous fly past from two EC155 B1 helicopters. One was trailing the Chinese national flag and the other the HKSAR flag – a white bauhinia flower emblem on a red background. There was also a display on the water by the Hong Kong Harbour Police. Chambers was pleased he'd seen the ceremony but equally happy in the knowledge he would never again witness this particular event.

It wasn't that he was agoraphobic, it was a word he'd never considered before in relation to himself, but this wasn't the first time in his life that the sheer weight of numbers left him desperate to escape the crowds for a bit of personal space. If he moved back a foot or so to give himself some room, sure as anything, a small bowlegged grandmother would be elbowing her way into the space. He sent Li a text asking her to contact him when she was finished with whatever other rituals and ceremonies she had to carry out. She had mentioned the restaurant was in or around Central, so he thought he'd make his own way there and wait for Li to give him the exact location. Getting out was a little bit easier than getting in; he made it to MTR Wan Chai Station in 30 minutes that wasn't too bad, although the station was only a few hundred metres away from where he had started. He contemplated jumping on a tram but decided to take advantage of the air conditioning in the MTR.

The train ride took less than ten minutes, but it was enough time for Chambers to scan and delete a lot of the pictures he had just taken as most of them had certain features in varying degrees of prominence: children, hands holding up cameras and the ubiquitous umbrellas. He'd snapped off about fifty shots, but only five were worth keeping; one of the fly-past had come out well, while he had also zoomed in and got one of Li marching by. He wasn't sure what it was about the photograph, but even with her uniform on and hair tied up she still looked lovely. Chambers certainly didn't have a fetish for uniforms and he'd been around the Metropolitan Police uniform long enough. The stay-press trousers looked bad enough on the men, but the women's uniform had no redeeming qualities in his eyes. It made even the most attractive WPC appear like a forward in a women's rugby team. Was that the point?

He decided to browse the shops of Central while he waited for the call from Li, just happy to be out of the crush of the ceremony. He looked on in amazement; he'd never seen such a concentration of flagship designer stores. He'd made the mistake of checking a few prices, and after doing some mental gymnastics with the exchange rate he finally understood how the likes of Ian Greening could so easily spend their vast salaries. Some of the labels he was aware of – Smith, Zenga, Gucci, Prada – but there were also stores that were located on equally expensive real estate that he'd never heard of before like Vivier, Pianegonda or Charriol. He considered himself up to speed on most things related to modern culture but since he'd been in Hong Kong he had really begun to feel all of his age and more. Musically, he didn't mind not being able to tell his breakcore from his neurofunk, but it made him cringe when colleagues his own age or older tried desperately to cling to their youth, following the trends to the point of wearing their hair like a young Rod Stewart and invoking phrases like 'the ironic mullet' to describe their latest follicle disaster. He wasn't advocating becoming prematurely ancient, but there had to be something to growing old with a semblance of style.

Fortunately for him the call from Li came after 15 minutes, directing him to a restaurant called Maxim's Palace in the City Hall building not far from the Mandarin Oriental Hotel. He had managed to get himself completely lost in the maze of walkways. He could see the trams passing below so he knew he wasn't too far from where he wanted to be, but it seemed to him he had been walking round in circles. It took him another ten minutes to realise there were actually two Mandarin Oriental Hotels within a close proximity of each other, the original and the Landmark. He had eventually escaped on to Ice House Street and made his way towards the restaurant. She had told him it was in a building opposite the Cenotaph that, quite rarely for an area in Central, was set in the middle of its own block surrounded by a neatly trimmed lawn. He found he couldn't cross the road and needed to go back and take the underpass that was also an entrance to Central Station, a vast underground network of tentacles stretching under much of downtown Hong Kong. As he walked back towards the underpass he got an unobstructed view of the IM Pei designed Bank of China building, a truly remarkable feat of engineering and design. In the foreground was the LEGCO building, a contrasting style that dated back to the Colonial era.

When he exited the lift on the third floor of the City Hall building he could see the place was busy and the noise impressive. The restaurant turned out to be enormous. There were waiters and waitresses everywhere wearing cream jackets, some pushing carts laden with bamboo baskets, others carrying trays of dishes, all under enormous crystal chandeliers that dotted the hall's ceiling. It wasn't hard to spot the police contingent; the amount of black jackets marked them out from the other diners. Li looked up and happened to see him. She beckoned him over to the group. Due to his delay he was the last to join and took the only seat available at one of the large circular tables. Unfortunately for him he wasn't next to Li, he wasn't even at the same table. The group from his department took up three large tables and judging by the noise it wasn't as formal as he was expecting. He squeezed in between an officer on his right who he recognised from his department and a young man on his left dressed casually like himself. He sat down and nodded to the officer who smiled back at him and moved up a little to give Chambers more room. He looked around the table, recognising a few of the police officers and guessing the others must be family members. Further to his left he saw Chief Inspector James Pang.

'Hello DI Chambers, perfect timing! We've taken the liberty of ordering, so grab your chopsticks and tuck in. This young man', he gestured to the casually dressed man seated directly to Chambers' left, 'is my son, Derek. Any questions I'm sure he'll be delighted to help. Won't you Derek?'

Derek grunted and nodded briefly in his father's direction.

Pang ignored his son's surliness and quickly introduced Chambers to the rest of the table. The policeman to his left, Mason Tan, offered him some jasmine tea. Chambers accepted and looked at the place setting in front of him. He had a pair of cream-coloured chopsticks, a white heavy plastic spoon, a small white porcelain bowl, teacup and saucer and a small plate. He saw some of the other diners washing their cutlery and bowls with the tea. He'd been in a few local restaurants and had seen this practice before, but usually with hot water. He decided not to do anything until prompted; including drinking his tea in case it was for washing the bowl. The food had already started to arrive. They were coming at the table from all angles and being placed on a large Lazy Susan in the centre of the circular table. He could see there were printed sheets of paper that looked like large lottery tickets, he picked one up to have a look at, it was covered in traditional Chinese writing, he guessed it must be the menu and put it back. All the while carts were brought to the table, Chambers was pleased to see these had signs in Chinese and English informing the customer of what delicacies were concealed within the steaming baskets. As soon as the first dishes landed on the table, the Lazy Susan was being moved this way and that, chopsticks were attacking the dishes. Chambers joined in. As he went to spear what he thought looked like a wet and floppy spring roll, Derek scolded him.

'Detective Chambers, we don't use our own chopsticks to take the food. We use the communal chopsticks,' he said in a condescending manner in perfect English.

Pang then leaned forward and picked up a pair of black chopsticks from the centre.

'Oh sorry, I didn't know.' Chambers felt it was in his best interests to avoid any conflict with the Chief Inspector's son.

For the remainder of the meal, Pang Junior was happy to point out all of Chambers' culinary flaws. Whether it was with his chopstick technique, or admonishing him for trying to stab an elusive item rather than pick it up with his chopsticks. Pang junior was making the lunch a less than enjoyable experience.

Chambers tried to humour him. His requests for information about what constituted the dishes' ingredients, were met by just the dish name and nothing more: Beef Rice Roll, Shao Mai, Chive and Shrimp Dumpling, Water Chestnut Cake. Whatever it was, Chambers concluded, James Pang's son was not a happy camper.

He admitted defeat and turned to Mason Tan on his other side, who was happy to point out some of the other dishes that he could recommend. Chambers fell in love with the white barbecue pork buns that were like little fluffy clouds of heaven, the rich and sweet sauce oozing out of the centre. He also took a fancy to the black sesame soup that appeared in front of him. Although his first impression was that it looked like a bowl of crude oil, it was only after much encouragement from the other diners that he gave it a go and thoroughly enjoyed the flavour and texture. The only thing during the meal he couldn't bring himself to eat was the Hainan-style chicken's feet. He watched Mason devour one that reminded him of a small child's hand, spitting the knuckles onto his plate like he was firing out machinegun bullets. When Mason pressed him to try one, he tried not to cause offence and surreptitiously put it on the side of his plate, hoping that no one would notice. Of course someone did.

'In our culture it's very rude to turn down a dish that's offered to you,' Derek said disdainfully and these were the last words he would offer Chambers for the rest of the meal.

Chambers was surprised by the speed of the service. The table of 12 had devoured at least 30 dishes of varying sizes and they were all finished in less than half an hour. The noise was intense as well, with bowls clattering, people chattering, waiters shouting. It was a cacophony of noise that oddly seemed completely in keeping with the elegant surroundings. When the bill came Pang senior would hear no objections as he put his credit card on the table. There was much smacking of lips and picking of teeth before small family groups began to make their way out amid friendly backslapping and laughter. As it was all in Cantonese, Chambers could only gauge the mood, and except for Derek, everyone seemed to have had a great time. The atmosphere was considerably more fun and lighthearted than he had imagined it would be.

He'd looked over in Li's direction a couple of times. She was sitting with her back to him so it wasn't easy to work out if she'd brought her partner along, although he thought not, as the men sat either side of her were both older and in uniform. He could see across the table and caught Brian Tang's eye, who nodded and gave Chambers one of his trademark friendly grins. He looked calm despite the commotion being caused by his two young children who sat on either side of him. Chambers figured the earlier ceremony must have been a huge success judging by the mood. He made a mental note to check with Li just what was up with Derek, who had left with barely a word to anyone except the briefest conversation with his father. Chambers noted the look of, what was it? Disappointment, resignation, that crossed James Pang's face as he watched his son depart. A couple of seconds later Pang had regained his composure and was chatting and joking with another officer, but Chambers had seen it and he felt the man's pain. He caught up with Li as the rest of the group headed to the exit.

'Sorry John, I tried to save you a seat, but I thought you'd got lost or had second thoughts. Did you enjoy it?'

'Hey, no problem, yes it was great. I tried some very interesting dishes, although I'm not actually sure I have a clue what most of them were. James's son Derek was next to me, not the most sociable or hospitable person I've ever met.'

'You can guess why that's where the only spare seat was. He's been like that ever since I've known him. I was actually surprised to see him here. He normally hates anything to do with his father. As long as he didn't ruin the experience for you.'

'No, no, quite the opposite.'

'Good. Sorry John, I've got to dash. I'm meeting up with someone. Have a great weekend and I'll see you in the office on Monday.' She rushed on ahead leaving Chambers standing on his own.

He was a little disappointed with the brush-off; he was hoping they could have gone for a coffee or a drink. He hoped she wasn't going off to meet her boyfriend, if she had one; he really needed to find out if she was single. For a detective he was doing a pretty bad job. He left the building and walked the short distance to Connaught Road. He was on the correct side of the dual carriageway to hail a cab and he got one almost immediately. As he climbed into the back seat he had an eerie sensation he was being watched. As the cab sped away from the kerb he looked out of the door's window and was sure he saw a man watching him from a recess in the nearby building. As he twisted round to get a better view out of the back window the person had disappeared from view. Chambers couldn't be sure but he thought the man had looked very much like Derek Pang.

≈≈≈

Li felt guilty. She knew Chambers was trying to ask her out on a date but what could she do? She liked him, probably more than was good for her. But how much longer would he be in Hong Kong? A few weeks – a couple of months at the most. She was sure he wanted to stay but it just wasn't going to happen. There could be no long-term future for them. In the short term it would lead to heartache for one or both of them, especially now, while they'd been working so closely

126

together. The negative implications on the case could potentially be enormous.

She had to admit she found him attractive, and she knew he liked her. He was very attentive and always trying to make her laugh, even if she didn't understand most of his jokes. Greening had also pointed it out his attraction to her, and if it was obvious to her, it would be obvious to others as well. Another time or place perhaps, who knew what was around the corner?

But there was also another problem and he went by the name of Kelvin Lau. He was Li's ex-boyfriend and he was becoming a major headache for her. They had dated casually for a few months after meeting through a mutual friend. Initially Lau had been charming and entertaining, but as the weeks passed he had become more and more controlling. He wanted her to stop seeing her friends and spend all her time just with him. Yet he would sometimes disappear for days on end and come back acting erratically, and be bleary-eyed and paranoid. She wasn't sure if he was abusing drugs or drink or maybe both. After a month of his disturbing behavior she had called an end to it. She hadn't seen much of him and she didn't need the hassle. Since then Lau had taken to phoning her at all hours of the day and night, calling her names and making vague threats against her and it was beginning to take its toll. She had planned to meet him later and give him an ultimatum. Either the threats stopped or she would be forced to get some colleagues to pay him an official visit.

≈≈≈

Chambers made the most of the hiatus in the case as he continued exploring Kowloon and other parts of Hong Kong Island. He couldn't put his finger on it, but Hong Kong was definitely beginning to get under his skin. He was getting a better feel for the city, realising it was a place that was at once beguiling and frustrating. After his trip to the dim sum restaurant he was getting more adventurous when it came to dining, and was no longer put off by the Hainan-style chickens he saw in restaurant windows. The style of cooking that looked to Chambers like the chicken had just been plucked bald and put on a plate, the head was on and the skin had an unnatural human-like look and texture. It seemed a common trait to leave the heads on the poultry in most of the local restaurants he'd seen. Another breakthrough was realising many restaurants were hidden away on higher floors of what at first appeared to be residential blocks. The more he explored, the more he was rewarded. Now when he dined out, he didn't mind if they didn't have an English menu, he would look at fellow diners' tables and just point out to the waiter or waitress who took his order. More than once, the other diners would engage him in conversation, often in perfect English, and make dish recommendations. Chambers was beginning to see Hong Kong in a whole new light. People who would be carelessly bumping into him on the street or in the MTR, closing lift doors on him one minute, would turn out to be hospitable, engaging conversationalists once they were inside a restaurant or bar. Apart from the exasperating lack of progress on the case, he was beginning to savour his time in Hong Kong.

When Asbury called to give him his deadline, he wasn't sure it was the case or the city that was keeping him here. Of course, there was one other significant draw, Li. Chambers knew he'd developed a huge crush on her and it was interfering with his usually methodical, logical mind. He tried to ignore it, but it was there all the same. He had tried subtly, well subtle for Chambers anyway, to ascertain her marital status, but even colleagues weren't clear or unwilling not willing to let him know. He'd even found himself at Jenny Greening's office, on the pretence of following up some forensic evidence, but as he directed the conversation on to his colleague Li, she had excused herself, claiming she had too much to do. Chambers had opted not to make a move on her on the boat ride back from Discovery Bay the month before and there hadn't been any further offers coming from her direction. He decided to play it cool and see what happened. If he was called back in a couple of weeks, he would make his move then.

≈≈≈

Chapter 14 – This little Piggy had none

Monday 1st August – Monday 29th August 2011

Dear diary,

Last night I got back from a 10-day break in Malaysia. I needed it - killing is a tiring business. I spent most of the time on the Perhentian islands, a great place to chill out. I even took an open water dive course. It was a revelation. I mean once you learn to become neutrally buoyant you can just sit in the water as weightless as if you are in outer space. The freedom is tremendous. Moving only with the current and able to get up close to an enormous variety of different coloured fish. I loved every moment of it. While I was there I met some nice people. No one asked what I did for a career or how much money I earned or what car I drove. The normal predictable questions you get in Hong Kong on a daily basis. The 'Arsehole Evaluation Meter' I call it.

The islands that are off the North East Coast of peninsula Malaysia are a very laid back place. It's the best time I've had in a very long time, maybe ever. When I finally come into my inheritance I'm definitely going to travel more. The escape also gave me plenty of opportunity to gather my thoughts, reflect on how my 'project' was coming along and, most importantly, to begin planning the next stages. By the time I got back to Hong Kong I felt totally refreshed. In fact, I realise this is the best I have felt in years. I feel like my life finally has a purpose. I know what I need to do, what my goals are and definitely, where I want to be. It's going to be very interesting when I meet with my 'family'. I go and visit them a couple of times a year. Any more and I feel like I want to do one, or all of them, some serious harm. Saying that, maybe I could accommodate them into my work. Now that is something I need to seriously consider.

Before I went on my break a few weeks ago it was imperative that I read the papers on what had happened, or at least what was perceived to have happened, in Tai Hang. The news was in the press the day after the murder, although this one didn't even make the front page. It was on page six, a couple of paragraphs about how the body of Mrs Penny Teo Li Wing, a publications' seller, had been found the previous afternoon by a deliveryman. Police and paramedics had been called to the scene but Mrs Teo had been pronounced dead on arrival at the nearby St Paul's Hospital. A police spokesperson was quoted as saying there would be a full investigation into the incident. The fact that the article was on page six made me think that it wasn't being considered as a murder. That was good news for now.

I booked a return flight with AirAsia to leave Hong Kong a few days after the murder, so I could read the reports and also to avoid being possibly flagged if they checked airlines' loading lists. You can never be too careful, and I didn't want to draw unnecessary attention; it was easy enough to book online even at quite short notice. The travel agents had tried to rip me off. As usual, if you want something done, do it yourself. When I got back from my trip there was no sign of any follow-up of the murder in the papers. I never knew it would be so easy to get away with so many murders.

ΞΞΞ

I had picked up a children's book the day before the murder. The character McDull was well known in Hong Kong, popular with both young and old; a bit like the bizarre hold that Hello Kitty

130

has over the Japanese. It makes you wonder how many gullible people there are in the world that are happy to waste their money on this kind of rubbish. There's one born every minute to quote PT Barnum. I think he got it wrong, the way society is developing, it is more like one every second.

For this particular task the victim wasn't important. This was good, as it just freed me up to wander the city and select any random arsehole. The only drawback with this procedure is often you've racked up 10 or more potential victims before you've gone a hundred metres from your front door. I left it until quite late in the day for several reasons. Firstly it was very hot and humid and not the type of weather to be out strolling around in the pollution in Kowloon, and secondly, I wanted to get into the action at or around nightfall for obvious reasons. I took the one-litre bottle of water out of the freezer and put it in my backpack along with a couple of ice packs; I donned my baseball cap and sunglasses, and headed out in the direction of Jordan.

The streets were teeming with people so it was nice to get into the relative peace and quiet of Kowloon Park. The place was still busy but fortunately a little less polluted and a bit more spacious. I casually followed a couple of people around, before I found myself at the pond that's got a large flock of flamingoes. Quite a strange sight in the middle of Kowloon, it has to be said. I stood up at the railings and watched people coming and going. That's when I saw my mark, standing off to my left; throwing what looked like sweets to the birds. He might have been in his early 20s. Old enough to know better anyway. As I looked over at him, he caught my eye and nodded conspiratorially, like he was letting me in on some secret act, as if I were now somehow involved as well. I averted my eyes. 'Yes, you'll do' I thought to myself. After several minutes of him shouting to the birds and throwing an assortment of food at them, he wandered off along the path that leads to steps up to the aviary.

In an ideal world I would take him in the park, as it had to be quieter than out on the streets. The sky was darkening and there were fewer people around but I'd still be lucky to get more than a few seconds to sort him out. I knew I still had a few hours to look for another victim if this didn't work out, so I decided to see where this one would take me. I gave him a fairly good head start and once I knew for certain he was going up the stairs, I went around to the other side to wait for him to exit down the other set of stairs. I was probably there for five minutes when it dawned on me that he was up there annoying more birds and this was a possible opportunity I should investigate.

I took the bottle out of my bag; it had only melted a small amount. I scaled the steps and walked round the circular path that surrounded the bird enclosures. The staff quarters for the aviary were down below on the ground floor, and it was only this viewing station that was upstairs. There was no one else up on the gantry looking at the birds at this late hour except my flamingo-feeding friend. As I walked towards him, he recognised me and smiled, before going back to carry on his bird-annoying antics. I moved past him before swinging the bottle back with all my might. Knocking him to the ground with one clean smack on the side of his head. He went down like the proverbial sack of spuds. I hit him quite a lot of times, the sound of the bottle against his head was drowned out by some cawing from one of the nearby sulphur-crested cockatoos.

When he stopped twitching I pulled the tea towel out of my bag and wiped the bottle down. I then stepped out of my tracksuit bottoms and pushed them in the bag along with my baseball cap but I kept my gloves on. I'd put the sunglasses in the bag earlier. I pulled the book out and placed it under the victim's arm while the bottle I left on the ground near his other arm. I surveyed the scene, unfortunately it was quite dark by now, so it would be difficult to see if I'd left anything behind, but at least there was no one around. I removed my gloves as I walked down the stairs and headed back the way I had come, making sure I kept my head down and my face averted from any potential witnesses. Within five minutes I was out of the park and had merged with the mass of pedestrians on Nathan Road, beginning my journey home.

ΞΞΞ

Chapter 15

Thursday 27th and Friday 28th October 2011

The call that Chambers had been dreading came as he was walking to work. The number came up as unlisted which normally meant it was from overseas and that could only mean one thing, or more correctly, one person, Inspector Asbury.

'Hello, DI Chambers,' he answered.

'John, it's Colin.' It was Inspector Asbury as he had suspected. 'How do you like it in the Far East?'

'Good, good.'

'Hmm. Well don't get too used to it. I've just got word from on high. We're pulling you out. We want you on a flight back at the weekend.'

Chambers had been taking a drink from a bottle of water and choked on it.

'What?' he coughed. 'You said early November.' Chambers was furious. 'You're only giving me two days to tie things up here and come back. I need more time.'

'Do you have anythning for me?'

'We are onto something here. I know he's involved in two other murders, the evidence should be with me by next week,' Chambers lied.

'Too late John. Book your ticket, and pay with your credit card. Don't worry, we'll reimburse you when you get back.'

'But.'

'No buts John, we need you back here. We're short-staffed as it is. It's as simple as that. Book your flight and I'll see you in my office for a debrief on Monday morning. Take the next few days off. The weather's wet and windy back here. I'd advise you to enjoy a couple of days of sunshine. Goodbye John.' Asbury hung up leaving Chambers standing in the middle of the street staring incredulously at his phone.

He continued on to the office. There was little point in resisting. He had been ordered back and he had no compelling evidence to keep him here. The only thing for it was to invite Li out for a drink, as he slumped down in his chair, Li looked up and saw his expression.

'John, what's the matter? You look awful. Another busy night in Wan Chai?' She tried to lighten the mood.

Chambers ignored her sly dig. 'Asbury called from London. I've been called back. I'm leaving on Saturday night or Sunday morning, depending on what flight I can get.'

'Are you serious?' She was stunned. Chambers had told her before that he only had a few weeks left, but not a few days.

'Yes, I'm done here. So no more chaperoning the stupid gweilo.' He smiled briefly to show it was meant as a joke.

'Come on John, you know I ... we've enjoyed having you here.'

'So.' he stalled a moment, drumming up the courage, 'Would you like to go out for dinner with me tomorrow night?'

'Yes of course,' she paused, 'I'll arrange it all now, hmmm, Brian, James, who else? I'll ask Jenny as well.'

Either she was playing more games or she really had missed his point. There was no point flogging a dead horse. 'Sure, the more the merrier. I'll leave it to you then shall I?' He got up from his desk. 'Look, I'd better go and sort out my ticket home. I'll call you later.'

'Sure John, take care, leave the dinner arrangements to me. Get out and enjoy the city, have you been up to The Peak yet?' she called after him as he exited towards the lifts.

Li had to think fast and the best she could come up with was deliberately misinterpreting Chambers' invite out on a date. Now she knew he had only a couple of days left there was really no point pursuing her feelings for him. Plus, life was complicated enough with the pressure of the case and the ongoing problems with her ex. The visit she had paid to him in October hadn't brought her the result she was hoping for. When she had confronted Lau, he had become very aggressive. He made more threats of a more violent nature. Li's promise to officially charge him had fallen on deaf ears. Her problem was she didn't really want to make it official, she was worried about the negative impact it might have on her career. She had left him with a warning that if he carried on harassing or stalking her then he would, without question, be arrested. He had countered with the veiled threat that he would be watching her even more closely in the future. She'd delved into his records and found that he had several priors for violent behaviour. It hadn't made her feel any better about her situation. She would need to be even more vigilant.

≈≈≈

It dawned on Chambers that he hadn't been up to what was probably the city's most popular tourist attraction. It was a one of those rare, beautifully sunny days in Hong Kong with no cloud cover or haze, and he had nothing better to do. He could always book his flight ticket after his trip. He spent the rest of the day as a tourist, queuing with the hordes of people waiting for the historic Peak Tram, the city's old funicular railway that was built to ferry the rich colonials and the wealthy local Taipans to their mansions on the lofty slopes of Victoria Peak, out of sight of the riff raff and the cloying humidity. These days the ancient tram took thousands of tourists daily up the steep tracks that offered spectacular views of the skyscrapers that appeared to be at bizarre angles to the viewer.

To say he was a bit disappointed by what he found at the top was an understatement: it was a multi-floored shopping trap. He avoided the chain stores and global restaurants that made a visit anywhere in the world feel decidedly similar, and escaped out onto the viewing platform. The view it offered on both sides of Hong Kong Island was truly breathtaking. He was lucky to have picked a clear day; often the view was so limited it was hard to see the harbour. Chambers leaned on the railing and absorbed the panorama. It really was an incredible sight. He looked down at the waterfront to where he guessed his building was. The view from his room was amazing, but now he was up here, it took on a new perspective. He could see beyond the numerous hills that circled Kowloon away on the other side of the harbour. He guessed he could also see the Chinese mainland disappearing into the horizon. He turned his gaze back to Kowloon. 'I know you're out there,' he said out loud to no one in particular. A couple of Japanese tourists walking past gave him an odd look and hurried on.

After he left the viewing station he was planning to return down on the Peak Tram until he saw the long queue and decided to go for a walk instead. He saw a few people walking towards a slightly higher peak and followed them. After a couple of hundred metres, the road veered right and he found himself at a park roughly the size of a football pitch. The park had a path around the edge and was packed with an wide variety of plants and flowers. Chambers took a leisurely hour alternating between investigating the flowers, while trying to memorise their Latin names that were affixed to nearby stakes, and sitting enjoying the cool breezes and refreshing aromas of the flowers. It was, he noted, the first time it had been cool outside and probably one of the few times while he had been in Hong Kong that his senses hadn't been overwhelmed by at least one unpleasant odour.

He tried not to think about the case. But there was no escaping it. He had failed. He'd been here for 10 weeks and had nothing to show for it. What about Kwok and Cheng? Kwok had been murdered, what was it? Eight weeks ago. Cheng had been murdered four weeks ago. There was something definitely odd about both of them but there was nothing connecting them. Chambers idly counted the days. It was 29 days since Eric Cheng had been brutally murdered in his apartment and then put in a bath, strangely thought Chambers as Cheng was probably already dead. The water had to be significant, was it symbolic of something, if so, what? He counted forward from there. Another 29 days brought him to today. An interesting coincidence. But it just proved to Chambers what little headway he had made with either murder, one about two months ago and one nearly a month ago. With nothing to go on, he sat back on the bench and closed his eyes for a moment.

The sound of people talking nearby woke Chambers. He must have dozed off. It seemed a bit darker. He checked his watch. Nearly 4pm. He'd only been asleep for 20 minutes or so. He looked up to see the sun was temporarily hidden behind a small cumulus cloud. As he stood up and stretched he noticed another object in the sky, he could just make it out faintly – it was the cusp of a new moon. He might not have noticed the faint sliver in the sky had the sun not been temporarily shaded by the passing cloud. He subconsciously withdrew his wallet and took out some banknotes. Facing the direction of the moon he turned them three times towards him. His grandmother had taught him this when he was a little boy. She told him it would attract wealth. He wasn't really superstitious, but on the odd instance he had seen a new moon he had always made sure he turned his money. He wasn't sure he had attracted much wealth so far, yet he performed the ritual whenever he saw a new moon. Plus in the expensive city of Hong Kong, he needed all the financial help he could get.

He wondered where he had been during the last new moon as he made his way back to the Peak Tram. He realised he still needed to buy himself a plane ticket back to London. The last thing he needed was to be told all the flights were sold out. He was leaving it late if he wanted to fly out within the next few days, he knew that, but it would hardly be his fault.

The sky was beginning to cloud over as he joined the queue for the tram, and after waiting about 30 minutes he took a seat facing down the hill. It was a most disconcerting view seeing the buildings tilted at such angles. The tram had glass panels custom-built into the carriage's ceiling so passengers could make the most of this peculiar spectacle. Chambers was idly imagining what it would be like to commute to work via this system. Some people still did, evidence of which was supplied when the tram made several stops at Kennedy Road, Macdonnell Road, May Road and Barker Road. The platforms were parallel with the horizon but seemingly at a crazy angle to the tram. The floor of the tram had crescent shaped tiles to stop people sliding down the carriage. Chambers looked back at the horizon. As he did so he caught another glimpse of the new moon as it appeared between the thickening clouds. It suddenly reminded him where he'd last seen one. He was in the back of the taxi with Brian Tang heading to the murder scene in Mong Kok. That time he hadn't flipped his money over. He'd been too conscious of having to explain his eccentric behaviour to a colleague and he was keen not to appear even crazier than some of them already thought he was.

~~~

Chambers was at his desk at 8am on Friday morning. Li was in not long after. She appeared surprised to see him.

'John, what are you doing here? I thought you'd be out sightseeing. Or at least nursing a hangover. Did you book your ticket yet?'

'No hangover, and no I didn't book a ticket.'

'Sold out?'

'No, I didn't go to a travel agent.'

'I know a couple of good ones if you need a number.'

'No. Thanks,' he said firmly.

She stopped what she was doing and looked over. 'What is it ?'

'I might have something. It could be nothing, but yesterday I was thinking of the dates of the two murders we have. Kwok and Cheng. We both think there's something odd about them and that they might be related. Well how about this?' he paused for effect. 'It appears they were both killed on a new moon.'

'Right,' she sounded suitably unimpressed, 'and?'

'And what?'

'Well we have two murders committed on new moons, that's a coincidence. We checked back the month before and nothing came up that appeared odd from the month before. I have to say, it seems tenuous to me, John. And if it's tenuous to me, then your man Asbury certainly isn't going to buy it. I'm just worried you are digging yourself in deeper with your boss at home.'

'Maybe. But I think it's worth looking into. I mean, what have I got to lose, right?'

'OK John, I'll humour you. I'll check the records for the month before the attack in the park. But then again that one could conceivably have been the first. So there may just be these two incidents. Moving forward, when is the next new moon due?'

'It was yesterday.' Chambers looked across at her. 'If my new theory is right, there must have been a murder reported last night, or at some time during the day.'

'OK, let me check. There was nothing I was alerted to. We are normally made aware of any murders; this is Hong Kong after all, not Caracas.' She pulled out her mobile.

Chambers waited expectantly. He felt this was his last throw of the dice. Li talked in Cantonese. Her body language and tone of voice gave nothing away. After a couple of minutes she hung up and turned to Chambers.

'That was James. If there was any news, he would know.'

'And?' Chambers was half out of his seat.

'Sorry John. Nothing came in last night. No reports of any murders taking place. Look, I've heard of murders occurring on full moons, but on a new moon? It just sounds a little desperate to me.'

'Shit.' He sat back down in the chair, looking seriously disheartened.

'I'm not giving up on this,' Li said after a pause. She knew this meant a great deal to him and knew her last comments didn't sound in the least bit supportive. 'Just because there's not been a report, doesn't mean to say that there hasn't been a murder, the other two were obviously going to be discovered sooner rather than later. Maybe this one won't show up for a few days.'

'Thanks, I know you're trying to help. I think my theory was a bit of a long shot. Worth a try though.'

'What are you going to do now?'

'As soon as the travel agents open, I'm off to book my flight home. Not much else I can do.'

Li went to the pantry and made him a coffee. She felt it was the least she could do. As she was returning to her desk her mobile phone rang. She answered it and as she spoke in Cantonese, she began waving her hand to get Chambers' attention. She listened for a couple of minutes, asking the occasional question. When she finished the call she was staring at Chambers, one eyebrow raised.

'What is it?' he asked, hardly able to contain himself.

'That was James Pang. He said he's just been informed a body was discovered at dawn this morning out on Lantau Island.'

~~~

Chapter 16 – Like a Drowned Rat

Tuesday 30th August – Tuesday 27th September 2011

Dear diary,

We all make mistakes. It's just some are bigger than others. Some have repercussions and some don't. At the moment I'm just not sure which category this one falls into, only time will tell. The good news was I was on the front page. The body was discovered less than an hour after I had finished with it. A staff member had made a final round of checks before locking the gates to the aviary; he had discovered the body and alerted his colleague by radio, who in turn had dialed 999. When the police arrived they closed off the area. The paper reported that the body of Peter Kwok, 21, had been found in the aviary section at Kowloon Park, he had died of head trauma and was pronounced dead at the scene. I used a similar technique on a lot of my victims. It was a fairly common method used in Hong Kong from time immemorial. For some reason, muggers would strike victims over the head before making off with a handbag or wallet. These attacks in the past had sometimes led to deaths. I started to think that maybe it would be better off for me to take valuables from the victim to make it look like a robbery gone wrong. But the more I thought about it, the more I thought the police were struggling to link any of my crimes so I figured it didn't really matter.

The one glaring issue the report failed to mention was what was found at the scene. I don't mean the things I had deliberately left there, the book and the bottle; I realised when I got home and emptied the bag into my washing machine that my sunglasses were nowhere to be seen. I could only think that as I pulled the book out I dislodged the glasses. I hadn't noticed them when I checked the area, but it was dark by then. I could have lost them somewhere else, but I had that sinking feeling. On further evaluation, I thought that maybe, if I did drop them by the body, that the police would assume they belonged to the victim. I was making several assumptions of my own, that the victim didn't have any sunglasses himself, and no matter how hard I tried to visualise him feeding the flamingoes the previous day, I just couldn't recall if he had shades on or not.

I can see him on the top step leaning on the guard rail, wearing a white polyester tracksuit with green piping, I think it had a Puma logo, and he's got white running shoes on, the make I don't remember, but did he have sunglasses on his face? No, I was sure, because he looked at me and I saw his eyes, but did he have them on top of his head? Folded and put in the neck of his yellow T-shirt? I couldn't say for definite. I was wracking my brains but it was no good. Well, whatever it was the police didn't mention them or the bottle or the book. I'm sure they'll be keeping certain information out of the papers. Would my sunglasses have fingerprints on them? Were there any witnesses? The answers weren't in the report. That much was clear. Police stated they were treating the death as highly suspicious and refusing to rule out murder, but were playing down any suggestion that this was anything other than a botched robbery.

ΞΞΞ

I needed to clear my head and keep a low profile, so I spent the next few weeks lying low at home. I just sat in messing about on my Mac, enjoying the air con and ordering takeaway. I went to the hardware store one day and bought some rat poison. Over the next few nights I put some down in the narrow alleys behind my apartment block. I sometimes played on my computer until it was getting light. When the sun started to show, I would nip down and check the alleys. If I found any dead vermin, I would pick them up in plastic bags and take them home, putting them in the freezer. After a week or so I was running out of room in the small frozen section in the top section of my fridge. Not to worry though, as it was nearly time for the next one.

ΞΞΞ

There was a man who lived in my block, his name was Eric Cheng. I sort of knew him a little bit. We knew each other by sight, occasionally saying hello and I sometimes saw him at the bars in Knutsford Terrace. He was one of these people that are instantly dislikeable. A mean, lean little person. You know the type; thinking he's the top dog, giving off an air of superiority to some and weaseling around others he thought might be of some use to him. It was rumoured that he was involved in the K19 gang. It was something he didn't try and deny; he loved the attention he got from some of the younger crowd. Whatever he was, he was a classic bottom feeder. He didn't work; he fenced a few bits and pieces, dealt a little on the side. But I, and it appeared quite a few other people, knew from the bar talk that he was a police informant. How he managed to walk this tightrope I was never too sure. He seemed to live a charmed life, until today that is.

I had literally bumped into him on the train a week before. I hadn't seen him around for a while. I was getting off the train at Mong Kok East, he was getting on. I nodded to him as casual acquaintances do, and he gave me a look as if I was the shit on his shoes. Un-fucking-believable. I might not be 'connected', like he gave the impression he was, but physically he was no match for me. I'm smart, well-dressed and get by in my own way. Whereas every day, he was doling out his own measure of misery to anyone unfortunate enough to enter his grubby little world. Oh

143

yes Eric was going to be next. And so convenient, I wouldn't even have to leave my building to do it.

He lived a couple of floors below me, I knew that. He was in apartment 1704. He'd lived there with his on/off girlfriend as long as I'd been here; I think her name was Sadie. I wasn't sure what she did. I had a vague recollection she worked in the electronics building near the ladies' market that sold all sorts of 'grey' goods at competitive prices, as long as you didn't expect a warranty. The few times I'd seen her coming into the building it was always after 10pm. So I just needed to make sure I had the time to get in, sort him out and leave before she came back. The only tricky thing was making sure he was going to be at home during my 'window of opportunity' on the day.

I thought the easiest thing would be to hang out in the lobby until I saw the Sadie woman leave. At around 11.30am I took a copy of the boring, free English newspaper from the stand and sat down on the black moribund fake-leather sofa in the lobby. The place really could do with a lick of paint, but I suppose you get what you pay for. I sat trying to look innocuous in the clichéd pose of holding the paper up in front of my face. I knew the electronics arcade opened at noon, so I guessed she'd be leaving sometime just before or around midday as the market was nearby. True to form she sashayed out of the lift about ten past, talking loudly into her mobile phone.

I watched her go past me, engrossed in the call and not giving me a second thought. She was an attractive woman – a little bit common about the edges – but she had lovely long legs. She reminded me of the bitch I used to live with. It seems like a lifetime ago now. In some ways I suppose it is. Many things have changed, me for one. I snapped myself out of my fug, picked up my rucksack and headed to the lift. I pressed the button and fished out my gloves and an old mug I had brought from my apartment. The lift doors opened and I pressed the button for the 15th floor. As the lift travelled upwards I put on my gloves. I knew it would draw a comment from him, but that was fine, it was all part of the plan.

The lift jolted to a stop and I headed straight for his door. I used the mug to knock on the door. I wanted to make sure he could hear me first time – I didn't want to be standing out here too long. I heard a commotion behind the door, and saw the light from the spy hole disappear as he decided to err on the side of safety. Wise man I thought.

'Hi, I'm from upstairs just after some sugar if you can spare it.' I said in the friendliest tone I could muster.

The door opened a crack. I saw his face looking at me, and obviously recognising me.

'I'm just a bit short of cash this week, if you could just spare a little, I'll buy you a bag next week.'

The door opened fully and he stood there, bare-chested, wearing just his sky-blue boxer shorts, a lit cigarette in his right hand, his left hand holding the top of the door. He was puffing out his pigeon chest like he was someone special. What a loser.

'I know you,' he said, an aggressive tone in his voice. 'I've seen you around, what the fuck are you doing begging at my door, do you know who I am?'

'Yes, sorry,' I feigned subservience as I pushed my cup a little further towards him.

'Hey freak, back off!' He raised his voice.

'Ok,' I moved my hand back.

'What's with the fucking gloves man? It's 35 degrees outside.'

'Well, it's because ...' I trailed off.

'Because fucking what?' he leaned aggressively towards me. Bingo!

'Because ...' I quickly pulled my hand back and smashed my mug straight into his ugly mug. He staggered back into his hallway, completely taken by surprise. I darted in, pushing the door closed behind me.

'Because I don't want to get your fucking blood all over my hands.'

I smacked him several more times with the broken mug. I flung the remains of the mug down. Punching him to the floor with my free hand and adding a few well-placed kicks and stomps to his body as he began curling into a ball. I needed to act quickly in case any of the neighbours overheard. He wasn't particularly big or strong. So it was easy for me to kneel on him and beat him some more around the head until he stopped moving. He was still breathing out of his now badly bloodied, pulp-like face. I went and did a quick reccy of the apartment, and on locating the bathroom I turned on both the bath taps.

I went back to the hall and dragged the body to the bath, pulling him up and pushing him into the tub. I flattened the body and left the water running. I took my backpack off and took out the plastic bag that contained the frozen vermin. I dropped one in the bath and spent a few minutes placing them strategically around the apartment. One in the oven, the fridge, the saucepan and one in his kettle. I'd read about a mass murderer in the UK or the USA doing that before. I forget his name, he left body parts in his kitchen appliances, that must have given the investigating team quite a shock if they had put it on for a restorative cup of tea! The remaining four I threw casually around the room. I turned off his air con unit. The corpses would thaw out over the afternoon, hopefully they'd be nice and ripe by the time his girlfriend got back home. That was assuming she'd come back to the apartment, as I didn't know if she stayed here on a full-time basis. Although I had a back-up plan to make sure the body would be discovered fairly soon.

I went back into the bathroom. The water was up to his chest. I sat on the toilet and waited until the water was deep enough. Then I forced him to turn over and held his head under the water for a good five minutes. The water was nearly up to the edge so I turned the hot tap off and lowered the pressure on the cold one, so it was more of a dribble. I waited another minute to make sure the pressure didn't ease off. Then I went for one last look around, careful this time to leave none of my possessions except for the broken mug. It was a one-off; I didn't have any matching ones in my apartment. I got it as a freebie with a box of Knorr soup. I took one last look at my victim. He looked a bit of a mess. The ceramic mug had made some deep lacerations in his face, plus the beating I had given him; I think it's safe to say he'd looked better. I'd broken a few of his teeth, so he wouldn't be sneering at anyone, ever again. I decided to roll the body over so he was face down in the water. For some reason it made me feel more secure that he wasn't going to have some kind of miraculous recovery. You read about these things. You know, how people drown but are revived hours later. Well he would be found, but surely not for a good while yet.

I picked up my bag and headed to the door. I leaned down to look through the spy hole. There were a couple of people coming out of the lift. I waited for them to enter their apartment. When I was sure they weren't coming back out, I left the apartment, closing the door quietly behind me. I walked through the fire door and walked the couple of flights back up to my apartment.

EEE

Chapter 17

Friday 28th October 2011

Chambers took his lead from Li. She was out the door moments after she had terminated the call from Chief Inspector Pang. He had time to grab his camera from the drawer, his mobile phone from the desk and his notepad. He jogged after her. They took a cab to Central and a ferry to Mui Wo. He took the relative calm of the boat to glean the extra information from Li.

'So what exactly did Pang say?' he asked.

'I don't want you to get your hopes up. He said a resident in one of the villages had gone down to the beach early this morning and had found a body. He called the police. As soon as James heard the news he'd called me. The body was discovered about an hour ago. Hopefully it will still be there when we arrive.'

'But you were on the phone for a few minutes. What else did he say?'

'He wanted to know why I'd called him earlier. What was going on? He wanted to know if you had a lead. That's all.'

'What did you tell him?'

'I haven't told him about your new moon theory if that's what you're getting at. All we know is a body has been discovered. At this stage it could mean anything. I wouldn't get your hopes up. Lantau Island is hardly a hotbed of Triad activity.'

They sat in silence for the remainder of the journey. Chambers enjoyed the ride. He'd been out to Lantau Island before, but this ferry was different from the Discovery Bay ferry in that it was open-sided. He enjoyed the breeze and the smell of the sea air. He felt positive that what they would find would link with the other two cases.

When they got off the ferry he followed Li as she headed to the nearby cab rank. Within a few minutes up and along a steep down they descended into Pui O. As they got out of the light-blue cab, Chambers could see there was a fair amount of activity around. There were several police cars and an ambulance parked just off the main road near a turn off on the right that was obscured by some hedgerows. A small crowd had gathered and was being told to stay behind the police tape. Chambers looked across the road at the village. There were a series of three-storey buildings, separate but closely packed together. Yet on either side of the village and on the other side of the road there were no buildings. The way the land was utilised in Hong Kong just didn't make sense to him.

Li pushed her way through the crowd and flashed her card at one of the constables on duty. He waved them through. They made their way down a quiet road until they passed a community centre that appeared to be hemmed in by disused shipping containers and an enormous pile of masonry. Next to it was an old dark-red Volvo, a couple of police cars and several members of the forensic team in their hooded white overalls sifting through the earth around the car. On the ground next to them was a monkey wrench in a clear plastic evidence bag. They could see a smaller crowd another couple of hundred metres further on. They walked on past a marshy-looking clearing that butted up to the beach. Chambers couldn't work out why all those buildings were tightly packed on the main road and not built here on the beach. In any other country this would have been prime real estate. He couldn't figure out why anyone would want to live in Mong Kok with a million other people when you could live here on the beach with the beautiful mountain scenery at your back in relative isolation and be less than an hour commute into the city. The logic, or lack of it, in the city continued to baffle him.

There was a mix of uniforms and crime scene investigators already there; they were searching through the flotsam and jetsam that marked the high tide line and in the scrub where the sandy beach merged with the tree line. As the pair got closer they could see the body was still in situ. The figure was lying face up, but judging by the amount of mud stuck to his face and clothing, it was clear the body had been found lying face down. There was a clear tidemark around the mottled face that indicated the level of water in the muddy puddle. Chambers noticed the large number of hoof prints in the dried mud around the body.

'Hey Lucy, what are these? They look like cow prints?'

'Not exactly.' She walked further onto the beach, taking a look around.

'Come over here,' she called to Chambers. 'Look,' she pointed up the beach past the restaurant.

Chambers couldn't believe his eyes. A couple of hundred metres away, sitting in the shade of a mangrove tree on the edge of the beach, was an enormous water buffalo. Further off in the distance he could make out several more. Apart from that, the beach was deserted. It was fairly secluded. He could make out a few well-worn paths leaving the beach at intervals along the tree line, but apart from the restaurant, another block and the lifeguards' towers there were surprisingly no beachfront buildings. He would have asked Li why, but he had more pressing issues.

'Are … are we safe here? That thing is huge! Look at its horns.' He was genuinely scared.

When Chambers was younger he'd got a huge fright from a cow when he was on holiday with his family and another family in Devon in southern England. He'd only been about seven or eight, and had been messing about with some friends in what they thought was an empty field when a cow had appeared from nowhere and run towards them. At the time he thought it was a bull and they'd run for their lives. When they climbed the gate, they'd looked back to see the animal had stopped 20 metres away. He was crying. It didn't help that his friends were laughing. The situation was made worse when they pointed to the cow's udders, proving it wasn't a bull. He'd cried in front of his friends, which was embarrassing enough, but even the realisation it was a cow and not a bull hadn't made him feel any better. The beast was huge, it smelled disgusting and the way its nostrils flared unnerved him. He didn't know what it was about the cow, but he knew it terrified him. The thing was he'd never conquered his fear of them. He didn't need to in one sense. It was hardly likely he'd bump into a herd of Friesian cows on Shepherd's Bush Green. But his fears had returned with a vengeance. Sure the beast was lying down. But if it decided to get up, Chambers was sure he would be the first one heading back up the road.

'What the hell is it doing here? Has it escaped from somewhere?' His eyes were wide with fear. Now he could smell it as well, or at least he was convinced he could.

Li was looking at him with a strange expression. She was weighing up whether he was faking this reaction or was genuinely scared. When she decided it was the latter she started laughing.

'John calm down. It hasn't escaped from anywhere. They're feral. They've been on Lantau Island for centuries. The local farmers used them to plough the nearby paddy fields. Some of them got turned loose when the farmers decided to give up growing rice a few decades back. There's a herd of them that roams around the island. They mainly stay around here. That flat marshy area,' she motioned to where they had just come from, 'that's pretty much where they live.'

'You are shitting me!' he said, walking back to stand a little behind her. 'A herd of these? Then where are the rest?' He was looking around anxiously as he said it.

'Stop it John, you're making me laugh. Sometimes they head down to one of the beaches for a swim late in the day. So I guess there must be a quite a few more of them nearby.'

'I'm glad one of us is finding this amusing. Can we get back to the body and then get the hell away from that thing?' He was pointing down the beach towards the animal that was closest to him.

As he did so, he saw the buffalo was idly looking in his direction. This didn't make him feel at all comfortable. He guessed the horns must be a metre from tip to tip. He tried to stop his mind from visualising the kind of damage they could do. The buffalo was a dull grey colour, the horns, almost white, forming a nearly perfect crescent. It looked very broad across the body. It must have weighed a least a tonne. He walked quickly back towards the victim, checking over his shoulder to make sure he wasn't being followed. There were a lot of hoof prints around the corpse. Chambers could see no obvious signs of injury. He called Li over. He took his small Canon Ixus from his pocket and snapped off a few shots of the body and the surrounding marks. As Li came up, he stopped taking photographs.

'Lucy, can you ask one of these policemen about the details?'

She nodded and moved towards a group of three uniformed officers. After several minutes she returned to Chambers.

'The body was discovered at approximately 7am by a local out walking his dog on the beach. The forensic officer thinks he died sometime yesterday. He needs some more time to give us an exact time of death. My guess is it would have to be fairly late in the day as although this is a relatively quiet beach during the week, you'd imagine if the body had been here any longer, surely someone would have discovered it earlier. It's not that far from the restaurant, I'll contact the owner and see if they were here yesterday.'

152

'Good point, so we are almost certain he died yesterday. That fits with my theory.'

'But John, at this stage there's no evidence he was murdered.'

'True.' He paused. 'Do you think he could have been killed by the buffalo? I mean there are plenty of hoof prints next to the body.' Chambers thought it possible the victim could have been scared to death if a herd of these beasts came charging down the path. He knew he would. His heart was still racing.

'Personally I doubt it. They might look scary, but they're actually very gentle. The only time you might see them get irritated is if you get too close to a calf, the mothers get very protective. I don't recall hearing of any incidents since they were set loose 30-odd years ago.'

'So it is possible, he could have come down here, met a herd of them, somehow got too close to a calf and the mother charged causing him to have a heart attack,' Chambers pondered.

'Maybe, but we'd just be speculating at the moment, let's wait for the medical reports. On first look there are no obvious signs, but then he is caked head to toe in mud.'

'Do they know who he was?'

'Yes his ID says he was Bert Yung. When they ran a check it seems he's a retired soldier. He's been the odd job man at the community centre we walked past earlier for the last 10 years. He lived alone in Tung Chung, which is a town on the other side of the island. That was his car we passed when we came down here.'

'The red Volvo? I guess you'd think he'd be used to the buffalo especially if they come down this way a lot. Let's take a look back up at the community centre and the car and then get the hell out of here.' He walked off quickly in the direction of the community centre.

When he arrived, he took a look around the building, stepping along the side of the enormous pile of masonry. Before he moved towards the Volvo he took some photographs, a couple of the car and several of the community centre. He walked towards the car and tried the door, it was locked. He put his hands on the window and peered in. Nothing out of the ordinary. He made his way back up the lane to where the uniformed police were keeping the crowd in check. Again he surveyed the village. Was it possible one of the residents could have seen something from the higher floors? The problem was, the buildings were only three-storeys high and the lane and surrounding area was quite heavily wooded. There were some buildings set further back and higher up but most of their views would be obstructed by the ones packed tightly in front. A couple of minutes later Li had caught him up. He asked her to get the officers to ask if anything had been seen. From there they walked past the crowd and waited for a cab. Chambers was anxious to put as great a distance between himself and the buffalo as quickly as possible.

When they were back in Mui Wo fifteen minutes later, Chambers finally felt able to relax. He no longer felt he would be gored to death by one of the feral buffaloes. He was just left with a sense of embarrassment. He tried not to dwell on it; instead he turned his thoughts to the body on the beach. Li was right, he knew that. They would just be speculating at this stage until the official reports came in. But here was a man working alone, who died on a new moon. The questions circling in his mind were: did the victim die by natural causes due to the scare induced by the buffalo? Did he get knocked down and trampled to death? Or was this something staged to look like an accident? What was the victim's connection to the Triads of Kowloon? The victim lived on Lantau Island and had worked in close proximity to the buffalo for years. It was unlikely, although not impossible, for him to have been killed by them. Despite what Chambers felt about the buffalo, he had to be rational. He hadn't noticed any of the other people at the scene even give the animal a second look. There were plenty of hoof prints at the scene, but then if they were known to swim and wander the beach then of course there would be prints.

Li had been to check the ferry schedule. They had 20 minutes to wait. She suggested they get a coffee and took him to a small café around the corner from a bar located on the waterfront. They sat down at a small circular table. Chambers couldn't help unfavourably comparing Mui Wo to Discovery Bay, the only other place he'd been on Lantau Island. There was a grey, almost austere, feel to Mui Wo. The drab and dreary buildings had that same run down appearance that at times threatened to overwhelm him with their bleakness on his excursions around Hong Kong Island. The waterfront had a series of small cranes set up for unloading boats onto an abrupt, ugly grey concrete concourse. But it was the sheer abundance of grey. The place was monotonous, filled with anonymous low-rise buildings. The sky perfectly matched the colour of the buildings and he felt like he was looking out at an old black and white photograph. The overall sensation was making him feel depressed.

Li snapped him out of his contemplations. 'What do you want to drink?' she asked.

'Oh, anything. I don't mind.'

'Well, I'll have a skinny latte, now get a move on,' she cajoled him in a joking tone.

'Sure,' he mumbled before getting up to go inside.

When he came back to the table she said, 'I've been thinking. As to whether or not this was a murder or an accidental death, it might not actually matter.'

'How do you mean?' he asked, sitting down.

'Well, do you think he was murdered?'

'Hard to say. Like you said earlier, we'd just be guessing at this stage.'

'Exactly my point. Think about it. If it's not obvious to us, then surely it's possible that if – and I know at this stage it's a big if – there is someone out there murdering people on new moons, they could easily have made their other murders look like accidents.'

He thought about this for a moment. 'Right, so what you're saying is, is that there could have been people killed on other new moons, but because they looked like accidents, they were never listed as murders.'

'Exactly my point.'

'When we searched before, we only went back to when? The beginning of July, right?'

The barista brought their coffees out to the table, interrupting Chambers' flow. 'So we need to go back a bit further in our search. Let's go back to say, May? That's another few months. We might need to widen the scope as well, let's look at all deaths that were reported either on a new moon or a few days after.'

'You're right, if people think they're accidents or the body wasn't found immediately, then the time of death might not have been recorded accurately. I'll call the office and get a search started on it right away.'

She stood up and took out her mobile phone. Taking her coffee she walked around to the waterfront to wait for the ferry back to Central while she made the call. Chambers followed and stood at the water's edge a little apart from her. After she finished the call she came and stood next to him. They both stared out to sea, lost in their own thoughts. Li was excited and apprehensive about where this investigation might take them. Chambers was thinking of a way to explain to Asbury that he wasn't coming back to London. Not quite yet anyway.

~~~

Chapter 18 – Buffalo Soldier

Wed. 28th September – Thursday 27th October 2011

Dear Diary,

Of course I heard about the last one before it made the newspapers. I stayed in my apartment until about 6pm that day. I showered, laundered my clothes and had something to eat. By the time it was beginning to get a bit dark I was itching to see what was happening. I am normally a lot more patient, but then this one was a bit different, it was right on my own doorstep so to speak. I decided to venture out and see what was going on. When I came out of the lift into the lobby there were several policemen waiting to take the lift. I kept my head lowered, not wanting to make eye contact. There was no one else about, but somebody had obviously found something. I went around the corner to the 7-Eleven and bought myself some milk and a Mars Bar. On my way back in I saw a couple of women talking. I milled around for a bit taking my time collecting another copy of the paper I read earlier and pretending to read it.

After a minute or so, the front doors opened and a couple of paramedics came in with a gurney. They headed over to the lift. After they'd entered I approached the women and asked if there had been an accident. One told me that they had heard from another resident that a man had tried to commit suicide in the bath and that he'd left the taps running. The water had flowed into the apartment below, the owner of which had called security. The guard couldn't get in to the flat so had called the police who had come and broken down the door and discovered a body in the bath. The women had it on good authority the man was covered in blood in the bath, so must have slit his wrists. Well these two were obviously wide of the mark, but the police would know exactly what happened. At least I knew for certain that the discovery had been made. I just needed to wait for the next day's paper to get all the gory details, as if I didn't already know them.

ΞΞΞ

Another day, another cover story. This was slap bang in the middle of the page. I'm officially the big news story of the day! The headline read, 'Triad Killing in Kowloon'. The gist of the story was that my poor unfortunate neighbour, Eric, was the victim of a retaliatory strike by the Sun Yee On, a rival Triad gang in the area. Police said they had found evidence at the scene that clearly linked the murder to gang activity. Interestingly they didn't say he was a police informant. They put the blame squarely on the other gang. Unless, of course, it was a smokescreen, put up to make the real murderer think he was in the clear. The nagging sensation that had been troubling me had been growing over the past few months. I was sure they had to know more than they were letting on. I mean even the dumbest policeman would work out the analogy of the rat and the fact the victim was a well-known snitch. And everyone knows snitches get stitches, eventually. So why were they deliberately being obtuse? I had no idea what clues they had, whether they had any DNA or whatever, whether my name was appearing on a list somewhere. I needed to find out what they knew. But how? Maybe a visit to the police station. No, that would be downright foolhardy.

ΞΞΞ

For my next victim I needed to go back out to Lantau Island.

Again, the who wasn't important but the location was critical. I decided to take a different route to the island; instead of the boat, I took the MTR to Tung Chung. From the station I caught a bus round to Mui Wo. The journey time was marginally longer, but the bus circumnavigates the island, so I got a chance to look and see what I needed to see. I got off at the same dismal, grey bus station where it had all begun eight months ago. I headed to the China Bear bar and sat down at one of the green plastic tables outside. Now that I had seen all I wanted from the bus, I just needed to make some final adjustments to my plan. I ordered a lime soda and a bowl of chilli. I wasn't sure how long this would take and I was keen to be prepared for a long wait if that was what was required. I stayed there for the best part of an hour. When I left at around 3pm, the bar and the surrounding town were relatively quiet. I didn't mind being seen this time, as I wouldn't be engaging in any nefarious acts here in Mui Wo. Where I would be was several miles away. I walked back to the bus stop and joined the queue to take the same 3M bus that would take me back towards Tung Chung. While I was admiring the scenery I put on my baseball cap and the new sunglasses I had recently bought. I had also let my hair grow out and hadn't shaved for a few weeks, just to change it up a bit.

I didn't ride the bus all the way back to Tung Chung, this time I got off after about ten minutes in the small village of Pui O. I quickly went down Chi Wa Man Road past a lot of dumped and rusting shipping containers and on towards the artificial sports field. I was already on the outskirts of the village and the trees lining the narrow road meant I'd be out of view of anyone in the village who happened to be looking out in my direction. There were a couple of little shops but this was a quiet street that ran down to the beach about one hundred metres past the empty plastic football pitch. I carried on and a huge expanse opened up on my left, it must have been an old paddy field as it was partially underwater. As I came towards the beach there was a solitary restaurant with a small camping ground attached. It was completely empty as it usually was midweek: The place was a bit busier on weekends with the some expats and teenage camping groups. It would be busy later but for now there wasn't a soul on the beach or in the two lifeguard towers.

I began walking back from the beach toward to the football pitch. On the way I noticed quite a lot of distinctive prints in the dried mud in an area between the beach and where the road began. Nearby to the right, among some scrubland, was a long but shallow puddle. Now I think about it, I'm not sure if it was filled with rainwater or it was seawater trapped by the receding tide. A little further back there was a small community centre. I decided to have a look around the back of the building as I could hear the sound of metal clanging on metal. Here I came across a man, probably in his 60s, tinkering under the bonnet of an old red Volvo Estate. I stopped and watched him for a minute or so. He had his back to me and was making a bit of a racket banging away at some part of the engine with what looked like a monkey wrench. There didn't seem to be anyone around, so I walked back around the building from the same direction I had come from minutes before. I looked in the window of the community centre. The lights were on, but it didn't appear there was anyone at home.

I checked my watch, it was after four now. I took my backpack off and crouched down, easing the zip open as I slid the bag gently onto the ground. I took out my black gloves and left the bag there. I scanned the area as I put on my gloves. There was an enormous pile of bricks and masonry to my left. That would do perfectly. I picked up a full brick and a broken piece, a bit bigger than a half. I took one last look around and in the window. Still there was no sign of anyone. I made my way quietly towards the old man. I was only a metre or so behind him when he lifted the wrench for the last time. As he brought it down on the engine block, I timed it to perfection to smash the half brick into the back of his skull. He slumped forward smacking his head on the engine. I leaned forward and brought both the bricks down onto the back of his head. I dropped the bricks and grabbed him round the throat. I was on top of him with all my weight. I could feel his legs kicking out between mine, he was pivoting on his waist on the edge of the car, but he could get no purchase. I was pressing him into the hard metal of the engine. The space was cramped by the angle of the bonnet. But he had nowhere to go, he was trapped and I was squeezing the life right out of him. I don't know how long I held him there but I felt the energy suddenly leave him.

I pulled him out from the engine and hoisted him over my shoulder. He only weighed 60kg or so. Heavy enough I suppose but I knew I didn't have to take him far. The walk was 100 metres or so back past the muddy fields. As I came back to the restaurant I skirted to the right to where I'd seen the large puddle earlier. I carefully stood him up leaning against me just in case there was anyone looking out from the restaurant. My mind was playing tricks as the building was in complete darkness. The man didn't appear to be breathing. I was careful to only stand on the hard, sun-dried mud as I carefully let him slump down so he ended up with his face in the puddle and his feet on the dried mud. I pushed his body in a few directions until I was happy with the effect. His face was partially submerged in the water. His body twisted like he had been hit by something hard and fallen awkwardly, one hand bent up his back and his leg crooked at an angle.

When I was happy with the position I took a long look at the scene. There was no movement from the man, no bubbles forming in the puddle that was beginning to smooth out after all the commotion. I looked at the prints in the mud, I hadn't added any new ones to hard crusted areas and the body was covering the scuffmarks I'd caused in the softer areas. I walked out onto the beach and had a look around; there was no one to be seen. There were no items of mine left at the scene this time. I made my way back to the car; collecting the two brick parts and throwing them back onto the huge pile I'd originally got them from. I peered into the window of the community centre and again there were no signs of life.

I returned to the car and picked up the monkey wrench from the engine sill. I hit on the engine for a few minutes with it. Why? I don't know, I just had a sense that someone might have noticed the lack of noise and come to investigate. Also while I was doing it I looked over the engine to make sure there were no signs of a struggle. After a few minutes I stopped banging and unclipped the pole from its stand and eased the bonnet down. I looked around for a minute before kicking the monkey wrench under the car. I checked the doors but they were locked and I couldn't see the keys in the ignition. There wasn't much more for me to do.

I collected my rucksack and made for the beach. Taking a left I walked along the sand for about 500 metres before following one of the paths on my left. As I walked up the path that led to an asphalt road I remembered to remove my gloves, putting them back in my bag. The lane I was on joined South Lantau Road. From here I could catch a bus back to Tung Chung and then home. To be on the safe side, I decided to walk a couple of kilometres along it until I came to a series of houses just before Cheung Sha beach. Here I waited at the bus stop for about 20 minutes. When the bus came I made sure I paid by cash and avoided making eye contact with the driver or any of the 10 or so passengers that were on the bus. I knew I had taken a bit of a chance hanging around the vicinity of the murder scene, and especially walking the main road. But I was hoping it was an educated guess, from my experience not many people went down that way.

☰☰☰

Chapter 19

Friday 11th November 2011

Chambers woke with a start. He was soaked with his own sweat and shivering. His thoughts were jumbled, his breathing short and shallow. He had been chased by a herd of water buffalo along a deserted beach at sunset. More buffalo were emerging from the sea and coming towards him. He could see past them to a state-of-the-art yacht, on which were Lucy Li and Ian Greening drinking wine while looking over in his direction and laughing. He had lost his footing and fallen on the soft sand. As he rolled over he saw the horns of the charging buffalo were about to penetrate his chest. That's when he woke, nearly leaping out of bed with fright. The digital clock showed 3.02am. He tried to remember the dream in its entirety but the images were dissolving like sand running through his fingers. What did it mean, Li and Greening on the boat? Chambers was confused and perturbed by it. He decided to have a shower and clear his head. It was two weeks on from his visit to 'Buffalo' Beach. The Crime Scene Team and forensic reports had come back in. It was official, the victim, Bert Yung, had been murdered.

But Chambers hadn't known this vital piece of information at the time he was due back at his desk in London. He had taken a gamble and called Asbury from Hong Kong at 9am GMT; intent on doing and saying whatever he needed to in order to prolong his stay. The seven-hour time difference, he had hoped, would have allowed time for the reports of what really happened to Kwok to have filtered through to him. Unfortunately, when he made the call at 4pm Hong Kong time there was still no news, so he decided to bluff it. He let Asbury know that they had a third murder by the same suspect. Also, since these murders had begun only after the man he was following had returned to Hong Kong, there was strong evidence linking the two cases together. Chambers assured Asbury that the evidence he was alluding to would be forwarded in the form of a report by the end of the day, London time. He had managed to dominate the conversation, leaving his superior with little option but to reprimand him for not returning and to assure Chambers that if the report wasn't with him by the end of the day he had better start thinking about another career.

He knew it would be a long night; he called in the services of Li to chase her friend Jenny Greening in the forensics team. At 10pm that night they finally got word that the report from the post mortem clearly showed signs of asphyxiation. The initial reports from the scene had shown some blunt force trauma to the victim's head, but whether that was from a one-tonne buffalo or something else couldn't be clearly ascertained at this stage. The post mortem report, along with evidence of murder, had shown there was no muddy water in the lungs, meaning he was dead before being placed face down in the puddle. There was also brick dust in the victim's mud-splattered hair. Chambers thought back to the huge pile of masonry he'd seen near the car. In his mind he had a fair idea of what had happened. He could picture the old man working on the engine. The monkey wrench found under the car had come back with a fingerprint match only to that of the victim. The man had been surprised, hit over the head and strangled. The body then dumped on the nearby beach that happened to be a popular hangout with the local feral buffalo population.

Was he murdered because of who he was? He had a military background that needed further investigation. Was he murdered because of someone or something he knew? Did he have any links to the K19? Or was he murdered for another reason? Was it because he was in the wrong place at the wrong time, or because he was in exactly the right place? But why move him to the puddle and make it look like an accident? The murderer must surely know it would only be a matter of days before the reports showed the victim hadn't had a heart attack or drowned. But then, Chambers thought, if he and Li hadn't been on the scene and been pushing hard to get evidence that it was murder, could it have slipped through simply as an accident? It was certainly a possibility. An old man dies on a deserted beach that was sometimes home to a herd of wild buffalo. It could easily have been reported as an accidental death. The body and incriminating evidence buried or burned within a few days.

Chambers busied himself with the report until nearly midnight; he highlighted the links between the 'Black Dragon' and the first two victims as members of the K19. He had no qualms embellishing the story of Kwok as being a former member and known muscle of the Triad outfit. He had no idea if or how he was really linked but he knew he was on to something. He needed time and he was quite sure Asbury wasn't going to check the details. As long as he had Chambers' name on the report it would exonerate Asbury if and when the shit hit the fan. He put the final touches to the report, indicating he'd need to be here at least until the time of the next expected hit. He hadn't told his senior about the new moon theory, he was sure that would see him on the next plane home. He had just outlined that the murders were taking place on what seemed to be a monthly basis and that it would be best if he was here until December and ideally until the New Year. He made it clear that this was the worst-case scenario; of course he would have apprehended him long before that. Chambers saved the MS Word file and attached it to the email he had drafted to

Asbury. He pressed send and hoped when he returned to the office in the morning all would be well.

The following morning he was relieved to see a stay of execution from his boss. Asbury was giving him an extension until Christmas to arrest the suspect or return. There were no alternatives this time. Chambers felt an enormous sense of relief. Whatever was occurring in Hong Kong right now, he had a sense he was very close to it. He just didn't know what 'it' was.

Li had been busy searching back through the database flagging any bizarre, untimely murders or any that looked out of place. A strange brief, she reflected, as when could murder ever be considered as straightforward, expected or normal? The previous search they had carried out went back to early August. This time she widened the search to the beginning of May. She was intrigued by the findings. There had been four murders in that time, but when she went through the reports of other deaths in and around the key dates of the new moons, there were more interesting findings. The four murders had included another case of a husband murdering his wife and a fatal stabbing outside a bar in TST that was suspected to be gang-related, but the date was 10 days from the closest new moon. She marked the file anyway as it had possible Triad connections. The one that caught her eye was the suspected murder in Tin Hau on the new moon in early June. She pulled the file up on screen and printed out the relevant information. At the time, the death had been reported in the newspapers as a possible accident. The investigation team was convinced it was a murder, but had no leads to go on. The other murder was the result of a neighbourly dispute that again had taken place a week away from the July new moon.

It was when Li began the painstaking investigation of all reported deaths that she turned up some surprising results. There were none for the period surrounding the new moon in early July. Nothing. She considered how Chambers would take this news. This was a clear indication to her that his new moon theory was significantly flawed.

For the new moon date in late July there was an interesting death that she certainly felt compelled to investigate further. This was the unfortunate death of a lady in Tai Hang. According to the report, she'd apparently tripped over her pet dog and fallen down the stairs to her death. The date matched exactly the second new moon of that month. She checked her calendar. There were 13 new moons during the year. One every month except for July that had two. She took a moment to think about it. The victim in this case was Mrs Teo, a 55-year-old newspaper seller; she'd been running a small street stall in Tin Hau for nearly 20 years. This was hardly K19 material. But for deaths occurring on or near the new moons in July it was the only match. Although Li felt the victim's links to the murders in Kowloon were tenuous at best, she had to admit there was more than an element of suspicion in the cause of death. She printed out the file.

She had covered the three dates with mixed success. She had one potential murder that was reported as an accident, one suspicious death and the other, a complete blank. She began searching around early May. Again there was nothing. She widened the search to several days after but to no avail. She called Chambers to arrange a meeting back at the office in the afternoon.

At 2pm Chambers came back to his desk. Li was already waiting for him.

'Good news Lucy.'

'I'm glad you're in a good mood.' She smiled at him.

'Yes I am. Is there any reason I shouldn't be? Asbury has extended me here for six more weeks and I'm sure we're onto something.'

'You asked me to compile a report going back to early May for murders or suspicious deaths on or around the new moons. I don't think you're going to like the news.'

'Hit me with what you've got.'

'OK, I went back three months but there were actually four new

moons in that period. May and June had one each, but July has two.'
She hesitated. 'I'll give you the so-called good news first. We have a
death that looks very much like a murder in June.'

'When you say looks like a murder,' Chambers interrupted, 'do you
mean like our buffalo beach killing?'

'More so. The victim choked to death on a chicken's foot, but at
the time the investigators noted down several strange elements at the
scene. But, and I think this is good for us, it was reported in the press
as an accident.'

'What benefit is that to us?'

'I took the liberty of calling Pang after the body was discovered on
the beach and asking him to inform the press team that this was death
by misadventure. I just think it's better for all of us to keep this thing
out of the media for two reasons.'

'And they are?' Chambers was pleased with her taking the initiative.

'Firstly, whoever's committing these crimes will think they're
getting away with it, maybe that will cause them to get a little
careless. And secondly, we don't want the press crawling all over this.
You might be used to a media circus back in London, but Hong Kong
is starved of front-page news. If – and I know it's a damn big if – this
is the work of the same person, then this is going to be the biggest
murder hunt in Hong Kong's history.'

Chambers thought about what she was saying. If his theory was true
and the murder she was talking about was in fact one of theirs, then
potentially they would have five or possibly six murders already, let
alone what they might yet discover.

'That's good, so at this stage only two of these have been reported
as murders in the media, and completely unrelated.'

'Yes, one a mugging with fatal consequences, the other a gang-
related murder. No logical link. That should keep the heat off us for a
while.'

'So, you said there were some suspicious findings at the scene.'

'Yes, in the report from the DI who investigated the scene, he states that there were no signs of a forced entry. The victim was found on the floor, as if his chair had tilted over backwards, with a chicken's foot stuck in his throat.'

'Odd I agree,' said Chambers, 'but surely not impossible.'

'There was also a plate of chickens' feet on the table, but no other dishes. No chopsticks, no drinks. Again a little strange, but maybe that's what he liked. However, they also found him sitting upright in the chair, but at a 90 degree angle. Surely if you were choking to death, you would get up, grab a drink, and move around? Do something. Not just sit in your chair and keel over backwards dead. He also had an almighty bruise on the back of his head. It was noted in the report that it looked out of place for simply falling back and banging his head on the floor.'

'So how come it wasn't reported as a murder or nothing came of the investigation?'

'The file is still open. He was a young, reasonably successful businessman. His business partner has a solid alibi; he was out of the country at the time. The victim liked to be seen as a ladies' man, but the report says his colleagues implied he liked to frequent gay clubs. He thought no one knew, but apparently the office gossip was rife with rumours about his sexuality. Saying that, it hasn't provided any leads.'

'What about other friends and family?'

'His parents just wanted the whole thing finished so they could move on. From reading the report, I think they knew about his secret life and maybe just wanted him to be remembered as a young and successful businessman, rather than the press or police digging too deep into his personal life. As I said, the case is still open but there were no fingerprints at the scene. No sign of a break-in and no sign of a struggle except the head injury. The building has a part-time security guard but no CCTV. There's access into the building through the main doors, which are often left wedged open, plus there's access to the lift from the underground car park.'

'If there is a killer, he could easily have followed the victim and trapped him in the lift, that way he could have got into the apartment without having to break in. What happened to the body?'

'He was cremated several days after he was found.' She continued reading from the report. 'The evidence that's been collected includes his possessions at the time and his clothing. You think it's worth a look?'

'Definitely, get his clothes sent to Jenny, see if there's anything she can find. The investigator was right; you surely wouldn't just keel over and die. He was surely tied on or something.'

Chambers was writing on a pad. 'So we've got a definite possibility for the new moon in October and working back: September, yes; August, yes; two in July, both blank at this stage; June, yes; and May, nothing.' He stopped writing and looked at her. 'That's four out of a possible seven. So what's the bad news about the other three?'

'I've searched comprehensively from 3rd May until the 8th and I can't find anything definite. A couple of deaths in hospitals of terminally ill patients but no strange, ill-timed or more importantly, accidental deaths.'

'Hmm, but that doesn't mean there wasn't one for sure though does it?'

'No, that's right,' she agreed. 'And it could mean the murders began after this. Hang on? Going back this far is when the man you're supposedly looking for wasn't even in Hong Kong?'

'I know Lucy. I think you and I have stumbled onto something bigger, and, the more I think about it, very unlikely to be linked to any Triad operation.'

'It's interesting you should say that. Because the only thing that turned up for either of the July dates, looks to have no Triad links at all.'

'Go on.'

'The same day as the second new moon, on 31st July, a Mrs Teo fell down stairs outside her apartment to her death.'

'What was the cause of death?'

'The coroner's report states death by misadventure. She died of a broken neck.'

'What did the investigation turn up?'

'Nothing, they never bothered. The report said that she was found by a deliveryman who saw her dog at the top of the stairs and her lying in a crumpled heap at the bottom with the dog's lead tangled around her feet. He called police and they assumed she had either had a heart attack and fallen down the stairs or more likely tripped and fallen. There was no thorough investigation.'

'Shit.' He scribbled something on his pad. 'Now we have a murder for every month going back to June. But nothing so far for May.' He looked up at Li.

'I know exactly what you're going to say.'

'What's that?'

'Widen the search, explore everything in May. And go back to the start of the year. Search all the new moons in 2011.'

'It's like you read my mind,' he nodded appreciatively towards her.

~~~

Chapter 20 – A Tiger in the Woods

Friday 28th October – Friday 25th November 2011

Dear diary,

I was surprised that on the following day the papers reported nothing. That made me a bit anxious. The logical reason was because the body hadn't been discovered. But it's a funny thing, when you're waiting for a report on your latest murder, logic tends to go out of the window. The news was delivered the day after. Page 4 of the *South China Morning Post* had a few paragraphs. It's not much for a life is it?

I think a few months ago I would have been quite pissed off at the realisation they had misinterpreted what had happened. I mean, nobody likes their hard work to go unnoticed, do they? The thing is, I'm getting very close to my goal and I think it's better this way. I'm seventy five percent of the way through my project now. Only a couple of little jobs to do before the big one, the finale. After that I can choose whether I begin to let people in on my little secret or not. Only time will tell.

The good news for me is, if the body wasn't discovered until the next day, it's hardly likely anyone will remember whether they saw me anywhere near the scene. Since then I've lost the beard and burnt the baseball cap. I've purchased one of those beanies instead. One drawback is that it doesn't have a visor, but the advantage is I can pull it down and cover my hair. Once you add a pair of cheap wraparound shades you are almost anonymous. I think I've overused the baseball cap. This next job will give me an opportunity to try out a different look; hopefully it won't have a negative impact on my success rate.

ΞΞΞ

The weather in November is nice and cool. The cloying humidity has finally disappeared and Hong Kong becomes so much more enjoyable to live in. This brings several problems for my plan, as the cooler weather means more people venturing out from the safety of their neat little air-conditioned homes.

Sometimes I have it all mapped out. Other times, like this one, I have to just run with an idea and see where it takes me. So far, maybe I've been a bit lucky as they have all come together nicely. Sure, I've made some mistakes along the way, but then who's perfect? I guess it's like anything in life, you get better the more you practise it, you learn from your mistakes and become more clinical, more experienced. I think my dedication has helped. I spend the weeks between jobs thinking things through, how I could have performed more efficiently, analysing my performance, looking for ways to improve. I guess the old adage of 'practice makes perfect' is true. Well let's hope so.

ΞΞΞ

Today went as well as I could have expected it to go. I woke up this morning and when I looked out of the window and saw what a beautifully clear day it was, I had already made up my mind. I packed my small rucksack with a roll of transparent plastic film you use to wrap food with, a hammer, some duct tape, a couple of pots of menthol ointment, sunscreen, a pair of gloves, camera, a bottle of water and my beanie. I put a spare white T-shirt and a pair of black cargo pants in my bag as well. I didn't need to leave my apartment until mid-afternoon. So I just took my time visualising what I planned to do later. I wanted to make sure I had it all clear in my mind.

I took the MTR to Shau Kei Wan Station on Hong Kong Island. From there I boarded the number nine bus at the nearby bus depot. I rang the bell when the bus was approaching Cape Collinson Road. I waited on the side of the road after the bus departed. It had been fairly quiet on the bus and I didn't want the driver to recall seeing which way I set off, just in case. When the bus had travelled out of sight, I crossed the road to join the hiking path marked by the Shek O Country Park sign. I was expecting to see quite a few hikers even though I was lucky enough to be there on a weekday. I had put on my sunglasses and hat before getting off the bus so I was quite confident no one would be able to point out exactly what I looked like.

The hiking path goes straight up the mountainside for quite a while; so most hikers have little energy to expend on deep and meaningful conversation with passers-by. They are more focused on where their next step is rather than exchanging anything but the briefest of pleasantries, which suited me just fine. It was quite tiring even though I had only joined the last leg. I could have just got the bus all the way to Shek O, but coming via the 'Dragon's Back' route is much more rewarding. When I reached the crest the view down the other side really was amazing. You can see down the slope to Shek O golf course which hugged the coastline, and the sprawling village of Shek O off to the right that joins the two beaches together. There is also a slightly raised peninsula further out and a pyramid-shaped island just off the coast. The sparkling blue South China Sea stretched as far as the eye could see. There are other scattered islands further out – it's truly a remarkable view. I took my camera out and snapped off a few shots thinking how blessed I was to be out on such a magnificent day doing something I thoroughly enjoyed. I wondered how many other people got such satisfaction in their work.

Often when I'd been up here, the sky was either a cloudy grey or more commonly hazy with pollution. I headed on down the path. From this aerial position I could pick out a good place to wait.

There were quite a lot of trees on the golf course, lining various fairways, but across the road a kilometre or so back from the village was a much bigger expanse of wooded area. That would do nicely. I made my way down to the bottom of the trail and found myself on the outskirts of the village. The hike had taken me just over two hours. It was half past five and the long shadows indicated it would be getting dark soon. I had timed it to perfection.

I took the road that headed out of the village and back along the side of the golf course; all the while I was checking the fairways. There were a few fourballs out, but it wasn't too busy and they were much more interested in their round than in who was passing by on the main road. I kept an eye out along the high metal mesh fence for any holes or unlocked gates. Half way along there was a quieter area with no houses anywhere near on my side and a row of trees obscuring a hole in the fence surrounding the golf course on the opposite side. This was what I wanted. I waited until the road was clear of traffic before I slipped into the wood behind me and hid myself about 10 metres back from the road. I could see a fair part of the way up the road in both directions, but unless someone was looking directly in at me, then they wouldn't know I was there. I took out the roll of clear plastic film, the hammer and the ointment. I pulled out a section of the cling roll and scooped out the balm onto the thin plastic membrane, before putting them in one pile behind a tree. I placed the spare T-shirt and shorts in another pile, to which I added my hat and sunglasses and the rucksack. It was too gloomy in the wood and I didn't need to disguise myself at that point. I put on my gloves and sat down to wait for my prey.

Maybe I was there for about an hour. A fair amount of buses, cars and bikes went past. As it was a Friday, and after 6pm, there were a lot of commuters and people heading to the beach for the weekend. Several people walked past. Mainly in couples or groups, the only singles went past at the same time as some cars. I just had to be patient; the traffic would eventually ease off. The course would be empty and the golfers long gone by now. The only lights coming from that direction were from the golf clubhouse that was several hundred metres from where I was waiting. Tall trees surrounded the building and by my reckoning there was no clear view out on to this stretch of road from there. In fact, due to the road bending away to the left as it approached Shek O village, it would only be the traffic on the road that would be able to see anything. The few streetlights meant it was easy to tell if a car was approaching. The only problem I faced was if a cyclist was coming along without any lights. I'd never be able to tell. I would just have to take a calculated risk.

That's when it dawned on me. I should actually target a cyclist. Another ten minutes passed before I made out the faint light of a bike headlamp weaving its way towards me. I stepped to the edge of the wood, still hidden from view. A last check to make sure there was no traffic. When the cyclist was about 10 metres away heading in the direction of the village, I stepped down from the wall that separated the wood from the pavement.

'Hello,' I called out, 'please stop.' I waved my arms slowly to indicate to the cyclist to slow down. As the rider braked, the lamp on the front of the bike was directed slightly away, allowing me to see the cyclist was an older woman in her 60s. She looked European although it was hard to say in the gloom.

'Do you speak English? Can you help me?' I needed to act fairly quickly to get her off the road.

'Yes, what's happened?' she said with a fairly strong northern European accent that I couldn't immediately place.

'Oh I was here earlier in the day looking for some wild flowers for my wife, and when I went back to my car I realised I must have dropped my keys somewhere in here. The trouble is it's very dark now. I was hoping you would lend me your bike light.'

'Of course, unfortunately it's quite an old bike and I've never removed the lamp before.'

'I can lift the whole thing up; the wall here is only low.'

'OK,' she said as she dismounted.

I moved towards her. She nodded to me as I picked up the bike. It was one of those upright ones with a wicker basket on the front. It must have been made from steel as the thing weighed a tonne. I placed the bike on its side a few metres into the wood then turned and beckoned to her.

'Can you direct the light for me while I look?'

'Yes, sure thing.' She moved towards the wall.

I stepped back down to help lift her up over the low wall. I could smell her perfume; it was some kind of rose water. I could see her better now, she was tall and slim, and a bit older perhaps than I first thought, her hair pulled back into a grey bun. I returned to the bike and wheeled it a few more metres into the darkness. The light was weak but enough to highlight about ten metres or so in front. I positioned the bike so the light shone further into the wood. Its position was beyond my two piles of clothing and equipment. She followed me into the wood.

'That's great, if you can just hold it here while I take a look.' I sifted through the undergrowth for about 30 seconds.

'It's no good.' I said. 'Hang on, I've had an idea; maybe if I use my camera flash; it might pick up on anything that's reflective. What do you think?'

'It might work,' she said, 'it's got to be worth a try, otherwise how will you get home? What an awful nuisance for you.'

'Hang on, my camera's in my rucksack. It's just behind you. I won't be a minute.' I smiled at her as I walked past. I moved to the first pile, put the shaft of the hammer in my pocket and picked up the partially unraveled roll of plastic. I carried on to the second pile and put on my beanie and gloves. I could see out of the corner of my eye that the old woman was diligently turning the handlebars to scan the area in front of her.

'I've just noticed,' she said 'there don't seem to be any flowers here. Did you pick them all?'

I had stepped to within a metre of her. 'Oh yes. There's none left.'

As I said it I stepped in and placed the clear sheet of plastic across her face with both hands. Holding the side of her face with my left hand I managed to get a complete loop of it round her face before she could comprehend what was going on. She dropped the bike as her arms thrashed up towards her face. I pushed her to her knees and knelt down on her back with my left knee while I managed to trap her right arm under my right knee. As she struggled I got the plastic around her head several more times before I was forced to drop the roll and subdue her free arm. I finally got into a position where I was kneeling astride her pinning both of her arms to her sides, while I could resume wrapping the film around her head; I did this until the roll was finished. She hadn't been able to make a noise apart from the trashing about. Within a minute she had stopped struggling completely. I reached over and turned off the bike lamp. It took me several seconds for my eyes to adjust to the darkness. When I was sure she was dead I rolled her over. It was hard to see in the dark and with all the plastic over her face and the way the ointment had smeared inside the plastic mask, but it looked like her eyes were wide open.

I stayed there for a good five minutes until my breathing had returned to normal. I crawled towards the road to see if there was anyone coming. I'd been vaguely aware of a few headlights rushing by. There was no one about. It was still early so I would have to wait. I dragged her body back deeper into the wood. It definitely couldn't be seen from the road but there was no point taking any risks. I packed up my rucksack, making sure I collected everything including the cardboard tube from the roll of plastic. I then changed my clothes and put on the fresh white T-shirt and black cargo pants. I carefully packed the red T-shirt and blue jeans I'd been wearing, making sure this time that I put the sunglasses in the bag before zipping it up tightly. I sat back down in among the bleak black trees, checked my watch and waited. I passed the time by searching in the undergrowth for some broken branches. I finally found one I liked the look of. I took out my Swiss army knife and whittled away for a while until I had the shape I wanted: a perfect '+'. I put it in my pocket. The only thing I regretted was not bringing a sweater, as the evening got quite chilly and it was an effort to stop myself from shivering.

When it was 9:30pm I picked up the body and put it over my shoulder, struggling under the dead weight. It felt cold now, but it was still pliable. I stood in the tree line and waited. I made sure there was nothing coming before I ran over to the hole in the wire-mesh fence. It was almost hidden from view by the dense foliage. I placed the body in the bushes and then dragged it through the hole after me. I stood in the rough and caught my breath. So far so good. I could see across the fairway to a small bridge across a stream. Next to it was a clump of trees. I put the body back on my shoulder and walked as fast as I could to the bridge. I lowered the body into the water and pushed it under the bridge. I knelt down on the edge of the stream and put the piece of wood I had cut into her hand. She was my tenth victim; I wanted to mark the occasion. I then made my way back across the fairway to the hole in the fence. Again I waited and then darted back into the wood opposite.

I put my backpack on and then wheeled the bike to the low wall. When it was clear, I lifted the bike down and cycled the several kilometres along the now deserted road back to the outskirts of the village. There was no sign of anyone. The only accompaniment I had was a faint sliver of new moon in the clear sky above me. I found a small car park on the right. I hopped off the bike and leant it against the fence of the car park. It was called the Imperial Car park and had its own booth, but it was far from regal. It was just a barren stretch of concrete, no lines or markings were painted. It was only the gaudy pink and black sign that distinguished it from the surrounding similarly nondescript paved areas. Both the park and the booth were empty. They would be full tomorrow as it was the weekend but maybe the bike might go unnoticed for several more days when hidden behind a parked car.

I took my gloves off and put them in my shorts as I walked through the town and across to the bus terminus by the beach. I went as directly as possible, past the low-rise shops that were shut for the night and a couple of restaurants with a handful of people patronising them. I took a right at the roundabout and jogged on past the closed shops selling beach paraphernalia and into another car park that was located right at the beach. This one was more official, painted lines, meters and a few cars. I ambled about at the back of the car park until I saw my bus pull in. I knew it would sit there for a few minutes, so I took a walk round the entire car park, keeping as far as possible away from the few people waiting in the queue. When I heard the engine growl to life and the interior lights flicker on, I made my way over to board the bus. I sat upstairs at the back, putting on my beanie and looking out of the window as the bus passed the scene of my latest triumph. I alighted at the terminus and took the MTR home.

ΞΞΞ

Chapter 21

Friday 18th November 2011

Chambers and Li had been busy over the past couple of weeks. Li had gone to the database and extended her search back to the first new moon of 2011. It fell in the first week in January. She was a little disappointed not to find any matches. It seemed that the harder they looked the less they found. There had been no suspicious deaths reported in the first week in January. She had drawn another blank. February was a slight improvement. There were three bodies found in the week after the February new moon. One was clearly a murder; a fatal stabbing in Mong Kok on the actual day, Thursday 3rd of February. While the other two could be described as unusual – there was a death from a suspected drug overdose in Tsim Sha Tsui that was reported on the following day, the Friday. On the same day the body of a hiker was discovered off of a mountain path on Lantau Island. She downloaded all three files and printed out the reports.

March was a different story altogether. There was a murder on the actual day. She recalled the story when it happened; a retired stable hand had been beaten to death at the racecourse in Happy Valley. This one was obvious. She knew most of the facts about the case but downloaded and printed the report and added it to the growing file. April was the same. There was a murder on the precise date. She knew of this one as well, but as it had taken place in Mong Kok, out of her remit, she had only the vaguest outline as to the specifics. She printed the report and scanned the case file. A young office worker had been beaten to death in an alley near his home, although nothing had been stolen.

This had to be the same man, Li thought. Although there was another possibly suspicious death that took place on the same day, she felt inclined to rule it out. A workman had been killed by falling masonry at a construction site in Ap Lei Chau. She added this to the report just in case. May was still coming up with no leads. She would have to come back to that one. It had taken Li most of the week to search through the police and hospital databases, cross referencing reports and going through the information in minute detail.

By the end of the week she felt she had enough to take to Chambers. She had a file that was over two inches thick of forensic evidence, crime scene reports and newspaper cuttings. She realised how it looked, most of the information was in Chinese. These would be of no use to Chambers, but she would need all of it to convince Pang just how big this case could really be. Chambers was right, but at this moment, she was the only other person who knew they were dealing with a serial killer. Pang was going to have to set up a taskforce and utilise most of the available team, this case had the potential to be enormous. Before she went to see Pang she wanted to show Chambers what they were on to, she wanted something simple yet effective. Before she briefed him, she summarised her findings in as blunt a manner as she felt it warranted. She typed a simple list into a word document, stating the month and murder that they attributed to their killer. The results put in this simple format had a devastating impact on the reader.

≈≈≈

Suspicious Deaths / Murders on New Moons in 2011 - Fri 18th Nov

January	–	None
February	–	Stabbing/Drug OD/Hiker death
March	–	Felix Cheung – Beaten to death
April	–	Daniel Lam – Beaten to death
May	–	None
June	–	Tony Fung – Death by asphyxiation
July First	–	None
July Second	–	Penny Teo – Death by misadventure
August	–	Peter Kwok – Beaten to Death
September	–	Eric Cheng – Asphyxiation / Drowning
October	–	Bert Yung – Beaten to Death
November	–	New moon due 26th November
December	–	New Moon due 24th December

~~~

She saved the document and attached it to an email she had already drafted to Chambers. It was late on Friday night when she sent it. Chambers had been out all afternoon and she had considered calling him but had decided against it. If only half of the murders were carried out by the same person, maybe it was best to let him enjoy his weekend. From here on, things were going to a whole new level.

~~~

Monday 21st – Saturday 26th November 2011

When Chambers read his email just before 9am on Monday morning, he called Li immediately. She answered on the second ring.

183

'So you've read my email then?'

'Shit Lucy, why didn't you call me on Friday? We could have had two extra days on this.'

'Look, maybe I should have called you. But we know one thing. If it's the same person responsible for all these murders, then we know the next attack won't happen until Saturday. Whoever did them isn't going to change his MO now.'

Chambers conceded she had a point, and at least they had several more crime scenes and evidence boxes to examine.

'We've got to take this to Pang. This is much bigger than either you or I had suspected.'

Again she had a valid argument. At this rate they were going to need all the help they could get.

'Sure, let's talk about it when you get in, are you close?'

'Just getting out of the cab now. I'll be there in five.' She hung up.

Chambers printed out the attachment and collected it from the section printer on his way to the pantry. He leant against the fridge and read the list again. From the start of the year he was sure that at least five were linked. He'd need to get Li to translate the reports on the others. What he couldn't fathom was why some like Cheng and Kwok were obviously murders, while the killer had tried to pass others off as accidents. It didn't make any sense. Whatever the reason, if they could positively link five murders to the pattern of new moons, and with a possibility of several more and another imminent, the reaction from Pang and those further up the chain of command was going to be interesting to say the least.

When he brought his coffee back to his desk, Li came in.

'I hope you made me one,' she called to him.

'Coming right up.' He returned to the pantry.

'Thanks,' she said as he came back with a coffee for her. 'Before you ask, I have this.' She took the thick folder from her desk drawer.

'I need to know more about the suspicious deaths, specifically the ones in February and late July.'

Li pulled out the corresponding reports and went through the details of the dead hiker, the stabbing and the overdose from February, and the death of the old lady who had fallen down the stairs in late July. She took ten minutes to brief him fully.

Chambers let out a sigh. 'My instincts are to rule out the drug one straightaway. The report says he got his fix and was seen by a neighbour entering his place alone. As for the knife attack, if I'd been here then I'd have been tempted to link it to the guy I'm supposed to be after. But all these other murders have taken place in quiet locations or some distance away from busy thoroughfares. The stabbing happened in broad daylight outside a bar. It just doesn't fit, it doesn't feel right.'

'So you think the hiker is the one?'

'I'm not sure. On its own it looks like an accident. But then the scene we found out at Buffalo beach would have looked like an accident if we hadn't been looking for a murder on that specific date.'

'Right, but I couldn't find any murders from the month before. How do we know they didn't start in March?'

Chambers leaned back in his chair and rubbed his eyes. 'We don't. That's the problem. They could go back much further. Your findings are certainly impressive, but are you not concerned there were three new moons this year with no murder?'

'I know. But that could be because the bodies haven't been located yet. It's worrying.' She paused. 'We need to go to Pang with this. This is explosive. Hong Kong has never had a serial killer before.'

'Really?'

'You sound surprised, do you think we Chinese like butchering each other?' She didn't look impressed. 'Serial killing is an Anglo-Saxon invention.'

'I just … it's a big city; I was just surprised that's all.' He tried to placate her. 'You're right though; we need to speak to Pang. What do you think he's going to make of it?'

'I'm concerned he's going to think the new moon link is unsubstantiated. We need to come up with something else to link this together.'

'Let's pull the evidence boxes from the February and July cases if there are any. In the meantime arrange a meeting with the Chief Inspector.'

Li called Pang, while Chambers thought about what their next move should be. He needed to insert the Black Dragon into this so he could maintain a valid presence on this case. He felt a buzz of excitement pass through his body. This was potentially the biggest case he'd ever worked on and although it wasn't the case he'd been sent here to solve, he was determined that he would be involved in this until it was resolved.

Li put down the receiver. 'He wants us in his office, now.'

She gathered up the case files and headed to Pang's room. Chambers followed. She knocked and they waited to be summoned in. They sat down opposite the Chief Inspector. Li took the lead in the conversation, outlining their findings in English, occasionally slipping into Cantonese to clarify a point. Every now and again she dipped into the files, pointing out certain facts. She also had a printout of the dates of the new moons of 2011. She showed the dates of the deaths and how they corresponded. She concluded by pointing out the relevance of the coming Friday as the date the next attack was expected.

Pang took several minutes to absorb the news. His face had become ashen as the details of the crimes and the full, horrible circumstances became clear. He was in an unenviable position. Whatever he decided now was going to have far-reaching and potentially irrevocable impact on the investigation.

Eventually he spoke. 'At this stage I'm not 100 percent convinced these are linked. But I'm not going to rule it out just yet, I'll keep an open mind. But If they are, then unless this can be resolved quickly and quietly, we are going to have the biggest and most intrusive media circus ever seen in Hong Kong.' He drummed his fingers on the table. 'If this gets out, the impact is going to be like a tsunami of bad feeling. Can you imagine what it will do for the image of the Police, that we haven't caught a crazed killer after all these months? God only knows how bad the general public's reaction will be.'

The three of them sat in silence. Pang continued drumming his fingers on the table, Li sifted through her notes. The tension was palpable.

'If I can just say one thing, Chief Inspector,' Chambers broke the silence. 'I think you're right and until we can gather more evidence to prove beyond a doubt these are linked then we need to keep a lid on this. But to get the information we need, you're going to have to provide us with more assistance.'

'What do you need?'

'At this stage I think we need to check back on all the new moons in 2010, that way we can establish when these murders started. It took Li a week to go through three months of records. Searching at that speed will take another month. If our predictions are correct, the next murder will take place in just five days time.'

Li pointed out Chambers' prediction for the next new moon.

'So you are both confident that there will be a murder this Friday?'

They both nodded.

'But you don't know by whom, how, when or where?'

'That's pretty much correct.' said Chambers, smiling weakly, aware that it offered little positive help. 'That's why we need a dedicated team to search for any possible victims in 2010, to dig deeper around the dates that have no victim and finally, we need forensics to go through anything we have for the new cases Li has just uncovered.'

'OK' said Pang, 'I don't know what evidence would have been collected if these murders were officially reported as accidents. But we'll hand over all the relevant case files to Jenny Greening. I'll let her know that she is to prioritise any requests from you two. I'll also find a team of officers to help you to thoroughly search the database. Give me an hour to set this up with Brian Tang.'

It was clear the meeting was over. Chambers noted some of the colour had returned to Pang's cheeks but he looked far from happy. The full scale of what they had just told him was yet to sink in. The pair of them got up and moved to the door.

'Hang on. One last thing. I'll brief Jenny and Brian about this and I'll tell them the same. I don't want a word of this breathed outside of this office. We cannot afford this getting out to the press. Do you understand?'

They nodded and left the room. They heard Pang on the phone to Brian as they headed back along the corridor to their open-plan office.

'What now then?' Li asked as she sat down. She picked up her coffee. It was cold. She didn't wait for his reply. Instead she got up and took Chambers' untouched cup to the pantry to make them both a fresh one.

'Where did the February and July murders take place?' he asked when she returned with the coffees.

'Lantau Island in February, and er …' she paused while she checked the file, 'Tai Hang for the July one.'

'Lantau Island again? Close to this last one at Buffalo beach?'

'Not exactly close, maybe 5 or 6km away. Closer to Discovery Bay, where we went for dinner that time with Jenny and her husband. You weren't a fan as I recall.'

'No, it was OK, what did you call it? Disco Bay?'

'I meant not a fan of her husband,' she broke into a smile. It was probably the first time either of them had done so all morning.

'From the report,' she continued, 'the hiker was bitten by a Chinese Cobra on one of the hikes up by a place called Tiger Head; it's directly above Discovery Bay.'

Chambers thought back. He could vaguely recall the high green hills stretching up above the tall buildings. It would certainly be an isolated location.

'What about Tai Hang, I've heard of that. But I can't place it.'

'It's not far from here. It's between Tin Hau and Causeway Bay. Come on John, you stay in Causeway Bay. Have you not even been and had a look around where you live?'

'Of course, I just didn't know where it was,' he hesitated, 'Where is it exactly?'

'You overlook Victoria Park. Opposite there is the library; it's tucked in around the back. Didn't you go and see the famous dragon dances that are held there every mid-autumn?'

Chambers drew a blank. Mid-autumn?

'I'll take that as a no then? I think it's going to take a couple of hours for the Chief Inspector to get everyone up to speed. Let's grab a cab over there.'

'Sure, we can give Jenny a call in an hour or so, I've got an idea we're going to be seeing a lot more of her very soon.'

Li and Chambers spent the next two hours examining the building in Tai Hang where the unlucky Mrs Teo had fallen to her death. As the door to the building was unlocked they managed to get in and take photographs of the staircase. They examined the accessibility, and more importantly, they noted the lack of security cameras. It would be relatively easy to follow the woman in, murder her and exit without being seen by too many people, if any at all. From the dark entrance

189

hall, the murderer just needed to casually walk out of the building and exit the area.

Li called Greening from Tai Hang. She had already been briefed by Pang and had been waiting for their call. They requested she pull the crime scene reports on both of the murders so that she could familiarise herself with the details. Li arranged a meeting with Greening in her office for as soon as they got back to the station.

Less than 20 minutes later, the three of them were seated in Greening's office, the files for the suspicious deaths in February and July spread across the table. Greening began with the forensic file for the February death.

'Michael Watson, aged 45.' Jenny read from the file. 'This indicates he died from a combination of snake bite and injuries suffered in a fall.' She pulled another sheet out of the file. 'This is the toxicology report. It clearly states that he had significant amounts of cobratoxin, cardiotoxin and hemotoxin in his system that is consistent with the venom from a naja atra. This snake is more commonly known as a Chinese Cobra, and is found all across Hong Kong. The post mortem report,' she slid another sheet from the file, 'states he had two puncture wounds on his calf that again corresponds to the bite of a Chinese Cobra.'

Chambers interrupted. 'But you said there were other injuries related to a fall?'

'Yes, that's right, he had several large hematomas to his back and leg areas plus some quite severe head injuries. But then if you look at the photographs that were taken at the scene,' she handed them a manila envelope, 'you can see that he fell about five metres, which accounts for those injuries.'

Li and Chambers studied the handful of pictures; the victim looked like a ragdoll, his arms and legs bent into painfully awkward positions.

'So it appears the victim came up the path,' Li said indicating the route on one of the photos, 'surprised the snake, which in turn bit him, he then stumbled back and fell to his death?'

'That's how the police reported it when they found the body the next day.'

'Or that's how it was supposed to look.'

'Chief Inspector Pang has briefed me on what you two think is going on. I'm here to give you all the support I can. It's not my place to tell you how to do your job,' Jenny trailed off.

'I can feel a but coming,' said Li.

'OK, but the thing I can't work out is – why go to all that trouble?'

'I see where you're coming from,' Chambers carried on her train of thought, 'if you want to murder someone, and at this stage it looks like quite a random choice, why climb halfway up a mountain and use a snake to do it.'

'And just where did he get a snake from?' Jenny asked.

She had a point. How could they rule this one in? There were no records of a murder in January, and this one in the following month felt like they were trying to force a square peg into a round hole.

Li came up with a theory. 'Jenny, sometimes I think you spend too long in Discovery Bay, you need to get back to the real Hong Kong now and again.' She said it in a light tone, 'when was the last time you were up in Mong Kok? At Tung Choi Street, you know the goldfish market. Well apart from fish they sell terrapins, turtles, lizards and snakes. I bet it wouldn't be too hard to put in an order in one of the less discerning shops up there to get yourself a delivery of a Chinese Cobra.'

Jenny conceded the point. Chambers had no idea where Li was talking about, but it kept the possibility alive – that was the most important thing.

Jenny pulled out the files relating to the July death. 'This unfortunate lady, Mrs Teo, has injuries that I would associate with a fall down a flight of stairs. I can see why it was written up at the time as an accident. The police report mentions they found a small dog at the scene, a schnauzer. Neighbours apparently confirmed it was the deceased's pet. It appears the dog got tangled in her feet and caused the fall, the dog's lead was found wrapped around her legs. The officers on duty didn't report any other suspicious findings at the scene.'

'Personally,' interjected Chambers, 'I just know this one belongs to our man. I can feel it. It seems to me he's an opportunist. Ideally he wants them to be seen as accidents, but equally, he's not bothered to use such excessive force when necessary that it couldn't be mistaken for anything else.' Chambers was thinking about what Li had told him of the murders that had taken place in March and April, two men's skulls beaten to a pulp.

'My initial thought about this one is that when he saw where she lived and saw the dog, he made an impulsive decision to take advantage of the situation. I'm sure originally he was planning to follow her to her flat and deal with her there.'

'Interesting,' said Li.

'You don't like my theory?' Chambers looked over at her.

'Not that, I just noticed you have started referring to this killer as a "he". Since you came to the conclusion it wasn't the man you followed from London, you have just been referring to "the killer" but now you seem sure it's a man.'

'That's my gut instinct. If it is the same person responsible for all these deaths, then we're talking about a serial killer. They're very rarely women.' He turned to Greening. 'Jenny, I need you and your team to re-examine everything available from the murders on the list Lucy has already sent to you, we need everything double- or triple-checked. I'm guessing a lot of things weren't looked into if the deaths weren't reported as suspicious, but DNA, fingerprints, blood splatter, fibres, anything, calling cards, whatever you can get me. In the meantime can I take copies of all the crime scene photographs now?'

'Of course John. We'll do our utmost to help. If there's anything there I promise you, we'll find it. I'll get my assistant Maggie to run off the copies, she'll have them on your desk shortly.

≈≈≈

Chambers spent the next few days examining the photographs, while Li kept Pang up to speed on the investigation. No new leads had developed, but Chambers and Li were now familiar with all of the cases. Apart from them occurring on a new moon there was nothing else they could see linking the crimes together. Chambers had lost track of how many times he had stared at the pictures of the unfortunate old man in the stable. The pictures showed the old man face down in the straw. There was a horseshoe placed on his back, but there was no blood on it and it didn't look like it had been used to kill him. This had to be placed there by the killer. Li had told him that he had died from hammer blows to the head, but the murder weapon still hadn't been found. He switched his attention to the photos of the death in Mong Kok. This time the murder weapon was at the scene. A putter from a set of golf clubs, the photos left him in no doubt that this had been used in the attack. The other thing that stood out was there were matches scattered over the scene. The box looked like it had been thrown, and it must have taken place after the victim was on the ground as there were matches on top of the victim. The report didn't show any evidence of anything combustible at the scene. Why would the murderer throw an open box of matches at the body? It didn't make sense. Unfortunately, like the horseshoe from the other scene, the putter and matchbox had come back without any fingerprints. He just hoped Jenny could find something.

By Friday lunchtime a small group of officers at the Wan Chai Police Station were on tenterhooks. Pang had requested assistance from other district police stations to get as many extra beat officers out across the city as was possible. He covered his tracks by informing them he had good information about a pickpocket gang from the mainland planning a citywide hit over the weekend. The problem was the specialist team had no idea of where or at what time of day the next attack would take place. Time passed slowly, occasionally interrupted by an email from Jenny Greening updating them on her findings, which so far just corresponded to the reports they already had. DNA samples were going to take a while longer and they would have to make a decision about requesting the disinterment of those who were originally believed to be accidental deaths that they now suspected of murder. When nothing had come in by 10pm and the rest of the office had gone home, James called together the small group assigned to the case.

'I'm not suggesting for one moment the intelligence we have on this matter is in any way incorrect. What I am saying is, judging by the MO of this suspect, there's a good chance if and when the murder takes place it's going to be in a remote place. I think the best thing is for you to go home and get a good night's rest. I think tomorrow is going to be a busy day, so keep your mobiles switched on and I'll be in touch as soon as I hear anything.

~~~

Chambers had gone back to the apartment. He doubted he'd get any sleep, but he had taken his shoes off and laid on the bed, surfing the channels on the television, finally settling on the discovery channel that was airing a show about sharks. As he watched the images on the screen of grisly shark attacks his thoughts instinctively turned back to the murders. In every case he had previously worked on there had always been a motive. When there was no clear suspect there was still the motive, whether it was greed, love, freedom, money or whatever it was, there had to be a driving force. So why could he not see one in any of these murders? What was this murderer's motive? If he could work that out, he might finally be able to crack the case.

194

The phone was ringing. Chambers was confused. He looked at the television; the show was about orangutans. He must have dozed off. The room was bathed in light; he hadn't switched off any of them. The alarm clock showed 5.56am. The phone was still ringing and vibrating in his pocket. He took it out and saw Li's name.

'Hello John, did I wake you?'

'Yes, but I bet you've got a good reason.' He held his breath, but he knew what was coming.

'There's been another body found. This time out near Shek O on the golf course there. It was found by one of the green-keepers, less than an hour ago.'

'Christ.'

'I'll be round to get you in a cab, be downstairs in 10 minutes.'

Chambers went to the bathroom to freshen up. He washed his face and brushed his teeth. It was a sickening sensation, knowing a murder was going to take place but being powerless to stop it, he couldn't help thinking he was in someway responsible. As he exited the room he grabbed his camera and went down to the street to wait for Li.

At that time of the morning, there was almost no traffic on the road. The winding path around the high hills of the island offered exceptional views down to Stanley as the sun broke the surface of the placid South China Sea on the distant horizon. The cab made a steep descent towards a coastal village; the expansive stretches of fairways nearby indicated their destination. As they pulled up Chambers could see an ambulance and two police cars. They got out in the golf course car park. There were a few dedicated golfers, resplendent in their Saturday finest of tasteless plaids and bright pastels, clearly distinguishing themselves from the drab-coloured 'plain-clothed' police officers, green-overall wearing ground staff and the white all-in-ones of the scene of crime investigators. It appeared that the amount of police had been kept to a minimum and then he saw why. Chief Inspector Pang walked over to them and he didn't look well.

'Good morning detectives, at this stage it looks like your theory might hold water. I'm glad you could both get here so quickly. I got word not long after the body was found. We were lucky, if I can use that phraseology, that it happened on Hong Kong Island. I got the news quicker than if it had happened in Kowloon, the New Territories or one of the outlying islands. This way we might be able to keep it just a little bit quieter.'

'What about the early morning golfers? What are you telling them?' asked Li.

'We have told them we're investigating a serious case of vandalism on the course; that it looks like an animal has been killed. But we need to complete a full investigation that could take some time. The golf course management has reluctantly agreed to close the course for this morning at least. They're not too happy as a Saturday morning is the busiest time of the week.'

'That doesn't explain the presence of the ambulance or what they'll say when they see a body bag.'

'That's right; so we'll need to act quickly. We need full cooperation from the staff to get the course closed to outsiders, at least that way we can get the body into the ambulance without too many people seeing it. I've already had the grounds-man taken into custody, more as a preventative measure for us. At this stage I seriously doubt he is involved, but it will stop him from speaking to anyone for the time being.'

'Where's the body?' Chambers asked.

Pang pointed down one of the fairways. 'As he was driving up to work on one of the greens, he spotted it half-hidden under that low bridge over there.'

They could see a group of four or five people several hundred yards away under a small stand of trees. Li and Chambers took their leave of Pang and headed towards them. On arrival they saw the body had been laid out on the perfectly manicured fairway. It was clearly a woman, although her face was covered by so much Clingfilm that the facial features were hard to make out. It wasn't helped by being obscured by some opaque material inside the plastic.

Li questioned one of the officers at the scene in Cantonese. After several minutes she returned to Chambers who was looking under the small bridge, where the body had been found, for anything that looked out of place.

'Mia Jensen, that's the name on the HKID card found in her pocket. Date of birth says 27/03/1941. I can run some more checks shortly. I think it's safe to say she was suffocated to death,' she said.

Chambers stepped back up to the fairway from the bank of the small stream. 'Well we can say for certain she wasn't killed here. There are no signs of a struggle. I think this has to be our man. The body is showing no signs of decomposition. I'm no expert, but the body doesn't look in a bad way to me.'

'So if he brought the body here last night or early this morning, where did he come from?'

He stood up and looked back down the fairway. He had to put his hand up to shield against the bright early rays of the sun. He could clearly see the footprints of where he and Li had walked up the fairway earlier, the dark footprints of compressed grass contrasting sharply with the shimmering early morning dew. There were a lot of other tracks heading to and from the car park that were created by the other investigating officers. He looked off in other directions. There were no signs of footprints in the damp grass going in other directions. The fairway he was standing on was the one closest to the road. Separating the road from the course was a high chain link fence that was overgrown with bushes and trees. No one could scale that with any ease, especially carrying a body. He crossed the fairway to have a closer examination of the metal barrier.

Li was set to join him when she noticed something in the shallow water of the stream not far from where Chambers had been looking a few minutes before. She moved a little further along the edge of the stream and fished out an item from the icy cold water. She saw it was just a piece of a tree branch, about four inches long. It resembled a small cross. She was going to throw it back when she noticed that the ends weren't jagged but had been whittled flat. She called back to one of the team that were busy photographing the body and got them to show her the exact position where the victim was found. She could see the wooden cross would have been very close to where the body had been dumped. She begged an evidence bag and placed the wooden cross inside.

Chambers had also found something. His investigation of the fence had shown there was a hole big enough for someone to have squeezed through. The disturbed ground on either side of the gap in the fence looked recent. He called to Li to get the team to search the surrounding area for any evidence. He snapped off a couple of pictures and returned to Li. By this stage the body had been placed in a body bag and onto a gurney. The ambulance, much to the consternation of the golf club management, had been driven along the side of the fairway to allow for the body bag to be removed with as little fuss as possible. It seemed logical to Chambers that if the body was dumped there, then whoever had done it would want the easiest access. He had seen from the aerial view of the course that they were offered on the way in, that the other side of the course was bordered by the sea. There were many entry points to the course for anyone determined to get in. But why would the murderer need to make it more difficult than it had to be? Surely they would have been trying to dispose of the body as close to the murder site as possible? And by leaving it on the course after dark that meant it wouldn't be found until at least daybreak, giving him plenty of time to be far, far away.

Chambers and Li made their way round to the corresponding place on the road to where he had found the hole in the fence. The traffic was getting heavier. Chambers glanced at his watch, it was now just after 7am, the sun was up and it looked like it was going to be a clear and sunny day. Several buses, taxis and private cars were making their way along the narrow road to and from the beach village. He and Li scouted around; there was a relatively dense wooded area on the other side of a small stone wall. This would offer the killer the perfect place to have committed the crime while remaining out of view of anyone passing by. Li phoned James to organise the crime scene team to come and investigate the area. While they were waiting, Li told Chambers about the piece of wood she had found.

'You think it has something to do with this?' he asked.

'Hard to say, but for the proximity to the body and the neatly cut ends. It could just have been something done by a bored golfer waiting for the players ahead to finish on the green in front, or a groundsman using it for something. But it's worth checking for prints all the same.'

Chambers agreed. If it was something left by the killer, what did it mean? Li had described a cross shaped piece of wood. Could it be a religious symbol?

~~~

Chapter 22

Saturday 26th November 2011

Chambers knew the case was desperately in need of a break. There could be no denying that his theory of the murders taking place on new moons was now almost a certainty. Although what was the use of that without a motive or a suspect? He had received news related to the cross-referencing of murders on new moons dating back into 2010. So far nothing had shown up. At least this relatively good news meant that the murders were probably limited in scope to 2011. Not much, but the way things were going it was better than nothing.

By the time he had got back to the station it was close to 10am. The initial investigation of the woodland had, after intensive searching along a 100-metre stretch, found some disturbed ground; with what looked like bicycle tyre tracks. Chambers had left the experts to uncover what they could, while Li had remained to assist Pang. Jenny Greening was waiting for him at his workstation. She informed him she was waiting to hear back about the results of the post mortem. They'd be on her desk by Monday, which was the best the coroner could do at this stage. She hadn't wanted to push it. They were all aware the tightrope they were walking, trying to keep this out of the media spotlight. The murder of an expat was hardly likely to help matters.

The first 48 hours would be crucial after that the chances of finding solid leads would begin to evaporate. Pang had organised interviews to be carried out in the area, but without speaking any Cantonese, Chambers would be of little use. He sat at his desk waiting for news. After going over the morning's findings repeatedly in his head, he decided to go and see if there was anything he could glean from Greening's reinvestigation of the case files of the other murders. He began by describing to her in detail the victim they had found earlier, the body dumped under a small bridge. He told her about the wooden cross that Li had found that could have been placed in the hand of the victim.

Chambers was aware of Greening's religious convictions and he wanted to tread lightly. She was not alone. Many of the team were active in their local churches. There was even a band of happy-go-lucky born-again Christians that held weekly get-togethers in the staff canteen. Chambers had nearly joined one of them as he was under the impression it was just a friendly Wednesday lunchtime team gathering. As he'd been making his way over, he only just noticed that the small thick black books on the desk in front of them were bibles. Fortunately for him he'd managed to veer away at the last moment and joined a couple of uniformed officers who appeared completely non-plussed by the sudden appearance of an inanely grinning gweilo. Luckily for Chambers they'd been too polite to make a fuss and he'd considered himself lucky to have escaped an hour of gospel quizzes and hallelujahs.

'Jenny, the crime scene team found evidence, including wood shavings, near the suspected murder scene. At this stage it points to the fact that whoever committed the murder is also likely to have carved the piece of wood that Lucy found. My first thought is that it could be a religious motif. With one leg on the ground it resembles a crucifix, tilted to one-side with two legs on the ground it represents

201

the saltire, either way it seems to me to have obvious religious connotations.'

'Possibly,' Jenny said as she took out her notepad and a pencil and sketched a cross. She tore the page out of the ringed pad and slowly rotated the image. 'There's another thing that strikes me,' she paused.

'Go on.'

'Well the saltire is a cross. But then 'X' also represents the number ten in Roman numerals.'

'Right. And?'

'Rotated through 90 degrees we get the '+' character, which in Traditional and Simplified Chinese writing also means ten.'

Chambers looked across at her as the realisation of what she had said dawned on him.

'Have you got the page that Lucy sent us with the list of murders this year?'

Greening was already moving to her files. She took out the document and placed it on the table between them. They now had nine suspected victims including the one found earlier that morning. But there were still no records for a murder in May or early July.

'Christ!' he yelled. 'I think that's it. I think you're spot on.' Chambers was suddenly aware of his poor choice of invective.

'But we've only got nine on the list.' Greening appeared to have ignored his blaspheming.

'We need to get back and check the details of those two other dates. I don't know why, but I assume that it's one murder a month on a new moon. That means today marks the tenth month. I've got a suspicion that there wasn't a murder in early July. But I bet there was one in May, it would fit the pattern of one a month. Can you chase up the investigating team?'

'Yes, John. Or would it be easier for you and me to go through it now? We know that Lucy looked on the date and a few days after. We know it can't have been reported prior to the new moon.'

'That's right, so if the new moon was on, when?' He checked Li's notes, 'The 3rd of April and she looked to the 6th, can we pull up reports from the 7th onwards?'

Greening logged on to the central database and began checking for any reports that might be relevant. Chambers ran back to his desk and began a Google search, typing in 'Hong Kong + body + 7 May 2011'. No matches. He tried the next date and was again unsuccessful until he found a link to the *South China Morning Post* website for the 11th of May. He didn't have a subscription to the account, but he could read the headline and opening sentence, the rest of the story was behind the paywall.

Hiker's body found on NT trail

Wednesday, 11 May 2011

New Territories: A police spokesperson today announced the discovery of a body in a forested area close to the MacLehose Trail. At this stage Police are … [*Read more*]

≈≈≈

It wasn't much but Chambers had read enough and raced back to Greening's office.

She looked up and saw him enter. 'John I've found something.'

'Tell me it's the same as what I've got.'

'I've got a dead hiker, found a week after he died on a trail in the New Territories. What about you?'

'The very same!'

'It wasn't reported as murder either, so I can see why it was overlooked. Plus the body wasn't found until a week later. But the time of death was given as 4th of May. So, obviously it wouldn't have been flagged for a death on the third.'

'But that wouldn't fit our man if it was the 4th, would it?' Chambers was concerned that maybe this wasn't the one.

'I need to check, but I think if the body was out there for that length of time, exposed to the elements and the particular type of fauna at that spot, I would hazard a guess that the coroner may have incorrectly determined the time of death.'

'Well that's good news, but what do you mean when you say "particular type of fauna"?'

'According to the reports I have, the body was found in an area of Hong Kong that's home to a number of wild troupes of long tail and rhesus macaques – monkeys to you and me.'

Chambers was surprised to hear there were wild monkeys in Hong Kong. He knew there were snakes and had come too close for comfort with a buffalo, but he hadn't expected to hear there were monkeys as well. He imagined what a horde of wild monkeys might have done to the corpse; it was an image he tried unsuccessfully to get out of his mind.

'This is really amazing news. This gives us our tenth victim which corresponds to your X/+ theory,' he nodded to Greening, 'plus, it also gives us a much better indication of when this whole thing started.'

'Yes, but that would indicate that the killings began on 3rd February 2011, with the hiker on Lantau and the tenth one was that of Mia Jensen this morning. I'm just not sure about the snakebite victim.'

'So what you're suggesting is it could be ten except the murders began in March with the killing of the old guy at the stables and that we're missing one; which would be the new moon at the beginning of July.' Chambers could see why Greening was still skeptical about the snakebite victim.

'Do you think it's worth a visit?' she asked.

'Up to where it happened on Lantau Island? Why not? The photos from the scene don't tell us too much.'

'I know the place. It's a bit of an effort to get up there. You might want to go and change into something more appropriate. Put some running shoes on and a pair of shorts. In fact go and pack a bag. You can get changed at mine if that would be easier.'

~~~

They met back at the station within the hour and took a cab to the ferry. On the boat they made small talk about the case. Chambers could tell she was frustrated with the lack of headway with both the DNA and CCTV coverage. She had managed to obtain some fibres from a couple of crime scenes, but with nothing to link them, this was currently of no use.

Chambers got changed at Greening's place and, fortunately for him, Ian was out playing golf. But Jenny, unaware of Chambers' dislike for her husband, was sure he would be back by the time they finished. As they walked back along the beach to the plaza, Greening pointed out where they were going. Chambers thought it looked quite an intimidating height, but he was fit and the temperature was in the mid-20s. He accepted her suggestions about taking a minivan up the steep route to the viewpoint. From the plaza they made their way up a winding road. The van turned off near the top onto a narrow concrete path that led to the isolated viewpoint Chambers had seen from the beach. It was set on a plateau that offered Chambers yet another amazing view. He could see back across to Kowloon and Hong Kong Island. Although there was the usual Hong Kong haze, he could just make out the skyscrapers of ifc and ICC on either side of Victoria Harbour.

He surveyed the steep path that travelled up steeply in front of them. The pale yellow path standing out in sharp relief to the verdant greenery of the surrounding grassy slopes that led up to the rocky outcrop that loomed down on them from above. He let her take the

205

lead and set the pace. About halfway up the steep gravel-strewn path, Chambers was pleased they had taken the van up to the plateau. It had probably saved them half an hour and he was beginning to notice that compared to Greening he wasn't as fit as he thought. After the third false crest they made it to the top. They stopped at a triangulation point for a drink of water and took a couple of minutes to regain their composure. Chambers took advantage of the 360 degree view that now offered the chance to see down the other side of the mountain. He could make out the airport built on the odd-shaped area of reclaimed land that reached out into the South China Sea. Further out across the bay he could make out the tall buildings of what he guessed was part of the New Territories.

He turned his head to look down on Discovery Bay. As they'd made their way to get the van from the bus station next to the plaza, the place had been as crazily busy as when he'd visited before. It was a Saturday afternoon, but again every man and his dog, quite literally, seemed to be in the plaza. And yet, up here, there was no one. They'd seen a few people walking up the road earlier, but since they'd started on the path up to where they were now, there was nobody to be seen. He looked along the ridge line. It was strangely treeless. The long grass was blowing in the wind. They put the bottles back in their bags and Greening had removed a white envelope, the contents of which were the few photos they had of the crime scene. They carried on along the ridge, it wasn't very steep on either side, and there were vast areas of long grass. In the distance, further along the plateau they had previously been on, Chambers could make out a golf course. It reminded him of what he had seen earlier in the day. On the left, just before the course, he could see a lake that was surprisingly devoid of activity. He asked Greening why that was and she explained it was a disused reservoir.

After travelling along the path for about 500 metres, they came to the spot that Chambers recognised from the photographs. Greening consulted the picture and moved towards the corresponding area.

She was standing at the edge of a precipice, the path went down away towards the left, but where she was standing there was a sharp drop of five metres. They both stood on the ridge and surveyed the surrounding area. One thing was clear: the location offered a wide panorama of the surrounding hills and the path for nearly a kilometre in both directions. Coming from the opposite direction to the way they had come, they could make out a small group in brightly-coloured clothing. They had time to travel further along the path to reconstruct the unfortunate hiker's last steps. They walked on 50 metres or so before coming back. As they breasted the ridge, it was noticeable that the grass on either side of the path was up to about waist high, but shorn close at the path edges – giving the trail the impression of being almost five metres wide.

Chambers recreated the supposed last movements of the victim. Which direction he had come from, where he was likely to have been bitten – which, assuming he hadn't decided to wander off the clearly marked path, was several metres over the ridge, and where he would have stumbled back and fallen to his death. Chambers thought it was definitely possible, but he still had nagging doubts. The victim regularly walked the track; he was in relatively good shape and would have been more than aware of the dangers posed by snakes. When he'd asked Greening for a description of the snake she said the Chinese Cobra was dark in colour, almost completely black along its back with a light-coloured underside. The snake's hood and parts of the body may be striped and it could grow to over a metre in length. The snake was poisonous but crucially, it was known to evade contact with humans.

Chambers and Greening watched the group of hikers struggle slowly towards the ridge, they waved and said hello before continuing along the path to the rocky outcrop and the descent back to the viewing point.

'It doesn't make sense,' Chambers said to Greening.

'I've also got reservations, but what are you thinking?'

'Look at the speed of that last group as they came over the ridgeline. They were slow moving. The last part before the crest is quite steep. You say this type of snake is likely to avoid confrontation with humans and as you come over the top you get a perfect view along the route. Surely a black snake is likely to contrast sharply against the pale grey of the path.'

'I agree, the police report said he'd had a few drinks, that makes me think he certainly wouldn't have been racing. It could however explain how he missed the snake, but he would literally have had to tread on it to get bitten and I just can't believe that he could have done that.'

'Were there any odd things found on the body? I'm just thinking about the wooden cross that we found near the victim this morning. It could give us some kind of link.'

'I'll have to check the records when I get back to my desk. Come on, I think we've seen enough here.'

Chambers agreed. He was still taken aback by the eerie remoteness of the place. No, that wasn't it; they weren't remote as such, just alone. Apart from the small group of hikers they hadn't seen anyone up on the trail since they came up from the viewpoint.

'Do you get up here often?' Chambers was thinking how he would definitely hike in these hills on weekends if he lived here.

'Not as much now, a few years ago we'd come up here a lot when the children were younger. Also Ian's not in the best shape these days, he prefers a round of golf,' she pointed away to the distant fairways, 'rather than anything as energetic as this. Plus I'm not as young as I look.' she laughed.

It was the first time Chambers had seen her laughing. He thought back to the dinner a few months previously, she had been the perfect host, a great conversationalist but he hadn't seen her laugh. She had an engaging laugh and Chambers found himself unintentionally joining in. They made their way all the way back to the plaza on foot.

Chambers was glad they'd been up there, he felt closer somehow to what had happened all those months ago. He knew this was a victim, but was that the first?

As they were approaching Greening's house, Chambers began making excuses to get back to Hong Kong Island and told her that he had several things he needed to do back at the station. As it turned out Ian wasn't there. But Chambers decided to head back anyway, turning down the opportunity of a glass of perfectly chilled white wine. Any other time, he thought, and this would be very welcome at the end of a hike, but not today and not if he thought Ian would be coming back any time soon.

He used the half hour on the boat to reassess the case. There had to be some common denominator in the murders but apart from the new moons he could see no other clear connection. There was no link between the victims or in the locations the killer had chosen. But if he was killing on a specific day then he would need to have a plan. It was surely too risky to be selecting his victims completely at random. The variety of different methods and murder weapons was also perplexing. The murderer had to be disposing of the tools he was using somewhere. But where? Unless he kept hold of them. He ruled this out. The man responsible for these crimes was too particular about his approach to be stupid enough to keep any kind of incriminating evidence.

Chambers knew the answers were tantalisingly close. There were clues. There were always clues. At some stage there was going to be a breakthrough, whether through DNA or some other evidence. He was sure of that. What he wasn't so sure of was when. They needed to resolve this case quickly before there were more attacks. There was something nagging at him. He felt that there were clues in the reports that they just weren't seeing. There had to be evidence that conclusively linked these murders together, a pattern that could possibly give a reason and from there lead to a suspect. Chambers knew he had to believe that was a plausible, explainable theory, without that where did it leave them?

≈≈≈

Wednesday 30th November 2011

Chambers and Li had been discussing the murder victim found on the golf course. There had been a strong smell of menthol coming from the victim's head. It was coming from whatever was smeared inside the Clingfilm, but neither of them could work out why it was there. There was no medical evidence associating menthol with either being an anaesthetic or a particularly effective poison. Greening had informed them that according to the Coroner's report, the paste found on the inside of the Clingfilm had been tested and matched to a popular local brand of Tiger Balm. Chambers had commented to Li that the Tiger Balm, which he'd been using to quell the itchiness of his all too frequent mosquito bites, was orange in colour. She had explained there were a couple of varieties of which one was the milky-white colour they had seen obscuring the victim's face. Although she was at a loss to explain what it might be doing there.

On the Wednesday morning Greening had called them both in to her office to discuss her findings in relation to whether any of the victims were carrying anything possibly left by the killer.

'I've been able to check the records in some cases, particularly if they were categorised as murders. That makes it a lot easier for me to check the evidence.'

'Please tell me you've found a pattern?' Chambers wasn't too hopeful.

'I did find some interesting things but whether they are relevant, it's hard to say. Let's go through them in chronological order, beginning with the snakebite death in February. At this stage we're all pretty confident this is the first. Although there is a possibility our hiker isn't one of them, we can't rule out that option.'

'Agreed' said Li. 'So what did you find? I read the crime scene report and I didn't see anything that was listed at the scene as profoundly exceptional.'

'That's right. There was nothing at the scene that couldn't be attributed to the victim. However, attached to the coroner's report, there was a mention that when the victim's clothes were removed a dead match fell out from the trouser leg. It was written on a separate sheet to the report more as an aside. They tend to note anything down as you never know if there is any significance.'

'And,' Chambers was thinking about the victim in the alley, 'the third victim…'

Greening cut him off, 'exactly, there were the contents of a whole box full of matches scattered over the top of the third victim.'

'So you think the dead match is a calling card of some kind?' Li looked puzzled.

'I immediately got a colleague to check the second victim's clothing.'

'The man at the stables? Don't tell me you've got a match?' asked Chambers, cringing inwardly aware that it sounded like a bad joke.

Greening ignored it, 'we did indeed. There was a dead match found in the man's back pocket. We're running some tests now to see if we can link the two matches we've found to the box and the other matches at the third murder scene.'

'Hang on though. Where are the photographs from the third victim?' Li asked.

Greening pulled out the file and placed the images on her desk. The three of them examined the images, passing them around. 'Why would he have thrown the matches when previously he'd been so careful placing dead matches in the victim's clothing? Do you think he was disturbed?'

Chambers was thinking about the last victim. 'What about the woman last weekend? Did you find any matches on her?'

'Hold on John, we need to work through them in order. The problem is we haven't been able to locate any matches on any other of the victims.'

'Maybe if he got disturbed he changed his method,' suggested Li.

'Yes it's possible, maybe he felt like it had brought him some kind of bad luck and changed his pattern?'

'Interesting theory,' Greening nodded, 'and it's one that might just hold water.'

'What do you mean? Has he changed his calling card? asked Li.

'The fourth victim – the one we only recently uncovered as a possible murder – was found clutching a lighter. Ok it's not matches but there's a common theme. Also the potential fifth victim; the one that choked to death. At the scene a Zippo lighter was found next to his body. Of course it was noted in the file, but no one would have linked it to another murder as he was a smoker, plus candles that had burned out were also found at the scene so it was logical that he would have a lighter on him. The lady who fell down the stairs was the sixth victim.'

Don't tell me, she had a lighter on her as well?' Chambers grimaced.

'Correct. So the first six victims all have something in common. Matches and lighters. The theme is clearly fire right? But then there's no evidence he's got any tendencies towards arson. The obvious place was the stable; there was a lot of straw and other highly combustible materials. Yet the killer was careful not to set anything alight. Personally, I don't understand what the link means.'

Chambers couldn't see what the connection meant either, 'I don't get it. Yes they both create fire, but why not just buy a new box of matches. I don't understand why he would change from matches to lighters. Can either of you see why he would do this?'

'John I think you are overlooking something quite simple. The fact that the first three all had something in common and the second three also had something in common surely proves that we can be almost certain that the same person is responsible for all of these.'

'Yes' continued Greening, 'we can work out the theme later. It gets more interesting when we move on to victim number seven. The man found in Kowloon Park.'

'Right, this is the first time that John and I went to the crime scene. Admittedly the day after, so there was little to see. What was found on or near him? I remember from the report there was a kid's book and a bottle of water. I can't recall anything else.'

'Two pairs of sunglasses?' Chambers was searching his memory.

'Yes, that's right, we're convinced the killer accidentally left his sunglasses at the scene, but we couldn't get any prints off them. Also we didn't recover either a box of matches or lighter from the scene.'

'So has he changed his calling card again?' asked Li.

'Perhaps, or maybe it just wasn't logged or got lost, because a lighter was found at the scene of the eighth victim. Although he was found in his own home, along with the remains of a cigarette. Judging from the scorch mark on the carpet and the DNA found on the stub it's clear the victim was smoking it at the time of the attack.'

'What about number nine? The older guy out on Lantau Island?' Again Chambers was trying to picture the scene. In his mind's eye he could only recall the water buffalo staring at him from down the beach.

'Again we've got no lighter or matches on or near the body. However, during the search of his car, a pack of cigarettes and a lighter were found on the back seat. Whether they were put there by the killer seems a little bit of a long shot.'

'We have a common theme linking the first three to each other, and the second set of three. Don't we need to be looking for something different to match the next three together? I mean let's get the inventory for the possessions of each of them. There has to be a link.'

'John, I'm one step ahead of you. I've done it. In common they all had mobile phones and wallets. In addition, the older man had a handkerchief, a wristwatch and a jade bracelet. The man in Kowloon Park had several gold rings and a gold chain; while the man in the apartment wasn't fully dressed, and being in his home it's too hard to rule out a lot of his possessions. He was wearing a small amulet around his neck and a silver ring on his left hand. In the pockets of the jeans we found crumpled on his bedroom floor there was also a penknife and several Mark Six lottery tickets from the Hong Kong Jockey Club.'

When no one spoke up Greening continued. 'That brings us to what we think is number ten, the one that took place last weekend. Apart from the wooden cross that Li found, she had a small amount of money in her pocket along with a shopping list. From what we can gather, she was cycling into town to get a few things according to her list.'

'What about the bike?' Chambers asked.

'It was found later in the day in a small car park off the road that ran past the golf course. Unfortunately, there are no cameras on the entrance and the basket on the front of the bike just held an empty recyclable shopping bag. We're running tests to confirm that the tyre tread matches the one we found at the disturbed ground opposite the hole in the fence.'

'Ok, we've got plenty to think about. Lucy, can you check with the golf course and see if there are any cameras that look out onto the road. If this is the victim's bike we can be pretty sure he rode it away from the scene. If he did, that means he had to ride past the entrance to the golf course to drop the bike off. If there's a camera there then we might just finally get a look at the bastard.'

~~~

Monday 5th December 2011

Li had quickly been able to establish that there was a camera mounted on the slip road leading to the golf course. The problem was they had misplaced the tape of that particular evening. After she had threatened to get a warrant, the tape miraculously appeared. It seemed the management was still irate at having the course closed for almost the whole day. A copy of the tape was duly delivered by courier to the station. She called Chambers into the only office handy that still had a VCR machine. The time stamp on the tape showed 18:03:32 25/11/11 at the beginning. The images were black and white and the picture quality, as they feared, was dreadfully poor. Li ran the tape on fast forward. They could see the evening darken to night. They were looking for a man riding a woman's bike. Every so often a cyclist passed by in full view. The camera was focused on vehicles turning into the golf course slip road, while at the top of the screen they could see the main road reasonably well.

On the table in front of them was a photograph of the victim's bike for reference. They would rewind and pause the flickering tape every time they had a solo cyclist. The amount of traffic on the road was getting lighter. At 21:44:21 25/11/11, after a hiatus of 20 minutes since the last vehicle had passed by, a cyclist entered from the right of the screen. It was hard to make out, the street lamp offered the picture very little brightness, just enough to see the shape. Within several frames the rider was out of the picture. Li rewound the tape and put it on the slowest speed possible. She paused it in the centre of the frame. The bike was an identical shape to the one in the picture.

'It has the same basket. It's a woman's bike, but the rider's male. That's got to be him!' Chambers exclaimed.

They studied the still image on screen. The cyclist was wearing a dark woollen hat pulled down so it was just above his eyes and covered the whole of the back of his head. He was wearing a light-coloured T-shirt and had a dark bag and shorts on. He was wearing light-coloured shoes. They ran the tape back and forward several times. The rider never looked anywhere except straight ahead. The tape was too grainy; it didn't allow them to make out any features.

'I'll get this tape off to the lab; see if they can enhance any of it and get a print out of that frame. I'll just run the rest of the tape to make sure there's no one else. But I think this is our man,' she said as she pressed the play button on the VCR remote control.

~~~

Wednesday 7th December 2011

With no other suspects emerging from the tape, the printout of the still from the CCTV footage now took pride of place at the top of the whiteboard behind Chambers desk. There were arrows pointing to the 10 possible victims. Off to the side Chambers had put a photograph of his initial target, Hak Loong – the Black Dragon. Although he'd been sure there was no link, he had to check the blurry image of the cyclist with the partially obscured image he had. The CCTV image was just too blurry for a positive identification but there was a clear difference in the two face shapes. The man on the bike had a lean appearance while the Black Dragon had a roundish face.

Chambers was aware that the lack of progress on the case he was supposed to be working on was putting him on a collision course with Asbury. He was due back in London six weeks from the last call he had from his superior, that would mean around Christmas. Chambers knew the next new moon was on Christmas Eve. He had less than three weeks to solve one of the cases, if not both. The problem was, since the death of the informant, there had been no new leads on his original case. The trail, that hadn't exactly been red hot to begin with, was now cold. He decided to concentrate all his energy on the serial killer. If his plan backfired and they couldn't stop him before the next attack was due, he knew he might as well pack his bags and head home. Technically he was out of his jurisdiction on this and was relying on the goodwill of the Chief Inspector for his longevity on the case.

Li had extended her CCTV search, but Shek O wasn't the most technologically advanced place on Hong Kong Island and the search was still ongoing. She had also requested the CCTV footage that would show the traffic passing by the golf course earlier in the day. The killer had to approach from one direction. She just hoped it was from the village rather than from the other way. Her diligence paid off. The earlier tape that she had elicited from the course initially looked like it wasn't going to generate a result. The tape ran from 12:04:17 25/11/11. The break came at 17:46:12 25/11/11. A solitary male walking along the pavement from the village towards the murder scene. Li wasn't sure when she paused the tape. She held up the photograph of the cyclist. The image of the walker was a little clearer due to the better lighting just before dusk, but he was wearing jeans and a dark T-shirt. There were similarities – his shoes, woollen hat pulled down and the black rucksack were identical, the face though was further obscured by a pair of sunglasses. She was convinced they were one and the same; he must have come prepared with a change of clothes. She sent the tape with the time code to get another hi-res image. Although this picture was better lit this time, the face was more obscured by the sunglasses.

Wednesday 14th December 2011

They had an image of the suspect, but the reports were producing no DNA or fingerprint evidence and the frustration levels in the department were increasing daily. Li had tried to find footage of the suspect from CCTV cameras in the area without success. She had requisitioned the on-board tapes from the different bus companies, unfortunately not all of them had cameras installed. The ones she and a couple of colleagues had laboriously checked had revealed nothing. Chambers had fared no better. He had been working with Greening in trying to uncover some link between the 10 victims. If anything, the more cases they linked together just muddied the waters. The original idea of the Triad gang that had brought them together on the first two bodies was now just a distant memory. They had expats, old ladies and hikers that appeared to have nothing in common except dying on a new moon. It meant the next murder, due in 10 days time, could literally be anyone, take place anywhere and at any time of the day. This was not the news Pang wanted to hear at the update meetings that were now held on a daily basis.

Chambers knew time was running out. He had installed a 10000:1 scale map next to the images on the white board. Again no pattern was discernable. There were two murders on Lantau Island relatively close together. A murder in Tin Hau, one in neighbouring Tai Hang and also one in nearby Happy Valley. The last one was also on Hong Kong Island but a long way from the cluster of the other three. The remaining murders had taken place across Kowloon and there had been the death of the hiker in the New Territories. He returned to the tapes. There was something about the discovery that Li had made earlier. The suspect was in the shot slightly longer as he walked across the screen. It was something about the way the man moved. That was it. He had the same rolling gait that reminded Chambers of someone he knew or had seen, but who was it? He just couldn't place it.

≈≈≈

Friday 23rd December 2011

Chambers had got no further connecting the man's familiar style of walking with when he might have seen it previously, but he felt the answer was tantalisingly close. He had a dream the night before in which he was following a man wearing a black beanie hat as he walked through the busy streets of Central, but no matter how fast he ran the person he was chasing continued to walk casually just out of his reach. Finally, he caught up to the man as he stopped and waited to cross a road. Chambers grabbed the man by the shoulder pulling him round and just as the face was coming into view he had woken in a cold sweat. He had actually yelled out in frustration. He was aware that there would be another murder the following day and neither himself, Li or Greening had any new leads to go on. Again they had asked Pang to mobilise as many beat officers as was possible, which was proving to be a headache as the staffing levels over the busy Christmas period had to be taken into account.

With everything that had been going on Chambers hadn't thought much about Christmas. He was pretty much alone in a new city; his parents were back in London. He wasn't married and didn't have children. What he knew was if – or more likely when – the killer struck, the chances were the body would be discovered late on Christmas Eve or on Christmas morning. Whenever the body was found it was certainly going to ruin someone's Christmas anyway, while Chambers had a fair idea how he'd be celebrating. He and the others had been working six-day weeks since the previous murder, meticulously going over the details and reports from all of the murders. He had almost full reports in English from comprehensively writing out the translations Li was making. Even when he got home he would look over his own and the photographs from the files but could glean nothing of any relevance. However, he knew that there were answers that must be held somewhere within them, more than likely glaringly obvious, but no matter how hard he studied each page, he couldn't see anything.

Late in the afternoon, Chambers was preparing to head home. He was frustrated and angry at their combined lack of progress. He knew everyone involved was trying their hardest. But on top of everything else he had to keep sending emails filled with bogus information to Asbury. The last email he had received from his direct superior had made it perfectly clear that he was expected back in to work in Central London on Monday 2nd January 2012. Asbury had given him the week between Christmas and New Year off, so he could refocus for his return to work. Chambers knew he wouldn't be taking a holiday then and the only silver lining to this was it had effectively given him a one-week stay of execution. Would it be enough? He was putting his jacket on as he waited to see Li before he left. He found it amusing that after the long, hot, humid summer he noticed the drop in temperature, even though at home he would consider this as T-shirt weather. He glanced to his left and caught sight of a man with a familiar walk heading away down the corridor to the lifts before the windowless office doors swung shut.

He paused for a second; unsure of what he had just seen, before setting off at a run across the office. As he got to the double doors one of them suddenly opened and Chambers had to halt abruptly to stop himself crashing in to the unsuspecting young uniformed officer coming from the other direction. He could see over the officer's shoulder as one of the sets of lift doors pinged opened, the man entered and before Chambers could get half way down the corridor the doors had closed. He ran to the fire exit and headed down the four flights of stairs, charging out of the emergency exit and into the main reception hall of the police station. He stopped and looked in the direction of the lift area, it was busy with people. There were two lifts. Chambers could see one was making its way down from the fifth floor to the fourth. The other lift was already heading back up from the first floor to the second. The man he'd seen was wearing a maroon polo shirt and blue jeans. He couldn't see anyone matching that description around the lifts. He ran towards the main doors, exited and looked up and down the street; there were hundreds of people, but nobody wearing that particular outfit. He made his way back to his office and sought out the young officer he had nearly collided with at the door. He knew his face from around the office but not his name.

'Hey you,' he shouted when he saw the officer in the pantry, immediately aware his tone sounded more aggressive than he meant. The policeman was understandably giving him a wary look.

'Sorry, I just need to know if you got a look at the man in the corridor a few minutes ago.'

'Which man?' The officer didn't sound surly, it was a fair question in the busy station.

'Just now, as you were coming into the office, we nearly collided, just before that. You must have walked right past him.'

The officer took a moment, as if he wasn't sure if the question was a joke. 'Just before you? I only saw one person. The Chief Inspector's son. I think his name is Derek. Yes, Derek Pang.'

<p style="text-align:center">~~~</p>

Chapter 23

23rd December 2011 – Christmas Eve 2011

Chambers hadn't known what to do with the information. When the officer had uttered Derek Pang's name, he immediately pictured Derek walking out of the restaurant back in October. That's where he had seen that odd pigeon-toed walk before, the same as the killer's. He knew he had to tread carefully. He couldn't go straight to James, not now, definitely not now. He would need concrete proof, not circumstantial evidence and not just the fact that Pang Junior and the killer happened to walk in a similar way. Chambers consulted Li. He felt bad keeping anything from her, but Li would be in this department long after Chambers was safely back in London. If he was wide of the mark, it would be her that would be left to deal with the maelstrom of repercussions. He called her in to go over the tape once again. She was happy to comply even though she had already watched the tape hundreds of times.

'Do you notice anything distinctive about him?' Chambers asked.

'What do you mean? Apart from the items he's wearing that match what the cyclist is wearing later?'

'Yes, what about his movement, his way of walking, anything that makes him different.'

She rewound the tape and watched it again. 'He's not shuffling exactly, but he's bent forwards a little. He sort of rolls his shoulders. Nothing apart from that. Why?'

Chambers ignored the question, instead responding with one of his own. 'Can you think of anyone else that walks like that?'

'There's lot of people that walk like that. No one in particular; John, where are you going with this?'

Chambers knew he had to be careful. 'What about me? Do I walk like that? Do you? How about Jenny? Maybe James or Brian? What about Derek Pang or anyone you actually know? You said it was quite common.'

She thought for a while, before deciding to play along. 'Hmmm, out of that list I'm not sure. I think Jenny's husband walks a bit like that if you're pushing me to name someone I know, as I say it's fairly common. Now tell me what you're getting at. I know you John; you wouldn't drag me in here unless you thought you were on to something.'

'OK, just hear me out.' He began, he was struggling to find a way to make this sound casual and not like he was about to accuse the son of their boss of being the cold-blooded murderer of ten people. 'It reminded me of Derek Pang, Chief Inspector James Pang's son.'

'For Christ's sake John, I know who Derek Pang is,' her voice was raised.

'Yes, right I just wanted to clarify,' he said quietly.

Finally she said, 'look John, this case has put an enormous amount of pressure on all of us. We're all saying, doing and definitely thinking, some crazy thoughts right now. We know there's due to be another murder tomorrow, but we need to remain logical about this. I think it's going to be one hell of a long day tomorrow and right now I think you ought to go home and rest.'

He knew she was just thinking about what was best for him and didn't take the rejection of his new theory too badly. 'Lucy I'm going home, but I want you to think about what I just said. And please, for the moment at least, don't mention it to anyone else.'

'Sure John, I promise I won't. I'll see you here in the morning, OK?'

~~~

The following morning Chambers had developed a plan. Initially he'd see what Li's conclusion was. If she was open to the idea, then, either with or without her, he planned to tail Derek Pang. Chambers had been at his desk at 8am and the first thing he had done after booting up his PC was to check the police database for any information on his boss's son. Unfortunately he couldn't find any reports that were in English. He would need to enroll the help of someone but whom? He needed someone he could trust, and someone who wasn't going to report directly back to Chief Inspector Pang. The only person he thought he could trust was Li. But the question was – would she be willing to help?

She came into the department just after 8:30am. She didn't appear to be surprised to see Chambers already at his desk. She offered a quick greeting and the chance of a coffee before making for the pantry. On her return with the two coffees, she informed him that Pang had called her earlier to arrange an update meeting in his office at 9am.

They sat tapping away at their respective keyboards for 10 minutes. John looked up at the clock behind Li; it read 8:47am. It was now or never.

'Lucy, have you had a chance to think about what I said yesterday?'

'Yes, John and to be honest it's put me in a terrible position.' She stopped speaking and nodded to someone behind Chambers.

He swivelled in his chair and saw Chief Inspector Pang standing there.

'Good morning. Sorry to do this, but I've been called to an impromptu meeting. I won't bore you with the details; suffice to say the life of a Chief Inspector is not a happy lot.' He rolled his eyes heavenward. 'Before I go I wanted you to know the good news is that I've been able to enlist a larger number of uniforms than we had for last month. But this is your last chance to give me any information on where you think the attack might take place. If you have any new leads then now is the time to let me know.'

Chambers could feel Li's eyes burning a hole in the back of his head. But what could he say? Yes we have one. It's your own errant son. 'No. Sorry Chief Inspector.'

'We've got a couple of ideas at this stage Sir,' added Li, 'but they're a little, how shall I put it, left-field.'

'Lucy, at this stage I don't think we're in a position to rule out anything. I'll touch base with you this afternoon when I get back from this wretched meeting.' He nodded and left them alone.

Chambers watched him go. When he was sure the Chief Inspector was out of earshot he turned back to Li. 'Well that sounded like our plan has been officially sanctioned if you ask me.'

'John, he did nothing of the sort. And it's not our plan; it's yours and yours alone. I'm not sure I want any part of this.'

'OK, just do me one favour then, I'll leave you out of it and will take all of the responsibility.'

''That depends. What is it?'

'Can you check Derek Pang's records on the database?'

'Only if you promise that's the end of my involvement. John, my career is everything to me, if this thing blows up in our faces it will be me that's dropped in the shit. Not you.'

'OK, OK. I promise,' Chambers lied.

She shook her head and began typing.

'Nothing's coming up apart from his basic details. He hasn't got any arrests or convictions against his name.'

'Were you looking under his …'

'John,' she interrupted him, 'I told you I would search and I've looked under his western and Chinese name. Nothing. My advice is that you should leave it there.'

'Yes, OK, you're right.'

Li's mobile phone rang. She didn't look amused when she saw the caller ID. She got up from the desk and answered it as she walked towards the pantry. Chambers checked that she was out of sight before darting around the desk to look at Li's screen. He could see the results of the search. There was an address in English. He noted it down on a pad of yellow Post-It notes that were sitting on her desktop. He was comfortably back at his desk before Li returned from the pantry.

'Tell me that was a breakthrough?' he asked as Li sat down.

'No, just a personal call.' She looked distracted.

Chambers typed the address he'd written on the Post-It note into Google maps. He got a location in Mong Kok. He printed out a screen grab and as he passed Li's desk on his way to the printer, he paused.

'Lucy, look all we know is there's going to be a murder somewhere in the city at some point today. I just feel I'll be of more use out there than sitting in here getting more frustrated. I don't know what I'm going to do, but I'll be on my mobile if anything comes in.'

She nodded. 'Sure, I'll keep you posted. And John,' she called after him, 'don't do anything stupid.'

Chambers grabbed the sheet of paper off the printer, folding it in half twice and slipped it into his back pocket as he walked to the lift.

~~~

226

According to the map he was in the right street. He was looking towards where the map suggested Pang's apartment block was. The place looked familiar, but then he'd spent a fair bit of time walking around this area, and after a while one busy street of high rises looks much like another. It was only just after 10am. Chambers searched for a café or restaurant that would offer him a position with a view of the building where Pang lived. He knew it was a long shot to see Pang, if he had a job he was more than likely already there, or he could simply have gone out earlier. But what other course of action was there? If Pang was his man, then this is what he had to do. He found a small place and ordered a slice of toast and a cup of yuanyung from the menu. When his order arrived the toast had already been buttered. He took a bite; it was extremely sweet but not unpleasant. He took a sip of the hot brew and nearly spat it back in the cup. It tasted like a mixture of very strong English tea and filter coffee. Chambers ordered an additional milk tea and settled in to begin his surveillance.

≈≈≈

Li had been disturbed by the suggestion Chambers had made to her yesterday. She had known Derek Pang for several years. She'd met him a few times at various department functions. She thought him hostile and anti-social. He had asked her out on several occasions, each time she'd been able to make what she thought at least sounded like plausible excuses. There was something about him she didn't trust, but she couldn't reconcile this view with him as a serial killer. She pictured how he moved. Chambers was right about one thing, there was a similarity in his gait to the man on the tape but that was hardly enough evidence to go and arrest the Head of the Department's son. She imagined the fallout from an action as extreme as that. If they got the wrong man they would all be looking for new employment the next day. No, she knew Derek was a bit sleazy and a creep, but a murderer? She just couldn't see it.

Li was wondering where Chambers was, hoping he wasn't doing

anything to get himself into trouble. She also wanted to keep herself busy. She took out the file on the first murder. What was in there that she was missing? She typed the name of the snake into her search engine and when she'd found a suitable picture she printed it off before leaving the office.

≈≈≈

Chambers had been trying to visualise Derek's face. It was harder than he thought, although he had sat next to him for an hour at dinner; he hadn't actually looked at him that many times. He tried to think back to the face he saw when he looked out of the taxi's rear window but frustratingly he couldn't picture anything other than Derek's father's face. At 1:45pm he saw a figure exit the building and head left along the street. Chambers watched for a few seconds until he was sure. Yes there it was – that distinctive pigeon-toed walk. He turned to the waiter and called out 'mai dan' in his best Cantonese. He paid, leaving a small tip and headed out. Pang was 50 metres ahead of him on the other side of the road. Chambers held back, as long as he could see the man that would suffice for now. Pang was wearing a dark jacket over jeans and had a black bag slung over his shoulder. He disappeared from view as he rounded the corner on to the main strip. Chambers sped up and caught sight of him further up the road. Following a suspect like this was always risky. Chambers could have done with a colleague or two to help, he needed to stay in touch but not too close that he could easily be spotted.

Then disaster struck, he saw Pang break out into a jog and board a bus. There was no way Chambers could get through the crowd on the busy street in time to catch it. He saw the doors close and the bus slide away from the stop. There was nothing else he could do but go back and wait for the news of the next victim.

≈≈≈

Chapter 24 – Here Kitty Kitty

Sat. 26th November – Sat. 24th December 2011

Dear diary,

After all my hard work for reaching double figures I treated myself with a visit to my favourite prostitute, Kitty. She makes me laugh. Not with her you understand, at her. She's about 25 and I'm sure she used to be very beautiful. I've got to know her quite well over the past months. It's not all about the sex. Sometimes I come and just pay her to talk. Not me, she likes to chatter on about herself and I don't mind listening, at least that's the impression I give. She was understandably quite guarded at first, but she's become more and more relaxed the number of times I've been to see her. I think she's developed a bit of a soft spot for me as I'm always kind and attentive to her.

I don't need to go to prostitutes. I have no problem in that area. It's more about the control I have over them. I like the fact it's my decision about the who, when and where. Other women can be so unpredictable. So poor Kitty has been sharing her life story with me and it's a sad, if predictable tale. She was a pretty teenager. Her father was Vietnamese, so she had a slightly different look from the other girls she grew up with. The older boys were always inviting her out to clubs and plying her with drink. She'd been a good girl, or so she told me, but over time she developed a fondness for champagne and began dabbling in amphetamines, just a little at first to stay up late. She didn't have a job and was relying on the generosity of her male 'friends'. Before long she'd fallen for a man who, in hindsight she realised, had clearly only been interested in getting her into harder drugs and eventually on the game. By the time she was 23, she was addicted to heroin and working as a prostitute out of a tiny bedsit in TST, handing over the majority of her earnings to her pimp.

Her story, I'm sure, is no different from those of millions of prostitutes the world over. What can you do? Tough luck I say. I don't have any sympathy for her. I can feign interest for the time I'm there. It's not that long a sacrifice out of my life. Her on the other hand, how long does she have left? Not long would be my educated guess. She tells me about her plans for the future, how she wants to kick the drugs, get a good job and go back to studying. All the time I'm looking at her knowing it's not going to happen, but happy enough to smile along with her.

The funniest thing about her is that she insists on speaking in English. She told me her cousins live in Essex, just outside of London. She used to go and visit her uncle and his family every year when she was a kid and had learned the language then. Her English is quirky, it's very good and if you didn't know you'd guess she was from the south of England with her accent, but every now and again she'll come up with a phrase that's purely Chinglish, some English and Cantonese words mixed together or she'll forget her grammar. Not often, it's like her English is slightly damaged, but then so is she. Like she has a tiny flaw that runs so deep inside her it's like the whole of her is rendered worthless.

We did have sex that time. After all I was celebrating. When I left I gave her a bigger tip than normal. I knew she would be injecting something into her arm that night. I always made sure I used protection with her, you can never be too careful.

The next morning I had gone to retrieve the paper. The report in the *South China Morning Post* wasn't on the cover. It was a fairly small piece on page three. That was a surprise, they could be in no doubt it was a murder. She had about two metres of plastic wrapped around her head, which for some reason wasn't mentioned anywhere in the story.

ⴲⴲⴲ

Woman Found Dead on Golf Course

The body of a 67-year-old woman was found on the Shek O Golf Course early yesterday morning.

According to police reports, the body was that of a Norwegian woman, a long-term resident in Hong Kong. Her name has not been released pending contact with her family who are believed to reside in Norway, a Police spokesman stated. The fully clothed body of the woman was found by a worker on the course near the 11th green.

ⴲⴲⴲ

So she was Norwegian! I hadn't been able to place the accent and it had been bugging me the whole time I was with Kitty. The article was sparse on details. This time I was sure it was because the police must have begun linking everything together. I know they are on to me. I knew they'd have a hard job with DNA. I was meticulous about how I went about things. I never had any desire to be sexual with any of them. I'm not some kind of twisted pervert who gets his pleasure from tying up some old lady and molesting her. No, I was pretty confident they wouldn't have anything from me on that side of things. My concerns were about being picked out by a nosey neighbour or a CCTV camera I'd failed to see when I'd cased out the crime scenes on earlier explorations. I was intrigued as to whether the police were putting my clues together yet. Maybe I was being too clever for them. Maybe I would have to make it a bit easier for them. Yes that's what I'll do. That way I can get back on the front pages where I belong.

When I began my project, I'd be lying if I said I didn't have doubts that I would complete it. Now I have 10. Two to go and I already know who the eleventh will be. For the twelfth I have the location, but I'm still juggling a few names. As this one is the special one, I want to mark the completion of my project with someone extra special. Of course that's going to make life a little bit harder, but then that's just how it's going to have to be.

☰☰☰

'Hello Kitty,' I said to her on the phone. It was my little joke with her.

'Oh it's you. I didn't recognise the number.'

'I lost my old phone, got a new one.' I lied. 'Are you free tomorrow? I'd like to come and see you. I've got you a present.'

'A present? What for?' She sounded strange, distant, stoned or something. It was only noon, how could she be so messed up so early?

'Come on Kitty. Tomorrow is Christmas Eve. You can't have forgotten that.'

There was a pause. 'Of course not,' she mumbled. 'Sure that's sweet of you. A present. Lovely. Hey?'

'What is it?'

'Will you take me somewhere? You know, of course we will have sex, my present to you,' she laughed softly. 'But I want to go out for dinner or something. I want to feel special.'

'Of course Kitty,' I said playing along. I'll be at your door at 7pm tomorrow.'

'Oh thank you. Thank you,' she sounded like she was already somewhere else.

☰☰☰

I had to spend Christmas Eve with my family; I'd made up a bullshit excuse for not being able to attend the following day so I had negotiated a lunch with them on the Saturday instead. I won't

232

go into much detail, suffice to say I hate them all with a passion. People joke about how you can choose your friends but not your family – it's a depressing statement all the same. How come it's so difficult to get on with your own flesh and blood? Every time my father opened his mouth I wanted to stick my steak knife down his throat; that would have shut him up, permanently. I haven't decided on my final victim yet, but there were a few candidates at that meal. My father did say something interesting. He mentioned where he would be in four weeks time. It's definitely something worth considering as he'll be in the right place at the right time.

I had taken my rucksack over for dinner. I knew I wouldn't need too many things with me for this one, and if there had been any prying eyes, carrying a pair of gloves and a woollen beanie would hardly look out of place on a chilly winter's night in Hong Kong. I was fairly smartly dressed for the occasion, the one in the evening I mean. I think my family was foolishly pleased to think I had made the effort for them. Of course they were mistaken; I had done it all for Kitty.

I made my way up the stairs to her place. She lived on the fifth floor of what could best be described as a grotty tenement building in TST. There was no security guard, I guess it's because there was nothing of value to protect. The building didn't have CCTV either, but as a precaution I'd put on my hat a few blocks away as I knew there were plenty of cameras in the surrounding streets. I guess it was hard on Kitty living there; the place was like a festering sore, hidden away from the glamourous flagship designer stores and fashionable boutiques that could be found in and around the Peninsula Hotel and the new development at nearby Heritage 1881. As I was walking up the stairs to her apartment I was thinking about asking her. I'd do it in a nice way, but really I'd be sticking the proverbial knife in.

I knocked on her door and I have to say I was taken aback when she answered. She looked incredible. The dark circles under her eyes had gone. She looked as though she had really made an effort. She was wearing makeup, but had done it in such a way as to make it hard to notice. Her whole face was radiant, she was literally glowing. I could see she had her long dark hair tied back and held in place twirled around a pair of wooden chopsticks. It showed off her face, which was actually quite beautiful. I could now see why she had such a following of men when she was younger, maybe she had been telling the truth. I couldn't put my finger on what it was but I felt myself immensely attracted to her at that moment. She was wearing a soft pink silk robe. She welcomed me in and told me to sit down.

She took a bottle of champagne and two flutes from the small fridge in her tiny kitchen off the side of her living room cum bedroom. She brought them back and placed them on the wooden coffee table next to me. I had a look round the room. It was much tidier than before, she had a couple of candles burning, they were scented with something. There was an iPod station with a couple of speakers, it had been playing some sort of elevator music as I'd come in. I had often wondered who bought that kind of shit music; I was surprised it was Kitty. Well, as they say, you can't judge a book by its cover.

'I brought you a present.' I said to her.

'Oh really! How sweet.' She was beaming at me. 'Let me pour you a glass of champagne.' She turned and began unwrapping the foil from the top of the bottle.

I opened my bag and took out a paper bag. I hadn't gone to much effort; in fact I hadn't even wrapped it. I just asked the woman in the shop to put a bow around it as they were geared up for the last-minute Christmas shoppers when I'd picked out the gift yesterday. The pop of the champagne bottle actually made me jump; I must have been tenser than I thought.

Kitty let out a little excited yelp as the foam began to gush down the side of the bottle. She quickly poured two glasses that were more bubbles than liquid.

'Cheers and merry Christmas!' She passed me my glass and we clinked them together.

'Here you are,' I passed her the bag. She put her glass down and didn't seem to mind the poor wrapping as she tore it open.

'Oh how lovely.' She held it at arms' length, before pulling it to her body and giving it a squeeze. It was a soft toy in the shape of a white rabbit. I'd picked it up cheap at a store that was flogging off crap. They were left with a surplus of rabbits as the year drew to a close. They needed to clear shelf space for next year's animal.

'I love it,' she said giving it an almighty squeeze to her chest. She leaned over and kissed me on the mouth. At that moment I was filled with lust and it took me enormous amounts of self-discipline to control myself. She really looked and tasted amazing.

'I've booked us a table at Felix.' I said in an off-hand manner.

She just stared at me.

'Oh,' I said with more than a hint of disappointment in my voice, 'I thought you'd be pleased.'

She began to cry softly. 'I'm sorry,' she said and rushed off to the bathroom.

While she was in there, I took in the room again, I needed to be ready for when she came out. It was only a couple of minutes before she emerged delicately patting at her eyes with a tissue.

'I'm sorry,' she began, 'it's been so long since someone was kind to me. I'm just being silly. I'm so delighted to be going for dinner at The Peninsula. I have a beautiful dress to wear but I didn't want to believe you would really take me out. Now I want to give you your present.'

I stood up and pulled her gently towards me. I gave her a warm hug and asked her to lean over the bed with her back towards me. She did so without question.

'Can I take your hair down? It's so beautiful.' I was laying it on thick now.

'Of course, would you like me to do it?'

'No, no. It will be my pleasure.' I stepped in close behind her and removed the chopsticks, dropping them next to her on the bed. Her hair fell about her shoulders. I gathered her hair behind her, pulling it gently so that it was straight. She let out a little moan. I separated the hair into two sections and let them drop across the front of her shoulders like pig tails. As I did so I kissed her softly on the neck and could feel her body tense like an electric pulse had run through her. She was trembling ever so slightly. I waited for a few seconds before putting my hands over her shoulders and taking the opposite end of her hair in my hands and crossing them over. Immediately I pulled them tight. Her upper body came off the bed and back into me. She was a petite thing so her weight was negligible. She was fighting to catch a breath. I quickly crossed my hands again, effectively forming a double knot. I was pulling as tight as possible; I was surprised at how little fight she was putting up. I grabbed for the nearest chopstick and inserted it in the knot, turning it as much as I could, like I was applying a tourniquet. There was no fight left in her. I held her like that for several more minutes until I was sure. I placed her face down on the bed; her hair was a tangled mess under her. I fished out the chopstick I had used, it was cracked from the pressure but not fully broken, I put it down next to the other one on the bed.

The struggle hadn't been long or violent, the room was largely undisturbed. I put on my gloves and took the bottle and glasses to the kitchen sink and poured out their contents, placing all three into my rucksack. I also had some baby wipes; I cleaned the chopsticks and wiped her neck at the same time. I tried to think of anything else I had touched. I wiped the coffee table, the door that I might have inadvertently touched and considered the cuddly toy that was on the bed, but decided against it. When I was happy with the cleaning job I packed the tissues back in my bag, had one last look around then carefully opened the door. There was no one on the landing, so I slipped out and gently closed the door behind me. As I took the last flight of stairs I walked straight into a man and his 'girlfriend' – and I say that in the loosest possible sense of the word – entering the building. I nodded an apology but neither of them turned to say anything. 'Merry Christmas to you too,' I thought as I exited into the winter evening. I dropped the bottle and glasses in a rubbish bin on the way and continued to the nearby TST Station for my short journey home.

☲☲☲

Chapter 25

Christmas Day – Sunday 25th December 2011

Chambers was woken by the sun shining through a gap in the curtains. He looked at the alarm clock: 8:32am. He reached over and took his phone off the bedside table. No missed calls. He was surprised, evidently the next victim hadn't been found yet. He had been expecting a call sometime in the night. He dragged himself out of bed and took a long shower. The first thing he did when he got out of the shower was to check his phone again. Nothing. He waited until 9am then called Li.

'Merry Christmas John,' she said on answering.

'Merry Christmas to you too, hope I didn't wake you.'

'Don't worry; I've been up for hours. Have you heard anything? Did you find out anything of any use yesterday?'

'No and unfortunately no again. What about you?'

'I went to Mong Kok. I wanted to see how easy it is to buy a poisonous snake.'

'I hope that's not my Christmas present.'

Li laughed, 'no I got you something much nicer. But I did find out it's possible to buy a Chinese Cobra from there; you just need to give them a week or so to arrange it. I would hate to think what else they could get.'

'So you think that goes to show our man was definitely responsible for the first murder?'

'I think it proves it's possible. Look John, I've got to go, I've got a family brunch to attend. I'll call you as soon as I hear anything.'

Chambers had nothing to do except wait for his phone to ring. Eventually it did. At just before 4pm the call came in. It was Li.

'John, they found a body. It's believed to be that of a prostitute in TST. I'm already over on Kowloon-side. Can you make your own way here?'

'Sure, give me the address.'

Chambers was in a cab a couple of minutes after the call. He had been sitting fully dressed all day just waiting. He knew the call would come; it had just been a matter of time. The taxi pulled up and dropped him off on Hankow Road. The driver pointed to the one-way sign on the T-junction with Ichang Road. He was close enough. He paid the driver and headed towards the police car further down the narrow street that was brightly lit by hundreds of garish neon signs. As he was walking he called Li. She told him to pass the phone to the uniformed policeman who Chambers could see standing in the doorway. When he got the all-clear he walked up the three flights of stairs until he saw Li standing outside an open door. She signalled for him to follow. The apartment was tiny. There was barely enough room for the six officers and crime scene investigators. The body was lying face down on the bed. There was a pair of chopsticks, one of which was broken; there was also a soft toy in the shape of a white fluffy rabbit.

Chambers looked at Li. He didn't need to say anything, she knew what he wanted.

'The ID says her name is Karen Nguyen which as far as I know is a Vietnamese name. Neighbours say she was a drug user and were pretty sure she was a prostitute, but as she kept herself to herself and didn't make a lot of noise, they tolerated her.'

'Who found her?'

'Her friend had been calling. When she didn't get a response she came by and knocked. When she still didn't get an answer she phoned again and heard the mobile phone ringing inside. She called a male friend and he broke the door down.' Li indicated the damage around the lock.

'Where are they now?'

'We've interviewed them, got their details and let them go for now.'

'How was she killed?'

'Initial reports suggest she was strangled with her own hair. One of these things could be the calling card,' she pointed to the broken chopstick and cuddly toy.

'The wood is a common theme with the last one.' He thought about Greening saying the cross could be ten in roman numerals or written Chinese. Two chopsticks side by side looked like 11 to Chambers. Too obvious? What did the rabbit mean? Was it the colour? The fact it was a toy? He couldn't be sure.

'Are the chopsticks wooden?' Chambers leaned in to get a better look. If it hadn't been broken he would have assumed from the smooth black surface they were metal. But he could see the splinters where the wood had cracked. 'Have they been touched? Were they in a cross shape?'

'No, I'm pretty sure no one has touched them. That's how they were when I first saw them.' She turned and asked the others.

Chambers could see from the headshakes that no one had touched them. 'Well let's get them photographed, bagged and checked for prints. But I think we both know they'll be clean.' He took out his own camera and photographed the bed, the body and the objects. The room depressed him. The place was minute. How could anyone live in such a small place? What sort of existence did this poor girl have? No one deserved this. He took a look around, there didn't seem to be any signs of a disturbance.

Suddenly Chambers stood bolt upright. 'Lucy, if the door was broken down by her friends, that meant the killer must have been invited in, or at least got in without a struggle.'

'You think our man might be a client of hers?'

'Possibly. Let's get her phone back to the station and check out the numbers on it. It could give us a link to the time of death anyway.'

'Was she sexually assaulted?' Chambers asked Li. It would be too much to expect the killer was going to leave his DNA in any form at the scene. But it was a question he had to ask.

'Forensics will go over the whole scene, but initial investigations don't show any signs of a sexual attack.'

≈≈≈

Boxing Day – Monday 26th December 2011

It was Boxing Day morning and Li, Greening and Chambers were in Greening's office. None of them were particularly pleased to be there. Li had already explained to Chambers that Boxing Day was present-giving day in Hong Kong and therefore everyone's favourite part of the Christmas experience. Of course the more religiously inclined Greening had pointed out the more spiritual side of the festive period. Chambers didn't care; it was just another day to him. He had no presents apart from the one Li had just given him; he told her he would open it later. He thought she had been joking when she mentioned it on Christmas morning and he hadn't got her anything in return. He lied and said that her present was back at his place.

240

Greening had been going through the call history on the victim's mobile phone. Chambers was hoping that one of them would belong to Derek Pang. The last outgoing call on the phone was at 5pm on Christmas Eve. The number had corresponded to the contact number of the female friend, Sarah Wong, who had alerted police the day before. So they knew she was alive at 5pm. They spent an hour checking numbers in her phone against the police database. There were several calls over the preceding days to known drug dealers, takeaways and friends that were saved in her phone as favourites. The only number they couldn't trace had come in at noon the day before. The call had lasted several minutes. They had tried calling the number but it rang out. When it was checked, the number appeared to be from a pay-as-you-go phone. There would be no way of tracking the user's identity. It was a possibility that the call at noon on the 23rd had been from the killer. They were getting closer.

While they were waiting for the results of the fingerprint analysis, Greening and Li were discussing their plans for the forthcoming January holiday. Chambers wasn't really listening; he was thinking about how he could get hold of Derek Pang's mobile number without alerting suspicion. The first thing was to check her phone in case Derek's name was on there. As he was reaching over the desk to pick up the Nokia off the desk, Greening said something that caught his attention.

'Jenny, what did you just say?' he asked.

'I was just saying the good news for January is that Chinese New Year Day next year falls on a Monday so we are finally entitled to three days off. Over the last three years they have fallen across weekends so we lose some of the entitlement,' she explained.

'But I thought you said a date?'

'Maybe I did, I'm not sure, anyway it's the 23rd of January.'

'That's what I thought. You know that's the date the next murder is due to occur.'

'No holidays for us then,' Li chipped in.

'Definitely, if we can't crack this,' Greening agreed.

'So, Chinese New Year. That means there will be plenty of firecrackers, lion dancing and dragons?' asked Chambers, thinking back on the tremendously noisy and vibrantly coloured events he'd witnessed over the years in London's Chinatown.

'More dragons than lions this year.'

'Why's that?'

'Next year is the Year of the Dragon.'

'So what is this year's animal then?' Chambers realised he had absolutely no clue.

'It's currently the Year of the Rabbit.'

'Ah, well that depends on where you're from,' added Li.

'What do you mean?' Chambers was confused.

Greening explained, 'It's the rabbit in Chinese culture, but the event is celebrated in other Asian countries. Take Vietnam for instance, the new year there is called Tet.'

'Tet?' Chambers recalled hearing that name before. 'Tet, why does that remind me of the Vietnam War?'

'The Tet Offensive,' it was Li, 'was a series of uprisings across South Vietnam by the Viet Cong in January 1968 that took place on the Lunar New Year, hence the name.'

'That's it! There was a huge battle at a place called Hue. I remember seeing a TV show about it on Discovery,' said Chambers, 'I recall that it was the old capital, it had such an evocative name, the Forbidden Purple City on the Perfume River.'

Li was laughing. 'Very good Detective Inspector. I've actually been there and you're right about the name, shame there's nothing left. It was attacked first by the North Vietnamese Army and then the resulting counter-offensive by the Americans and South Vietnamese knocked the palace flat. There's nothing to see now, just an outline on the ground, in the forest where it once stood. Oh, and another thing, I don't know what perfume they were using, but when I was there the river was brown and had an odious smell.'

Chambers was impressed with Li's military and geographical knowledge. 'But what's all this got to do with rabbits?'

'Well back in the day, there weren't any rabbits in Vietnam, so in their traditional calendar they use a cat instead,' explained Li.

'And that's not the only one they change, in some countries it's a wild boar not a pig, also the goat is replaced by a sheep,' Greening added helpfully.

'Even the rabbit sometimes gets called a hare,' Li turned to Chambers, 'can you tell us what the diff...' She paused mid-sentence. She turned to the desk and began searching for something among the files.

'What is it Lucy?'

'John, I said to you the last victim had a Vietnamese name, right?' She was now reading from a sheet of paper she had retrieved from the file. 'Oh my god!' she looked at Chambers.

'Lucy what the hell is it?'

'The victim is down here as Karen Nguyen, her family name is Vietnamese. But her friend kept calling her by her nickname – Kitty.'

'Right, and?' Greening said expectantly.

Chambers saw it. 'And next to her on the bed was a rabbit.'

'Oh Christ, and she was killed by her own hair,' added Li.

'Just in case we were in any doubt, we've got references to a hare, a cat, a rabbit and we also have a Vietnamese victim.' said Chambers. But it hadn't all dawned on him.

'Hang on a minute. Oh my god, how didn't we see this?' Li looked shocked.

'See what? I'm completely in the dark here,' said Greening.

'Get on the Internet and get the list in order.' She realised she wasn't making sense. 'Get a list of the Chinese Zodiac of animals in order.'

Chambers rushed to the PC and opened the browser, he typed 'Chinese Zodiac' into Google. The first hit was one called chinesezodiac.com, he clicked on it. There was a menu that ran down the left side of the page. It read:

Rat

Ox

Tiger

Rabbit

Dragon

Snake

Horse

Goat

Monkey

Rooster

Dog

Pig

He lowered his head into his hands, rubbed his face and looked again. He read the names out loud while the others looked on in dismay.

He made a mental checklist of the victims. The hiker bitten by a snake. The death of the old man at the horse racing track. He couldn't link the third, the fourth was the hiker killed in the area full of monkeys. The next choked to death on chicken's feet, the old lady who fell to her death, suspected of tripping over her dog, the man in the aviary, he couldn't figure what the link was there.

He groaned out loud.

'What is it John?'

'The informant in Mong Kok. I just assumed the rats were left at the scene because he was a grass, a rat, but it had nothing to do with that. It's so obvious now. How did we not see it?'

The ox?' Greening asked.

'In Vietnam it's the water buffalo,' gasped Li.

'The woman on the golf course last month, the paste on the Clingfilm was Tiger Balm,' Greening said.

'Well, if it's any consolation, we know what the next one's going to be. A dragon,' Chambers offered.

'But how does that really help?' Li snapped. 'It could be anything. Where's the file for the third murder?' she asked Greening.

'Here,' Greening handed the brown file across the desk.

Li spread the contents and read out the victim's name. 'Donald Lam. Lam? Oh shit.'

Chambers picked up the copy of the newspaper report. A policeman holding a golf club. He could read the make of the brand name written vertically in white on the black rubber handle. RAM. A second sheep reference. It was all becoming sickeningly clear.

Every new moon was marked by a murder. Every murder contained its own clue. Fundamentally linked to each death was an animal from the Chinese zodiac.

'Put me out of my misery,' Chambers said to neither of them in particular. 'There are no birds on the list so how does the murder in the park link in?'

Li was already there. 'Remember there was a book at the scene John? A kids' book.'

Chambers could see the colourful hardback cover, showing a cartoon pig wearing a baseball cap. That completed the set. Eleven murders, eleven animals. 'Yes,' he groaned, 'McDull was a pig wasn't he?'

They stood in silence for what seemed like an eternity.

Greening eventually spoke, 'so were we completely wrong about the calling cards? The first six all had lighters or matches.'

Li pondered the question. 'Could it have something to do with the five elements? All of the animals in the zodiac have an intrinsic element, outside of the sexagenary cycle, of course.'

Chambers interrupted, 'You've lost me, the sexy what?'

'There are 12 animals, plus there are five elements: water, earth, wood, fire and metal. So in each 60-year cycle, you have five complete cycles of 12. Let me give you an example. Say year one is a dragon year, and the element is fire, 12 years later in year 13, it is a water dragon, year 25 is an earth dragon etc.'

'OK, I'm with you now. But you said each animal has a, what did you call it, an intrinsic element.'

'Yes. Although for example you can be a metal dragon, fire dragon etc, but the dragon itself is always the wood sign, wood being the animal's fixed element.'

'And these five elements are wood, water, earth, metal and fire?' Chambers asked.

'Correct. If memory serves me correctly, although there are five elements, only four of them are fixed elements. Wood, fire, water and metal. But why there is no earth fixed element, I couldn't tell you.'

Chambers was already thinking of the calling cards. 'So what animals are linked to the fire sign?'

Li was thinking while Greening checked on the Internet. It was Li who spoke first, 'I think it's snake, horse and sheep.'

'So that corresponds exactly with the dead matches at the first two scenes and the box of matches at the third scene. He must have been interrupted. His change of calling card to lighters had nothing to do with him being disturbed.

'No,' began Greening, leaning over and reading from the Internet, 'it says here, that the metal animals are chicken, monkey and dog, that corresponds to the three metal lighters found on the next three. We were looking for a fire link between all six. The killer had simply changed elements.'

'Yes but there was such an obvious correlation to fire, we just didn't see it.' Chambers was picturing the scene in the bathroom where the victim had been put in the bath after he was strangled. It now made sense. 'Water. That's why the rat man was drowned, or at least made to look like he had drowned. The killer needed a water link. The man on the beach was found face down in a pool of water. What was the other one in the three?' His head was reeling from all the information.

'The victim in the park,' it was Li, 'bludgeoned to death, we suspect with a frozen bottle of water.'

Greening continued the momentum, 'so who came next? Was it the lady on the golf course? She had a wooden cross, right?'

'And finally our most recent victim, Kitty, with the wooden chopsticks left on the bed next to her.'

'So now we know the next victim is going to somehow involve wood and a dragon, and we know what day he will strike, but that's not much to go on and we still don't know who he is or where he's going to kill his next victim,' Greening said with an air of resignation.

'Jenny, I have a theory. Take a seat, I'm not sure you're going to like what I'm about to say.'

≈≈≈

Chambers thought Greening had been more receptive to the revelation of whom his prime suspect was than Li had been, but it was all relative, he guessed. He also wouldn't say she fully embraced the notion.

The problem they faced in the lack of any new evidence appearing – whoever the killer was, whether it was Derek Pang or not – they wouldn't be doing anything out of the ordinary until the next new moon, which was also the Chinese New Year, on the 23rd January. The first day of the Year of the Water Dragon.

≈≈≈

Chapter 26 – Enter the Dragon, Part 1

Monday 26th December – Sunday 22nd January 2012

Dear diary,

I had to wait until the Tuesday before I saw any news of the death. I had mixed feelings when I read the report, it feels like a lifetime since I was on the front page. This one was reported as an overdose. Now I know they're onto me. Otherwise how could you explain the lack of coverage? Well, I guarantee I'll be back on the front pages next month. There's no way they can hush up my next one when I'll be performing in front of quite a large audience.

Everything is on track for my endgame. I've still to decide whether I'll put an stop to it all then. I guess I'll see how it goes. This one will have a much more personal touch about it. I'm sure the police will have some kind of criminal psychologist working on a profile of me and why I have used the techniques I have, or why I linked my victims to the Chinese zodiac. They'll be sadly disappointed when they find out the truth.

I'm going to take my time planning the next one; I already know who it is and where they're going to be on the day. I'm not saying it's going to be easy; there'll be at least a million people about either witnessing it live or on TV. This one will require a very different approach. I just need to make a few calls to be sure everything is in the right place. Someone's going to die.

ΞΞΞ

Chapter 27

Wednesday 28th December 2011

Li had compiled a report based on the discussions of the three of them held in Greening's office several days before. She had called Chief Inspector Pang to let him know they had made a breakthrough of sorts, as they were no closer to finding the killer – apart from Chambers' outlandish claims, which she had made a point of not adding to the case file. She felt bad about Chambers. He was due back in London soon and although he was a critical player in the case, part of her was willing him on to the plane home. Not for any malicious reason, she was just genuinely concerned for him. She wanted him back there saving his own job, and, more importantly, not creating waves that could destroy the very fabric of the team and along with it a series of personal and professional relationships.

She conceded he had a point, there was no one else that could even be considered as a suspect at this stage. They had no forensic leads, the only thing they had was the grainy images from the CCTV from the golf course. She decided she would appease Chambers and agree to personally investigate Derek Pang as long as he agreed to return to London to establish whether he could get clearance to come back to

Hong Kong. She hoped in the time it would take, she would be able to conclusively rule Derek Pang out of the investigation.

~~~

Chambers knew there was only one course of action left open to him if he wanted to keep his job. He booked a flight to the UK with British Airways and went back to give Asbury the bad news. He was at his desk in the West End of London for 9am on Monday 2nd January, just as he had promised his boss that he would be. Asbury called Chambers in to give him the opportunity to explain what had happened and why, not only had he come home empty handed, but also at a cost. Asbury would have to explain to his bosses where the money went and why he had nothing to show for the expenditure.

Chambers studied Asbury. He was tall and thin with short grey hair that was plastered to his skull, not in the sense of a comb-over but almost like it had been painted on. He had a particularly annoying habit of clacking his false teeth as he paused for thought. The whole upper set was false, allegedly from a rugby injury in his youth. Chambers couldn't help thinking it was more likely from a right hook someone had thrown trying to close the mouth of this tiresome man. Asbury, blissfully unaware of Chambers' seething animosity, proceeded to give Chambers a serious talking to about departmental policy and procedure while the recipient sat quiet and unemotional, accepting everything that was thrown at him. When Asbury had tired himself out – and the surprising lack of fight offered by Chambers meant Asbury didn't get the satisfaction he was looking for – the pair of them sat in silence for several minutes, save only for the occasional click clack of false teeth from the inspector whose eyes never left Chambers' face.

Eventually Asbury said, 'Come on John. I've been defending you here since the day you flew out to Hong Kong and you've done nothing but bullshit me the whole time. There's no physical evidence you've even laid eyes on the man. What happened over there? You've come back different. I want an explanation or I'm going to have to take this matter further.'

Chambers slowly reached into his jacket pocket and removed an envelope. He ran his hand over it as if he were smoothing out an imaginary wrinkle, before casually tossing it onto the table between them.

'What's this John?' Asbury's hand had already snaked out and grabbed the envelope.

Finally Chambers spoke for the first time since their meeting began 20 minutes ago. 'Sir, with all due respect, I'm requesting a period of leave. I'm owed nearly a month in annual leave plus several more weeks' time off in lieu. I hope you won't find any reason to reject it.'

Asbury tore open the envelope. He unfolded the single sheet that had a solitary paragraph that was a formal version of what Chambers had just told him. He read it again and looked over at Chambers. 'John, tell me you're not planning on doing anything stupid.'

Asbury was well aware of the other case Chambers was involved in, as he had received reports alluding to the serial killer's activities and the Black Dragon's supposed involvement.

Chambers knew how it looked, but he was entitled to a holiday and there was little Asbury could do to control what he did when he was off work. Chambers nodded to his superior, got up from the desk and made his way to the door.

'Just one thing John,' Asbury called after him.

'I'll approve it on one condition. I don't care where you go or what you do as long as you don't try to join the Organised Crime and Triad Bureau in Hong Kong. If you are on leave, then you can't, and won't, go to work for someone else. I'll be in regular contact with Chief Inspector Pang. If I so much as hear you have set foot in a police station over there, then you're going to be drummed out of the Met Police quicker than you can say "unfair dismissal". Don't slam the door on the way out, there's a good chap.' Asbury was already folding the letter and putting it back in the envelope as Chambers closed the door firmly behind him.

Fully aware of what the consequences of his actions would be, Chambers had predicted exactly the line his boss would take. He was always covering his own arse, in that sense he was a very predictable individual. This didn't make the news any easier to bear. He would just have to go back and work the case more carefully. He had requested six weeks off. He had expected Asbury to maybe negotiate the period down but he hadn't. Chambers wasn't sure if six weeks would be enough, he just had to hope it was. He booked the date for his flight back to Hong Kong for a fortnight's time. That way he'd be back in Hong Kong exactly a week before Chinese New Year which would give him plenty of time before the next attack was due. The less time he was in Hong Kong before the due date, the better for all concerned.

His thoughts turned to Li. He'd left in a hurry, only sending her a text from the airport. It read, 'Got to go and face the music. Hope to see you soon.' He hadn't really known what else to write. Things had definitely been cooler between them. He wanted to put it down to the stress of the case, but deep down he knew it had more to do with his assertion that Derek Pang was the killer. He had expected some reaction from her, but he had completely misjudged what it would be. He expected her to do everything in her power to support him. He couldn't understand why she wouldn't at least want to see if it led anywhere.

Chambers spent the best part of the next fortnight reading as much as he could about subjects he thought might be relevant. From books and websites on Chinese history and culture focusing on anything relating to the Chinese Zodiac, especially dragons, to Hong Kong's cultural activities, Google maps and finally Expedia.com to book his hotel room. He chose The Langham Hotel on Peking Road in TST. It was in very close proximity to where two of the murders had taken place. That didn't have enormous bearing on his decision. More importantly he'd been reading about the celebrations to mark the Year of the Dragon. Every year for the past two decades there was a huge float parade around the Kowloon peninsula. That meant the place would be packed with Chinese Dragon merchandise, symbolism and other assorted paraphernalia.

The other link he had to a dragon and the TST area was the statue of Bruce Lee on the waterfront at a place called the Avenue of Stars. He was vaguely aware Lee had featured in a film with dragon in the title, Enter the Dragon, but was surprised and interested to learn his Mandarin name was Li Xiaolong, or 'young dragon'. He knew both ideas were tenuous to say the least, but he was going to have to take a gamble. He needed to be somewhere and this was as good a place as any. Also, he wouldn't be too far from Derek Pang's address and he had a week to see what this man Pang was really all about.

~~~

While Chambers was away, Li was keeping the promise she made to herself. She had received Chambers' text message from the airport and she wasn't sure if or when he would be coming back. She was pleased for him, happy that he had decided to do the right thing. Although his departure date was known, the time leading up to the actual day was a blur of activity and before she knew it he was gone. She knew if it was at all possible he would be back in Hong Kong before Chinese New Year. He had invested too much energy and got so close to this case, she knew he couldn't leave it alone. He would be in touch when he returned, of that much she was sure.

Li had checked Derek's records, she hadn't lied to Chambers – there were no convictions or arrests or any reports of misdemeanours. She took down his address and mobile phone number and decided to see if she could get anything from his father. She called James on the pretence of updating him on the case and brought the topic round to the forthcoming Chinese New Year celebrations – the most important

Hong Kong family occasion on the lunar calendar. She asked him whether he would be celebrating at home with family or out with friends. Pang had explained that he was expected at the Chinese New Year Night Parade event in TST. He would be there in an official capacity, "full battle dress and best behaviour" he had joked. The following day he would be having dinner with his wife and son. Here was Li's chance to ask him how Derek was getting along, she said she had seen him at the National Day but not had a chance to speak to him.

Pang went silent, before muttering something about Derek acting very strangely over the past few years, mixing with the wrong crowd and not studying hard enough. He was living in Mong Kok and had little to do with his family. He told Li Derek would turn up for family events if it was demanded, like the other week for the Christmas weekend and again for Chinese New Year but apart from that they had little contact. Li could hear the loss in Pang's voice. From the time she had known the Chief Inspector, he had doted on his only son. Whatever had happened to the two of them was tearing Pang's heart in two.

He surprised Li by making a plea to her. She knew Derek, would she do the Chief Inspector a favour and ask Derek to accompany her to the forthcoming Night Parade? Li was put on the spot. If Derek was the killer, he would either have already killed or would be looking for a victim that very night. However, she thought, this might actually work in her favour. She agreed and Pang told her his son's mobile phone number. She wrote down the same details for the second time in just a few minutes.

Li waited several days before calling Derek. She wanted to get her story straight, plus she was in no particular rush to speak with him. She waited until the morning of the 11th before ringing. He answered and they made small talk, of course he remembered her, the good-looking cop that worked with his dad. Sure he'd like to go for lunch. Was he still living Kowloon-side? She had an appointment up there next Wednesday, how about they meet for lunch? That would be perfect. He told her where he lived and she would call him on the following Wednesday morning. She hung up. She noticed her hands were shaking almost imperceptibly. Was she beginning to suspect Derek as well? There was something in his voice that had unsettled her.

Li spent the rest of the week corresponding with Greening and rereading the case files, trying to find anything that would link any of the victims to Derek Pang. The more she looked into the files and reconstructed the events in her head, the more the killer's appearance began to resemble Derek Pang.

~~~

Monday 16th January 2012

Chambers arrived back in Hong Kong and checked into his hotel in TST. His first thought was to call Li, but he decided against it. He wanted to have a few days tailing Pang, hopefully finding something of interest before alerting anyone at the OCTB that he was back in town. The longer he went incognito, the longer it would take for Asbury to find out what he was up to. On Tuesday afternoon he felt suitably refreshed from the long flight to take a walk along Nathan Road to Mong Kok. He was back at the same restaurant opposite Pang's building that he had been at several weeks previously. He took up a position and waited. He knew he was unlikely to see much activity as it was after 3pm before he got to his viewing position. Not long after 7pm he saw Derek walking along the street, obviously heading home. He was dressed casually with a black rucksack slung over his shoulder. While he was waiting, Chambers was formulating a plan. If he could establish that Pang had a routine, even a job, then there was a possibility that he could gain access to Derek's residence while he was out. That way he could hopefully find the evidence he needed to get back to Li before it was too late.

The next morning Chambers was back at the restaurant shortly before 7am. He wanted to make sure he was there if Pang happened to be an early starter. He needn't have bothered. The first time Pang left the building was around 10:30am. Chambers got ready to follow him, but he went to the nearby 7-Eleven, bought a paper and a canned drink and went back into his building.

Another couple of hours passed before Pang emerged again. He was talking on his mobile phone and looking both ways along the street, finally he began waving. Chambers looked up the street and couldn't believe his eyes. Lucy Li was walking towards Pang, calling to him and waving. Chambers immediately grabbed for the nearest menu to hide his face. What the hell was going on? Was this why Li had been reticent when he had told her of the link to Derek? Was she dating Pang?

Chambers' world had just been turned upside down. It was a hammer blow to think that she was dating him, and if she was, just how much information had she been passing on? No wonder the murderer was always one step ahead. He knew he needed to be rational; he was letting his personal feelings for Li cloud his judgment. Right now he needed to act like a detective.

Chambers followed them as they walked back along to the junction with Nathan Road; they were talking and laughing but not holding hands or being particularly close. They picked a restaurant on the ground floor. He couldn't do much more than walk past and carry on towards TST and his hotel. Then he changed his mind and circled back to his restaurant of choice. He just needed to confirm something. Within an hour Pang returned alone, and headed into the apartment block. It was nearly 2pm. At least Pang had returned alone, that was something positive, but what was he doing having clandestine meetings with one of the investigating detectives? He knew he owed Li at least the chance to explain.

He decided against sitting and waiting for Pang to make another move, as it appeared to Chambers that he didn't work, but realistically, his best source of information on Pang was now Li. As he made his way back on foot to The Langham he walked past two of the murder scenes, taking time out to have another look at the aviary in Kowloon Park as it was only a couple of hundred metres from his hotel.

≈≈≈

Li hadn't enjoyed the lunch. Pang had been superficially friendly, but had then spent the rest of the hour responding in a guarded manner. He had been particularly anxious to find out why she would have got in touch all of a sudden, had it been for personal reasons or was his father involved? Li had tried her best to get him to relax and enjoy the lunch, skirting around his questions, although she was aware he could see through her pretence. As the meal wore on, she brought the subject around to the Chinese New Year.

She told him a story of splitting up with her boyfriend who had been planning to take her and now her best friend was heading out of town. She enquired if he was going to attend and whether he would mind escorting her. Li had been hoping to elicit a response that could effectively rule him in or out of the investigation. If he was relaxed and agreed to take her, it would indicate to her he had nothing better to do, like killing someone for example. Unfortunately his reaction was quite the opposite. He wanted to know why she was interested. They hardly knew each other, and surely she had more than just one friend. He had no inclination for being nearly crushed to death with thousands of other people on a cold night just to see some gaudy floats go by, it was his idea of hell. He had more important things that demanded his attention.

When she pressed him, he refused to answer. She had to be careful this didn't turn into a police interrogation. She knew she was already on thin ice, and tried to change tack although it just meant asking him more questions. She asked him how his work was going and was surprised to hear he was out of work. She knew he was bright and had a degree, so why wasn't he working? For the first time over the meal he opened up slightly. He told her how he had been delighted to get his degree in Traditional Chinese Medicine, but had struggled to find work. His father had been less than supportive since he made his university choice as he believed his son should have been studying to be a doctor or lawyer, rather than this old-fashioned hocus pocus that no sensible modern Chinese person took seriously. It had affected their relationship irrevocably. Of course his father would still maintain in public he was the injured party and would put on a great show of offering his son an olive branch, but when he showed up at the family home it was business as usual. The patriarch issuing orders to his wife and son and letting them know in no uncertain terms who was the wealthy and successful one in the family.

As the meal came to an end, Li again offered Pang the opportunity to escort her to the forthcoming celebrations and again he declined. Instead he offered to take her out for dinner on the night after. She felt she had little choice but to agree, even though she knew it might mean dining with a man who had killed his twelfth victim just the day before. They parted company and Li had mixed thoughts about the man. More than anything, she felt sorry for him. She'd heard another side to her boss, one she couldn't immediately associate with the kindly but firm Pang she knew from work. She did know that many of her colleagues were vastly different to the personas they showed in the office. The only one she thought was the same in and out of the office was Chambers; she wondered what he was up to in London right now.

Thursday 19th January 2012

By the afternoon, Chambers felt he had spent enough time drinking strong tea laced with condensed milk and staring at the building across the road. His teeth hurt and Pang still hadn't set foot outside so far that day. Plus he had hardly slept. He'd tried to blame it on jetlag but he knew it was the nagging in the pit of his stomach about Li and Pang's relationship. He went for a walk towards the Ladies' Market that would soon be opening its stalls of copy watches, knick-knacks, fake clothes and anything else you could think of from T-shirts for dogs to the latest iPod covers, there was something for all and everyone in between. He pulled his phone out and called Li's number.

'John, hi, how are you? Are you back?' She sounded genuinely pleased to hear from him.

And why wouldn't she? They were colleagues, they worked well together; he needed to put these negative thoughts out of his head. 'Hi Lucy, guess what?'

'You're back in Hong Kong!'

Chambers paused; did he want her to know he was back in the city? Would she tell anyone? He realised the signal from his phone would probably identify that he was calling locally rather than internationally. 'Yes, I'm back, but I need you to keep it to yourself.'

'Why John? What's happened?'

He lightened the tone with a chuckle. 'Nothing serious, I'm just waiting for the paperwork to be authorised. It should be cleared by Monday, until then I want to do things by the book, so I'll stay out of the station, just easier that way for all concerned.'

'OK, sounds like the less I know the better.'

'So how's the investigation going? Any new leads?' He tried to sound casual, but was not sure that he succeeded.

'No, not really. No further on since you left a couple of weeks ago. We're looking at possible attack sites. The obvious ones are along the parade route in TST.'

'Exactly what I was thinking, but then the other ones didn't have any such obvious connections.'

'Right, but this is the one that completes the cycle. The twelve animals, beginning with the snake and ending with the dragon. My guess is that this one is to be his pièce de résistance if you like.'

261

'You think it's going to be more obvious?' He hadn't considered the option.

'That's my guess. I think he wants people to know. We've managed to keep a lid on the murders so far, some by luck, but latterly through the interventions of James Pang.'

'I know some of the early murders were mistakenly identified as accidental death in the press. But what has James been up to?'

'Since you've been gone, he managed to keep the whole of the last murder out of the paper and personally intervened with the family of the Norwegian lady killed on the golf course. He told them it was imperative to the success of the ongoing investigation. He's worked wonders.'

'He's done very well. I think you're right, I think our killer is looking for a big pay off with this next one. Talking of killers, any further evidence on Derek?' Chambers tried to make the comment sound light.

'I see you haven't moved on John.' There was a long pause. 'Personally, I just don't think he did it. I think you're wasting your time and energy there.' She sounded annoyed.

'I don't see why you're protecting him. His father is doing a great job, yes, but does that mean the son can't be a killer?' His voice was much louder; he received several quizzical looks from passersby as he walked through the market.

'This isn't the time or place to be having this discussion. Are you back in the same place? I'll come over tomorrow if that's OK with you.' She appeared to have calmed down.

'No, I've moved. I'm now at The Langham, the TST one. Call me when you're on your way. How about lunchtime?'

'Sure, speak to you then.' She hung up.

Chambers was left standing in the market, not sure what he'd gained from the call. He felt more confused than ever about Li's relationship with Derek Pang. She had got him thinking about the parade that would be taking place in a few days. He walked back out to Nathan Road and took a cab to the Star Ferry pier. He knew there was a tourism centre there. He wanted to collect any literature on the forthcoming parade.

When he arrived, he found the office decked out in colourful cartoon dragons and red lanterns. He asked one of the staff for parade literature and was duly handed an assortment of pamphlets, guides and maps for the event. He asked the lady serving him to point out where the parade route would run, so he could visualise the basic map that he was now holding. Once she'd pointed out a couple of nearby landmarks it became much clearer.

He decided to walk the route. He began by heading out to the right along the pedestrianised part and took a detour to visit the Avenue of Stars, the city's tribute to its famous celluloid history. The walk offered Chambers some great views of the harbour and Hong Kong Island. He stopped to look at the names of the 'stars' on the pavement; they'd copied the Hollywood style of putting palm prints in the wet cement. He had to be honest, he didn't recognise many of the names, but he immediately recognised the statue of Bruce Lee. Already there was a throng of tourists getting their pictures taken while pulling the same pose as the iconic statue of the kung fu legend. Chambers stopped to assess the location as a possible murder site. It was too open, there was nowhere to be easily concealed, and on the night, the place would be packed with tourists and locals.

He walked all the way along to the end and then back towards where workmen were busy building the temporary seating that would mark the beginning of the parade. They had already fenced off another area where, Chambers guessed, the performers and floats would gather before the parade began. This was definitely a place that could be considered. Judging by the pictures in the brochure from the previous year's event, there were an enormous number of artists in costumes both on and accompanying the floats. Would the killer choose the waiting area? There would be plenty of activity before the parade, making it relatively easy to slip into the backstage zone and murder someone in one of the many shadowy recesses of the Hong Kong Museum of Art building that hemmed the area in.

He walked the rest of the route around the tip of Kowloon; it was still too early for the roads to be blocked off. From how busy these streets were, he guessed this would only take place on the day, maybe even the afternoon of the event to allow the traffic to flow as long as possible beforehand. Until the barriers went up he couldn't imagine how packed the place would be. He would need to try again on the day, and hope he had picked the right place or all this planning would be for nothing.

Friday 20th January 2012

Li arrived at 12:30pm, she had called him in advance and they had arranged to meet in the Main St. Deli, on the ground floor of the hotel. Chambers was surveying the menu when she arrived, he was thinking about the Ultimate 54 Burger, but when he saw the prices he regretted choosing this place to dine and not one of the local places just across the road. The cost of the hotel was making a sizeable dent in his savings.

'You must have money to burn John,' she waved to him as she entered the small ground floor restaurant.

He got up and greeted her, not sure whether to shake her hand, kiss her on the cheek or give her a hug. He tried to do a combination of all three. She simply stepped back to avoid the clumsy attempt, then leaned in and gave him a peck on the cheek.

'Great to see you.' She gave him that special smile of hers.

They ordered and made small talk. The case was no further along, Pang was drafting in more officers. She had been able to persuade him to focus on the parade. It seemed logical to everyone. If the murder was going to take place in the far reaches of the New

Territories or on one of the outlying islands, there was little they could do to prevent it.

She gave him an update from Greening. Forensic examination had linked wool fibres from seven of the crime scenes that could be from a piece of the killer's clothing or more likely, Greening concluded, from a pair of gloves. This was positive evidence, although they both knew the man who was responsible for one was responsible for the other ten. There had also been a photo fit of the man seen at the golf course. This was done to give Pang a chance to get more people out on the streets. Li had brought a copy. It was fairly generic, Chambers didn't think there was much of a resemblance to Derek Pang, but the details below the picture which stated that the man was 25-40 with a slim build did fit the description of Pang – as well as most of the young male population of Hong Kong. Next to the photo fit was an enhanced still from the CCTV camera. This picture did remind him of Pang, but it was very blurred. The face was impossible to see. Just the shape of the face. It wasn't much to go on and if anyone was inclined to make a citizen's arrest – the stations across the city would be inundated with people fitting this vaguest of descriptions.

The conversation moved on to the plan for Monday. They really had precious little evidence, while Chambers wasn't officially supposed to be there. It was agreed that Li would follow the plans of the Chief Inspector. Chambers, on the other hand, would try to find the best vantage point.

'I was looking into the 60-year cycle you were talking about. It's fascinating stuff, I have to say.'

'Yes, the whole philosophy is of great interest to me. Did you find your birth element and animal?' She knew it was the first thing everyone would look for.

'Sure, I'm the year of the monkey and the element is earth. Maybe that's why I was scared of the water buffalo that day, a little monkey and that huge beast on the beach,' he laughed.

'Oh yes I remember, big tough DI John Chambers, frightened of a harmless buffalo that was lying down at least a hundred metres away,' she joined in laughing.

'So what's your animal and element?'

'Come on John, if I told you that, then you'd know how old I am! You should know a lady never tells,' she was back to the old Li, toying with him.

He realised he had given away his age, it would be easy enough to ascertain his birth year. When he'd been reading about the cycles it dawned on him the killer had to be very familiar with the intricacies of the zodiac. Could it be possible that he was a dragon sign? There would be a certain symmetry to it. For that theory to work it would mean the murderer had to be 24, 36 or 48.

Chambers knew it was an abrupt change in direction and the dynamic of the conversation but he had to ask.

'Just out of interest, do you know when Derek Pang was born?'

'No John. Look we've been over this before and I'm not going to tell you again. I'm not following up on Derek Pang. I have no idea about such details.'

'So you haven't seen him since he was in the station a month back.'

'No John. Now let's change the subject. In case you didn't know we've got a murder investigation taking up a lot of the department's time.' She signalled to the waitress.

Chambers had watched to see if she would make eye contact, but she hadn't when she denied having seen Pang.

'So who do you suspect? You must have someone in mind?' Chambers knew the words sounded vindictive.

'I've changed my mind, I'm not hungry. I'm going back to the station. Call me when you've decided to act like a normal human being. I've got too much to do to be worrying about your madcap schemes. I thought the trip back to London might have shaken some sense into you, obviously not.' She got up from the table and put her jacket on.

Chambers waited until she got to the door before saying 'Are you sure you're going to Wan Chai and not for lunch with anyone in Mong Kok?'

She stopped at the door and looked back at her friend. She stared at him for several seconds before shaking her head and walking out. He ate both their dishes when they arrived and contemplated on how he possibly could have handled the situation better. At least she knew he was aware that she had been lying to him. Maybe that would force her hand in explaining things to him. The next move would have to come from her.

Saturday 21st January 2012 – Sunday 22nd January 2012

Chambers had spent the afternoon back in Mong Kok, hoping to see either Pang or Li or both of them together. He would give her until Monday morning to get in touch, if she didn't he'd give her a call. If she was still unwilling to explain why she was with Pang earlier in the week and why she was covering it up, then he would have to take matters into his own hands.

Over the weekend, he made several sightings of Pang, but none of Li. He followed Pang as best he could; he certainly didn't want to give away his presence, which meant he lost Pang every time. However, Chambers hadn't been too concerned as Pang's activities were mainly grocery shopping and the occasional lunch out. There was little in his activities to suggest he was planning a murder.

~~~

Chapter 28 – Enter the Dragon, Part 2

Monday 23rd January 2012

Dear diary,

Today is the big day. I've been working on my 'special' project for almost a year now and if everything goes to plan, then by the nightfall I'm going to be the most famous person in Hong Kong.

I've packed my bag already. I've got my trusty gloves; I've used them on every occasion. Although I'm not sure if I'll need them this time, I'll bring them along for luck. I have my tape, camera and a hammer, but they are just my essential toolkit, my good luck charms so to speak, they've been with me on every job so it seems foolish to leave them behind this time. Plus I picked up this fake gun the other day from the a toy shop down the road. It's just a kid's plaything, but it looks particularly menacing from a distance. When I need to make my getaway, I think I'll need it, wave that in a few faces and people will be sure to let me go past without any bother, plus it will hopefully knock the wind out of any 'have a go' heroes.

This is it. I'm ready. Everything is in place. It's time for me to pay a little visit to the man who has made me like this. Through his mental and emotional bullying over the years he has moulded me into the monster I know I now am. This creature of hate, that thrives and survives on causing misery and destruction to others. But I feel no remorse. The world is full of arseholes. All I have done is remove a few grains of sand from the beach.

Wait. Someone's just knocked on the door, that's very unusual. I seriously hope it's not the police. That wouldn't be good, not when I'm so close to completion. Please not now. Don't let it be them.

ƎƎƎ

Chapter 29

Monday 23rd January 2012

Chambers woke at 8am feeling decidedly uneasy. He knew that the events due to unfold over the day were going to have far reaching consequences on his career. He felt even more anxious when he looked at his phone and saw there was still no attempt from Li to get in touch with him. He needed to speak to her to coordinate their plan for the day. He showered and headed down for the hotel's vast buffet breakfast, although when he entered the restaurant the smell of the sizzling bacon, normally so appealing to Chambers, this time just increased his queasiness. He settled for tea and a slice of dry toast. The nervous sensation surprised him; it was a long time since a case had affected him physically. Maybe it was because he knew this would be his last chance to catch the killer. There was no way he could afford to stay here for another month. When the clock showed 9:30am he called Li. He was a little surprised when there was no answer – it just wasn't like her. Maybe she was still pissed off at him. He waited a few minutes and tried again but hung up when it connected to her message bank. He sent her a message – 'Sorry about the other day, call me when you get this. Pls.' Not the kind of positive omen he was hoping for today of all days.

Instead of sitting idly waiting for his phone to ring, he decided to walk the parade route once again. The heavy barriers still hadn't been placed across the street but sat piled along the kerb. The streets were now covered in all manner of red and gold decorations on every conceivable surface. There were also banners stretching high over the main streets. He tried to imagine just how busy it would be later in the evening. The parade was due to start at 8pm so he would need to be back before then to establish a good observation point, but to see what exactly? He had no idea. The grandstands that had been getting built a few days before were now finished, with ticket booths set up at the entrance points. He went back to the tourism office near the ferry to purchase a ticket for a grandstand seat that overlooked the beginning of the parade. He needed hassle-free access to as much of the evening's proceedings as possible.

≈≈≈

Li had been angry with Chambers when she first left the restaurant, but she wasn't one to hold a grudge or let a disagreement cloud her judgment. She was convinced he acted and said things out of genuine belief, not because he was naturally malicious. But the thing that bugged her was how had he known she had met with Derek Pang? The only way she could see, was that he'd been following her and had obviously been back in Hong Kong longer than he had initially said. But why would he lie about it? It simply didn't make sense to her.

She put it to the back of her mind and focused on one of the more positive points he had raised. She had picked up on his comment about the killer, whoever it may be, possibly being born in the year of the dragon. When she got back to her desk she checked Derek's file and compared his date of birth to that of a Chinese Zodiac chart she found on the Internet. It was a match. She was pleased that Chambers wasn't privy to this piece of information as she knew what he would do with it. But did it really mean anything? Everyone had a one in twelve chance of being born under the dragon sign.

When she arrived at the office early on Monday morning, she had gone the pantry and taken out two mugs from the cupboard, before realising Chambers was no longer there. She thought about putting one back before proceeding and making two cups as normal. Instead of going back to her desk, she headed down the corridor carrying the two coffees. She rapped her knuckles on the door and waited. She heard the scraping of a chair on the tiled floor before the door opened. She handed one of the mugs to Jenny Greening, who invited her in.

'Wow! Thanks.' Greening said taking the cup, 'you're in early,'

'Today's the big day isn't it? But can I ask you a couple of things?' Li felt confused, normally she was decisive and clear headed, but since Chambers had become so obsessed with Derek as the killer, she had started to see evidence linking the crimes to him. Was she making more than was really there? Surely Greening would give her an objective opinion. 'It's about Derek Pang.'

'Oh no, not you as well.' Greening raised her eyebrows. 'Sorry, I just think John's theory is a bit desperate.'

'So you don't think it could be him? I've got serious reservations, but there are a couple of things that point in his direction.'

'Like what? I thought the only thing John has is the passing similarity in walk and build.'

'Yes, plus his date of birth shows he was born in the year of the dragon. Also the criminal psychologist's profile that Pang authorised last week suggests our killer is a loner, under 35, single, unemployed, who has serious relationship issues with his father.'

'Lucy, I've read the report as well, but let's be honest, whenever we've brought in a profiler, they always come up with the same results. Single, problems with holding down a job, making friends, etc etc. In my opinion that's about as accurate as that photofit we've got. It rules more people in than it rules out, it's just so generic.'

'Yes, but as you say, it's not ruling him out, is it?'

'No, but your idea of the year of the dragon, it's a coincidence. I mean, there's two of my family born in the year of the dragon. Ian is, I know that. A long time ago when we first met, it came up in conversation. Of course Ian being Ian dismissed it as a lot of mumbo jumbo. It hasn't stopped me though, I love buying him birthday gifts that have some relationship to a dragon, admittedly just to annoy him,' she laughed.

Li appreciated the lighthearted break in the conversation. 'Like what?' she said before taking a sip of her coffee.

'Oh you know, a tie with dragons on it, a lovely red silk dressing gown with a huge golden dragon on the back, which he loves by the way, that sort of thing. Think about it, I bet you've got family born in the year of the dragon.'

She was thinking of what ages – 12, 24, 36, 48, 60 – her father was 60 so he was probably one of the people born in the dragon year. She nodded, ' yes I see what you mean, it could be a coincidence. But what else have we got to go on?'

'There's one thing that's been nagging away at me but I don't know if there's anything in it,' Greening seemed unsure of something.

'Go on,' prompted Li.

'It could be nothing, but I've got a notion the murderer is well versed in forensics. Nearly every crime scene is clean. There are no fingerprints, fluid samples or anything of any forensic value. Apart from the sunglasses, what he leaves at the scene, I think is deliberate. He intends for us to find it. The murder weapon is normally removed and we've yet to find one except for the golf club and judging by the brand, I'm not so sure it wasn't left there on purpose.'

'Are you saying he could be a policeman?'

'I wouldn't rule it out, or he could work in the medical profession or had some forensics training. Either that or he's read or watched a lot on the subject of murder and murder scenes. As I said though, it's just something to consider.'

Li thought it over, it was a possibility and no worse than any other ones she had at the moment. She changed the subject. 'What are your plans for today, are you rostered on all day?'

'I'll be in here until 6pm or so, then I'm heading to the parade, Ian has got himself nominated to make one of the welcoming speeches. God only knows how he did it or why.'

Li knew exactly why. Ian Greening would have the chance to rub shoulders with the Chief Executive of Hong Kong and all his cronies, plus there was the salient fact that the whole show would be televised, not just in Hong Kong but all over China as well. He really would do anything for publicity. 'How nice for him.' She couldn't conceal her sarcastic grin.

'Don't get me started. You know what a media whore he is.' They were both laughing now. 'What about you?'

'I have a few things I want to look into. Then I'll be working at the parade, I'm just waiting for confirmation of the briefing time. He's going to strike again today or tonight unless we can stop him. I think it's going to be a long 24 hours.'

'Hmmm, it's not going to be a lot of fun. I'm on call for the next 24 hours so get in touch with me if you need anything.'

'Will do, see you later.'

Just as she got back to her desk she had a sudden thought. She put the coffee cup down, woke her PC and began typing. When she found what she was searching for she took a pen from her top drawer and wrote the address on the pad of yellow Post-It notes that were on her desk, peeled off the slip of paper and quickly headed in the direction of the lift.

Something Greening said had resonated and led Li to a disturbing conclusion: it couldn't be, could it?

~~~

It was nearly 2pm and Li still hadn't called Chambers back. He had tried several more times with no response. He had left several voice messages. This wasn't like Li at all; she was too professional and conscientious to be ignoring him. Although he didn't want to let too many people know he was back in Hong Kong, he knew he had to call Jenny Greening.

'John, how delightful. I didn't know you were back in town.'

'I've not been back long, trying to keep a low profile, you know? Sorry to be so short, but is Lucy with you?'

'No, she was in earlier, about half past eight, but I haven't seen her since then. Is everything OK with you?' Greening thought it was strange Li hadn't mentioned seeing John.

'Can you do me a favour and give her a call?' He didn't want to have to explain the whole story to her.

'Of course, I'll call her now. And call you back in a minute. Any message you want me to pass on?'

'Just ask her to call me, it's urgent. Thanks Jen.' He hung up and waited.

Two minutes later the phone rang, Jenny's name came up on the caller ID.

'Jenny, hi, what's the story?'

"John, she's not picking up. She's probably in a meeting offsite, she told me earlier she'd be going to a briefing about tonight so she could be at that. I went and checked and she's not at her desk. I think she went straight out after she left my office.'

'What time was that?'

'Before nine. What's going on John?'

'I'm not sure, look when she calls let me know as soon as you can, OK? And if she contacts me first I'll let you know. One last thing, how well does she know Derek Pang?'

'I couldn't say, not very well to my knowledge. She was in here earlier talking about him being born in the year of the dragon, but she never mentioned them being friends or anything like that.'

Chambers couldn't believe what he just heard. 'I've got to go, I'll call you soon.' He rang off.

So if Li had followed up on his question about when Derek was born, it suggested to Chambers that Li might not actually be involved with him. She could have been following up her own line of enquiries into Pang, but why was she being so elusive about it? Right now though, he knew the most important thing was finding her. She'd been out of contact for about five hours. His instinct told him something was wrong. It was time Derek Pang received a visitor.

~~~

Li had taken a taxi to Mong Kok. There was one man she was keen to see, although she wasn't sure he would be particularly pleased to see her, but she wanted to keep the meeting as informal as possible. She waited outside the building, steeling herself before she entered the rundown lobby and calling the lift. As she stepped out onto the landing she looked both ways before locating the right apartment. She took a deep breath and walked over to the door, it was imperative to appear as casual as possible. She knocked three times. From inside there were noises, there was no mistaking that someone was inside. It was now or never. She definitely heard the sound of typing, then some heavy footsteps and something that could have been the sound of a zip opening.

The footsteps got closer, finally the door opened and the man who now framed the doorway said, 'Come in Lucy, I've been expecting you or one of your colleagues for quite a while now.'

Before she could say a word, he brought his arm from behind his back to reveal a revolver pointing directly at her stomach. 'I said come in, and don't say a fucking word.'

Immediately she knew she had made a mistake. Her police-issue pistol was still in its holster at the back of her belt. She was regretting using the informal approach, and as she stepped in he directed her to sit on the sofa. She took in her surroundings, she saw a black rucksack on the coffee table in front of her, she was trying to visualise the one in the picture from the golf course, was it the same one? Suddenly she felt something being yanked down over her face. She realised he had pulled a balaclava or something similar over her head.

'Now unclip your gun and police radio. Do it nice and slowly.'

She did as she was told. She took her Sig Sauer P250 and placed it down on the table in front of her. She was aware she could just make out shapes through the material of the hood. She had to stay calm. When he went out, which he would surely have to do, she could make good her escape. She felt a shiver run through her body as she realised that maybe she had just given him his twelfth victim. It was imperative that she regain some semblance of control of the situation. As she opened her mouth to speak to him, she was slammed forward, a searing pain in the back of her head. Then nothing.

≈≈≈

Chambers was back in Mong Kok, the cab dropped him outside the restaurant that was fast becoming his second home. He waved at the owner who was outside wiping down the Formica tables, but declined the invitation to have a cup of his powerful tea. After jogging across the street he slipped into the building's foyer. There was an old man who was probably the security guard, but he showed little interest as Chambers marched past and pressed the lift button. As he waited, he pulled out the piece of paper he had scribbled the address on. When the lift arrived he rode it to the 15th floor.

The lift doors opened and he peered out on to an empty hallway. He looked at the sign and followed it to the door he was after. He banged on it several times while shouting 'Police open up'. There was no sound from within. He waited 30 seconds and when there was still no response, he took a few steps back and shoulder-charged the door. He felt the lock buckle but it didn't break. He leaned back and used the sole of his foot to break the door's remaining resistance. On the third kick the door flew open. He cautiously leaned in. He could see the place was quite small. The distance from the doorway across the room to the far wall was only about 10 metres, with three doors off to the left in an alcove in the wall and a small galley kitchen immediately on his left. These two areas were clearly empty.

There was a sofa half-way into the room, facing the television on the far wall. He crouched down so that he could see under the sofa, there was no one there. He stepped into the room, and could see a small balcony leading off from the far right wall, but it was small, only big enough for one person maybe, but again it was empty. He made his way past the small dining table to the recess on the left that had three doors, one on each side. He was vaguely aware of some voices coming from back out in the hallway. Nosey neighbours surely alerted by the commotion he made smashing the door down and now coming to investigate.

Chambers paused then leaned in and listened at the first door. He couldn't hear anything over the hum of the refrigerator and the voices outside that were gradually getting louder. He reached down and turned the handle, opening it a crack. The room was dark, almost pitch black. He opened the door further, but still he couldn't see anything. He slid his hand in and along the wall, luckily finding a light switch. He flipped it, the single bulb in the ceiling snapped into life, revealing a room with a desk on which was a computer. Next to the modern looking flat screen of the PC was a journal of some sort, there was an office chair and a fully laden book case, but nothing else. He stepped back and slowly turned to the second door. The light switches for the room were on the wall outside; he flipped them then turned the handle, gently pushing the door open with his foot. It was a bathroom, just long enough for a small bath and sink on one side and a toilet at the other end, the white shower curtain was extended around the bath. He leaned in and pulled the opaque shower curtain back, to reveal nothing but an empty bath.

There was now only one door left. He listened again but could hear nothing from inside. He turned to see two people standing in the doorway looking at him quizzically. By putting his finger to his lips he signaled for them to be quiet; they looked on transfixed but, fortunately for Chambers, in silence. He tried listening again but still there was silence. He took a deep breath, then turned the door knob, opened the door and charged in. He got two steps before he banged his shin on something solid that sent him tumbling onto a soft landing. The room was dark save for the light coming in from the now open door behind him. Before he could move, the room became bathed in light.

He looked up to see the old man that had been standing at the door was now in the doorway with his hand on the light switch giving him an even odder look than before. Chambers sat up and looked around, he had tripped on the corner of a bed that took up most of the room and was now half sitting, half lying in the middle of an unmade bed. The place was clearly empty. So where the hell were Pang and Li? Had he got there too late? He fumbled for his police card and flashed it at the old man, before escorting him back to the hallway and closing the broken door as best he could.

Chambers was now alone in the apartment. Even though he hadn't found what he wanted, he finally had the perfect opportunity to find substantial and conclusive evidence of Derek Pang's involvement in the murders. He started by looking through the drawers and cabinets in the living room. There had to be proof somewhere. He searched the cupboards hoping to find the black gloves or the black rucksack or even better, a blood-stained murder weapon but could find nothing. After nearly an hour of frustrating searching he admitted defeat. There was nothing here that linked Derek to any of the murders. Chambers knew this didn't prove anything one way or the other. The lack of matching gloves or bag could simply be due to Derek having already taken the equipment to do his next job. As Chambers was walking to the door his phone rang.

'Hi Jenny, any word from Li?' he asked hopefully.

'I'm afraid not John, are you OK, you sound a bit out of breath?'

'I'm fine.'

'John, I just had a call from Pang, he was looking for Lucy, she was due at a briefing an hour ago and didn't show up. It's not like her, and what with you asking me to track her down earlier, I'm starting to get a bit concerned.'

'Shit. Jenny I'm coming in to the station. See if you can find anyone who sits in her section and ask them if she gave any indication of where she was going.'

'Will do.'

≈≈

It took the cab nearly 40 minutes to get to the Wanchai Police Station. Chambers could feel his stress levels increasing every time the cabbie braked suddenly then accelerated too hard, as if he'd never driven in traffic before. He finally met Jenny at Li's desk.

'John, you look terrible, are you OK?'

'I will be when we find Lucy. What did you find out?'

'Constable Tong,' she indicated a young uniformed officer sitting at one of the desks off to their left, 'says he saw Li about 8:45am, she came out from my office, typed something into her computer and left.'

'Did you have a look at the screen? Do you know what she was looking at?'

'She had several windows open, the Internet, her email, and the database. But she appears to have cleared whatever she was looking at.'

'What about her emails? Anything there?'

Greening's phone rang. She looked at the caller ID, 'It's Pang. I'd better take this. I suggest you have a look for yourself.' She gestured to the screen. 'Hello Chief Inspector,' she set off back towards her office.

Chambers pulled up Li's email account. He scanned down the list of mail she had received for the past week. There were familiar names on it, mainly from the office. He didn't see Derek's name anywhere. He went back to the most recent. He was looking for any emails that came in between 8am and 8:45am. There was one from Ian Greening, inviting her to a family lunch the following weekend. It was timed at 8:12am, why hadn't Jenny mentioned that? The signature at the bottom of the email had Ian's work number. Chambers thought it had to be worth a call, there was something distinctly untrustworthy about the man, what it was he couldn't put his finger on, but there was something that Greening was covering up, he just knew it. Chambers reached for the pad of Post-It notes and was just to jot down the telephone number when he stopped and stared at the pad.

As he had moved the pad, the light reflected off the plain surface, revealing a vague imprint. He pulled open the drawers and searched desperately for a pencil. He found one in the second drawer, grabbed it and as he started to lightly shade on the top of the pad, it began to uncover Li's handwriting in relief. When he could read what she'd written he copied it out, took the note and ran for the lift, banging the call button in the futile hope it would make the lift arrive quicker.

He contemplated getting the MTR, it had to be quicker than a cab especially at this time, but he didn't really know where the street was that he was looking for. He ended up hailing a cab and just hoped the traffic was lighter going back to Kowloon than it had been coming across to the island half an hour before. It was now 6pm and almost dark; soon they'd be shutting off the roads around TST if they hadn't started already. The cabbie was signaling that he had to take a different route. There was little Chambers could do but sit back, look out of the window and try to remain calm. The journey was torturous, Chambers desperately trying to blank any images from his mind about what might have happened to Li. Would it already be too late? It was dark by the time the cab pulled up outside the address Chambers had instructed the driver. He checked his watch: it was coming on for 7pm. The parade was due to start in an hour. He knew that whatever happened he had to be there with or without Li.

He raced into the lobby of the building and slammed his hand against the lift button. He took a step back while he waited and noticed the place looked familiar, the crappy-looking old black sofas, and then he realised why. This was the same building he'd come to with Brian Tang, this is where the rat man was killed. A coincidence? Surely not. He took the lift to the 17th floor, trying to recall from the notes which floor the murder had taken place on. It wasn't 17, but which one was it?

He exited the lift and cautiously approached the door. He knocked lightly, but there was no response. He waited, his ear pressed hard against the wood. When he was satisfied there were no sounds emanating from inside, he, for the second time that day, took several steps back before charging the door with his shoulder. He was surprised when the door gave in the first time. His momentum carried him into the middle of the room as he spun around quickly, fully expecting to be attacked. It was then his worst nightmare came true. There was a female body lying face down next to the sofa in a pool of blood.

He swiftly moved across to kneel next to the body. The victim's head was covered in a black balaclava, the eyes holes turned to the back of the head. Softly he lifted the head and worked the mask free; he could feel her hair was matted with sticky, congealing blood. Slowly he began to turn the body over, fearing the worst. It was definitely Lucy. His heart sank. He placed her head on his thighs, and opened her mouth, trying to clear her airways of blockages. As he did so he felt her neck for a pulse. He felt a surge of relief, she was breathing, although it was shallow and her pulse was weak, but she was alive. He moved her gently into the recovery position before taking out his phone and dialing 999.

He needed to make a decision and it needed to be made urgently. Should he wait for the ambulance and make sure Li was in safe hands? What if the killer came back? Or should he go to the parade where he was sure the killer was planning to go? Whoever lived in here had to be the murderer. But why hadn't he just killed Li when he had the chance? Did that mean he had a specific target in mind? Chambers could see the place was empty; the door to the only bedroom was open, the ceiling light bathing the room. Chambers knew that he needed to find something, some evidence either revealing the identity of the next victim or that of the killer, preferably both.

He could see a large Apple iMac on top of a solid looking, dark wooden desk in the solitary bedroom. It was showing different images as part of the screen saver; every three seconds or so a new picture in the form of a Polaroid-style photograph appeared on the screen. The screensaver programme then dropped it into an artistic collage of other images. Chambers watched this cycle repeat several times but couldn't quite make out the details, just the white frame that was wider at the bottom than at the top. He was drawn towards the screen but it took a moment before he realised what he was looking at; then the horrific realisation that these were grotesque images of the murder victims. He darted to the mouse and moved it to get rid of the screensaver and its appalling images; he knew the screensaver would be accessing images from a file somewhere on the hard drive. When the screensaver disappeared it revealed an open word document on the desktop. Chambers quickly scanned a line before scrolling up a few pages and reading more. The content was a first-hand, detailed account of the murder at the golf course. This document, combined with the photographic evidence, proved beyond any doubt that the killer lived here. So, whoever owned this computer was responsible for the murders.

He scrolled down to the bottom and read the final entry. This gave Chambers a reference to the next victim, but without the identity of the killer the reference was redundant. He began a desperate search of the apartment but couldn't find anything that would identify the killer; no bills, no mail, no photos – nothing. At regular intervals he had checked on Li's condition; he didn't want to leave her side, but he needed to find the killer's identity. His suspicion was that the killer knew they would be coming at some point and had destroyed or removed all the evidence. He went back and sat with Li, holding her hand. At least she was still breathing. Where was the ambulance? His watch read 7:23pm. He had to stay with her.

The paramedics arrived just after 7:30pm; he heard the commotion as they brought the stretcher out of the lift. Chambers met them at the door, flashing his police ID and directing them to the body. He knew they would have a lot of questions for him, but he needed to be elsewhere. He had to continue his search of the apartment. While the paramedics were busy taking care of Li, he turned his attention back to the kitchen, searching through several drawers, before his eye caught on something just sticking out from under the corner of the fridge, tight against the wall. With difficulty, he managed to fit his hand into the gap and at the third attempt retrieved a greetings card. The card had a lame cartoon on the front but Chambers didn't take the time to read it, he opened it and written in an elegant hand was the message, 'Happy Birthday Bradley! All the best on your big day!!! Auntie Pat & Uncle Mike xxx'. This was his killer. Bradley. Not much to go on but it was something.

He raced out of the apartment and jammed his finger on the lift button. He could hear one of the paramedics calling after him, fortunately the lift came before they caught up with him. He took his phone out. He felt that now he knew it wasn't Pang's son who was a mass murderer it would make life a hell of a lot easier to go straight to the Chief Inspector.

Chambers was out of the lift now and making his way across to the front doors. He knew now that this was definitely the same building where the informant was killed. That could explain why the CCTV footage didn't reveal anything from its vantage point further up the street. They had put it down to the fact that the killer had come from another direction. No-one had thought it was because he had simply come from another floor. He dialled the number now that he finally had coverage.

'DI Chambers, lovely to hear from you. To what do I owe the pleasure of this call? Are you back in Hong Kong?'

'Hello Chief Inspector, please just listen to what I have to say with no interruptions, please.' He took a deep breath. 'The man responsible for the 11 killings lives on the 19th floor at 133 Sai Yeung Choi Street South, on the corner of Bute Street in Mong Kok. I know because I've just been to the address. I found Lucy there; Unconscious but alive. I don't know how long she's been in there. Don't worry, the paramedics are with her now. As for the killer's identity, all I know is his name is Bradley. Also I found a journal or blog on his computer. The last line is a reference to his father. That's who he is going to meet and, I presume, to kill.'

Chambers could hear a great deal of noise at the other end; he guessed Pang was already at the parade. He recalled that Pang would be there in an official capacity as well as being there in his capacity to coordinate the operation.

There was a pause before Pang spoke. Initially it was several Cantonese words, then 'Chambers, you put me in an awkward position. I have received correspondence from your superior, Inspector Asbury, informing me that I should contact him immediately if I hear or see you connected with the case. However, from what you just told me, obviously we can deal with that later. I need to pass on the information and run a check on who lives at that address. Let me call you back.'

Chambers could see a cab with its roof light on pulling up at the traffic lights at the junction with Nathan Road. He ran towards it shouting for all he was worth. He caught up with the vehicle just as the lights changed. He banged on the back to alert the driver, before sliding round and opening the door. Before the driver could say anything, Chambers was in the back seat telling him to get him to the Peninsula Hotel as quickly as possible. Whether the driver understood the urgency, he couldn't be sure, but he knew the name of the hotel and that was enough. The cab screeched away, taking a left onto the main thoroughfare.

Chambers' phone rang, it was Pang.

'I called it in. The place is owned by a man called Hoi Fan Fung, he's a 57-year-old from Mainland China, so I doubt it's him. We're trying to track him down right now. He rents it out, so we need to find out who he rents it to. Where are you now?'

'In a cab heading towards TST, I'm nearly at the Peninsula Hotel. Yes, I think it's safe to say that it's not the old man; the card was written in English. Could it be his son?'

'We certainly can't rule it out. OK, meet me at the main entrance of the hotel. I'll be there in five minutes,' Pang said then hung up.

Chambers was at the Hotel before the Chief Inspector. He had got out of the taxi when it hit solid traffic a couple of blocks up from the hotel. He jogged the last few hundred metres along Nathan Road, before heading inside to the lobby to gain respite from the chilly winter air. As he looked out of the window he saw the enormous crowds lining the parade route. He could hear the announcements over the tannoy in Mandarin, followed by Cantonese and then English. How he was going to find the killer or his potential victim among the throngs of spectators made his head reel.

While he waited for Pang, he called Greening to give her an update on Li.

She answered on the third ring. If it was possible, it sounded even noisier than when he spoke to Pang a few minutes earlier.

'John, have you heard from Lucy?'

'I think she's going to be alright. She ...'

Greening interrupted, 'What's happened? Tell me John!'

'She's in an ambulance. I tracked her down to a flat in Mong Kok. She had been following a lead of her own, and it looks like she got lucky.' The words caught in his throat.

'Oh my god! You said she's in an ambulance. Is she badly hurt?'

'Jenny, I'm not going to bullshit you, she's received a serious head injury. But she is alive. I think we have to focus on the positives.' He could hear her crying at the other end of the line.

Chambers was scanning the crowd outside, looking for Pang. He checked his watch: 7:58pm. The parade was about to start.

Greening broke the silence, 'John, you said you were at the killer's apartment, does that mean you've caught him?'

'No. I did find something, but to be honest, it's just a lead at this stage. We're pretty sure the next victim is going to be his father; I found a document on his computer. It was written in English and there were no other documents I could see in Chinese.'

'So he's not local then?'

'At least not one that writes Chinese. We have a first name as well. Wait a minute, Pang's just arrived.' He saw the uniformed figure of James Pang break through the crowds and make his way up past the hotels' impressive fleet of dark green Rolls Royce Phantoms sitting proudly in front of the hotel.

Chambers stepped towards the lobby doors as James spotted him and raised his hand in recognition. They met at the door. Chambers

287

still had the phone pressed against his left ear; he shook James's hand with the other.

'We have a name,' Pang skipped the pleasantries. 'You're right, the man who rents the apartment is called Bradley. His family name is Greening.'

Before Chambers could respond, a shrill scream pierced his ear. It was Jenny. Chambers thought at first she must have witnessed something? It took him a couple of seconds to figure out what was really going on.

'Christ, Jenny are you there?' Chambers shouted into the phone. There was no reply. He turned to Pang. 'Inspector, I think the man we're looking for is Jenny Greening's stepson. Do you know him?'

Jenny was back on the line, 'John, oh my god, oh my god, it's Ian's son – Bradley! I saw him about 20 minutes ago.' She was struggling to get her words out as she choked back tears. Chambers held up his hand to stop Pang from speaking.

'Where Jenny?' Then he added for Pang's benefit. 'Where did you see him' He was looking straight at the Chief Inspector as he uttered the words and saw the look of shock on Pang's face.

'I was coming off the ferry, he was hanging around there. He said he was waiting to meet some friends.'

'What did he have on him? Can you give me a description of what he was wearing? Anything at all is going to be a big help.'

'I can't …' she was crying hard now, 'I think he had a black beanie on and a rucksack; he seemed impatient to get away. He was wearing a grey jacket, like, sort of a hiking jacket and blue jeans, I think.'

Chambers repeated this out loud for Pang who now himself was telling this in Cantonese to someone else via his Police radio.

'That's great Jenny, is there anything else? Did he say where he was going? How was he?'

'Nothing, he just said a quick hello and it was clear he was uncomfortable, but then that's normal for him. We've never got along, he shows a lot of resentment towards me; I know that he thinks I stole his father away from his birth mother.' She was rambling now.

Chambers butted in, 'Ian, shit! Jenny, where is Ian?'

'He's up in the VIP section of the stand; he's going to give a speech soon. Oh no, Brad asked if I knew where Ian was. That's all he said. Oh my god, he's going to kill Ian isn't he? I need to call him.' She rang off before Chambers could say any more.

Chambers turned to Pang. 'Did you get all of that?'

He nodded. 'We need to get to Ian Greening immediately, follow me.'

He was already moving quickly back down towards the wall of people lining Salisbury Road. Chambers followed Pang, who was announcing his presence as he pushed through the crowd to the recently erected barriers. The main parade had yet to come this far, so it was easy for the pair of them to clamber over the waist-high barrier and make their way to the other side of the road across the central reservation, darting between the jugglers and clowns who were the at the vanguard of the evening's entertainment, sent out to keep the crowds amused before the main event. A steward initially came towards them but nodded when he recognised Pang's uniform and ran ahead to unhinge the barrier on the far side of the road. They squeezed their way through the crowd on the other side until they were in the shadow of the domed Space Museum building.

Chambers became aware of his vibrating phone. The number was Jenny's.

'Jen, what is it?'

'I can't get hold of Ian. His phone is going to voicemail. I can see him; he's in the grandstand opposite me. But the parade has just begun so it's impossible for me to get over there.'

At least he's still alive, thought Chambers. 'Jen, try and stay calm,

I'm here with Chief Inspector Pang, we're just at the back of one of the stands. We'll be with Ian shortly. Just tell me his exact location in the stand.'

She told him the approximate row and that Ian was in the middle of the stand. Chambers thanked her and rang off. They were on the edge of a high fenced-off area. On the other side of the chain-link fence they could see the performers and the floats that were preparing to join the parade. This was the area Chambers had visited a couple of days before when it was quiet. Now it was a riot of colours, noise and excitement. There were performing groups of various sizes talking or going through last-minute practice routines. Pang was ahead of him and had found a security guard manning the exit. He had a curt conversation with the guard and the gate was soon opened. The pair of them stopped just inside the gate.

'John, let me go on to see Ian, I think it's going to look at lot more natural if they see a uniformed Chief Inspector heading towards the VIP section. Keep an eye out here and I'll bring Ian back out this way so we can get him out of here as quickly and discreetly as we can.'

The plan sounded logical, plus it would give Chambers the opportunity to monitor the performers heading out to join the parade that would be passing close to the VIP section. If Chambers was right, the murderer would be trying to blend in here, probably in a costume that he had picked up from some unfortunate person around here. He didn't want to waste time looking around the back lot, there were simply too many places for someone to hide, the best he could do was try to keep an eye on the groups as they went out. The next float was an African tribal group about 20-strong. They were dressed in what looked like brown suede micro shorts and tops. There was no float with the troupe and if Chambers was right about who he was looking for, then he didn't belong to this group. As they waited to go, he turned his attention to the next group. The parade appeared to alternate between dance troupes and floats. The float that was rolling slowly to the start line – as the African dancers leapt into their routine – belonged, according to the words emblazoned on the side of the float, to Amazing Thailand. It was huge and decked out in golden colours featuring some Thai dragons and an elaborate miniature version of a golden Wat. Escorting the float were serene looking, beautifully made-up Thai dancers, resplendent in carefully embroidered silk outfits.

Chambers was thinking back to the image he had seen of Bradley Greening in the photo on the wall of Jenny Greening's house. Looking at the faces of the few male Thai dancers, it was clear to Chambers he wasn't among them. The float lurched forward to join the parade. Chambers could see there was little more than 45 seconds for the organiser, a fraught looking lady with a clipboard and walkie-talkie on the other side of the float, to get the next group ready. The float briefly lined up at the start position underneath a specially designed arch that served as the entry point. The arch was decked out in loud colours that also promoted the name of the event in huge letters. The theme of the year's parade was – World City. World Party.

Chambers looked back along the line. Next up were a group that caused him some consternation – a dragon dance group. The dragon looked to be made up of over 30 people, plus a supporting group laden with a variety of drums, cymbals and gongs. Was it possible that his target had somehow got himself a place under the body of the dragon? He scanned towards the grandstand; there was no sign of Pang and Greening. He could see the stand was less than 50 metres long; they had to be making their way back shortly.

Chambers pulled out his police badge and moved towards the enormous red, green and gold oversized head of the dragon. He reached it and tried in vain to lift it. The thing weighed a tonne. The man underneath could obviously feel the disturbance and pushed up the head a little. Chambers crouched down to get a look. It was a middle-aged Chinese man, not his target. He waved his card and moved along, lifting the lighter body of the dragon at intervals to get a look at whoever was under the shiny red fabric. He hadn't seen anyone that could be Bradley Greening. As the dragon dance team began their performance, Chambers was forced to step back out of their way. The next float behind was decked out like a pirate ship pulled by a colourfully decorated Land Rover. The float had a group of 30-or-so giant pirates, with gigantic caricature heads, walking in front. They had to be eight or nine feet tall. It was more likely that the killer could have infiltrated one of these solo suits than joined a specialist team. The thought made Chambers relax momentarily, but he still had a nagging doubt that he had just let the killer walk by hidden somewhere in the body of the dragon.

Behind the pirate ship, there was a group of stilt-walking women dressed in shiny, frilly ball gowns that looked like those he had seen in Wild West films. But the gowns were enormous; they were designed to make it appear that the parading women stood over 30 feet in height.

He turned his attention back to the parade in time to see Pang and an irate looking Greening exit the barrier and begin walking towards him along the edge of the grandstand. By taking that route Greening and Pang were now on the wrong side of the barrier, making them an easier target. Chambers' heart was in his mouth, the pair were now level with the dancers. The dragon moved erratically across the road, making sharp darting movements in time to the clash of the cymbals, then it jerked suddenly towards the two men. Chambers started towards them but before he had even got a couple of steps, the dragon had dipped sharply and moved harmlessly away. Pang was waving to him and then pointed beyond Chambers towards the gate they had entered earlier.

There were a series of loud bangs just as he turned to walk back to the gate. The sudden sharp cracks made him instinctively crouch down as he scanned for the source of the noise. Was that the sound of gunfire? He looked back to the parade but no one else appeared to be reacting. Silver slivers of paper began to float down from above. He realised the noises had come from the oversized party popper-like fireworks and not thankfully, the sound of gunshots. Chambers continued on his way towards the gate when he happened to look into the cabin of the Land Rover that was now level with him. The driver was unmistakably Bradley Greening.

Chambers froze. The vehicle was less than five metres away and rolling slowly towards the start line. He had to act quickly and this realisation snapped him out of his apathy. He tried to subtly change direction but the driver spotted him approaching and began grinding the gears while the engine revved ferociously. As Greening and Pang walked under the arch and came into view, Chambers grabbed frantically at the passenger door handle. He pulled it open and dived in as the vehicle's gear caught and the car accelerated towards the two men.

Chambers used his momentum to try and tackle the man in the driver's seat, struggling to grab him by the throat. The driver was trying to fend him off with one hand while steering with the other. Just as Chambers got a decent hold on the driver the vehicle slammed into the barriers close to the base of the arch. The impact broke his grip and smacked him hard against the dashboard - winding him. Chambers was able to quickly scramble back onto the seat in time to see Greening anxiously pulling at the door handle. Chambers was just able to stretch across and grab the snub-nosed pistol sticking out of the back of Greening's waistband. Greening felt the tug on his trousers and he turned to look at Chambers, the unemotional expression quickly changing to one of bewilderment as he realised his gun was now in Chambers' hand.

In one swift move Greening stepped away, swung the black rucksack off his back and pulled out a large carving knife as he made his way around to the front of the vehicle. Chambers opened his door and leapt out. He could see Pang was lying face down next to the vehicle; it was hard to say if he was alive and there was no time to check. Where was Greening? Chambers took three steps before he could see what was happening. Ian Greening was lying trapped under the front wheel of the car, while his son stood over him holding the knife in his left hand pointing it towards his victim.

Chambers instinctively fired a shot. The bullet hit Greening in the right shoulder, knocking him backwards and off balance, temporarily halting him, before Greening regained his composure and lunged towards the sprawling figure of his father. The recoil from the shot had caused Chambers to nearly lose his balance, the violent kick from the gun had caught him by surprise making him take a step backwards. Regaining his composure he took a firmer grip on the weapon and fired again, this time hitting Greening in the left side of the neck, just as the knife made contact with the prone figure. Bradley Greening slumped backwards and released the weapon, clutching at his throat as thick jets of blood began pumping throught the gaps in his fingers.

Chambers stood still for several seconds, the gun still raised. He wasn't able to comprehend the events that had just taken place. He abruptly became aware of the noise; it was deafening, it was as if the volume had just been turned back up, and everyone was screaming. He could also hear the sound of the engine revving as if the accelerator pedal was stuck. He looked around to see people running in all directions, it was sheer pandemonium. As Chambers stepped forward to check on Ian, he saw a uniformed policeman in front of him with a gun levelled at his chest. Chambers shouted out that he was police, but knew better than to argue. He tossed the gun to the ground and put his hands up in the air.

He felt a heavy blow in his back that knocked him to the floor. Evidently there were more police behind him. From his position he could crane his neck to see over to Bradley Greening, who was still lying on his back holding his wound. He had an odd expression, not one of shock exactly, it was more one of confusion, as if the events that were taking place couldn't or shouldn't be happening. Ian Greening was dragging himself across the tarmac towards his bleeding son. Chambers watched as the father held his son, crying and begging him not to die, and trying desperately to stem the flow of blood.

≈≈≈

Epilogue

Monday 6th February 2012

When Chambers met up with Li at Hong Kong Station it was a solemn affair. She appeared with her bandaged head wrapped in a fashionable headscarf. Chambers was intrigued as to how she remained so attractive and attentive to fashion having just escaped death. On the evening of Chinese New Year, the paramedics had rushed her to Kwong Wah Hospital in Mong Kok. At the hospital she had been put into an induced coma for a week before being sent for observation in the intensive care ward. When the doctors were happy there was nothing more serious than a compound skull fracture and severe concussion, she'd been able to go home to finish her convalescence.

Chambers had left plenty of messages on Li's phone and had been in several times to visit her in the first week while she lay unconscious. It had been a difficult few weeks for everyone.

The immediate aftermath of what happened at the Night Parade had been a blur for Chambers. Several uniformed officers had, on instruction from a groggy Pang, bundled him through the throng of bewildered onlookers, into a police car that had whisked him away to the relative safety of the Wan Chai Police Station.

Chambers later found out from different sources that Ian Greening had refused to let go of his son to receive treatment for himself. The ambulance had taken them both to the Prince of Wales Hospital in Sha Tin, that had been selected for security reasons. Miraculously, Bradley Greening had survived being shot in the neck. Several hours of emergency surgery had saved his life. He was now under a police guard while he recovered sufficiently to face the charges and eventually a trial. He was initially going to be charged with the attempted murders of Detective Lucy Li and Chief Inspector Pang along with the murder of Karen Nguyen. A team of Investigating officers was looking into possible charges relating to other murders and would present their findings in due course. This much Chambers had learnt from Li when he'd spoken to her on the phone to arrange their final meeting.

The major problem that had faced Chambers was that he had fired a weapon, albeit Li's police service sidearm, while not officially affiliated to the Hong Kong Police. Initially, it looked likely he would face court and a possible custodial sentence. The only person who could negotiate a path out of the mess was Chief Inspector Pang, who himself spent the first week in hospital recuperating from his injuries. These included a broken wrist, chest injuries and mild concussion. Whether Pang did it out of gratitude for Chambers saving his life, or because he saw him as one of his team, Chambers wasn't sure. But when the Chief Inspector was released he had immediately put the paperwork in place to make it appear that Chambers already had high-level clearance and had formal approval to act as a member of the Hong Kong police.

Chambers had been told to go and stay with Brian Tang and his family until the initial paperwork could be sorted out. He was not to leave the house without permission. The only time he had disobeyed the order was to slip out and visit Li in hospital. Chambers was aware that Pang's effusive support was only made available to him because Pang must have still been unaware that for the last two months of the investigation, Chambers had been on a one-man mission to prove Pang's only son was guilty of being the city's worst ever serial killer. It was possible that one day Chambers would come clean – but certainly not until he was safely out of the city.

The only other people that knew about his theory were Li, who at that point had still been in a coma at that point, and Jenny Greening. Chambers had been extremely fearful that she would say something. Several days after the event he had received a call from Jenny. The last time he'd heard from her it was a few minutes before the shooting occurred. Since then he had shot her stepson in the neck and her husband had been badly injured. He wasn't looking forward to the call.

Greening sounded calm and almost friendly considering she was speaking to the man who had nearly killed her stepson. She explained that her husband was still in deep shock and denial that his son, no matter how errant, could be responsible for trying to kill him and also for the deaths of 11 people. It became apparent to Chambers that there was no love lost between Jenny and her stepson. Jenny explained that her worst fear was that Ian would be killed, and without actually saying it, in a way she was grateful for Chambers actions and certainly had no plans to tell Pang about Chambers' fanciful theory relating to the killer's identity. She was more worried that Ian was planning to defend his son in court as soon as he had recovered from the injuries he sustained on the night. Greening had convinced himself he was to blame for his son's behaviour and was planning a defence case based on diminished responsibility citing Brad Greening showing classic signs of having borderline personality disorder and that his unwillingness to help his son had caused his extreme behaviour. Whatever the outcome, it was clear Jenny had more important personal matters to attend to for the foreseeable future. While her complicated relationship with Bradley Greening had meant it had been a relatively easy decision to accept the gardening leave offered to her by the Police department. She was now free to support her husband in his futile quest for his son's salvation.

Ten days later Chambers had finally begun to relax. Jenny Greening was out of the picture and unlikely to say anything, while Chief Inspector Pang was doing all in his power to help. The media had been informed that Chambers' role was that of lead investigator on a case that was suspected to have had its roots in London's Chinatown. This allowed them to develop a legitimate cover story to be constructed and disseminated to the media. The press, who had been disappointed with the amount of hard facts surrounding the wild events of the Chinese New Year Night Parade in Kowloon, were desperate for answers and scapegoats. It was decided the best thing was to get Chambers out of the city. He would have to come back of course, when the case went to trial. Pang moved swiftly and drafted more paperwork so that Chambers was allowed to leave and head back to London.

He had booked his flight for the 6th of February and was delighted to hear from Li the day before. He needed something to look forward to before heading back to potential redundancy at the hands of Inspector Asbury. They arranged to meet at Central Station before Chambers caught the Airport Express.

When he saw her he was almost overcome by emotion. Her successful attempts to look good failed to hide her obvious fragility. He wanted to go and hold her rather than lean in and give her a gentle kiss on the cheek. She looked like a porcelain doll, so vulnerable and delicate, her skin colour was deathly pale. Their conversation was stilted and awkward. He had so much to say to her, about how he had failed to believe in her, while he had charged along convinced of his ability to 'know' a killer when he met one. His gut instinct had been wrong, that's all there was to it. He thought back to when he had cradled her head in Bradley Greening's apartment. He had been quite sure she was going to die. How could he tell her it meant the world to him to see her alive. She was quieter than usual. There were things she wanted to tell him too, but where to begin. After an awkward pause and just as she was preparing to explain how she felt, he blurted out a goodbye, leant in to kiss her on the cheek.

As he walked away towards the barrier he turned to look at her. She stood upright and elegant. Chambers could not think of anything else to say, he gave her a wave and took one last look at her beautiful face, he was sure he saw a tear fall from her eye and run down her cheek. He turned and quickly walked through the barrier to the waiting train. Only when he found a seat and controlled his breathing did he dare to look out of the carriage window, but she was no longer there.

He closed his eyes, lost in his thoughts and didn't open them until the train eased into the station at Hong Kong Airport. He checked in and made his way through immigration and customs and onto the shuttle train as if he was on auto pilot.

He sat in the departure lounge waiting for his flight to be called. He took out his camera and began looking through the pictures from his time in Hong Kong, in particular, the ones that had Lucy in them. He flicked through to the ones from the National Day Parade. This one was his favourite, the one of her marching past in her uniform. He zoomed in to get a closer look at her face. The viewer automatically zoomed in to the middle of the shot, onto some people in the grandstand just above Li's head.

A face stood out in the crowd. How he had not seen this before? The man in the crowd was undoubtedly Hak Loong – The Black Dragon or whatever his real name might be. Chambers didn't know whether to laugh or cry. Finally he had proof that all along the man he was looking for was right here in Hong Kong. On one particular day back in early October the pair of them had stood less than 50 metres apart. Had he passed him on his way to or from the venue? Chambers consoled himself with the knowledge he would find the man he was looking for – one day.

He texted Li: 'Good news - I know Hak Loong is in HK. I'll email and explain all. But I'm coming back. Get well – I need you healthy! John'.

≈≈≈

6149781R00180

Printed in Great Britain
by Amazon.co.uk, Ltd.,
Marston Gate.